HIDING

by Jenny Morton Potts
For Gramps

ISBN: 9781976862816

Contents

Chapter 1 Killer Road April 2007 1

Chapter 2 Death Row June 2021 9

Chapter 3 The Party 23

Chapter 4 The Hunters 33

Chapter 5 The Library... 50

Chapter 6 The Atlantic.. 61

Chapter 7 The King 77

Chapter 8 The Shooting 83

Chapter 9 The Staircase... 101

Chapter 10 The Aunt 113

Chapter 11 The Reaper 138

Chapter 12 The Visitors.. 150

Chapter 13 The Brother.. 172

Chapter 14 Arrivals... 188

Chapter 15 The Secret 217

Chapter 16 The Coupling 230

Chapter 17 The Wigwam.. 246

Chapter 18 The Browns.. 256

Chapter 19 The Uncle, the day before 267

Chapter 20 The End 282

Acknowledgements 319

CHAPTER 1

Killer Road
April 2007

They died, Rebecca Brown's mum and dad. They were killed on a road with a big reputation. Rebecca could only imagine it. She was hundreds of miles from the scene of the crash when it happened. When she thought of that road, she pictured it covered in ice, black ice, since the accident took place on a bitter December night. The A42, was the road's alphanumeric name. The Killer Road, they called it back then in the papers. *The Killer Road has struck again!* The headlines came into Rebecca's mind like a voice, like Vincent Price, as if the road arched up into vertical life, a tarmac monster stalking its victims.

Rebecca Brown was four years old when she became an orphan, alongside her sister, Colette, and her brother, Austen. Rebecca was the youngest. She couldn't even remember the moment she was told. What had they said? *'Mummy and Daddy have had a terrible accident, dear. In the car.'* At the time, she knew little more than the fact. They were gone. They'd been there all the days of her life, and then they were not. Of the circumstances and detail, she knew next to nothing. Perhaps Rebecca hadn't thought to ask questions. Perhaps there was little more to say to a child so young. As Rebecca grew, though, so did her thirst for knowledge. But it seemed that, even if there had been a window of opportunity to make her enquiries, that window got bricked up years ago. There was a solid wall now between Rebecca Brown and the truth.

Julia and Stephen, her parents had been called. 'Julia and Stephen,' Rebecca liked to say aloud when she was alone in her garret bedroom. She could barely remember them but she thought they sounded really nice. She was sure that they were kind people, with ready smiles and lovely clean clothes.

It was their grandparents who raised the Brown children. It was the Grands who took the youngsters into their care at *Taransay*, a red sandstone mansion in the north of Scotland. *Taransay* was only partially restored. It had vast, austere rooms and draughty, wood-panelled corridors; a real *Amityville Horror* of a home, scary even on a cornflower sky summer's day, and a weird contrast to the heavenly Highland surroundings. They lived high up on a plateau that could have been made for a view. There was an imposing tree-lined driveway and the steading, as Rebecca's grandfather Ralph liked to call it, overlooked the magnificent Morar Sands. The golden beach met the Atlantic Ocean which unfurled itself like ruffled navy silk on the calmest of days, but the fierce ones were just as precious to Rebecca, as she stood at her dormer window looking out across the sea's tossing and turning. She loved it best when the gods got angry down there in the depths and rose up, throwing the spray right at her face.

The land surrounding *Taransay* was mostly meadow, with the churn and splat of their cattle's hooves and excretions. Their cowhand, Murdo Hendry, tended the animals. They had mostly Friesians but some Jerseys whose milk was creamier with more butterfat. And they had five Swedish Reds, the strongest and healthiest of the herd, and Rebecca's personal favourites. They sold their high quality milk to a premium ice cream manufacturer but the income from such a small herd fell considerably short of supporting the Brown clan.

Murdo also tended a half acre of vegetable patch which their grandmother Primmy was inclined to call 'the potager'.

She was often found to use French substitutes for every day words. Austen told his younger sisters that this habit of their grandmother's was part of her general denial and dislike of where they had ended up. He claimed that her French references were a deliberate barrier to assimilation. Primrose Anctillious Brown described herself as *English to the core* and it had not been her choice to relocate to Scotland.

The henhouse was Rebecca's domain. They had a couple of dozen hybrid laying hens which produced far more than they could ever eat, so they supplied their excess to Moss Mills Nursing Home which made them all feel they were doing their bit for the community. However, the Browns were utterly insular and rarely met the community. It was Murdo Hendry – himself a man of very few words – who delivered the eggs.

The perimeter of their land was marked with stone dyke walls, upon which Rebecca could balance, even on the windiest of days. She was certain that this was a skill which would be good for something.

In many ways, the Browns were living in paradise, albeit a rather unpredictable one weather-wise. The blot on the landscape was really the house which was such a strange hulking abode. There was barely a smooth exterior surface. The builder had lumped on every possible feature: turrets, balconies, oriels, buttresses, corbels and a dozen chimneys. And all of the downstairs windows had metal bars fitted on the outside. Not the pretty ones you get in Spain, but the kind you get in gaol. *Taransay* looked more like a Rhenish correctional facility than a family home. No, this abode was not for the faint-hearted and yet the bereaved children were brought to its huge oak door, for re-settlement; like little refugees with their suitcases and their sorrow.

The rambling, shambling, freezing house was often cited as the reason that guests could not join them. They had moved into the sprawling mansion after the accident, so that there would be room for all of them. And there certainly was. A small regiment would have found it spacious. The house was only partly restored and some years into their tenure, it had become obvious that not only would *Taransay* never be finished whilst under their guardianship but that nobody had the slightest ambition to try.

No other relatives came to call, except for Uncle Neil. He was from England, Rebecca could tell from his voice. None of the children, or indeed the Grands, ever called him Uncle Neil during his visits. Uncle to whom exactly was unclear to Youngest Brown, as the family called Rebecca. Uncle Neil didn't appear at times of festivities but rather any old time, usually in the morning. He was ushered into the drawing room and was gone before lunch. Any enquiries Rebecca made about the man were smartly rebuffed. Apart from Uncle Neil, visitors were strongly discouraged by Primmy Brown and as in all her wishes, her husband Ralph went along with it.

Questions relating to the dark time of *The Killer Road* were virtually taboo also. So when the burning need to know came to Rebecca, there was no-one to safely ask, except for her siblings and they were even less helpful than the Grands. The only useful snippet of information Rebecca ever got was exactly that, a snippet; a fragment of a torn cutting she found in her grandfather's study:

'... The A42 Killer Road has no central reservation. This makes it a lethal stretch of dual carriageway. Regular users have been complaining to the Highways Agency for ...'

That was all there was, but she could see that the cutting was from a newspaper. Rebecca rubbed the paper between her thumb and forefinger. She sniffed at it, like it was a clue, a paper trail. She needed so badly to understand what had happened. It gnawed at her as she lay in her wrought iron bed with the dormer window open. The longing to know swirled in on the Atlantic wind. It slapped her dark hair against her face as she looked out of the window and watched the ocean spume, as if it was daring her.

Rebecca Brown made up her mind on her 10th birthday. She was going to get some answers. She'd waited long enough.

There was to be a party. Just the three children and their grandparents. Austen, who was seven years older than Rebecca, had come home from boarding school especially, though for years he'd chosen to stay at Beaton College over the weekends. Rebecca tried very hard to hate her older brother but she knew from the paddling in her tummy that she was excited to see him. In age, her sister Colette was almost exactly between them, the distinctively middle child.

The 10th birthday party was to be later in the day. No invitees of course, no outsiders. Not even Murdo, whom Rebecca loved more than all of them put together.

'No dear, not the staff,' Primmy had said a few days ago.

And Rebecca had not even bothered to plead for her best friend, Maria Theresa, to be included. Being turned down was just getting too painful.

Breakfast on her birthday was nothing special. The Grands were seated as usual around the farmhouse table in the kitchen, munching their toast and Ralph Brown was chalking up credits in compliments for Primmy. He liked to start early in the day, storing valuable brownie points so that he'd earn himself some peace in his study for a few hours. Rebecca listened to them from just beyond the door, out of sight.

'Wonderful jam, Primrose! Simply marvellous. I do *not* know how you do it.'

'Course you do, you old sop. In a copper jam-pot with a hundred weight of sugar.'

'Is that cardamom, the spice?'

'Cinammon.'

'Oh yes, I knew it ended with a *mon*.'

'Why'd you say cardamom then? Which ends with a *mom*, not a *mon*.'

Rebecca wanted to shout through that *mom* was American for *mum* but she knew by now all the words that were to be avoided. And *mother* was number one on that list.

Ralph nudged Primmy, as if they were having some private wordplay but his wife just frowned in mild disgust at his offending elbow.

Rebecca waited outside the kitchen, waited for the right moment. But how was she to recognise the right moment? She was suddenly sure of nothing. Except that it was her birthday. It was April 16th 2007 and she was ten, and she must be entitled to something.

The child looked down at her bare feet. They were tinged purple with the cold and she clutched her arms around her middle to retain some warmth for her vital organs. Austen suddenly whooshed by and banged her over the head with his rolled-up newspaper. He'd read it all evening rather than talk to anyone when he arrived from Morar station yesterday and it seemed he wasn't finished with that paper yet.

'What are you doing there, skulker?'

Rebecca opened her mouth to reply but he was already at the kitchen table, reaching for the teapot. And since you really could never tell when Colette would surface on a Saturday morning, Youngest Brown reckoned that this would be the largest audience she could expect. She wanted the discussion out of the way well before the party and decided this was the moment to go ahead with her formal request. Rebecca walked awkwardly into the kitchen, like a stage-struck performer. The double aspect windows were flooding the room with April morning sunshine, belying the frigid outdoor temperature, and the fire was roaring in the grate. Rebecca had a fireplace in her bedroom too but it was never laid and she was forbidden from making a fire herself. The kitchen was so warm though, she was tempted to just snuggle among them and tip up her face to the sun. But no, she had a job to do and anyway, she could see through the window suddenly that bulging rainclouds were chasing down the sun. Quickly, while she had her grandparents and brother under this brief sunny spotlight, Rebecca began:

'There are things I need to know. I want you to tell me about mum and dad. For example.' Rebecca held up her palms. 'Did they die very quickly? Right away, I mean? Did they feel it?'

Primmy stopped chewing, her jaw slackened and her knife clattered on the side plate. Ralph took hold of his wife's hand. Austen sipped at his tea, his eyes unreadable over the top of his mug.

'Are they in heaven? If they are, can they still miss us? Maria Theresa used to say they would be angels. Since it wasn't their fault. But I don't know how she really knows that. And anyway, she's an atheist now.' Rebecca took a breath and tried to remember her other questions. 'Oh yes, also: where are my other grandparents? MT has two lots.'

Before anyone could consider an appropriate response, Primmy Brown's face was preparing for martyrdom and Ralph was scowling at his dashed prospects of a peaceful day.

Rebecca thought that her tenth birthday party would be cancelled. Things were often cancelled if Grandma became upset, they were all used to that. Rebecca had once asked her Grandad why an event had to be cancelled. Why could none of them go to a place because Grandma was upset? Why couldn't Primmy stay at home and cry and let the rest of them go ahead and have a nice time? This suggestion had not gone down well.

Ralph had a coughing bout at the table now. He had a chronic bronchial condition and was dislodging phlegm much of the time. He even tried to make a feature of it on occasion, by clearing his throat to Strauss's *Radetsky March*.

Since all, it seemed, was lost anyway, Rebecca thought she would switch tack entirely and have one last crack at requesting the presence of her friend Maria Theresa.

'Since I am now ten, that's two figures, can MT come over?' Rebecca bit her bottom lip and tried to look appealing. 'And play,' she added, though the girls would never use such a babyish term to one another now.

Her grandmother began to answer whilst searching her dressing gown pockets for a tissue. The answer was of course, 'No,' though it took Primmy many grief-stricken sentences to say this.

If Rebecca had been just a little older, she might have identified this trait in her grandmother as a kind of lazy misery. But she was just ten years old, today, and she was a practical child. She ran from the room before Grandma could cancel the party.

CHAPTER 2

Death Row
June 2021

Keller Baye made sure to find the shade of a tree when he drove into the parking lot of Ashvale Mall. The weesatch branches hung over the hood of his Chevy Silverado, leaves just inches from the windshield. In a light wind, those leaves would reach down and stroke the glass. But there was no wind on this late June day in 2021 and the sun was already relentless in the North Carolina sky. Keller watched a bug dance across the dashboard, looking for an exit. Was this a good day to die? Keller thought that it was as good as any.

The Chevy pick-up was his pride and joy. He worked three jobs to keep up the payments. But he wouldn't be making a payment next month, or ever again.

Keller Baye had lived his whole life in this State. It never occurred to him to look elsewhere but now everything had changed. He'd been on this earth for twenty five years but he felt he was only just starting to really come alive. Up till now, he'd never been further than Charlotte, which is where he was headed right after his meeting with the bounty hunter, day after tomorrow. Of course, Mr Blonk did not like to be called a bounty hunter, preferring instead the term skip tracer. But essentially, Blonk hunted folk down for money. And since Keller was paying, he'd call the guy whatever the hell he chose.

It was the last thing to be sorry for, abandoning the pick-up truck. The last thing to leave behind, that's what Keller was hoping. Had it all planned out. He was going to drive to Charlotte

Airport and pull up in the Park'N Go. *No waiting, no walking, no worrying.* That's what the website said, and he liked the sound of that. Six dollars fifty was all it cost at the Park'N Go, to leave your life behind. And he wasn't even going to pay that. He would just walk away and get on his plane to London Heathrow. The flight ticket was here in the glove box, along with his six month work permit. Couple of other guys from the Hickory Recycling Plant had taken advantage of the new permits too. Now or never, they said, chance of a lifetime. They intended to work their asses off in London for a few weeks and then party their way round Europe till the permit expired. People said the agreement wouldn't last, that the UK/US exchange for the under 25s was just a gimmick, a vote seeker. They said the Republicans were trying to woo the young who had started running in droves to the Democrats.

Keller's boss, Frank Delacroix, said the scheme was an admin-heavy load of hooey. He hadn't voted for it and he wasn't happy that Keller was leaving. The boy was a good worker. A little creepy, his colleagues said when he first started but they got used to him soon enough. He was a sound worker, reliable and productive. When Keller gave a month's notice, Frank said, 'You're a loss, son, I'll be honest. I had high hopes for you.' Delacroix slapped Keller on the shoulder and his employee just smiled that inscrutable smile of his, thinking: *You kept those hopes well-hidden.*

Keller hadn't voted for the Republicans. He'd never voted for anyone or anything. He'd never even considered voting. He could care less if the US/UK agreement lasted or not. Nothing lasted. And he had no intention of partying in Europe. He had just one mission. You might call it revenge but he didn't. He called it duty.

Keller leaned forward to take out his flight ticket and work permit from the glove box. The permit had the Governor's stamp on it. That same Governor who was responsible for today's foul business, with Prisoner 72259-931.

Keller almost caressed the smooth documents and stretched out his long limbs. It felt so good to have a plan. He could actually feel the adrenalin of the changes he was making to his life. The sensation was running through his body. He was acutely aware of his every action now, as if he had walked clear of a choking gas. He could fill his lungs finally, inflate his chest. He was listening like never before. He heard the creak of his leather jacket, the sound of his own breath. Every move he made had an effect. Why had he never realised this before, that he had such power.

A Ford minibus drove swiftly into the parking lot. It was a pristine white with black tinted windows and *Harfield Correctional Institute* emblazoned on its side.

Keller checked the clock on the dash: 9.17am. The *Harfield* officers got out of the bus and looked around for their passengers. They had penitentiary badges stitched onto their breast pockets and light sweat patches two toning their shirts. The minibus looked brand spanking new but perhaps the aircon was on the fritz. Or perhaps their perspiring bodies were simply unable to conceal the fact that they were scared shitless on such a day.

North Carolina had not invoked the death penalty since 2006 but the incumbent President Descher was a firm believer in it. More and more, capital crimes were receiving the ultimate punishment, but not widely enough, in Descher's opinion. He had campaigned to accelerate the process for inmates awaiting judgment. Fifteen months into his term, the President was getting impatient with some of his States. The Death Row argument was never off the headlines. It started with the row in Arkansas over hasty executions before the lethal drugs' *best use by* date and had raged every other month since. Today, it was the turn of North Carolina's Governor in Raleigh to satisfy his President.

*

Keller had never been to the Ashvale Mall before and he would never return. He was going to be free, in a matter of forty eight hours or so. Malls were not for guys anyway. Right from sixth grade at Jefferson Middle School, the girls in his class would get so excited about their trips to the mall. It was the shining light of their weekends. Even at Weaver High, Makayla hung out at the mall, and he'd kind of hoped she had a mind for higher things. How small their ambitions were, Keller sneered, and pulled down the vanity mirror. He took an electric shaver from the map pocket and ran it slowly around his jaws. He was smiling under the buzz. How small his own ambitions had been till now.

'Looking good, Kell.' He nodded to himself.

As Keller began to run a comb through his fine blond hair, he saw an older gentleman approaching the *Harfield* prison officers. The old guy was a little stooped. He had used-up shoulders and an anxiety in his fingers as he opened his wallet to show some identification. The side door of the minibus was opened so that he could take his place. The man handed over the light blazer he'd been carrying and a leather dossier bag, leaving his arms free to hoist himself inside. Perhaps he was a freelance journalist who couldn't quite afford to retire, Keller mused. Or a writer. He could have been anyone. To Keller Baye, he was no-one. Everyone he met today would be no-one, except for the man who was to meet his death.

Keller swept his eyes around the parking lot again. A young woman with red hair and stupidly high heels was coming out of the Mall. Instinctively, Keller knew she was to be one of the minibus party. Is this what they looked like now, those girls from school? Had Makayla traded in her athlete track shoes for the likes of these? He didn't want to think about his first love. Well, his only love. That was the good thing about moving to Greensboro: getting away from Jefferson Middle School and meeting Makayla at Weaver High. That, and his friend Steve Truffaut ending up there too.

Keller could never have recovered from the humiliation. The day the police came knocking at the classroom door at Jefferson. The kids' eyes bored into his skull. He could feel the reddening starting in his neck and rise up through his jaw till his own eyes burned with shame. Behind him they started to bang on their desk tops with their fists. To his side, someone leaned over and hissed in his ear, 'Kell, boy? You gone got yourself arrested?' As he walked down the aisle between the desks, their faces all turned to him. A foot shot out to trip him up but he saw it alright. The two blue uniformed officers marched him out of there. He could barely keep up. He was not allowed to fetch his things from his locker. He did not know where they were taking him, nor why.

*

Now a tall skinny guy came into view in the parking lot. He looked barely adult, and was clutching *Chicken Express* takeout. He was one of the party too, Keller could tell. He felt a certainty about everything, a clarity. Keller got out of the Chevy and locked her up. He touched her flank and the metal burned his fingertips. Lord, he was going to miss his Silverado.

Folk were clustering around the minibus, seven of them now, and the officers put the passengers' bags into a secure box at the back of the bus. He asked for their cell phones and tablets so that he could put these in a temperature controlled bag, much like the one Keller's aunt used to take on picnics up in Greensboro. They used to start out on their picnics early so that they could walk the Uwharrie Forest till their feet were tattered from blistering. Funny that a woman as evil as Aunt Joya would even own a picnic bag. Unless it was for keeping roadkill at a conservable temperature; or dropped off body parts from frostbite. *'You forgot your mittens, Kell, we sure as fuck not turning back now.'*

'Cell phone, Sir?'

Keller held up his hands which made the officer frown. 'I don't have a cell phone.' He couldn't see the point. All the phones he'd had got stolen and anyway, he had no-one he wanted to talk to. The computer in his apartment had a core processor which left cell phones in the dust.

'iPad, tablet?'

Keller shook his head. Aunt Joya had never allowed anything like that in the house when he was growing up. That's most likely why he bought the most powerful PC in the store when he got away from her. Joya thought that computers and such were the devil's work. Not that she was a churchgoer, but placing expensive items which a child might wish for in the devil's work category, freed up her purse at the gas station for Powerball Lottery tickets.

*

The thin man who was tearing into a chicken leg, was asked to finish his meal before they set off. It was unclear whether this was mandatory or simply preferable. To moderate the request, the officer added, 'We have time, sir.'

'Sorry. Been on an assignment all night. Didn't get to eating.'

Keller wondered what kind of assignment and reminded himself that only his own life mattered.

The others in the party began to exchange details: why they were here, on behalf of whom, had they been to one of these before. Keller physically took a step back when these exchanges began and pursed his lips if he felt any eyes of inquiry upon him.

The skinny guy gave up with his takeout and threw most of his chicken at a trash can mouth, but missed. He stooped to make amends and Keller could see ketchup bleeding from his lower lip.

The woman from the Mall had two bags. A small one which might have been jewellery and a large one from *Foot Locker*. Her red hair barely moved when she did. Perhaps she'd been to the blow dry bar too, asked for extra lacquer. Reluctantly, she handed the bags over for inspection and they were put in back with everything else. So, this young woman had combined the execution with a shopping trip, and possibly the hair salon. She looked nervous now though. Keller hoped she would drop dead of fright.

There was also an androgynous student with a plaster cast. And a lady who could barely catch her breath, though she'd been stationery for some minutes. Possibly angina. She was the permanently harassed kind, mopping at her brow with a grubby bandana.

Keller took his place among them. Without offering an explanation, he asked the chicken guy if he could have his seat by the window. Keller found that you could ask people to do things for you without giving a reason and often they did. If they said no, well then he was none the worse off, was he. Now he sat at the window and kept his big green eyes fixed on the outside.

As the *Harfield Correctional Institute* minibus pulled out of the lot and turned west onto the US170, the passengers were advised not to open a window or door between now and alighting the vehicle. They might as well have been told to shut up too, since conversation stopped abruptly. They were on their way now to their final destination and no-one had the stomach even for talk. An air freshener dangled from the rear-view mirror. It cast a sickly fruity smell and then was sucked away by the AC system. A woolly bear caterpillar crawled its way along the seat in front of him, inches from the collar of the 'journalist'. The caterpillar was getting caught in the seat fiber and its progress was slow. Keller knew a lot about car seats, since right from high school, he'd been working at the Hickory Plant in Greensboro, recycling plastic bottles and post industrial waste into the likes of those Ford seats.

The officers said nothing on the journey until on the far side of the Highway, they passed the facility where the prisoners were held on death row. This was five miles, the driver told them, from Turville Unit, the building where the executions took place. There could be no further doubt then. The words had been said aloud.

*

When they arrived at Turville, there were many cars in the lot. You might have thought you were attending a concert. There was no landscaping, nothing to soften the bricks of this death house which had been painted grey some time ago and had begun to flake. The *Harfield* logo hung on a large metal plaque. It too was faded and chipped.

Without a word of leave, the escorting officers walked away from the passengers and new staff took over. The minibus occupants were told that their belongings would be locked in the van until post-procedure. They were asked if they would like to take quarters into the building as there was a vending machine with snacks and drinks. But not even the skinny guy reached for quarters.

Then another officer, a woman, just young, set about asking them security questions and issuing tags on neck bands. 'You have to sign your name in a ledger. That's first.' She made herding movements with her arms and the group passed through a body sensor and then there was a cursory pat down. The officer held her thumb and forefinger up, like a diver's affirmative. Good to go.

Keller noted that indeed the older man he had marked out as a journalist, was permitted to take a notepad in with him. The redhead girl was also permitted writing material. Their pens were tested in a small scanning machine and he overheard the girl saying that she was preparing her doctoral thesis.

'Nice subject for a PhD,' Keller muttered beneath his breath. 'Classy.'

Somehow, he thought there would be a long walk now, time for contemplation but almost straight away the group were led into a small waiting room. The walls were solid, there was no viewing window. This was not the place then. But there was a vending machine. Keller could see fresh apples in the bottom row.

The redhead sat opposite Keller. He wondered if she would like the look of him. Women usually did, at first. It wasn't really the time or the place but a woman like her was hardly one for etiquette. She looked at her watch and said to the student wearing the plaster cast that she could barely cope without her cell. She then realised that there was some sort of joke to be made of the pun on 'cell' and actually laughed. Keller had a sudden vision of being in a lifeboat, sitting next to her, and pushing her over the side. She scribbled away in her big A4 pad, a ring with a diamond on her wedding finger. She was engaged then, and no doubt believed that she had everything to live for. The death penalty has a way of driving home a point like that. The girl sighed, like she had done a hard day's work. As if taunting him, she let the pad rest upside down on her lap, so that he could make out the words. She had big, babyish writing. Not like the American cursive they were taught. She had a bit of an accent too. Probably went to one of those expensive schools in Europe. Keller looked down at her notes.

...2002 Uzbekistan authorities boiled men to death in water... China have mobile death units, small buses with in-house execution equipment which travel to far lying provinces.... Neighboring South Carolina executed a 14 year old in the electric chair...

Keller stared hard at the redhead. What a charming companion for the day. Fleetingly, he wondered if he should follow her home tonight and get in a bit of target practice. He could get himself match ready and make the world a better place without this member of the population. He dug his knuckles into his thigh and told himself to stop getting distracted.

Keller knew that there would be no stay, and no clemency. He knew that the procedure would begin at 12 noon prompt. He closed his eyes and let his head rest against the cool plaster of the wall behind the bench. Without vision, the thrum of the AC filled his ears fully and he shut out the hushed voices and fell asleep, as he had done in moments of stress as a child. He had Aunt Joya to thank for that technique. Every time she locked him out of the house, he'd nap, no matter what the temperature.

If he were to have died of cold before waking, that wouldn't have been much of a tragedy. There was a point in the coldness when you stopped noticing and the sleep just washed gently over you. He trained that sleep to come to him when he needed it, like a faithful dog.

When Keller was woken in the Turville waiting room, his legs had loosened and sprawled out before him. 'It is time,' someone seemed to have said in his ear. As the day's reality cleaved through his head afresh, the redhead opposite had the nerve to offer him a look of disapproval. She picked her way through his sleepy limbs and walked out of the door, sober and straight-faced.

There was a walk now. They passed doors, like random choices. They all looked the same, all the colour of pale nicotine. But some of those doors were in the business of living and some were not. As you walked past them, you could feel hope slipping away. Which door? Which one? It was like a game the devil might play as you entered hell. Eventually the passengers reached the end of their journey and were shown into another room which was similar in size to the last but with what looked like a window on one side. The window was dark for the moment, with a black blind pulled down and opposite, there was a gallery with seating. The seating was slightly raked, like a theatre. They were here for a performance.

'That's 11.30 gone now,' someone said from the far end.

'Show must go on.' Keller mumbled.

There was a crackle and then an audio test from the speaker in the corner. Keller imagined that President Descher had arranged a televised viewing and that all over the State the people could see and hear this: factory workers, grandmothers, schoolchildren, stopping what they're doing and watching. From the audio speaker, Keller recognised words from the phonetic alphabet, then the date, today, June 23rd 2021, the location, the prisoner's name and number HCI 72259-931 and the time scheduled for execution.

Keller knew that the duration for the poison to act was ten minutes maximum and that the ratio to be injected was set against the inmate's weight and height.

Somewhere behind him, Keller could hear mumbling about the victims' families and an officer explained that they were seated separately, in another viewing room. He imagined that the families' room was crowded, since eight victims had lost their lives that day.

At 11.45 am, the time was announced once more on the speaker and the blind was pulled up manually, revealing the execution chamber. Keller had forgotten who was seated directly next to him now, but whoever it was flinched.

The prisoner was already strapped onto the gurney. There was a sheet over his body but you could see where the constraint buckles jutted up into the clean white cotton. His left arm was exposed however and the intravenous tube was already in. He was clean shaven. Keller had never seen him without a beard. He could almost pretend he did not know him.

Three *Harfield* guards came into the chamber now. They did not look at the window, which to them was a mirror. Who would want to see themselves doing what they were about to do, even if it was their duty. The three guards were each handed a syringe. The content of one of the syringes was deadly and the other two contained a harmless fluid. The guards would never know who among them administered the lethal injection.

The condemned man's chest began to rise and fall. He blinked rapidly and his Adam's apple bulged in his throat, as he struggled to find an impossible place between dignity and the screaming of his nerves to stay alive.

Keller murmured, 'There is nothing to do now but die.'

A man in the chamber who had been out of their view, moved into sight. He was dressed in a plain dark suit. He identified himself as Warden James and held up a chart. His hand was steady enough, his white knuckles though suggested a very tight grip on that chart.

Keller stared down at the inmate who seemed to be staring back, though Keller knew that the glass was one way and that all the condemned could see was a reflection of his own final scene. All the same, their eyes met.

Warden James turned to the prisoner. 'Is there anything you would like to say or read before we administer this lethal injection?'

'Yes.'

Keller frowned down at the neighboring lap. It was the redhead next to him, the PhD student, twisting that engagement ring. The girl who more than likely had it all, the girl who could not cope without her cell, was barely coping at all. Keller could feel her trembling against the length of his torso and the anger in his veins burned. The young woman held her hand up to her mouth and whispered into it, 'God, dear God.'

The Warden lowered his eyes to Prisoner HCI 72259-931 on the gurney and blinked several times. He said to the inmate, 'Go ahead, what do you want to say.'

'I would like to ask a question.'

'What is your question?'

'I would like to ask a question and have it answered.'

Warden James looked around the room at the other officials.

'Go ahead and ask your question.'

'Not until you tell me that I will have an answer.'

Keller smiled and nudged the redhead. 'You see? Make the most of every goddamned moment.'

The young woman was on the edge of her seat and on the edge of tears.

In the chamber, the suits and uniforms huddled and muttered amongst themselves and the Warden came free of the pack once more.

'We shall try to answer your question. And cannot commit beyond that. I ask you therefore again, is there anything you would like to say?'

The inmate tried to lift his head but the strap across his brow was held tight. He cleared his throat and said in that thick Carolina accent that Keller thought he'd forgotten but which now reignited in his memory and ripped through his heart.

'I want to know if my son can see me.'

CHAPTER 3

The Party

After the appalling start to Rebecca's 10th birthday at the breakfast table, her hopes rallied when she found a cake in the fridge. Colette must have baked it. And though as Austen often declared, Colette must be *the idlest of girls*, she did make exceedingly good cakes. On the occasions Colette made a cake, and Austen was at home, he would call her 'Kipling' for the entire day. Colette seemed to like this and since she and Austen did not get on at all otherwise, everyone brightened when the smell of Colette's baking rose from the kitchen. And now there it was in the fridge, a glorious gateau, with the light shining upon it. Gosh, it looked amazing. Rebecca felt a sudden surge of love for her big sister.

Colette never ate even a morsel of cake herself, since she was always aiming for the kind of body weight where your bones clacked together. But she loved to make them, to set them on a table and pace around them, to be praised copiously for her genius and selfless commitment. This cake was chocolate, with creamy filling and snowy icing and red writing, with a new number atop and Rebecca's name in extravagant swirls over the crown: *Ten Today Rebecca!*

At 4.00pm, as was customary for such events, the family were all seated in the high-ceilinged dining room. Rebecca's tummy turned over, like a pancake was getting flipped in there. She didn't settle her eyes on any of her party companions but gazed around the walls at the hunting scenes and seascapes. Where had they come from, these enormous oil paintings in their gilt frames? Who had painted them or hung them here? Rebecca's awakening was not confined to the history of her parents. She was now curious about everything. Who had lived here before? Why did they put metal bars on all the downstairs windows? Why did they leave? Did they all die?

'Stop your gawping, birthday girl.' Primmy said but with almost a smile. 'Or if you must gawp, gawp at that.' She pointed to Colette's wonderful cake in the centre of the grand table.

Colette herself pushed back her chair and stood up. 'I have something important I want to discuss.'

'Oh God, another one.' Primmy squirmed with discomfort.

Ralph's expression was open. Austen's face was highly amused. And Rebecca's inquisitive nose almost twitched; indeed she was so curious to hear what her sister was going to say next that she forgot to be annoyed at having her birthday thunder stolen.

Colette took a deep breath. 'Thing is, the actual thing is, this house is going to rack and ruin.'

Austen sniggered. Without even looking, Rebecca knew that her brother's mouth would have taken on that twisted sneer and she knew also that her sister's treacherous stammer would take full advantage of Austen's mocking.

Colette cleared her throat. 'I'd expect nothing less from you, Austen. But you don't really have to live here, d-d-do you. Oh yeah, you come by, in the holidays, or for the odd occasion. Like t-t-today. When you know the grub'll be d-d-decent. But the rest of us, we four…'

Austen burst out laughing. 'Fuck me, it's the grand orator.'

Primmy picked up her napkin from her plate and threw it across the table like a gauntlet. 'How dare you use that kind of language in front of your Grandfather and I. How *dare* you!'

Rebecca ground her elbows into the dining table. The cloth moved as she huffed and puffed with distress. She'd been hoping they could have used the whole length of the table but as usual, they were huddled down at one end, near the fire. The dining table was covered with enormous pads to protect the wood. What was the point of its grandeur if you were never to see it? The French polisher had come a few months ago but as soon as he'd finished treating the mahogany, it was hastily covered again. Perhaps it was like a Greek myth and its glossy surface couldn't be looked upon, or you'd be blinded. Rebecca scratched at the eczema in the crook of her arms.

'Don't!' Primmy Brown fixed her stare on Rebecca.

'What did *I* do?' Rebecca could feel the flaking skin under her finger nails and put her hands in her lap.

Colette wasn't finished with them yet. Normally, this level of tension would have got the better of Colette Brown. She had a sort of lock gate emotional release. When sadness or injustice rose too high, it all sluiced through. Her younger sister generally found it safer to stand back a little when Colette reached this flashpoint but today, she seemed to be holding it together. Colette laid her palms on the table and looked desperate. 'We're not managing. Are we? Well, are we?'

'Hey. Are you wearing lipstick?'

'Oh shut up, Rebecca. For a minute.'

'It's my birthday.'

'Well, duh, this we know. Look, all I am t-t-trying to say is that we have to... we're going to have to b-b-buckle down. We can't just accept things. Not as they are. We're... not pathetic, but like that.' Colette looked at her brother.

'We're apathetic, Kipling.'

'Yes, thank you Austen. We're apathetic. And I don't want us to be. I want us to make an effort. I want us to fix up this house. There, that, for a start, we never call it *Taransay*. But that's its name. We treat the house with d-d-d, with dis-dis...'

'With disdain, Kipling.'

'Yes. Like we don't care about it. I mean Austen calls it *The Orphanage*. Like it's all a big joke. But I don't think it's funny.'

'I don't either. It isn't funny.' Rebecca looked down at her empty plate.

Primmy closed her eyes and spoke in her medium at a séance voice. 'Once upon a time there were three little orphans who lived with their wicked grandparents in a creaky old house by the sea. *Taransay*.'

Ralph Brown didn't like his wife's sinister tone and steered them back towards debate. 'Insofar as a house really has a name. It's just something plucked from somewhere. An idea that—'

'You see, Grandad, that's exactly the kind of thing I'm talking about. You're d-d-d.. deh, deh, den...' Colette looked at Austen once more.

'You're denigrating the idea. You're putting her down, Ralph. She's had enough. And look at Rebecca, bless her. She's about to explode. I fear for the crockery.'

Colette's ambivalence played in her expression. Normally, she'd be rolling her eyes at her brother's absurd Lord Byron way of speaking but he did seem to be kind of on her side. Colette's knuckles bore down now on the linen cloth, as she leaned across the table like some emaciated silverback. 'I want us to turn over a new leaf. I want us to have a sort of... sh-sh-schedule of works. Put some love back into this place. Into *Taransay*.'

Primmy had heard enough. She had turned puce with outrage. 'My God. Dear God above. You ungrateful brat. All of you.' She stared down Colette and then she cast her eyes among them, like she was making a silent spell. 'As if we hadn't done enough. Given up our entire lives. Our very lives. For *you.* Might I remind you that we lived in England. That we were English. *Are* English. And yet we came up here. To Brigadoon. Moved into this godforsaken house, in this godforsaken land. And why. *Why?*'

Ralph reached up, almost to his wife's trembling lips, but thought better of it.

Rebecca opened her mouth to say, *Yes! Why?* But her grandmother held up her hand and her words kept tumbling. 'There's a strangeness here. And you children are infected with it. Austen talks like an eighteenth century bard. You, Colette, steal food from the fridge, always the best stuff. Oh God yes, you think I don't know? I'm *paying* for it. Scurry up the stairs to your bedroom, like some giant rodent. Then you come down again, weighing next to nothing. You think we don't know what's going on? *Honestly?* You think we don't hear you in the bathroom, chucking it all up? And as for *you*!' Primmy Brown pointed at Rebecca.

'It's my birthday.'

'You, Rebecca. With your silly make-believe games. Doctors is it? Surgeons? You, with your blood transfusions, your re-starting of hearts. Your crossing yourself! I suppose Maria Theresa taught you that, did she? You don't have any other grandparents. Alright? They had your mother by mistake when they were nearly fifty and now they're dead. We're all you've got, Emma. Sorry if we don't pass muster.'

'Emma?'

'Rebecca.'

'You called me—'

'For pity's sake child, give it a rest.'

Rebecca's eyes filmed over with sorrow. She looked at the cake, still round and proud but it was wasted now, pointless.

She wanted to run to Murdo and sob in his arms. She wanted to run to the sea and drown herself and make them sorry.

Austen's eyes gleamed maniacally. 'Fucksake, Primmy man, you're killing our wee lass.' He lifted his hands into the air and reached over to his little sister with imaginary defibrillator paddles and shouted 'Clear!'

Colette grabbed Rebecca's wrist in a tight cuff and snorted, 'Leave her out of this. Rebecca is innocent.'

Rebecca nodded vigorously and Austen clutched at his ribs, near hysterics, saying, 'And to think, I nearly didn't come for this.'

'Wheesht, Austen,' Colette held her finger up to silence him and they each stared at her. 'What? Don't all look like that. So I said *wheesht*. Why do we have to avoid Scottish words. We live here. I go to school here. This is my life. I didn't grow up in England. All I'm asking is that we make the house warm, comfortable. A *home*. Everyone else has one. Why not us? And then we can, well, get through these years as best we can.'

'Till we can escape.' Austen dried his eyes with the back of his hand.

'Yes, well, you've always escaped, haven't you. Always gone to a posh boarding school. Not us though. Why? Just why is that?'

Ralph took a measured breath and quelled a coughing fit. 'There wasn't, that is there isn't enough money to go around. Please understand, fair Colette.'

Rebecca did not like it when her grandfather made reference to her sister's flaxen hair. Rebecca felt she was missing out, being dark, and she worried that blondeness was connected to goodness, that she was shut out. Although Austen was fair too and the goodness had certainly run out for him.

Youngest Brown had never thought about their education and the financing of it. Her head rose now, like a gopher from the burrow. How could a girl, just ten today, really understand that her brother attended an eye-wateringly costly boarding school and that her sister went to a middlingly expensive grammar school, while she herself knocked about at the local comprehensive up in the nearby town of Mallaig.

'Rebecca?' Grandma Primmy straightened and stiffened. 'Rebecca, could you look at me when I am addressing you, please.'

'Yes.' Rebecca tried to shake off her sister's grip which still cuffed her wrist but in so doing, unsettled her plate which was still cakeless. The whole day was cakeless now.

'Well?' Primmy's nostrils were at their widest flare.

Ralph's bronchial tubes could stay quiet no longer and he sounded like he was attempting to gob forth a small amphibian. He croaked: 'I think your grandmother wishes to know if you would like to carry on with your party. I think that's it.' Ralph smacked his piscine lips together, which is what he always did when awaiting a response.

Rebecca began to cry.

'Oh stop that, Rebecca. Heaven's sake.' Primmy was losing her temper. 'You're not a baby anymore. So keen to point out to us how grown up you're getting and now look.'

Austen looked at Youngest Brown with an anthropological eye. 'So we *train* children not to cry. It's their natural response, yet we diminish them for it. Extraordinary really.'

Colette pressed her fingers against Rebecca's throat to quell the gulps which had become so regular, her little sister was burping too. 'Oh come here, Becky.' Rebecca couldn't look up, but she sensed her big sister was probably making some kind of open arm gesture. She did do that once a year or so and

Rebecca tried to shift her chair closer to Colette's. 'Becky, I think your games are fascinating. I do. Because they actually are. Especially the blood transfusion. Can someone cut the cake. Come on, let's do her birthday. Why are we always giving up?'

Ralph creaked into action and took up the bone handled hunting knife which he admired greatly.

Austen lit a cigarette. 'They're not games, are they Becky?'

Rebecca could feel Austen tapping the leg of her chair with his big Brogue.

Primmy took the first slice and sighed, flapping her hand at the cigarette smoke. 'Might I remind you, and I hardly have the strength at this point, that my husband has emphysema.'

Austen did not look at his grandmother, but answered, 'He doesn't. He does not have emphysema, does he, Grandma. No doctor has ever diagnosed that. No doctor ever diagnoses anything. Because you keep us all in here.' Austen rolled his eyes over the ceiling. '*You* diagnose us. Treat us. General practitioner. Child psychiatrist. And on occasion, surgeon. No wonder Becky plays those games. She's practising for what she believes is adulthood.'

Primmy bridled. 'Austen, for a smart boy, you can talk the most unutterable tosh. Put out that cigarette. Right now.'

'Ralph has chronic bronchitis, which has every chance of clearing up if you'd just let him put the fire on in his study.' Austen took a long drag on his cigarette, then turned his attention back to his youngest sister. 'The blood transfusions, Becky, are just the tiniest bit weird. No? Since you turn pale at the merest—'

'It's just pretend! There is no blood. I'm making it up. I have my imagination. And anyway I haven't done that for years. You people need to let me grow up. I'm ten!'

Austen was laughing again now. 'I like it when you take the pulse and you look at your little watch. Eh, my wee lassie

MacGraw? Your watch, which doesn't even have a second hand.' He shook his head affectionately. 'I love that.'

Ralph had now given each of them a slice of cake and Primmy let a forkful sit in her mouth.

'Mmm,' Ralph waved his dainty cake fork, like a hatpin in his great mitt. 'Good, Colette. Excellent. Your own recipe?'

Colette ignored him, determined on resolution of some kind. 'I really mean this, about the state of us. I don't want to spend another winter here. Under these conditions.'

Primmy swallowed her cake to free up her mouth. 'Well now Colette, I can't imagine quite what you think your options are. But if we can all pull together, perhaps something can come of this plan. Uncle Neil is visiting the week after next and I'm sure he'd be more than—'

'What on earth does this have to do with Uncle Neil?' Colette was genuinely dumbfounded.

Austen too. 'Who the hell is Uncle Neil anyway? Why does he come here? He never stays. Never eats. He's like some vicar, without the neck thingy. Is he dad's brother? Or mum's?' Austen shook his head. 'I think he'd be much better suited to appearing in an Agatha Christie play and leave us well alone.'

'Yeah. I don't even like him. And it's my birthday.'

Colette nodded, 'Rebecca doesn't like him. I don't like him. He's not like a real person. No-one knows who he is. He's like a spy.'

'The Uncle from U.N.C.L.E.' Austen said.

Colette was bolstered with this united momentum. 'I think Uncle Neil is having cosmetic surgery. He never looks the same twice. Why is he always, like, ushered into the drawing room, as if he's a criminal. We shouldn't have to have him here. Creepy guy. What we need around here is more d-d-d, demock...'

'Democracy.' Austen put his hand in the air. 'I vote we get rid of Uncle Neil.'

'Steady on.' Ralph looked longingly at Austen's cigarette.

'All those in favour, say aye.'

'I,' Rebecca said wistfully and crossing her arms, slid them over the table, letting her head rest upon her hands.

Ralph got up to put another log on the fire.

'Don't bother, Ralph,' Primmy said. 'We've done enough for one day. Out!' She got up to leave.

Ralph did not move. 'Excuse me, dear, I wonder if you wouldn't mind re-phrasing that. *Out?* I will not be spoken to like a dog, Primrose. I will not.' But he did not get up to tend the fire. Instead, he sat very still.

'Oh for God's sake. Why does everything have to turn into a ding dong?' Primmy said, as this was her preferred phrase for the many arguments which took place at *The Orphanage*. But this was not like one of their usual ding dongs. This was rebellion. This was cake carnage.

CHAPTER 4

The Hunters

Keller sat in the stationery Chevy. He had his father's ashes strapped into the seat belt on the passenger seat beside him, along with a bag containing Othaniel Baye's personal effects:

A wedding ring – no inscription.

A fake Shinola watch, which was still keeping time but the Roman numerals for IX and X had fallen off, so that the time between eight o'clock and eleven o'clock stretched eerily. Keller put the watch on his wrist and looked through the rest of his father's belongings. Mostly they were from the first prison, before his crime was upgraded to capital.

There were several certificates detailing qualifications in mechanics and an Enhanced Driver's License. Othaniel would have been hoping, back when he was first incarcerated, to land himself a decent job as a prisoner.

There were some faded pajama bottoms.

A diary, with no entries. Keller shook his head at that. 'Dumbest thing I ever saw.'

Couple of pair sneakers.

A wallet with photos. Keller took out the picture of his father and Aunt Joya. They looked younger there than Keller was now. They were going somewhere in fine clothes, laughing, both of them. His father wore a suit with a vest. There was still hope in Othaniel's eyes.

Keller got out of the Chevy with the carryall and walked towards Greensboro's South Main Street. He slung the bag up on his shoulder and slowly ripped the photograph in half, dropping

Aunt Joya on the sidewalk. He walked up to a homeless man outside *Kitty's Nails*. The guy wasn't begging, just sat hunched by the doorway. His foot was rattling, in the aftermath of some substance ingestion most likely, and the little sandy dog at his side fixed his stare on that trembling foot. Keller stared at the man's shoes, as he did every time he passed a homeless person. But there was nothing remarkable about these scruffy loafers. Keller put down the carryall next to the odd couple and walked away. Neither the man nor the dog seemed to notice.

For the ashes, Keller had no idea where to take them. He'd hoped something on the landscape would speak to him as he'd been driving from the mortician's, but nothing had suggested itself. If he was honest, he could barely remember living in a place with his father. His memories were more an awareness of a time when his father was simply present, there in the house, there in his life, but he struggled to see him at a table with a plate of food in front of him, or shaving at a bathroom mirror, or ever being out in the yard. Keller had no photographs of their own home, when he had lived with his dad down in Fayetteville, but he guessed Joya had ditched all that. There was nothing left of them.

In the end, Keller took the ashes down to Horsepen Creek which held significant memories for himself at least. Lots of alright memories and one very bad one, in the denser part of the forest. He would stay well away from that area. Keller walked by the river for a half mile or so to be clear of the dog walkers and then studied the urn to see how it opened. It was easy enough, just newly sealed.

The water was moving slowly on the Creek as the heat built to full summer and the ashes settled on the surface as one shape, like a grey continent, breaking only when it slipped over boulders. Keller took off his shoes and sat on a rock near the edge of the river, with his feet in up to the ankles. He wished his father could have been to this place with him just once. He tried to think of something meaningful to say, not a prayer exactly but something about the man who gave him life.

His teacher had told Keller he had a way with words. He couldn't remember her name, Miss Rake or Miss Rooney or something. She'd taught him over at Jefferson too, when he lived with his dad. Always seemed to have a word of encouragement for Keller. She used to call him 'son'. *C'mon son, nice looking boy like you. Get your head down into those books. Make something of yourself. I know you can.* She'd pick up a hunk of his untended blond mop and pretend to tug. She even brought him novels from home, *White Fang* and *Johnny Tremain*. He could see the book covers now in his mind's eye. That teacher came to see Aunt Joya on one occasion but she didn't get past the front porch. Now Keller couldn't even remember that lady's name. Was it Rook? Miss Rook? Many times, he thought he'd seen her since school but it was just wishful thinking. Whenever he got close, it turned out to be someone else. Even after the execution, he thought he saw her at the press conference, sitting near the back but when he looked for her afterwards, there was no sign.

Keller turned the empty urn around in his hands. There was no inscription, Keller couldn't see the point. He wasn't keeping the urn. The mortician had just typed up a sticky label with his father's name and date of passing. Keller peeled off the label and pressed it inside the back pocket of his new jeans.

There was nothing in Keller's head to say to his father. He looked around the huge tulip poplars lining the Creek. Impossible to tell which one had held the old rope swing he'd used as a boy but Keller left the urn at the foot of a particularly grand specimen.

It had taken Othaniel Baye just under nine minutes to die.

It had taken just seconds for that old drifter to die, back there in the thick woods of Horsepen.

Keller tried now to remember what year that would have been. You didn't think about years in four figures till you were clear of school. Every recall was in terms of which grade you were in. Eighth grade, Keller guessed. He could see Angelo's pale face still when they found the cat pinned to the tree.

There had been four of them in their gang. Steve, Keller, Lemi and Angelo. All a bit misfit, none of them ever part of the main event. The four of them were like the scraps Lemi's mom would pare from her pastry pies. But those boys balled themselves together to make something, and it kind of worked. But then Steve Truffaut, with his thick milk bottle glasses, got leukaemia and died. Seemed every kid at school was crying the day they finally heard, even his teacher who'd given him books.

Soon after Steve's passing, a white cat appeared in the woods. Keller took him home to Vandalia Road but Aunt Joya shooed the pair of them straight back out. Fastest she'd moved in years. Joya hollered at them so loud, half the street could see his shame and the white cat's ears flattened against its head. They went back to the thickest part of the forest, where it felt safe and soundless of people. Keller made a shelter for the cat and as he talked to him, Keller began to believe that his friend Steve Truffaut had reincarnated himself in this feline form. Keller did not share this belief with Lemi and Angelo, who would have whooped with laughter and derision for his theory.

The rumble of anger Keller felt towards his Aunt grew and grew, as he made a den for the cat from thick branches and ferns. The following evening, Keller stole the last of Joya's fried chicken from the ice box. The cold fat slathered over the chicken bones would work its way onto the animal's skinny haunches. When she found the chicken was missing, Aunt Joya jumped out at her nephew with the handle of her old cane banging at his shoulder blades, but Keller figured it was worth it if the animal was still at the shelter the next day. And indeed the white cat was. When Steve Truffaut smelled that chicken, he forgot his fear and nipped at the meat right from the human hand. Keller stayed till late into the night, even though it was fall and the temperatures were going down quickly. The white cat slept up against his body and Keller looked around at the darkness slipping down through the tree canopy. Would there be a way of living out here? Just him and Steve? With Lemi and Angelo visiting?

Within a couple weeks, the cat would come to a call. Of course, it was expecting food and he did not disappoint it, though Keller quickly learned that the white cat did not like peaches. For tuna however, Steve Truffaut would sprint through the red and golden leaves. That cat had such a bright expression on his face when his human arrived. Perhaps it wasn't a smile exactly but it made Keller feel happy. This was such a peculiar sensation, he held his hand against his chest.

One day, Keller brought Angelo to the little den. Angelo had never been that deep into the forest and was afraid that they would not find their way back, though he could quickly see that Keller was familiar with the route. But when they got to the shelter, the cat did not come scampering. Keller called over and over and over. Then he saw it. The cat was nearby, fixed to a yellow pine, with a bolt through his middle. Dark blood stained the white fur like a rust. Steve Truffaut's eyes were open and strangely unsurprised.

'You boys been feeding this one? I saw the dish.' The boys jumped when they heard the man's voice behind them. 'Shouldn't a done. Makes 'em real lazy.'

The man had all the hallmarks and trappings of a person belonging to nowhere and no-one. *Hobos*, Aunt Joya called them. He looked like he'd been living rough for a good while.

Paper bags containing his life's necessities sat at the foot of a tree. His clothes were spattered with every kind of stain. But in his hands, he held a spanking new mini crossbow.

'This is, well, this is a birthday present. I gave it to myself.' The down and out looked at the crossbow and then doubled up laughing. 'Got it from a store-keeper. Told me to fetch the supper. I think that's what he said. Supper. And all I found me was this lil' fucker.' He pointed at Steve Truffaut, hanging like a pajama case. 'How d'you think I got him up there? Maybe he could fly? Like a squirrel?' The man started to laugh again, folding over on himself.

There was no thinking to be done. Keller ran straight for the drifter and head-butted him in the stomach. The cat killer and his crossbow fell to the ground. The man's shirt had ridden up, exposing his white flesh. Keller leapt upon him and sunk his teeth into the tramp's flank. A scream took a swoop of birds out of the trees and Keller staggered to his feet, wiping at his mouth which was sloppy with blood. The man let out a roar of rage and got up unsteadily. He swung his arms around, like a drunken discus thrower and lunged forward. He took hold of the boy by the neck. Keller clawed at the man's grip.

'Angelo! Shoot him! Shoot him!'

Angelo was clutching at his own hair but moved towards the weapon. Keller could no longer speak as the breath was wrung from him with tight, filthy fingers. There was a fizz in the air, a sound like a speeding firework. Suddenly Keller was released and snatching at the air for oxygen. The drifter's face creased in agony and he fell backwards into the foliage. A bolt was fixed deep in his thigh and Angelo's eyes were pinned wide with terror. He dropped the crossbow and tears started tumbling down his cheeks.

'Kell, no, no, no. I thought he was gonna kill you.'

The tramp writhed on the ground. He got one hand firmly around the bolt and then pulled hard so that it came free. Blood gurgled in the wound then spurted upwards, like the water fountain at school. The man was trying to get to his feet. Keller picked up the crossbow. It had a trigger just like a gun and two more bolts were loaded and ready. The man hesitated as he saw Keller take aim. He reached out his arm, the fingers on his hand splayed in appeal.

'Now boy, don't be insane. This has to stop right here right now. There's no sense in—'

The bolt thumped into the man's breastbone, more or less dead centre.

*

Clem's Diner was still on the corner of West Friendly Avenue in Greensboro. It was a traditional fifties diner with chequered floor, red leather seating and aluminium ribbing around the counter. Keller had not had the best of experiences in *Clem's*. As soon as he was earning decent money on the weekend, he tended to find comfort in burger bars and spooning up *Turkey Hill* ice cream. When his body started to give away his pastime, the punishment came thick and fast from his classmates. So Keller was surprised to find himself with a smile on his face when he saw the old *Diner*. Why would he be smiling just two days after seeing his father put to death? And then it came to him. He was smiling because this would be his very last visit. Nothing much good had ever happened to Keller in *Clem's Diner*, yet as he pushed through the door, warm nostalgia flooded his chest. He was passing through his past, like his own spirit. This was an exorcism.

Clem himself was a rodent-faced oddball who really had no business being in hospitality. But that was part of the attraction for the high school kids. Clem was the guy they loved to hate. Anyone who was getting a rough ride – often Keller Baye when he'd grown out of the woods – could run for the *Diner* after school, where the taunting would abate and switch right over to Clem. It was like a sanctuary for the unpopular.

Keller half wondered if he'd run into someone from school today. That's how it happened in films. You'd be minding your own business and then someone would tap you on the shoulder. *Hey, it's Keller isn't it. Looking good, buddy. We should get a cold one. No, better, come for supper. You remember when you'd come by my mother's? Her pot roast?*

But Keller didn't remember anyone's mother, except Lemi's when they were young. From senior high and on, he'd never been invited back to anyone's house, let alone eaten their mom's pot roast.

Keller hopped up on a stool. 'Clem not here?'

The older waitress dispensing coffee further up the bar tilted her head back to answer. 'Well, good afternoon. Clem retired, oh two years since. Could barely see him for the dust. Still owns it though. I'm the manager. Ha! You wouldn't know it from the pay check.' A bitter laugh burst from her, scaring an elderly lady with a hearing aid who was only just maintaining balance on a nearby stool.

A younger waitress in a lumpy pinafore came back to the counter and turned to Keller. 'Clearwater, Florida. Brand new condo, Clem's got. Alright for some. There's a couple postcards over there on the board if you're interested.'

'I'm not.'

'Coffee? Soda?'

'Mountain Dew.'

'Regular or diet?'

'Regular. You think I need to drop a few pounds?'

The waitress ignored him and Keller went over to a booth. Let her bring it over. Why would she say that? He'd been bench pressing for years. She wanted to take a look in the mirror a little more often and drop a few of her own pounds. He wouldn't touch her with a ten foot pole. Not even in his practising days, when he'd zone in on a girl who couldn't get any in a month of Sundays.

He never spent any money on the practising girls but he'd take them down to Horsepen Creek, over beyond the Longleaf Pines. There was a bird hide there with tattered pictures on the wall. The girl would always say something about those pictures. Just trying to make conversation, Keller guessed, but all the same, the low opinion he already held of her, diminished further. He saw in them no originality and much worse, he saw that in himself.

The last time he went there was with a girl called Emily who had acute asthma. Some days she brought oxygen to school on a little two wheel trolley which looked like Aunt Joya's shopping cart.

Keller flopped down at the back of the hide. He was around fourteen and his legs were too long at that point for the rest of his body. He watched Emily breathe. She seemed ok. He wanted to make her come, that was all. He didn't want to put her in any danger.

Predictably, Emily focussed on the bird pictures. 'I don't know these. Do you? Oh I heard of the chickadee.' She put her fingertip on the names and read aloud. '*A chipping sparrow is a spizella passerina*. Huh. Wonder why they have two names.'

'It's latin. They have a common name and a latin one. Don't ask me why. Just come and sit down.'

'Kell?' Emily turned to him and she suddenly seemed much more attractive. 'I never done anything like this.'

'I know. There has to be a first time. It won't be intercourse. You know that, don't you. I just want to touch you, to make you feel good.' He used the word *practise* just the once, with a girl whose name he had long forgotten. He wouldn't make that mistake again.

'You want to make me feel like a woman?'

'Yes.' Oh that was a good one. He made a mental note of that and was to use this often in the following years.

It was all about the timing. They wanted to do it just as much as he did, otherwise why were they here. To begin with he'd say something kind of funny, that always put them at ease. He might start out like, 'Hey, should I put the *Do Not Disturb* sign on the door?' Then he might ask them a bit about their family. That reassured them. He would begin to touch them lightly, almost so's they didn't notice, on top of their clothing, on the sleeve or his finger lightly just inside her collar. He smiled a lot. Then he'd compliment them. They'd shrug that off because they weren't at all used to that type of nicety. But he'd insist. Then he'd tell them how they made him feel. 'Hot. You know? Kinda sweaty. I don't know, just sort of crazy.' He'd shake his head, as if he was trying to get a grip of himself but that the task was impossible, since she was so irresistible. If he could get her to the point that she made the first direct move, perhaps leaning in with her lips almost pouting, breath just a little raggedy, then he was home and dry; though in fact dry was not at all what he was aiming for.

They were good memories. Pleasurable at the time and pleasurable in the recall. He built up dozens of those memories at the hide at Horsepen but nothing could ever shift the mass of that dark memory in the forest, when they killed the drifter. Angelo completely lost his mind. Keller had to send him into the

Creek, had him sit in there on a rock to let the temperature chill him down. Then Keller sent him on his way. 'Go! Get! Tell your mother you fell in the Creek.'

Keller said that he would take care of everything, that no-one would ever know and that even if they were to find out, all's Angelo had done was defend Keller from strangulation. 'I mean it, Angelo. I will take care of this. Stop your crying and wash those tears off before you go.' Once Angelo had stopped crying and was simply shaking, Keller told him to keep the fading sun to his right-hand side till he got to the lighter woods and found the path.

Then Keller got to work. He unpinned Steve Truffaut and laid him carefully on the ground. His bloodied body was stiff and he maintained the same shape lying among the leaves. Keller had a little box of supplies in the shelter and now he spread honey and sardine oil over the spot where the bolt had driven into the tree. He figured the weevils and sweat bees would get busy right away and sure enough by the time he had extended the fire pit perimeter some, dozens of insects were gnawing at the bark of the yellow pine.

Keller tried to assess how much the tramp weighed and then chided himself for wasting time. He pulled the man by the feet towards the fire pit. It was hard work, inch by inch, and his shoes kept coming lose. They weren't his size. The drifter had stolen them of course, what would a man like that want with Italian leather shoes. But it was harder to pull the body without them. Keller put the shoes back on him and tightened the laces. Where in the world would a deadbeat like this get those fine shoes? With the laces tight, it was easier. He got into a rhythm – pull, stop, one two three, pull, stop, one two three - and dragged the dead man into the fire pit. He'd heard that bodies get all hard when they die, like the cat, but this guy was floppy and warm still. Keller pushed the man's knees up to his chin to make the pyre more compact and as he did so, the drifter said, 'Gaaaah'. Keller leapt back, tripping over a boulder and falling on his ass. What was that sound? He got up gingerly and held the man's wrist, as far away from his own body as possible. He couldn't feel a pulse. Perhaps it was just air inside him soughing out. He looked at the tramp's dead, swollen fingers, pink and black, like the charred brat sausages which dropped off their sharp sticks on cook-outs. The boys just wiped off the ash and stuck the brats back on. But oh those dead fingers. Keller felt the first wave of nausea then. Those fingers which had squeezed his neck so tight. He would have to wear a scarf tomorrow or what was that high-necked thing? A turtle neck, yes. But he didn't have one. Keller felt the vomit making its move. He remembered the way the tramp had laughed. Looked like he had those fake teeth, the kind you glue in. Would those teeth burn? He looked down at the corpse, bile rising. 'There. How funny is that now?' Keller's legs began to wobble and he threw up. He kicked dirt and leaves over the sick and took some larger rocks over to the fire pit to make a neat circle all around the body. There was a crack nearby, a branch snapping under the weight of something or someone.

'Angelo?'

Nobody answered and Keller went back to the shelter for the barbecue gel. There was three quarters in the bottle and he smeared it over the drifter's clothes. But he took off the leather shoes, somehow suspecting that they would take too long to burn, or would leave residual evidence. They had been very smart dress shoes in their day. He imagined the tramp lifting them from some locker at a country club. He put the shoes in a tree hollow a little way off. Returning to the fire, he made a note of the tree's position, in degrees, from where he stood. 'A human protractor,' his teacher used to call him.

He analysed the pyre. Would that be enough of the flammable gel now? Does flesh melt or burn? Or does it just cook. They say it's like pork. He'd have to get the body burned down to as small as possible and then he'd figure something else out. Should he take out those dentures. Keller imagined opening the corpse's mouth to remove them and the false teeth suddenly biting into the bone of his fingers. Keller shivered and pointed his stove igniter at the smeared gel and click, the body came alight. Better take all this stuff home when he was finished. Get rid of all his supplies and kick the shelter out of shape. The clothes caught on fire easily and Keller raided his supply of dry pine cones which burned really well too. He put them all around the folded over body. Too late, he saw that the tramp was wearing a watch. Something else he'd stolen probably. The flames were too great to get to the watch and he made a mental note to find it from the ashes later. He picked up the man's stuffed paper bags and was tempted to look inside but he really had to get this finished fast. Keller dumped the bags into the flames. Then he gathered up all the leaves where the body had fallen and every leaf around and about where he could see a drop of blood. He bundled everything on top of the body and looked up at the smoke already climbing a hundred feet high. It rose in a vertical plume, true in the sky, with no wind to speak of. He wondered about burning his own clothes but could hardly stroll back to Vandalia Road naked.

Keller stood back as the heat became more intense. He watched the man's skin blister and sizzle. He was really doing this. Him, Keller Baye. He'd killed a man and now he was incinerating him. He was not afraid, not right now.

'Nobody fucking kills Steve Truffaut twice. You hear? You hear me?' Keller had no idea what he was feeling as he held his arm up against the heat, but it might have been something akin to pride.

The sweat bees who'd gotten started on the honeyed tree did not like the smoke and wove furious figures of eight in the air. Keller blinked with the sting of the smoke and with disbelief. He tried to remember what life had felt like an hour before but already, he could not.

*

The hunter came into *Clem's Diner* with a little ting-a-ling of the bell as the door hit it. This was Mr Blonk with whom Keller Baye had been in contact for some time, though they had never met.

Blonk got himself a coffee from the older waitress before turning around to assess the clientele. When Keller tipped his head, Blonk came over to the booth. Keller liked that, a man following his direction.

Blonk had said when he last called that he'd be wearing a blazer and tie. 'No carnation though.'

Keller couldn't place his accent during their exchanges on the phone. 'Blazer. Got it. Two o'clock sharp then. Of the P M. I'll give you a nod.'

Blonk was rather dapper, Keller thought, with his pale linen jacket and silk necktie. Completely out of place of course. Shouldn't *'America's Foremost Internet Hunter'* try to blend? No, he was too arrogant to blend. He had always come across as arrogant, and particularly on the telephone, but Keller thought that was probably part and parcel of being the *Foremost* in a field. Anyway, it didn't matter if Blonk stuck out like a sore thumb, since this was the end of their journey together.

They shook hands. 'Good to meet you.'

'Likewise, Mr Blonk.' That was not his real name of course.

'Can I get you a coffee?'

'No, this girl here has my soda.' Keller gestured to the serving girl hovering behind Blonk. 'Finally.' Keller rolled his eyes. 'Thought for a minute there, it was too far to drag her fat ass.'

The waitress gasped and her mouth stayed open. Then she closed it and looked suddenly tearful. Keller hadn't been expecting that and he regretted his behaviour in front of his associate.

'Well now let me see,' Blonk was clearly embarrassed by his client's behaviour and began shuffling some papers on the table between them. 'This place takes me back. College years. Mind you, I've been in this game, well, of sorts, for getting on thirty years. Fact is I dropped out of my studies, it took off so fast. Different now of course, with the internet. I kind of miss the legwork.'

'The internet, yeah.'

'Hard for the young to imagine we had a life without it.'

'I never been to college. Did you make 'em proud?'

'Who? My kids?'

'No, Blonk. Your folks.'

'My line of work doesn't really generate pride.'

'But it pays well. I'm picking up your money right after this.' Keller leaned forward and lowered his voice. 'I've never seen twenty thousand bucks in the flesh, so to speak. Shit, I never seen five hundred.'

Blonk stretched his neck up from his collar. He hadn't dealt in cash since the late nineties. 'It's seventeen thousand eight hundred dollars.'

'I know, I know. Selling my car. It's a Silverado.'

'Chevy?'

Keller nodded. 'For twenty grand. The change is holiday money. Matter of fact, the paperwork's already done. But the new owner extended me the courtesy of keeping her till I get to the airport.'

'A friend of yours?'

'Yeah, I know him. From work. I mean, he got a bargain and all but you know, that's a rare kind of trust, don't you think? I just leave the parking ticket in the visor, keys under the rear left wheel arch and pshoooo, I take off. In the air, I mean. But I could just as easily drive up to Canada with my twenty large ones. You Canadian?'

Blonk looked out on the street. 'Where is it?'

'Where is what?'

'Your car?'

'Oh you can't see it from here. I don't park it near other vehicles. When I first had it, always had to be in sight, you know. If I'd had a leash long enough, I'd probably have used that. I even slept in it, first couple of nights.'

'Well now that's a hard thing to part with. I hope you will consider the money well—'

'You are from the north, aren't you? I never really heard it before.' Keller could feel the smile returning. 'I don't think I've been paying proper attention.' He was changing so fast now. All his senses heightening with purpose.

Blonk did not respond on his whereabouts. 'You know it's sold, this *Diner*. The owner's shipping it to England, on a boat. Can you imagine? Little British kids, slurping their shakes and wolfing hot dogs.'

Blonk had all the detail. The man lived for detail, sucked it up like a line of cocaine. It was typical that he would have the lowdown on *Clem's Diner* before agreeing to meet there. Urge for detail was in his DNA. It was necessary in his line of work.

'In the old days, we had the bounty hunters, Mr Blonk. Didn't we. But I suppose, with the complexities of globalisation and the internet, a suede clad mercenary on horseback just wouldn't cover it these days.'

'You're good with words. I'll say that.'

'Nothing stays the same. Clem's in Florida. *Diner's* shipping out.'

'Yes sir, Uncle Sam's loss is Coventry's gain. Not Coventry Connecticut. Coventry England.'

'Perhaps I'll go visit.'

Blonk tapped the manilla folder. 'You need to be a little north of there. Pack a sweater. You're going to the Scottish Highlands.'

Keller sipped his Mountain View and pulled the dossier around so that he could read the right way up.

Blonk seemed uncomfortable that the file was out of his control.

'Can you let me have access to the trace software, Mr Blonk? I'll pay extra of course.'

'I'm afraid I can't, sir, no. It's not under license. Just something I have developed myself over the years.'

'You mean it's illegal.'

Blonk smiled and patted the file with both hands. 'Everything you have asked for is in there. You don't need software. You don't need to keep searching. We found her.'

CHAPTER 5

The Library

Shortly after the birthday party, Rebecca was on a school trip to Fort William. The children were walking double file along a pavement and as they passed the Library at Airds Crossing, she happened to look in the window and saw someone there, sitting at a table and looking at a newspaper. Quite relaxed, they looked, as if it was their own kitchen. She wondered about that all day. She wondered so hard about that anonymous person reading a newspaper comfortably in a public library that the wonder scooped out a small section of her brain and made its home there.

When she got home, Rebecca asked her grandmother if she could join that library at Airds Crossing and Primmy said, "No". This was quite usual and did not daunt the girl in the least. Her grandmother said "No" to everything, whether she had properly heard the question or not. When Rebecca asked next, Primmy said there was a perfectly good mobile library provided by *High Life Highland* each Thursday morning in the *Co-operative Supermarket* car park – Primmy never called it the Co-op – and indicated that this was a duty, to support the mobile service.

Rebecca didn't ask again but instead arranged to go swimming with her friend Maria Theresa at the weekend. She gave MT five pounds. Two pounds fifty of that was to go swimming by herself in the municipal pool at Fort William. One pound fifty was for a Slush Puppie afterwards. The remaining pound was to keep her mouth shut.

During the bus ride however, the duplicity now properly underway, Rebecca became increasingly nervous. The bus stopped suddenly and when she heard the hiss of the door opening, she felt the game was up and stiffened, ready to be accused. But the driver was just getting out to usher a few blackface sheep off the road. Maria Theresa was pleased with the driver's intervention, since she enthused for rare breeds. MT's family had begun to specialise in Castlemilk Morrit on their farm.

When Rebecca suggested to her grandmother that they too acquire a dozen or so sheep, she was told the answer was no. Primmy did not hold with sheep. And the children's grandfather took no interest in the *Taransay* livestock, full stop.

At the bus station in Fort William, Maria Theresa and Rebecca synchronised watches, agreed to meet again in ninety minutes, and parted ways. For a moment, Rebecca thought they might shake hands. But then she settled for saying, 'So Long'.

Rebecca felt like a criminal once again, as she stood at the library reception. She blushed easily and her cheeks were aflame.

"Gosh, is it cold out?" a quite young lady said to her and pressed the back of her fingers (the nerve of it!) against Becky's cheek. But Rebeca was used to people touching her cheeks because of her dimples. 'Irresistible,' her grandfather often said.

She was not sure the order in which to arrange her words and began to stammer a bit, like her sister Colette did when she was upset, but the librarian seemed to understand what was being said and took charge of Rebecca Brown's Lochaber (Under 12) Transport card which had her address. In just minutes, the girl was signed up to membership of this lovely warm library in Fort William. The peak of this victory suddenly troughed as a vision came to her of Maria Theresa alone at the Leisure Centre, at the deep end of the big swimming pool, her hand just out of reach of the edge, her legs oddly still beneath the surface and her torso sliding into the water, then her open mouth. Rebecca held her breath, as if she herself were going under.

'Is there something in particular I can help you with?' the librarian wanted to know. Rebecca hesitated, so the librarian continued, 'Just to get you started.' Rebecca mumbled something about liking newspapers and the young woman smiled, gesturing with her head that she should be followed. Rebecca was instructed how to log on at the monitor and how to make the selections from the menu. And then she was left to it. She knew the date. 7th December 2001. The newspapers: *Glasgow Herald, Scotsman, Daily Record* all carried the story on their front page the next day, after the accident.

But it wasn't a crash involving just her parents. There was a pile up, lots of vehicles, and from the pictures, it looked like they had been dropped there by a crane; the kind of crane which had a giant magnet hanging down; as if the cars had already been scrunched for scrap. Though the vehicles had not been neatly cubed. You could not tell from the photos if there were any ripped persons inside. The shots were too grainy. It looked like one articulated lorry had eaten a small hatchback. The end of the little car poked out from the open bonnet jaw of the truck. There was no particular sense in the photography that this was winter but you could tell it was night. *Just after 9.00pm,* according to survivors. The pictures were black and white. There were no bodies strewn on the tarmac. There was nothing red. There was a number: 11. That's how many died. Her parents were mentioned: … *couple leaving behind three young children.* Another phrase that has remained with Rebecca is 'visibly shaken'. *Officers and medical personnel were visibly shaken.*

Later, during her teens, Rebecca was to add detail to the crash scene. From her imagination, she augmented the photographs over the years, adding Highland cattle slaughtered and strewn along the dual carriageway too, with legs bovine and human twisted together. She made the horror more real, with eyes popping or swollen shut, and horns splitting femoral arteries. She was able to make the images move, she flung a bony tail over a windscreen and lying in her iron bed at night with her eyes tight shut, she could make sound too, with hooves beating on the metal bodywork. Her grandmother was always shaking her head at Rebecca's imagination, and with fair cause. One peculiar day, Primmy said, 'It's no use hiding. Life will still be here when you get back.'

*

The youngest Brown didn't even know where her parents had been going that night, nor for what purpose. 'Visiting' is the most Rebecca had been able to glean from her family. The accident happened *Yards from the Moffat exit*, the papers agreed. Were Julia and Stephen Brown planning to get off the dual carriageway at a place called Moffat? Had her parents been just yards from living?

Who, visiting who? Who was it then that heard: *they've died trying to visit you. Julia and Stephen Brown. They're dead. But for you, their visit to you, they'd still be alive.*

The Grands were button-lipped on the subject. *That fateful night*, was all that her grandmother would say and looked longingly through the huge bay window of the drawing room and clutched herself around with her two arms. Once, after a visit from Uncle Neil, she said, 'My son,' and pulled her pearls sharply from her neck. The pretty pebbles plipped over the parquet flooring. 'Ralph!' she shrieked, as if acid were sizzling on the wood. He stooped, then got down on his hands and knees, to retrieve the scattered gems but she kicked his hand away and he fell forward. 'Not that!' she screamed at him and he looked up from where he knelt on the floor, holding his kicked hand by the wrist. 'Not that! Our *son*, you complete fool! We have lost our *son*!' Then she noticed Rebecca standing in the doorway and spittle flew from her mouth when she shouted. 'What are *you* doing here?'

Of course, they had lost their son. Rebecca's mother was their daughter-in-law. The Grands' loss differed to the children's. Their daughter-in-law was a professional bridge player. Their son was a biochemist. Colette had told Rebecca that their mother was away a lot but that their father always went to the same place to work every day. Rebecca couldn't remember that, nor where they had all lived together back then. It was England somewhere. Again, any mild request for more detail, was shushed or something more pressing needed urgent attention and the person Rebecca had tugged by the sleeve with her questions, left the room.

There were some bright images though from that remote past. Rebecca flipped through the catalogue of them often. She remembered riding a blue trike which had an enormous boot with a label, *Duckham's Oil*. She remembered the pleasing sound the garden gate made when the latch shut and the noise it made when you were behind its bars, rattling it. She remembered a tall thin girl at nursery who punched people as they ran by.

Rebecca knew that she lied a lot and the shame when she was caught out gave her a fizzing in her belly. There seemed to be a sort of universal horror about lies. Rebecca didn't understand that lying was a rudimentary coping strategy for very small people. She thought it was just the devil in her personally. She would take the cooking chocolate from the larder and guzzle away. Once she'd had her fill, the chocolate stayed plastered on her face, beyond the circumference reachable by tongue. Grandmother lifted her up to the mirror. 'Now, Rebecca, all I'm asking is that you admit it. Tell me the truth. That you took it. You ate it.' Primmy was fond of recounting Rebecca's misdemeanours to Austen when he came home from boarding school and since this was often done with affection, Rebecca liked the attention. Grandma made it all sound quite jolly, as if Youngest Brown was rather clever to be such a fervent and committed liar.

That's mostly what Rebecca remembered of her beginnings. And then more concretely, there was some movie footage. There was a video of her mother preparing for a trip to Sofia, which Rebecca thought was a person, but turned out to be the capital of Bulgaria. A family holiday on a beach in Sardinia. A cottage in Wales. Austen's first day at school. These movies were begged for but rarely made an appearance. It was as though they were held in a vault somewhere. They had to be requested weeks in advance, requisitioned; a special screening arranged and then when it was done, the videos were whipped away. Mostly the footage was of the children. Colette unwrapping Christmas presents. Austen furious with a kite which would not do as it was told. There was not enough of their parents.

'There's just not enough!' Colette would screech. She cried the whole way through the home movies.

Austen said nothing.

*

Colette had stuck to her guns and drawn up a schedule of works for the house and the surrounding land. Austen collaborated with his sister and Rebecca too was allowed to attend their meetings, though not encouraged to speak. They claimed that Becky had a habit of straying from the point in hand, and her name appeared on the schedule only in relation to caring for the hens (which Rebecca already did) and keeping her bedroom tidy (which she was never likely to do). There was nothing for Rebecca to get her teeth into during the meetings but she liked to be sitting with her brother and sister, to be united against Primmy's Rule.

'What it's come to, it seems,' Austen said at the initial meeting, shortly after Cakegate. 'Well, family life for you girls is just a big tally sheet of misdemeanours.'

'Austen, you've asked Becky to keep her trap shut but you could at least speak in words that she will understand.'

'But I do understand. I do. Oops, sorry. Shutting up.' Rebecca slapped her hand over her mouth but her eyes were alight.

Austen pretended to scowl at Rebecca. 'All that they hold sacred, the pair of them, Old Ralphie's just as bad, is this ridiculous idea of peace. Peace! When was that ever going to be part of the equation, taking care of us. *Peace?* What the fuck do they think they're running here, the United Nations?'

'If *only* they hadn't died.' Rebecca couldn't help herself. She wasn't built for silence. 'Did you go to the funeral, Austen? Did you, Col? No-one was here. No-one 'cept me and Murdo. Do you remember the cows died too? Sometimes, sometimes I don't know what's real.'

*

On the day of her parents' funeral, Rebecca spent an unusual amount of time in her bedroom. If they hadn't died and the house had been empty for reasons other than death, then for sure she would have been capering around the policies - as her grandfather called the house and grounds - poking her nose and fingers into every banned nook and substance. But she had no wish to investigate *Taransay's* emptiness on such a day.

She lifted her toy panda from its chair and settled its plump kapok-filled body in the crook of her arm and lay on her bed. Belle had been with her from beyond memory and comforted her now with her special, lightly perfumed panda scent. Which perfume exactly, Rebecca did not know, but it might have been left there by her mother. She treasured that smell. She didn't want it to ever run out, so she sniffed at it just now and again.

Rebecca banged her socked feet together, wondering how it would feel not to be able to get your eyes open due to being dead. She went through the habitual shapes she identified in the rough wooden ceiling of her attic room: the back end of a lion, a pitchfork, a pram, most of a treble clef. Is it possible that at some point she became slightly bored on the day they buried her parents?

Rebecca went down to the first floor landing and looked out of the high arched window in the freezing December morning, at the linden tree driveway. Everyone loved the trees, even Primmy. The winter-stiff lindens thrusted their white finger branches into the air, like a row of conductors, frozen mid orchestration. The cold weighed so heavily in the air, nothing dared move in the garden. The birds were speechless and the sun shunned. Everything was in mourning.

That's when Rebecca saw one of the cows leaning against the stone dyke wall, with a much smaller cow, protruding, well more than protruding, from the larger one's bottom. Both animals were still, absolutely still. None of the other cows seemed to have noticed this odd phenomenon and were mostly at a distance, snorting their condensed breath in the late morning December air. Rebecca heard her own breath, gathered in a gasp. The cow by the wall with its half-delivered calf had no breath.

She felt the running come for her body, and thundered down the baronial staircase, staying well over on the banister side, just as she had been trained; away from the bloodstained oil paintings of the Battle of Culloden, more than a metre away from the celtic knot framed mirrors. She had to find Murdo.

Murdo Hendry had himself been slow to protrude from his own mother and this was the reason for his 'ways', everyone said. But Murdo had lots of ways which were not slow at all. He knew all about cattle, and rawl plugs, and hydrangeas.

Rebecca realised once she was outside that she had no shoes on but there was no time to spare and she paid no attention to the sea of brown ills underfoot as she approached the doomed cow pairing. There was ice forming on the puddles in the grass, but it was thin. It cracked easily, like the Christmas brandy snaps she'd already been stealing. And beneath the ice was a cold wet earth filling her socks.

The stone dyke wall was a good deal higher than the little girl but she was used to scaling the slippy, mossy dykes and finding footholds with mindless ease.

The Holsteins weren't branded or tagged. Murdo knew them individually, though without naming them. He was a man of award-winning emotional restraint in a community satiate of the trait. Murdo would scan his cattle's black and white pattern and knew who was who and what was what.

Rebecca climbed up beside the mute cow, so that she was next to its big boned head, and far from the undelivered calf end. She shifted along a bit and placed her two hands on the rivets of the mother's spine. The skeleton beneath flashed before her eyes, like an x-ray. Rebecca rubbed her palms upon the coarse hide which was cold but still able to hold dust and pump out smell. The cow was not as chilled as the air around but there was no warm blood running beneath her skin. As a small child, Rebecca always reached for the cows' ears but generally whoever was holding her would draw her back just before she could get to a soft black ear with its mud spattered pink interior. Now though, as she held the mother cow's ear, there was no give at all. She could have snapped it off. Not even the world's most powerful defibrillating paddles could bring this pair back.

Rebecca was just about to get down and investigate the baby end of this stiff business when she felt a hand upon her shoulder and in her alarm, fell backwards into the icy squelch. Murdo was shaking his head, as he did almost every time he saw Youngest. He didn't say anything though. He couldn't talk all that well. He could never tell a story.

'I remembered my anorak, Murdo.'

He righted the child and zipped up her anorak, pulling up its hood. He tightened the cord at her throat, much too much, but she wouldn't say. Then he lifted Rebecca up with great ease and tucked her into the crook of his arm, as if she was a young turkey. He held her tightly until her breathing had to quicken, just to get enough air. He smelled of wooden baskets and old hair and road tar. Almost wrung dead from his love, Rebecca was set gently down on the ground. Murdo pointed roughly to the calf end of the cow and shook his head again and wiped his face with his brown whiskery jacket sleeve. He looked down at Rebecca's feet which were covered over in a caramel slush of water.

'Butcher won't like it, Becky. Not like that, he won't. Nor she.'

Rebecca knew 'she' was her grandmother. The little girl went back to the house and put her socks in a bucket in the kitchen. Then from her bedroom window, she watched Murdo feed a chain through the hem of some filthy canvas which had been folded for so long, he could barely prise it open. He rigged up the cloth and chain in a sort of stretcher and attached it to the tractor which he drove alongside the stricken beasts. When he pushed the mother and baby cows onto the stretcher they fell hard sideways. The ground did not shake of course but all the same, this was momentous, like a prehistoric find. The giant mound of flesh was taken to Barn Three where the animals would be broken into pieces.

That is what Rebecca Brown remembers from the day of her parents' funerals. Two dead cows.

'Cow and A Half', the episode became known as, at home, and in the wider district. Something to properly discuss, considering the alternative topic: three children losing their parents just before Christmas.

There's a strangeness here, Primmy was fond of saying - and none of them doubted it - *at Taransay*.

It would be many years until something truly strange occurred to Rebecca Brown and it was this: if her grandparents had been drafted in to look after them, subsequent to her parents' death, why then were they already installed at *Taransay* at the time of *The Killer Road* crash?

*

The librarian came back in due course. 'How are you getting along? It's nearly lunchtime. Oh those are just thumbnails. Headlines. If you click on that triangle, yes there at the side, the whole article will appear. See?'

Rebecca smiled at the lady and she scrolled down till she found her parents' names but she didn't find what she expected. They weren't calling her mum and dad The Browns. They were calling her parents *Julia and Stephen Seawhite*.

CHAPTER 6

The Atlantic

This was Keller Baye's first trip in an airplane. Frankly, he'd been expecting something bigger. What was he supposed to do with his legs, they were six inches too long for economy. The stewardesses were attentive though, he'd give them that. He liked to watch them stretch up to the overhead lockers. He liked the cloud of perfume which wafted into his nostrils each time they walked by.

When he took his seat, Keller was pleased that he'd had to tighten his seatbelt. Some lardass must've been in it last. And he was pleased with his passport. Got a haircut specially for the photo and treated himself to a close shave at the barber shop. It had been months in the planning, this trip. He bought his flight to London Heathrow on a no-refund basis. If the execution had been stayed, he'd have lost the ticket. But here he was. A window seat too. It was breath-taking when you got up high above the Atlantic and into the clouds. He felt like an astronaut. The view alone was worth a thousand dollars. Nobody else seemed much to notice.

The toddler who'd been yelling at take-off was quiet now. And the airplane personnel were getting busy with something. The gentleman seated next to him was already asleep, jaw hanging. Keller wouldn't want to look like this guy, not in front of those stewardesses.

But Keller could sleep just about anywhere. He'd nearly nodded off at the press conference after the execution. Of course, that may have been partial concussion. Something which felt like a rubber dumbbell had been brought down on his head as he banged at the glass of the window. If they weren't going to answer Othaniel's question about whether his son was watching, Keller would let his dad know. He pounded at the window to the execution chamber but the glass must have been inches thick. Nobody on the other side of it reacted.

The guards hauled him back to his seat and threatened to throw him out if he moved again. Keller's shoulders heaved up and down but he remained in his chair and watched his father die in silence.

He had no idea the press conference would go on for so long. But there had been many victims and of course each of them had a family. And it seemed as the afternoon sun slipped down the wall of the conference room, that these families would never shut up. On and on, all saying the same thing. They were good and mad at the journalists for asking Warden James about the prisoner's state of mind leading up to the procedure. They were irate when the Warden was asked about any suffering that Othaniel Baye may have felt as he endured those dying minutes, at the mercy of the Midazolam. A reporter from UNC-TV questioned why a doctor with a stethoscope had had to be present when the heart monitor already confirmed death. That question annoyed the relatives too. What difference does any of that make, they wanted to know. It seemed each and every one of those relatives wanted to take the stand.

Venting spleen the PhD redhead wrote down in her A4 pad. Once the execution was over, she recovered quickly and was eager to make notes once more.

Venting just about everything, Keller thought, as the relatives ranted:

'What you people fail to understand is that Baye's feelings, Baye's so-called suffering has nothing to do with it. *Nothing*. The point is the victims. The point is my father had to watch his own daughter die right in front of him. He had to see that happen. And then face the same thing himself, in the hospital. His ass hanging out, couldn't even lie down. Days we waited. Five days and five nights. And then he died anyway. Who gives a fuck about stethoscopes and laboured fucking breathing? Who gives a good fuck?'

Warden James tried to create some calm and took the stand himself again. He was asked by a magazine lady what Othaniel Baye had requested for his last meal. Keller leaned forward. Suddenly he knew what the Warden would say. Keller felt almost omniscient, all the power was draining from these weaklings and channelling into him. The press perked up too. Hey, who didn't love a last supper question.

'Mr Baye asked for chicken tenders with fries and a side of corncakes. That is all. No, um, no appetiser. No dessert.'

'Did he ask for something special to drink?' a journalist wanted to know.

'Any alcohol?' another asked.

'No. He did not ask for anything special. He just had water.'

The wife of the relative who had spoken last stood up. 'What is *wrong* with you people?' She rushed to the stand and almost pushed the Warden aside. 'Who gives a rat's behind. Cold dish of cyanide and save us all the trouble of this ugly day. Know what? I thank God this Governor ain't gonna have any of this twenty five years in jail shit. Waiting, waiting.' She shook her pretty, long hair. Keller thought she may also have been to the hairdresser this morning. 'They took 'em out. In broad daylight. Our family members. Yours and mine.' She poked her finger at the other victims' families, as if their response was lacking. 'Shot 'em all up. In cold blood. All what's happened here today is justice. Some of you people just not getting it. Justice! You media people are fucking full of it.'

She was ushered away and the rest came then with the same thing. Brothers, cousins, a grandfather. No end to it, till Keller felt his eyelids getting heavy and excused himself. He had been attracting attention these last years, since working out at the gym, but he'd always had some, with his square jaw and his blond hair.

'That's him!' One of the victims' families, a boy with a chuck of freckles over his face, stood up and pointed. 'That's the son!'

Keller was too tired for this. He turned around slowly. The boy looked barely out of his teens. 'What? You gonna lynch me too?' Keller wagged a lazy finger and exaggerated his southern drawl. 'I think you done had your money's worth for one day. Y'all take care now.'

The boy lunged forward unsettling several members of the conference, their aluminium chairs clashing. The boy was restrained by his family.

Outside in the Turville car park, a few of the passengers were also waiting, had also had enough of their time there, but the bus would not leave until the press conference was over and all of the visitors were reassembled for return to their lives.

Keller's father was dead at last. After all these years of struggling with the loss of him, here it was finally. And at last, a proper memory had come to mind: they used to have chicken tenders and corncakes every paycheck when he was little, just him and his dad. Before the devil rode in on horseback and set fire to their small world.

*

Othaniel Baye had allowed his son to visit him only once on death row. On the other occasions Keller had made the trip, his father had declined to see him. Keller's letters were unanswered and Othaniel had sent just one, explaining to his son that no good could come of their continued relationship and that Kell should build a new life for himself, renouncing the past and all of its hardship. That was all. There was no talk of regret, no reminiscence. There was no mention of love.

On one single occasion though, Othaniel agreed to see his son. It was not long after the verdict of his death sentence. Keller arrived on media day, which ended at noon. One of the guards must have tipped off the journalists because two of them lingered and asked if they could meet Keller after the visit with his father.

Keller felt confused, unprepared. 'I don't know.'

'Well,' the fat pressman rubbed the back of his sweaty neck and smiled indulgently. 'You need to know, son. One way or the other. I got things to do today.'

Keller remembered the weight of the crossbow in his hands, as he took aim at the tramp. He felt the anger rising now in his chest. Something pulsed under the skin of his left cheekbone. He had come to hate the word *son*. Keller thought of that slick weapon he'd buried in the yard after setting fire to the tramp. The crossbow was sitting patiently in its plastic lined crate, inches beneath the dirt, and ready to be disinterred. Now Keller's loathing for the newspaper jerk had brought menace to the edge of his mouth, almost a smile.

'Nother time.' The press guy waddled off.

The other journalist watched this exchange, then turned so that his back was to the surveillance camera. He took a wad of dollar bills out of his inside pocket. The guard could see the roll of dollars but did not react. The money man raised his eyebrows to Othaniel Baye's son but Keller walked on by, his shoulder knocking on the journalist's.

Keller was permitted to have two hours with his dad, though in fact their exchange lasted barely thirty minutes.

First off, Keller sat in the wrong booth.

'That's for attorneys, boy. Only attorneys. You don't look like no attorney.' The guard moved Keller off to the far end. His father ambled into the communications room, in no hurry at all, it seemed. He sat opposite his son but there was no smile and he barely made eye contact in those first minutes.

'Hey dad. They let you keep the beard then. But not the moustache?'

'Beard's ok. Moustaches ain't allowed. Some nut religious reason. Can't figure it.'

'So did you keep on with the reading program?'

Othaniel shook his head slowly. 'Don't have it in this one. What would be the point? We're allowed four books from the library but I didn't pick none out.'

Keller wished he had prepared some questions. He saw something in his father's beard. Egg? 'What's the food like? Look like you lost a pound or two.'

'Food's cold. I mean on purpose, cold. We get a hot one just about once a week.'

A baby cried further along the line.

'Well you look like you need to eat more. You're disappearing before my very eyes.' Keller tried to smile but his smile muscles were rusty with disuse.

'You wouldn't say that if you tasted it.'

'Oh hey. I read something about pets. You can get one. If you like. I mean I could get one for you. Just a cat, I think. No dogs or nothing. But a cat, yes. You can have it in your cell.'

'This place ain't fit for an animal.'

'I mean one of those older ones. The kind that you get from the rescue—'

'He visit you? Master?'

'Uh yeah, Master. Sure. He came to get me from school.' The guards were a few yards away but Keller could almost feel their breath on his neck. 'My friend Lemi nearly had a—'

'What are you doing, Kell, looking all around? You wanted to see me. All those letters. Pleading.' Othaniel shook his head again and then looked hard at Keller. 'Well now here I am.'

The fuck's his problem? The anger started to broil in Keller's depths once more. Seemed it was never far from the surface these days. 'Could be I'm not used to prisons. You'll have to forgive me.'

'That Master's a piece of work, ain't he. Master of the Universe, how he sees it. Thinks I'm a hero too. Keeping it all close to my chest.' Othaniel beat his hand against his caved in chest. 'You take my meaning, Keller?'

'Yeah. He's something alright, Mister Master.'

'You take his advice. You take whatever he gives you. Do we understand each other?'

'I do. And I did.'

'Billy Ray Master knows what I want. You do too. You know it, Kell. Don't you?'

'Yes. I know what you want.' This conversation was not what Keller had had in mind at all.

'Just, do the right thing. You make your father—'

'Make my father what, Dad?'

Othaniel leaned back, exhaling loudly, like some punctured inflatable that could do no more.

'Kell, I am here for one reason. My execution will be the responsibility of one person. That person told the world that I was a killer. That person lied.'

'Billy Ray is taking care of that.'

'Billy Ray Master is not my family. And how many years I been locked up in hell holes like this, waiting for Billy Ray to get the job done. Fucking dozen more than I care to recall. That's how many. He's scared shitless of his mama. That Billy Ray, he looks like he's built for this stuff, but he ain't.'

'Dad, I think you need to trust—'

'I trust *you*. I am placing my trust in *you*. Hear? Those Seawhites died, Master says, all solemn, like that's an end to it. He wants my silence, he gonna have to work a little harder than that. They had kids. I saw that bear, in her arms. Big old black and white bear. There is only one way. An eye for an eye. You see that, boy? You see it clear? That is what I am asking of you. It's only right. Now, you know what right is, don't you? I hope at least you know right from wrong. I hope I learned you that.'

'Kind of subjective, right from wrong.'

'Do what?'

'See, I was thinking bank robbery would be more on the wrong side. But I'm no expert.'

'Get the fuck on out of here.' Othaniel got out of his chair. It was the last time Keller would see the man standing.

*

The journalist with the cash offer was hanging around in the lot. He leaned on the hood of his Nissan Rogue and dragged hard at a cigarette. When he spoke, it was more of a growl.

For every hotdog his colleague was putting away, this guy was smoking twenty Marlboros.

'Must be real hard, your visits with your dad. No car?'

'Kids let the tires down. I didn't have time to get 'em pumped up.'

'Fuckers. Where you headed? Bus station? I can give you a ride. Look. Here's my identification.' The man pulled a tag out of his open necked shirt. 'Name's Quindt. Thomas Quindt. Work for the New York Daily.' He held out his had but Keller did not take it.

'What do you want?' Keller stopped in his tracks. He'd been hot in the prison but now black clouds bumped around in the sky and Keller could smell rain.

The journalist stubbed out his cigarette. 'Just to talk. Say, that's quite a bump you got there.'

Keller touched his forehead. 'It's fine.'

'You going back to Greensboro?'

'You know which town I live in?'

'Listen, sometimes it's good to talk. I might even be able to help.'

'Help with what?' But Keller was already decided to get in the car and take the money if it made another appearance. The more he could put in his savings account, the quicker freedom would come.

It turned out that although the writer's credentials were real, he wasn't here for his newspaper. He was researching for a book.

'It's about the heist.'

'Heist?'

'Well, the robbery. The one your father—'

'Oh yeah.'

'I spoke with your dad, I expect you know that. Couple times.'

'No. I'm pretty much out of the loop. The guards tip you off I was coming?'

'They did. I'll be honest with you, Keller. They tell me any time Othaniel Baye has a visitor.'

'That's real sweet of them.' There it was again, the blood red fury. If he didn't find a way of releasing it, Keller thought he would burst. Like his insides would explode with vitriol. He had never thought about his father visiting with anyone else. He had turned down his son, his only son, for a very long time and Keller would have assumed therefore that his father had seen no-one at all. But maybe there were lawyers or other professionals.

'That happen a lot? Kids getting to you?'

'What?'

'You said they'd let your tires down.'

'Oh yeah. I don't care. Just, inconvenient today.'

'I'm sure. You know, Keller, it might be an idea to get your side of the story out there.'

In the passenger seat, Keller looked straight ahead on the highway. It would take more than an hour still to get back to Greensboro. The rain lashed at the windshield and the wipers could barely keep up. The writer guy, Quindt, had some kind of shake going on in his hands, each time they strayed from the wheel. Maybe he was a junkie or had some kind of post traumatic stress. He sure could talk though, droned on and on. 'I appreciate that it might feel, I don't know, wrong somehow. But your dad, he wanted me to give you that money. That's all he cares about. Getting the best for you. And it's not a bribe. I'm paying for… a service.'

'Pull over. Pull the damned car over.'

'What? I can't. Not here. What's the matter? Did I say something to—'

Keller popped his seatbelt and opened the car door.

'What the fuck are you…' the man grabbed at Keller's t shirt and veered the Nissan onto the berm.

Keller got out of the car and so did the driver. Immediately, they were drenched but Keller took no notice. He shouted through the downpour. 'You see those strips of rubber, mister? Some old tires that blew up? You see all this litter?' Keller fluttered his arms around the berm.

'I see it, yes.'

'Just things that got damaged. Or had no point no more. That's me.'

'Look, son, rain's coming down pretty hard. I have a Thermos in the back there. What say we—'

Keller took off.

'Wait! You left your jacket. Keller, this is crazy. Wait!'

Keller ran alongside the highway traffic till he could see a path down to civilization. Last thing he heard the writer yell was, 'Ok, I'll bring it.' Why would that guy know where to bring his jacket?

*

On American Airlines Flight AA730, the drinks trolley came by and Keller ordered a soda. He liked the look of the air stewardess very much.

'What kind of soda would you like, sir?'

See now, that's proper waitressing. 'You choose.'

When the drinks wagon was well away and his companion of the hanging jaw was still out for the count, Keller opened Blonk's dossier. It wasn't what you'd call bulky but it had everything Keller needed. He'd had a hard time even getting it. Blonk wanted to give him a USB stick, in the post, and never to meet at all. But Keller wasn't having that. He wanted to see his bounty hunter face to face.

Many of the pages were picture downloads. Keller liked the photographs a lot. Especially the ones of her on stage. She would look a lot better with more make-up, but she had the basics, the girl did: good body shape, shiny dark hair, nice almond eyes. You couldn't tell exactly what colour the eyes were from the pictures but on her typed profile, they were stipulated as green. She hadn't smiled in a single shot, so he couldn't tell what her teeth were like and when he'd asked Blonk, the hacker was a little taken aback. 'Well, let me see, actually I don't know. I didn't get these pictures myself you understand. When a search is international, we subcontract of course.'

'I don't remember sanctioning that.'

'I don't remember asking permission. Your bill would have been astronomical if I'd flown over to Europe. And to get this stuff would have taken me four times as—'

'Yeah ok. Don't sweat it.'

'He, or she, the liaising skip tracer that is, doesn't even know your name. And you don't know theirs. Happens all the time. That's the business.'

'I said, Mr Blonk, don't sweat it.'

So a *colleague* had taken the photos. They were a network, of course they were. Hackers, skip tracers, bounty hunters. They helped each other get the money by unearthing unwitting citizens from their lives. Keller imagined a miniature crowd of folk, blinking, holding their forearms up against the glare of a giant torchlight.

'Rebecca Brown', born 16 April 1997 (24 years old)
168 cm
132 lbs
good health
no scarring or known birthmarks
heterosexual

Currently living in Muirhouse, Edinburgh which is thought to be one of the most deprived areas in Scotland. Lives alone in a two bedroom apartment which she rents. Does not appear to be in a relationship. Her sister Colette lives nearby in salubrious Marchmont.

Rebecca Brown had been working in Scotland's capital for an events company where she rose quickly in the ranks. Now is a professional comedian, performing stand up throughout the United Kingdom, but remains Edinburgh based.

Brown grew up in the West Highlands of Scotland and attended Maillaig High School which she left abruptly just prior to sitting her Higher exams (you need to pass these to graduate high school). The reason why she failed to sit those exams is unclear. Her closest friend there was Maria Theresa Millerson (née Cairney) who is now married with twin boys and still lives locally.

Brown lived with her grandparents, Ralph Edward Brown and Primrose Anctillious Brown. She has a brother Austen and a sister Colette. (None of the children appear to have middle names.) Austen is in the oil business, working in Dubai in recent years and is now based mostly in the Antipodes. Colette is a fostering social worker. None of the Brown children are married or have children.

Rebecca Brown is professionally known as 'Beck'. Her email address (which is rarely used) is Beck_a_Brown@gmail.com

Cell phone 00 44 (0) 7939 629279

Brown does not appear to have a Facebook or Twitter account and there is no record of her on Snapchat, Pinterest, Instagram, LinkedIn. She receives no notifications in relation to any popular sites.

She shops online at a supermarket called Tesco and there is nothing remarkable in the contents, except to say that she buys a lot of vodka. Clothes, she gets on Ebay.

Special interests: The Jacobites. Bonnie Prince Charlie et al. Growing up, Rebecca Brown borrowed every book on the subject, according to library records in Fort William.

These details Keller knew by heart.

Of course, skip tracers usually locate fugitives or weed out debtors but Keller's mission was to find a girl who was neither of these things. Rebecca Brown was innocent, in almost everyone's eyes.

Blonk was really a computer and phone hacker. The summary of Rebecca's *Salient Internet History (0.3% of overall searches)* was a dozen pages long. The keyword was *Seawhite*. Keller's trip to the United Kingdom rested on that one word, that name: *Seawhite*. Blonk had been trawling the world wide web for searches of 'Seawhite' and on January 1st of this year, Beck_a_Brown flashed up on a gmail account. And the holder of that account was looking for:

Julia Seawhite
Stephen Seawhite

Car crash 7 december 2001
Killer road moffat
Biological mother find
<u>www.adopted.com</u>
the adoption contact register
Births, marriages, deaths
Census Scotland
Stephen Brown
birth certificates

January 1st. That intrigued Keller. Perhaps some kind of new year resolution, Blonk said. Hardly a genius observation but certainly plausible. The date had to have a significance and then, once the Seawhites had been searched for by Rebecca Brown, she just couldn't get enough. Every single day, often dozens of times, the girl searched for Julia and Stephen Seawhite.

Keller Baye determined to find out why. He would find out from the horse's mouth, that's what he swore.

*

Keller built up his own profile from Rebecca's general internet searches. She was often to be found in the web pages of exotic locations like Mauritius or the Maldives or Bora Bora. She was constantly getting quotes for water villas on turquoise oceans, though her living and working environment suggested that in reality these ambitions were out of her reach. She was a dreamer then, Rebecca Brown. Keller kind of liked that.

According to the timeline records, Rebecca sometimes watched porn towards the end of the day. Her desire for this was erratic. Perhaps she used porn to wind down, to help her sleep. She didn't subscribe to sites, but just relied on free films. She almost always keyed in 'real couples' and never anything deviant. Straightforward in bed, therefore, Keller surmised. And looked forward to finding out for himself. But he doubted any of that would have figured in his father's plans. Keller's sexual designs on his victim were very much extra curricular. Othaniel would not have approved of this physical indulgence. But Othaniel Baye was dead and gone.

CHAPTER 7

The King

As it turned out, Maria Theresa came to no harm at the municipal swimming pool at Fort William and later the girls logged onto MT's father's computer at home, to have a look for *Seawhites*. But the only result was a stockist of educational and art supplies in Brighton. There was no mention of a *Julia* or a *Stephen*. It was a proper conundrum and curiosity swelled within Rebecca. She pleaded with Maria Theresa to make enquiries of her own parents who were fairly laid back and forthcoming generally. But the girls had had this conversation between themselves on numerous occasions and the answer from MT was always the same: *they don't know anything, they don't like discussing it either, they think it's all a bit creepy.* Oh my goodness, Rebecca didn't like that last comment at all. That she, and her forebears, had the whiff of creepiness did not sit well with sunny Becky Brown.

MT had seen a tv programme on regression to past lives and suggested they try that and though Rebecca couldn't quite see the point in relation to her personal parental mystery, they give it a whirl. The whole tenet of regression appealed hugely to the girls' dramatic natures and they had a whale of a time inventing various past lives, but of course by the end of the day, they were none the wiser about the Seawhites.

Later, in the garret, Rebecca lay on her bed and squeezed her eyes tight shut. She tried to think of her earliest memory and though she was looking for a remembrance of her mother and father, there was one incident which lodged itself on her mind's screen. She was around three years old and dressed in little pink checked shorts. She wore a white t shirt with a flower on it, perhaps a daisy, and a hand-knitted navy cardigan with shiny, gold, anchor buttons. Rebecca was sure she had seen a photograph of herself in this outfit.

With her eyes closed now, she was seeing herself as if she was appearing in her own film. She knew she had to try to remember the truth and not embellish the scene. She had to leave her imagination behind and just look. It seemed to Rebecca that the child was much younger than she had been on the day of the funeral. But she was at *Taransay*. She saw the child hovering at a doorway, making a decision, outside her grandfather's study and going in. But it wasn't her grandfather's study then. There was a card table there and she wanted to touch it, to press the metal clips which made the legs fold but she knew she had to be careful of her fingers. There was a cherry red velvet cloth on top of the table and underneath the cloth was green baize, the child knew that. She had seen her mother sitting at that table. But she was not there now. She didn't live there anymore. She was gone.

'She's dead,' Rebecca said aloud now, as if reminding the child memory, helping her along.

Upon the velvet cloth were two packs of playing cards. She knew that the cards were very important. That her mother had several sets but that these were her favourite ones.

It was starting to feel like a regression to Rebecca. She felt very calm, as if she were an elder sister to this little one, both searching for their mother.

The child's red lips were wet and slippy and Rebecca couldn't tell whose breath she was hearing now, her own or the memory's. She could see the kid's chubby fingers, almost feel the sensation of touching the perfect playing cards. And Rebecca felt the child's fear too; their fear. The idea came suddenly: that this was not allowed. What? To be in there, in the study? Then the little girl noticed something on the King of Diamonds. What was that? That yellow mark? Like glue, in the middle there?

The child looked at her fingers, brought them to her nose and took a tentative sniff. Golden Syrup. Her sniffing skills were more advanced than her decision-making skills. She caught her breath and coughed. Looked at the door. Ajar but empty. She thought to neaten the cards back into a block and gathered them together with her two hands, but several in the middle were now sticking together. The Golden Syrup was infecting the pack. She looked at the door again but there was no-one coming. She was hot and could feel the red blotch crawling onto her neck and the backs of her knees where her brother would point and laugh. She crammed the cards inside her cardigan. Two dropped out onto the floor and there was an eight of clubs still on the table, but she hadn't noticed this. She had no way of knowing that there was a requirement in number, to make a pack. She didn't know anything suddenly, except what mattered: wiping off the Syrup.

She hunched over her cardigan and snuck along to the kitchen. She let the cards tumble out onto the draining board and checked through them but as her syrupy hands were still unwashed, all the remaining cards more or less (though two more dropped out en route to the kitchen) now carried the mark of wrongdoing.

Now, yes, now at last, she thought of washing. She poured cold water, since she knew that she was not allowed to touch the hot, into the basin. There was something she should squirt but she couldn't see it. But there was a bar of soap. She emptied the cards into the basin and although another fell to the kitchen floor, this time she saw and retrieved it. She was not tall enough to see into the basin and cast around for a stool. But there wasn't the size of thing she was looking for. A chair! She went into the adjacent dining room and dragged a chair down the two steps into the kitchen. She was so hot now, she pulled her cardigan and t shirt over her head and off. Her hair electrified and she paused to think about that. But she had made such a noise on the steps with the chair, she had to hurry to finish. 'Noisy noise,' she muttered. Really, she was too high on the chair but busied the soap in the cold water. Every time she got the cards separate, they clumped together again. She pulled them all out and threw them onto the draining rack. They were completely changed. The colour had darkened. They were sodden and thick with ruin.

Then she had an idea, a great idea. She wobbled on the chair with excitement and the need to accelerate a plan, to move away from this heavy, dark wrong. She jumped down and wiped her hands on her chest.

She knew how to use the grill. She had used it before, just to see if it would come on, and her mother had been horrified.

'There! My mum was there! I know she was. She was.' Rebecca felt the tears springing into her eyes but she brushed them impatiently away as she fought to continue remembering.

The child was pulling out the grill pan and reached up blindly to pick the dripping cards from the draining rack. They had become one swelling clump.

Quick, quick now. She looked at the entrance to the kitchen because people can come without talking. But there was no-one there. She peeled the cards from one another and laid them out on the grill. Instinctively, to shield those with people heads from the heat, she placed the cards face down. There wasn't room for all of them. Never mind, she could hide the rest, in a minute. She straightened them up so that they were in neat rows and turned the heat up to full. Her small, sharp teeth were gritted as she watched the element come alive with orange.

A flash of her mother in the car came. Rebecca remembered her mum's hand leaving the gear stick to squeeze hers. Where? Where was that? Not in Morar, no. Rebecca shook her head and concentrated.

In the kitchen, there was a smell of burning. It pierced her troublesome adenoids. As she turned back to the grill, she tripped over her own feet and fell. She saw an angled wisp of blue smoke heading for the ceiling. She would never get that back down. She scrambled up off the floor and pulled out the grill pan. The cards were black, utterly charred.

There was something terrible here now in the air. Was this death? Was this part of her mother's death?

Rebecca lay trembling. Tears rushed from the corners of her eyes, into her hair and ears. Why did death come to the little Becky in the kitchen? How did death decide to come for someone? Why had it chosen her mum and dad? Was death like a person itself, hooded. Was death cooking something of its own, somewhere else but suddenly alerted to their family, on the A42? Had Death been at home in a kitchen? Did Death put down its spoon, check its clock, sigh, pull on its great cloak against the chilling night and go to The Killer Road?

Yes, it seemed so. It was never neglectful of its duty, Death. It never got bored, never took time off.

Rebecca pressed on her wrist artery, like she had in her make-believe games, when injuries were life threatening. The terror she had felt back then suddenly romped through her body. The end could come at any time. She remembered now, hiding in the bathroom, from Death, years ago. She would sit on the cold floor tiles and pull grandmother's bath robe over herself like a shroud but when she looked out, the cloaked figure was still there: tall Death, at the sink, washing the blood from its hands and drying them on a fine, fresh towel, quietly. She knew then that if it should ever turn for her, it wouldn't matter if she was ready or not.

The King of Diamonds sizzled on the grill in front of little Becky. And then she heard them, soft footsteps. Acoustically, her skills exceeded even those of sniffing, and she was certain that someone was standing in the doorway.

The child looked down and saw herself half naked. She saw that the chair must have fallen as she jumped down. It was on its side and the grey blue satiny seat had a dirty scuff. Now the child saw the angry glow still determined from the grill and as she reached out to turn it off, her mother behind her screamed: 'Don't touch that!'

Rebecca took deep breaths and after some minutes, came to herself. This regression hadn't been any fun at all. She was exhausted. Her eyes were swollen with grief. 'Don't touch that,' she whispered and decided never to play regression again.

CHAPTER 8

The Shooting

Keller Baye was nine years old when his dad shot Will Yearwood in downtown Winston Salem. William K Yearwood was a retired Supreme Court Judge from Albany, New York. He was a grandfather of five. The elderly gentleman was in North Carolina, visiting with his son and daughter-in-law, both doctors at the Wake Forest Medical Center, when he was killed. The Yearwoods were ardent charity raising folk and regular church attendees.

It took the jury five and a half hours to find Othaniel Baye guilty and to unanimously convict him, though the case itself was far from simple: a bank robbery which was disguised as a terrorist attack.

Bogus explosive devices had been placed around the town, in the rail station, under benches in the parks, and in the Bank itself. It was an inside job. One of the robbers was an employee of the Legacy Federal Bank. Her name was Lillius Queen. She was the disaffected Manager, with an expensive cocaine habit and almost a million dollars of debt. With a name like that, Miss Queen had certain expectations of life, it seemed. Her haughtiness throughout her testimony suggested that she still had those expectations. She set her mouth in a horseshoe downturn and she looked down her nose at them all: judge, jury, attorneys and gallery. Every spare chance she got, Lillius ranted, incredulous, about how near those thieves had come to success; as if somehow the wider public had been careless, or even the members of this court, rather than responsibility lying with the Bank itself. The judge threatened her with contempt, but the contempt was all Miss Queen's. And although every one of the jury felt that she was most likely guilty, there was insufficient corroborating evidence to convict her, thanks to the tight lips of Othaniel Baye.

In her own mind, Lillius just couldn't accept that they had come so close to pulling off the heist, yet failed. All that careful planning but still there was one unforeseen problem. They wanted to create chaos and they did. They wanted the authorities running every which way and they did. But that chaos was also the gang's undoing.

Othaniel Baye too owed a lot of money. Not a million bucks, nothing like, but he had no way of catching up with his payments to the loan sharks. He'd thought of upping sticks, just disappearing and going down to Guatemala. He knew a guy who did that last year and he could see that this was a viable solution. If your life is working out badly, get a new one. But it wasn't so simple for Othaniel. His boy was doing well in fourth grade. That teacher of his, Miss Rourke, called Othaniel in to show off Kell's IQ. All excited, she was. Nice lady, gave him some books to take home. He couldn't take the child off to South America just because his daddy had fucked up, it wouldn't be right. And if truth be told, Othaniel just didn't have the energy to run. He had the ambition for nothing much, since Keller's mom left for Portland with that guy who laid asphalt out on the highways.

Othaniel Baye had not been in on the heist during its planning. He was a last minute replacement and it was likely that the pressurised haste of this decision, was his downfall. The opportunity to take part in the robbery had been presented to him almost as a gift, as if he was the luckiest guy in North Carolina to be offered this chance. And in fairness, Othaniel liked the sound of the operation. *No violence* they had told him, right up front. They had *no wish to do real harm*, they just wanted the loot which would be covered by insurance and *affect no-one personally*. Seemed they couldn't affirm this often enough.

Othaniel listened keenly. It had been a long time since anyone had been enthusiastic for his attention. They wanted him. These smart people really wanted him. They took him out for a steak dinner and offered him fine Californian pinot. They knew he was a hard worker, getting on fifteen years with the same security outfit, Prolock.

'You're a steady man,' they told him. 'A man with a reputation. We admire that. We know you'll be there.' They gripped him by the shoulder. 'We trust you.' Well, Othaniel Baye could not remember when he'd last received praise. When they told him the worst that could ever happen was of course being caught, they reassured him that as a getaway driver in a heist with no casualties, he'd serve just a few years. But getting caught was never going to happen. That was *point five per cent of a chance, or less*. Whereas if they pulled it off (and they definitely would), he could have the kind of life for himself and his son that up till now he could only have dreamed of.

One of the robbers, Othaniel was told by the 'Ops Build Team' over his 12 oz t-bone, had done this kind of thing several times, though not with the brilliance of this plan. And he'd gotten away with it every time. The trick was always to find a disillusioned senior employee who could literally open doors. Enter Miss Queen. Though she did not literally enter the restaurant during their meetings. She was the mastermind, hidden away, not to be paraded in front of the lowlier elements in the operation. And for all their flattering and fawning, Othaniel was not stupid. He knew he was the very lowliest. But he said yes.

'In that case, we are going to need you to swear an oath?'

'An oath? What kind of oath?'

'We need you to swear on your son's life, that when the operation is over, you will never speak of it again.'

*

The heist was all about confusion. At 7.00 am, word went out to the police, newspapers, tv and radio stations, that a terrorist incident was about to take place and that devices were placed among the community. Two of the devices were genuine and exploded early in the morning. The first was at the bus station on West 5th Street. It was in a trash can near the coach which was boarding for Raleigh. Nobody was hurt but the bus station was the first of the day's evacuations. The second bomb was detonated by the Memory trees in Bethabara Park. Too early there for many visitors to be visiting the ghosts of their loved ones and again, nobody was injured, just a few pigeons had their feathers ruffled in the small blast.

The public buildings and shops were beginning to fill by 8.00 am. It was clear that a general alert had not yet gone out. As the vehicles of the security forces began to rumble and screech into action, four robbers gathered in the coffee shop next to the Bank. One by one, they went to the restroom, each with their carryall and changed into their 'terrorist' clothing: khaki pants and t shirt with Cordura bullet proof vest over. They each wore a shemagh, the Arabic check headscarf, covering their face and leaving only the eyes exposed. They exited the restroom together and marched straight out of the café and into the Bank next door.

Once inside the Legacy Federal Bank, the robbers raised their weapons and ordered the doors to be locked and the electronic security shutters to be brought down. As the whirr of this commenced, the lights were switched on full. One of the robbers looked around at the surveillance cameras, but the gang were not recognisable and made no request to switch these off. A mistake, since it was this footage which incriminated Lillius Queen, in the opinion of the District Attorney. Lillius had hoped that her starring role under surveillance would secure her innocence in court but the DA did not believe that the robbers would ask a Manager to write notes for them. The prosecution thought that this was staged, that the intelligent move, in what appeared to be an eminently intelligent operation, would have been digital instruction, requiring no live voices, or at the very least, prepared scripts. Miss Queen's performance, they insisted, had backfired. The District Attorney called expert witnesses by the dozen: body language and communication specialists; behavioural psychologists and voice pattern consultants. And yet their lengthy testimony could not get Miss Queen behind bars.

The robbers commanded all customers and staff to dress exactly as they were dressed. The clothing was quickly passed around from the carryalls.

Lillius Queen stepped forward to ask that the children – there was one toddler and a baby in a pushchair – be allowed to leave the building with their parents. The robbers had rehearsed several eventualities. They wanted the staff and customers to place Miss Queen in a position of trust so that they did her bidding. They held a gun to her temple and told her to keep her mouth shut. She then got into her costume and encouraged the others to do the same. Men were stripped of their pants where they stood, and women of their dresses. The outfits were all large but waists were elasticated. One customer was too large around to come anywhere near wearing the khaki pants. He was handcuffed to an executive chair in a back office.

A gang member had a gadget for locating cell phones, which were quickly collected from the pockets and handbags of the terrified clientele. All their other belongings were gathered and removed. The robbers hung fake submachine guns around the necks of the customers. Some of the innocent stood stalk still with expressions of pure bewilderment. Others were shaking with terror.

In less than three minutes, you would struggle to tell the guilty from the innocent, except for the large man chained to the swivel chair.

One elderly lady collapsed and was dragged up onto a sofa at the *Home Mortgage* area. She tried to catch her breath and asked for her handbag so that she might have her medication. She was told that her pills would have to wait. The baby was asleep in its pushchair. Its father's fingers were prised from the handle and the buggy too was parked in the *Mortgage* corner.

The toddler who was watching his mother dress up as a masked terrorist began to sob and could not be consoled. He shrieked for his confiscated teddy. And then the child himself was confiscated and cuffed to the lady having the chest pains. Later, the District Attorney would make a great song and dance about this: *Consider that for a good moment, ladies and gentlemen of the jury. The kind of people who will source carbon steel handcuffs, for children. I'm talking about the size now. Handcuffs made for children.*

Two of the gang marched Miss Queen up to the vault door leading to the safe deposits. Lillius let out a whimper, causing her captor to elbow her sharply in the ribs.

The carryalls which had held all the getup and weapons real and unreal, were now empty and ready to be filled with the contents of the safe deposit boxes behind the strong door.

Cash held at the *Legacy Federal*, held no attraction for the thieves. They were not there for paper money. Othaniel Baye had felt disappointed when he heard that. A lapful of dollar bills would have felt so nice. Something he could count on, literally; something real.

They had settled on stealing forty deposit boxes. The ones they wanted were the medium size: 4" x 10" x 12". It would be easy to fit ten in each of the carryalls. It was necessary that their selection seemed random, so that no suspicion would fall on Lillius Queen or the target boxes, but it was only the contents of six of them which were of real interest. Specifically, the gems deposited by one of the Bank's Kuwaiti customers, Mr Nabil Al Mutairi.

Nabil Al Mutairi and his older brother, Bader, had come to *Legacy Federal* almost a year ago. They had a meeting with Lillius Queen and arranged to rent six safe deposit boxes for a term of twelve months. They were co-lessors to the boxes. Nabil opened a small attaché case and let the gemstones roll out of their little purple velvet pouches. There were pink diamonds and black opals. The smallest but most spectacular was a rainbow opal. The stones scattered majestically on the melamine of Queen's desk. One diamond danced and tapped almost to the edge. What if it were to drop on the floor? Was it then, at that second, that the idea took hold of Lillius?

'Can you close the blinds, Miss Queen? And the door too please?'

Lillius did this and Nabil Al Mutairi gestured for her to retake her seat. He got up and turned off the light.

'Look, Miss Queen.'

Lillius Queen looked down and from the darkness the tiny rainbow opal shone its spectrum of colors.

'Madam, this stone was millions of years in the making. Isn't it magical?'

It was magical. It took Queen entirely under its spell.

And there were other jewels in their collection which Lillius had never even heard of: benitoite, musgravite. But she was soon to learn that these were the most precious gemstones on earth, some worth more than a million dollars per carat. Lillius Queen itched to touch them. Her throat was dry with longing. The sound of the jewels had made as they pattered on the desk, played and replayed in her mind's reel.

Less than two months later, Bader Al Mutairi drowned in a diving accident at the Blue Hole in Eastern Sinai. Nabil was in North Carolina at the time and he came to see Lillius Queen with the news. She explained to Nabil that once the paperwork was in place, there would be no difficulty in terms of sole access to the deposits. The young man was in tears and she consoled him. When Nabil got up to leave, Miss Queen extended her hand and suddenly, he was holding her close to his chest, sobs of grief wracking him. Poor little rich boy, she thought, and stroked his plump shoulder.

Once Nabil had left her office, Lillius looked at the date of expiry on the boxes' lease. Almost five months still. The opportunity to share in the Al Mutairi fortune was just too hard to pass up. She resolved to make good use of those five months.

*

Since everyone but the babies were now dressed like terrorists, the police could have no idea who the perpetrators were. The real robbers carried blowback Uzis but there was no quick or easy way of telling which weapons were real or fake, since the Bank's customers and staff held such realistic toy ones. One of the robbers went around with an industrial stapler, fixing the shoulder strap of the gun to the clothing of the unwitting collaborators. Of course, the greatest difference in weaponry was that the Uzis held by the robbers could fire off six hundred rounds per minute. And contrary to what the 'Ops Build Team' had promised Othaniel Baye, the robbers made good use of the Uzis' capability, in the end.

Within an hour of the terror alerts being declared, the ensuing mayhem more or less ground the town of Winston Salem to a halt.

Othaniel sat sweating in the getaway car, a black Subaru. The car was a de-commissioned taxi. It still had the rooflight but it didn't shine for custom anymore. Othaniel wore regular clothes and wiped his palms on his denim knees. As the siren wails became constant, he watched his exit routes blocking in all directions. He could see for certain that this eventuality had not been properly planned for. They thought the spot chosen for the Subaru on Marshall Street North was sufficiently distant to be free and clear. They were wrong. The getaway driver could only hope that the streets would begin to decongest some, but it seemed the very opposite was happening. Without a contingency for this, Othaniel's mouth dried right up and his armpits flooded with dread.

The police and army units needed the routes cleared too but the contagion of fear was causing people to simply abandon their vehicles in the middle of the road.

On the radio, Othaniel had heard the broadcasters describe the explosions at Bethabara and the bus station. Whole sections of the town were declared no-go and then the evacuations began.

The getaway driver could feel the sweat bubble above his top lip. He wiped away the perspiration and looked from one mirror to the next, trying to find an exit route. How was he going to get the men and the carryalls out of this? He turned the radio up above the noise of the sirens in the streets. Maybe there was a road free someplace near, a direction for trapped vehicles.

The broadcaster announced that they had closed the schools. They were interviewing on the street. 'The army are crawling everywhere,' he heard. Othaniel hadn't seen any soldiers yet but it was only a matter of time.

Comparisons were already being made. Oklahoma. Twin Towers. Hospital patients were attempting to flee their beds.

Othaniel thought of Keller out on Sally Kirk Road. What were all the kids doing at Jefferson Middle School? Crying beneath tables and waiting for a gunman to burst into their classroom?

The chaos was complete. If someone had announced World War III, Othaniel Baye could not have envisaged more havoc.

Inside the Bank, the robbers handled the Manager roughly. They told Queen to get out some paper to write a note. She did this and one of them began dictating. Once the note was finished, the gang took hold of the elderly lady in *Mortgages*. They asked her if she was able to walk and when she said yes, they told her that the lives of the people in this Bank would now depend upon her giving a note to the police officers outside. Did she understand, they wanted to know. She nodded solemnly and looked around her. She was deathly pale and her breathing was very shallow. They instructed her to take her handbag from the collection of belongings. She thanked them and tears ran down through her thick face powder as she got out her pills. Her hand trembled as she swallowed what seemed like half the bottle. She was an excellent candidate to deliver the note. She could not be anything other than what she seemed.

At first, the lady seemed almost too frail to get to the front door but then she raised herself up with a lifetime's accrued dignity and went outside.

The note informed the police that all of the customers had been taken as hostages and were now dressed as terrorists.

There was no way that the police could discern that four among them – the real threat – wore more specific neck ties, so that they might be distinguishable to each other.

In the cacophony of car horns and pedestrian holler, there was no clarity to get anywhere near a grip on the situation. All the police units could do was wait for the next communication, whether that would be from the Chief of Police, the Governor or from the terrorist/robbers, they had no idea. It seemed that anything could happen.

Inside the Bank, Queen and two of the gang went into the vault behind the strong door. The customers and other staff were lined up facing the wall. One young woman was murmuring aloud, as if she was reading out the adverts on domestic improvement loans which were plastered before them. Or perhaps she was praying.

With the four carryalls now filled, ten deposit boxes apiece, Lillius was instructed to write another note to the police, informing them that all of the occupants would now be leaving. Queen asked aloud why the robbers could not write these notes for themselves. Sassy, that was her reputation, though she knew her job back to front. Queen held up her hand with the pen. It was shaking. Nice touch.

'Do as you are told if you want to stay alive.'

Queen wrote down the robber's words once more, as he trained his Uzi on the line of hostages.

The note said:

We will leave the Legacy in five minutes from now. The Manager will come first. Then the rest of us. We will be walking close together, all of us, forming a tight circle, arms entwined. The baby and toddler will be held, but not by their parents. If any shot is fired, or any overt move made towards the circle, a hostage will be shot in the head. A copy of this note is simultaneously being sent out on social media, so the world will know if you choose another way.

Lillius Queen was ordered to read the note to the hostages so that they would understand what was required of them. Then the Manager keyed in the codes to unlock the door once more. Lillius Queen went to the door. She was to be first on the outside. If shooting were to begin, she would be the first to die. She raised her arms high into the air and walked to the front doors which now opened automatically. Queen took several long strides, as if she were measuring, and very slowly, laid the second note in the centre of the road. (*Ridiculous*, the DA would later say. *What if there had been a howling gale? What if there had been torrential rain? You wanted to write the notes in this heist, Ms Queen. You wanted the cameras on you. You wanted to be the leading lady. But you haven't convinced a single person in this courtroom.*)

Once Lillius Queen had placed the note on the road, she carefully reversed her steps, and indeed, the lightest of winds flicked up the corner of the note and it flapped its way a few yards, before being stamped under a police boot.

In the Bank, the customers looked at their captors who gestured for them to move. They shuffled up to the door also, behind the Manager who kept her arms raised, the sick joke of her toy submachine gun swinging at her waist.

Then with arms linked, the hostages and robbers went through the double doorway and into the world once more. With a thousand weapon sights upon them, they formed a tight circle.

The baby was no longer visible but the toddler who was hitched up in someone's arms, wrenched his tender neck back and forth at the vista of flashing lights, police cars and uniforms.

A shot rang out and a police sergeant screamed, 'Hold your fire.'

It could have been an officer who pulled that trigger, or it could have been a member of the public. It was never clear, although speculation went on for years, since that one shot altered the course of dozens of lives. Within twenty seconds another shot was fired and then all hell broke loose.

There was no way of telling where all the shots were coming from now but clearly it was both sides, all sides. Impossible to know who was innocent and who was guilty. All the same, the bodies started to fall to the ground. It was a total catastrophe.

Later, more heads would roll. The Chief of Police and the Mayor lost their jobs, as the town grappled with who was to blame for the bloodletting and unnecessary loss of life on that day.

The survivors in the circle dispersed. Some half dead, their injuries gaping and gushing. Some sprinting as fast as they could. Others disrobing the garments they'd been ordered to wear like they were made of acid. The plastic submachine guns clattered on the street. One man just stood with his hands over his ears and wailed. The toddler had not made it out of the circle and lay in a thick, bloody puddle.

In the Subaru, Othaniel looked up through the traffic signals along the street. They changed from red to green and back again. Nothing was moving. When the gunfire started, his hand grabbed at the door handle. He wanted to run. Everywhere people were running and every instinct told him to take flight. Then he saw two of the robbers, fifty yards down Marshall Street North. They each carried two carryalls and were weaving their way through the gridlock of vehicles. They had discarded the Uzis, but idiotically, one of them was still wearing his Shemagh mask scarf. He thumped on the window. Othaniel could see a maniacal glint in his eyes. The second man banged on the trunk for Othaniel to open it, so that he could throw in the carryalls. But there was no point in stashing them in there. This car was going nowhere. He started shouting to them that there was no way out, the streets were totally jammed. But they couldn't hear him above the racket.

Othaniel got out of the car. 'You have to run. Run! It's the only way. But take off those clothes. Quick!'

'We can't keep running with the bags. They're shooting at us!' They ripped at their clothing like it was on fire. 'Keep them in the trunk. You keep them in the trunk till Billy Ray calls.' Othaniel popped the trunk of the old cab and the men threw the disguise costumes in along with the stolen goods. Then they took off like Olympic athletes, in different directions. One of them only got a hundred yards, when the shots rang out. The defeated getaway driver watched in horror in the rear-view mirror. The second man got twice as far, before he was taken down too. Othaniel could not know at the time that all but one of his accomplices was shot dead, as well as six innocent customers of the *Legacy Federal Bank*, and one of their children. The dead lay in their shocking attire, some gunned down as they fled on the road, the others still on the sidewalk.

The Bank Manager, however, stood in the exact same spot and was untouched. Lillius Queen held her arms aloft. They shook, though she tried to keep them taut. Queen squeezed her eyes tight shut as the bullets rained all around her and piss trickled down the inside of her thigh. She hoped for mercy. She begged for it.

Othaniel sat in the Subaru and waited for them to come for him. He had a weapon with him but he did not intend to use it. He had to think. Would Billy Ray call? He checked his phone. They'd showed him how to look for calls on the cell they gave him. But there was nothing there. Why in the fuck wouldn't Master call?

Othaniel put the phone down and listened. The firing had stopped and the shrieking was more focussed towards the centre of Winston Salem. Couple of cars in the lane beside him eased forward and around the abandoned vehicles. If a path could become clear just to the next street, he could go for it.

Evidently, he wasn't nearly as suspicious as he felt. The police had been by earlier, before the gridlock. They'd seen him alright, but they left him alone. And in the last twenty minutes, many officers had skittered by, faces like thunder. They all ignored Othaniel Baye. They thought he was just stuck, like everyone else. He felt like he was carrying a big sign saying *Arrest Me!* but nobody seemed to take account of him in the crime.

Did anyone see the guys come to the car though? Othaniel checked all around again. He didn't think so. His knees began to bang together with the horror of what just happened. Fear was liquid in his veins. If only he hadn't told them to run, they might still be alive. How the hell did the police know who they were? Or were they just taking down anyone who was sprinting? Bastards.

Helicopters were coming in low overhead. Were they feeding the ground troops information from long lens surveillance? Othaniel's lips stuck to his gums. Pressure was in a red zone, inside his own head. He couldn't take much more and he started to murmur, over and over, 'I can't do this. I can't do this.'

When the old guy rapped on the driver window, Othaniel's heart slammed against the wall of his chest. He had to get out of here, with or without the getaway car, with or without the carryalls.

'I ain't working.' He shook his head at the old man who was undeterred and kept mouthing off and rapping his knuckles on the glass. Othaniel tried again. 'Sir, I am not working. I'm on a break. Can't you see what all's going on around you? Get inside one of them stores, for God's sakes. Ain't safe.'

'Damned right. Damned right it's not safe.' The old boy's nose was practically up against the glass of the driver window.

A couple were looking out now at this new scene from the florist's, just a few stores down the street. They too were rapping at the window of the store, and signalling for the old man to get back in there.

Othaniel let down the window a fraction. 'Sir. Do yourself a favour and get inside. What is *wrong* with you?'

'Me? *Me?* I saw you. I saw those boys you were with. I saw those bags they're all talking about. We've got it all going on in there.' He thumbed over his shoulder to the florists. 'On the radio. You're one of them. Think I can't tell? I've been putting people like you away for decades. I'm going to need you to come with me.'

For a split second, Othaniel almost laughed. Was this octogenarian going to attempt a citizen's arrest? The day had gone totally crazy. The sky might fall in. Anything was possible. Othaniel's shirt was clinging to his skin. He was drenched in sweat. His breath was getting away from him and he was dizzy, couldn't think clearly. There was an extra space now out on the lane of the street and he could see a path up on the right. That looked like a possibility. If he could just see off this old timer.

'Sir, like I said. I'm off duty. I'm just waiting here till—'

'I saw them. I saw those men running.' The senior citizen was almost jumping on the spot with rage. 'I saw you talking to them. I know you're one of them. Get out of the car and put your hands in the air. Get up now!'

Suddenly more shots rang out and the cracks bounced around the buildings. It was impossible to tell what their target was. No point in trying to make sense of it any longer. There were no more pedestrians scurrying here and there. Just this old one.

'I'm Bill Yearwood. Judge Yearwood. You think I don't know a thing or two about your type. Get up out of there. Now!' The old guy reached into his pocket and Othaniel felt a surge of panic burst through his veins. He had been issued with a handgun, a Smith & Wesson Bodyguard 380, only in case of emergency – *No way you're going to need it. See, it's essentially a defence weapon. Has a green laser, to assist with targeting.* The gun was on his right in a small recess next to the steering wheel. He reached down for it. His hand was shaking as he lifted the pistol slowly up.

Through the small gap at the top of the window, Othaniel's words were slow and deliberate. 'I want you to go away. Just move away, sir. You are in danger.'

The old man gave up searching his jacket pockets and started to tug at the door handle of the driver door. Othaniel raised the Smith & Wesson and his finger felt tight, locked, on the trigger. Suddenly a shot went through the glass of the window. Othaniel Baye had shot William K Yearwood in the belly. The glass shattered over both of them, one piece lodging in Othaniel's eye but he barely noticed. The blood boiled over the old man's belt and down his pants, like a giant's tongue. The victim took a good look at what was happening to his lower body and then sank to his knees which cracked hard on the sidewalk. Part of his small intestine slipped out of the wound. Othaniel threw the gun onto the passenger seat and turned over the engine. He watched his fingers rattling on the steering wheel and tried to get his breathing under control.

They made a point of saying during the trial: *shot in cold blood, murdered in cold blood.* But that blood looked red hot. It steamed out of the old judge. It flowed, thick and warm and nothing could stop it. Bits of offal tumbling out of him, like something in a butcher's shop.

Othaniel looked to his right and saw that the couple who had been trying to call Yearwood to safety were staring at him in stark horror. Their faces were frozen with the truth of what they had just seen. Othaniel looked at the pistol and picked it up. He looked at the couple again and they thought he was going to go for them but he just had to get that weapon out of the car. He dropped the gun over the jagged edges of the window and it fell to the gutter with an insignificant clunk. He started to brush at the glass strewn over his body, like rough diamonds. Mostly the shards were embedded in him, each piece with its own frill of blood around the entry point. He stopped trying to clean himself off. He looked up at the florist's shop again and saw the woman staring at him in disbelief. Her mouth was open and her eyes wide with shock. The man, probably her husband, grabbed at her jacket sleeve. He tried to pull her out of harm's way but she stood her ground. He would never forget her face, and she would never forget his.

In the florist's, Julia Seawhite's arms did not hold a bunch of flowers, but a panda teddy.

CHAPTER 9

The Staircase

Rebecca began to rely more and more on her grandfather. Standing alone, away from his wife, Ralph Brown was a different person. He could be very entertaining. He was kind, and a font of knowledge. Ralph taught Rebecca more than she could ever learn at school, that's what she thought. Out of his wife's earshot, he was keen to apprise his youngest grandchild of the history steeped around them. He told her about the Jacobite Rebellions and how Bonnie Prince Charlie dressed up as a woman to flee the English. He told her about the navvies who dug out the Caledonian Canal. But his favourite topic of all was the Highland Clearances.

'They brought them simply to the beaches. By cart or just on foot. They herded them, like cattle. It was all about the cattle, you see, Youngest Brown. About getting rid of the cattle, their livelihood. The English and the Clan Chieftains, they destroyed the Highlanders. Oh Rebecca, it was a wicked part of our history. We should all be ashamed, even you, Youngest.'

'Why did they take away the cows?'

'For the fight with Napoleon. The cattle had to be cleared to make way for the sheep. The wool, do you see, for the uniforms. They needed the grazing land. Well, it had to be somewhere big, child, didn't it? And by crikey, Scotland was big. Scotland was the very place. The Highlands. It was perfect. And so they paid off the Chieftains and The Clearances began. They left the Highlanders by the coast, at the water's edge. In all weathers. And they mostly died there. Some died at sea. Some made it, of course, to North America. And then later, there was the great renaissance for Scotland, when Victoria filled the glens with stags and the rich came. As if that could ever make up for what was done to them. And oh those merchants in Edinburgh did well with the laying out of the Highland playground.'

Unlike his wife, Ralph loved Scotland and he loved the Scottish. Primmy would barely allow a Scottish accent in the house. Mrs Scattergood, who came to clean, soon got the hang of this and was more or less mute throughout her employment at *Taransay*, much to Primmy's relief. Rebecca thought perhaps Murdo Hendry, with his few words, had been chosen for this very reason. But old Ralph, he admired the natives enormously and gathered their stories wherever possible.

It was her grandfather who would come up to Rebecca's room at bedtime. He would put his head around the door to say goodnight but then pretend that someone had grabbed him from behind and was throttling him. Funny, but inappropriate before bed.

He had a soft accent, Ralph, with something of post war BBC running through it. But just exactly from where the Grands originally hailed was a well-kept secret. They never mentioned it. And Primmy left very few topics unmentioned. It was as if they themselves had been born as elderly, had arrived here on the Morar Sands with no previous life lived.

The restoration plans from the 10th birthday party never really got underway. No-one was impressed with even the bits of the house that were already quite well done. Nobody who actually lived at *Taransay* liked the Morris wallpaper or the de Morgan tiles. The house smelled bad. The fust and decay ran riot in most of the rooms, since the thistly stained glass windows stayed invariably shut against the mind-made-up Caledonian weather.

The weather didn't bother Rebecca at all, however. She was out in all of it. This was her land, even if *Taransay* and their family's place in it was a mystery. Blow by blow, Rebecca had recounted the events of her birthday party to her best friend Maria Theresa, but when she had finished the retelling, Rebecca felt oddly disloyal to Primmy.

'It's not that she's terrible.' Rebecca would say now and again to MT. 'She's not. Sometimes, she's almost, well, fun. I love her. I do.'

In later years, when the children were well past the mothering stage and Primmy could at last just behave like a grandmother, she turned out to have some talent for it. And even during the *Taransay* years, she could be genuinely quite sweet, docile on occasion. In the (smallish compared to most rooms in the house but still large) sitting room, which was easy to keep warm and where delicious coal fires danced on winter evenings, they watched films on a Sunday evening. And if the plot was complicated – and to Rebecca, they all seemed to be – she naturally would ask questions. Colette would tell her to be quiet or say, 'We don't know yet. We don't know the answer to that. No-one knows. You'll just have to wait, for crying out loud.'

And Primmy would reach out for Rebecca with her snakeskin arm and the girl would feel obliged to go and sit by her grandmother's side, on the floor, by her prime-position armchair. And the old lady would rest her oddly large hand on Rebecca's head, so that the girl had to stay like that for a while. If the hand got too heavy or unbearably sweaty, Rebecca would suggest that Primmy get out her chocolates in the black, satin smooth, rectangular boxes. Rebecca didn't really like doing that, it was a last resort, because no sooner had Primmy wolfed her more than ample share, than she'd be heading off to the cloakroom to throw them all up.

'It's just the wicked chocolate.' She'd wink at Rebecca and harrumph back into her chair, post-puke. 'One wouldn't dream of heaving up one's balanced meal.'

As the complexities of *The Odessa File* or some such spy thriller took hold, Rebecca's questions would become intolerable for Colette who would screech at her little sister. Old Ralph would wag his hand towards the door which was Rebecca's cue to get the hot cloths for his face. She would exit on all fours to show how caring she was, not to get in the way of the screen. She would run the hot tap upstairs where she declared that the hot always seemed to be hotter, though no-one believed her. Then she'd squeeze out two or three facecloths (which is what they were called at school, yet they were 'flannels' at home) and race downstairs to her grandfather's chair. He would close his eyes shut like a big cartoon cat smiling as wide as he could and Rebecca would lay over the first flannel. The steam would float gently around the mould of his face. If he pointed at his ear, Rebecca was to lift the flannel and say to him, 'You are my protector,' deep into the folds of his ear. Then she'd find his tortoiseshell comb in his inside waistcoat pocket. As she combed, Ralph would purr, infuriating Colette. Grandma might pass Youngest an elastic band or two from her odds and bobs basket which she fiddled with during films and Rebecca would snap the bands into ponytail horns for her grandfather. He'd walk right up to bed like that.

After school, if he was alone, seated, Ralph would instruct her to sit very close to him and he'd say 'Rebecca, I am your protector. Tell me, tell me.' He'd lean his head towards her and she was to whisper that he was her protector deep into the pink hairy cave of his ear.

'Well, Becky? Did you tell me?'

'Course I did, silly.'

Rebecca didn't quite understand her grandfather's games, his ways. She didn't understand that his need for her was even greater than hers for him. But what she did understand was that they were close. They hadn't been at first but now they were.

She felt it under the skin of her palms and in her chest. There was a sensation, a flow of affection, for him. She knew that she really had someone.

That study which had housed the card table with the red velvet cloth became Ralph's. The card table disappeared and was never referred to again. Nor the playing cards.

Her grandfather would wait for her to get home from school in Mallaig. 'Youngest? Youngest Brown, is that you? Want your advice on something.'

He didn't of course. He didn't need advice. He needed companionship, from a warm source. He needed friends, or a friend. Rebecca didn't know why her grandmother disallowed him, actively discouraged him, to find a friend or a backgammon partner or a trout-fishing pal. But if anyone ever came near, Grandma would usher them away, sometimes literally, off the grounds.

Ralph showed Rebecca photos of his own father in the Royal Air Force. He knew the names of each of his father's friends, whilst having none of his own.

So Rebecca and Ralph worked together to make the study their kingdom, the oldest and the youngest. They catalogued all the vinyl records. Over twelve hundred. Rebecca wrote out all the names on lined foolscap on his clipboard. She would re-align the sheets under the bulldog clip. Sometimes he would have her check through them, though with no burglary and no interest from any other family member, nothing was ever moved from its spot. Mrs Scattergood wasn't allowed near the stereo. If anything was out of place or lost, it had to be their fault alone. Whereas in the rest of the house, anything which was hard to find or damaged in any way was blamed entirely on Mrs Scattergood. Primmy never tired of berating her, once the cleaner had left for the day, once she'd judged her beyond the driveway and safely aboard her old navy blue bicycle.

Richard Strauss days were good in the study. Rachmaninov ones were great. Vaughan Williams was the one to look out for. Ralph Brown would cry. He could make it through *Lark Ascending* but barely got past the cello overture for *Fantasia on a Theme by Thomas Tallis* before he reached into his copious trouser pockets for his parachute of a hankie. He never played Vaughan Williams when Primmy was home and if Rebecca returned from the High School during it, she waited outside the study till it was over and then went in quietly to lift the needle, not daring to look at her grandfather till he had rallied a little.

Rebecca liked to think that her grandfather had had someone who truly loved him once, a long time ago, but that this other love had been unable to leave her own husband because he'd been paralysed in some war-torn location. Rebecca liked to think that Ralph had loved this amazing woman deeply and that she'd returned his passion. She looked through all his photographs. She looked into the eyes of every possibly eligible pair but couldn't say that she ever got any feeling of finding Ralph's true love.

One early autumn day, when she was thirteen, Rebecca couldn't find Ralph when she came home from Mallaig. He had just that week taken delivery of a Berlioz set which he had ordered from Japan. There were ten vinyl records and a booklet and a canary yellow baby duster. They had begun working their way through the collection after school with hazelnut Rittersport. This flavour was Rebecca's find and when he tasted it, Ralph lifted back her fringe and kissed her. He hadn't been so crazy about a flavour since crunchy peanut.

Before they began a new record collection, her grandfather would tell her all about the composer. In Hector Berlioz's case, Rebecca was particularly enchanted. 'Listen to your gut, Becky. If you know in your heart you must be a lion tamer, then you will have my blessing to go to the circus.'

Oh dear, Rebecca didn't like the sound of that at all.

'Or a tree surgeon, Becky. Or a welder. What you want, is my point. Do what you want, Youngest. Take Berlioz. He was sent off to study medicine. His father, who by the way was the tadger who brought acupuncture to Europe, didn't even let him learn piano.'

'What's a tadger?'

'It's Scottish for todger.'

'What's a todger?'

'Never mind. Don't say it in front of your grandmother. You'll have her clutching for her *Persephenie* smelling salts.'

'Did Berlioz want to be a lion tamer, Grandad? Which is more important, the heart or the gut?'

'Um, the heart. No, the gut. Let me think about it. Anyway, this Berlioz, he was remarkable! Had to spend time reviewing musical works when he should've been composing. There wasn't the money, you see. Dickens was the same, with writing.' Ralph leaned into Rebecca. 'He nearly murdered someone. Actually, three people.'

'Dickens?'

'No. Hector Berlioz. He travelled from Italy to murder his fiancée. And to murder her mother, who had called off their engagement. And to murder the man, some big piano manufacturer, to whom she was now betrothed. Want to know what happened?' He held up his arm for her to come close on the sofa but she was getting too old for that. Rebecca nodded and carried on wiping the vinyl they were about to spin.

'It was a very long journey. Perhaps you'll think about it, one day, when you're travelling the world. He had with him a disguise, a woman's disguise. He was going to do the deed, the murders, dressed as a woman.'

'Like Bonnie Prince Charlie! He's my favourite.'

'Yes, darling.' Ralph beamed at her and then suddenly frowned. 'Gosh, you look so much like…'

'Like what?' Rebecca looked down at herself.

'You know that I love you, don't you.'

'Yes.' Rebecca nodded vigorously. He had that sad look and she wanted it to go away. 'Did he have a beard?'

'Who, darling?'

'Hector Berlioz. Just thinking about the disguise.'

'No. I'm sure he didn't have a beard. Anyway he could have shaved off a beard. Listen.' He smacked his hands on his knees. 'He stole pistols for the murders and loaded the gun. Keeping one bullet for himself. He even had strychnine just in case the pistol jammed.' Ralph broke off a piece of Rittersport.

'Well? What happened?'

'Oh he didn't go through with it. Go ahead, get the needle down.' Ralph put his feet up on the Moroccan leather pouffe.

'After all that, he didn't go through with it?'

'Changed his mind. He was a handful, that Hector. Geniuses are. I knew someone like that once.'

He rubbed his index finger along his eyebrow and the sadness was back. Rebecca imagined some flaxen-haired Viennese flautist who had spurned him. How dare she have turned on her dainty Austrian heel and married the conductor instead of her Old Ralph!

'That was your father's middle name, you know. Hector.' Ralph's blue eyes were suddenly bare with loss.

Rebecca picked up the back of the Berlioz album and began reading aloud, hoping for her grandad's quick emotional recovery. *'Such is the strength of this recording, you'll believe you're in the thick of the action.'*

*

Just a week or so later, Rebecca came home from school as usual and went into the study. There it was, that date, on the desk calendar: September 17th. And although her grandfather had in fact not changed the date for two days, so that it was actually the 19th, Rebecca would always think of him on September 17th.

But he wasn't in his study on that day and so she flugged into the kitchen, her body and its step exhibiting its usual mix of post-school exhaustion/boredom. She made herself a tomato sandwich with pepper and salad cream. She wolfed it in the kitchen, as eating was discouraged in her attic bedroom, to starve rodents. (Though not discouraged, on occasion, in the Grands' bedroom, Rebecca noted as the pair of them shuffled and skulked along the landing around midnight, with fridge pickings.)

Replete now, Rebecca grabbed her schoolbag and was heading upstairs. She saw Ralph's arm first, on the half turn of the staircase. His twigletty fingers were dangling over the edge of the tread. Rebecca thought at once that he was dead and not collapsed. She dropped her heavy bag and went to the phone in the hall. There was a leather-bound blotter with a fresh page. If they wanted to write down a message at the secretary table, there was a separate pad in the exquisite mission oak drawer. Rebecca found a cartridge pen in the drawer. She'd asked to take this to school the day they dressed as Victorians and were trying out fountain pen script, but she wasn't allowed.

Now Rebecca unscrewed the cap and shook the pen over the vast blotting pad till the blue ink spattered out on the white.

She dialled 999. They wanted to know her name. They wanted to know if 'the man' was breathing. They wanted to know if he had a pulse. They wanted to know who else was in the house. Rebecca said no-one, though it was possible that Murdo was on the grounds. Surely there was no time to check. Surely they should just be coming this instant.

'He's just lying there! On the stairs.' Rebecca looked up the staircase where the light flooded down onto the turn in the landing, from the beautiful arched window which looked out onto the linden tree driveway. For a second it seemed like the light itself had come for her grandfather, that angels might appear with little harps.

The voice in the telephone wittered on. They wanted Rebecca to give them the address. Then they said the ambulance was on its way but there was a chance that she could save him.

'Take the phone with you, Rebecca. Go up the stairs. I'm right here. I'll keep talking.'

'No, I can't.'

'You can, Rebecca. Take a deep breath.'

'No, you don't understand. The phone has a cord. I'd have to put it down to go on the stairs.'

They told her that she didn't have to worry about that. They wanted her to go check the pulse on his neck, the breath from his mouth, the colour of his skin, then come back to the phone. And they would be waiting still. *Go on now*, they said. *You can do it.*

Rebecca held the phone down at her side. She could hear the mouse-like pleadings coming from it, as she set the phone on the secretary table. Her legs started shaking and she grabbed the banister to pull herself up to her grandfather and then almost fell upon him. His knees were up near his chest. Was he in pain?

She held his cold, silky hand in both of hers. He looked asleep. She had to wake him up. She wondered about playing the Ravel waltz at full volume. His favourite. 'The greatest waltz ever written, Youngest!' They'd tested the volume to this waltz, when no-one else was in. And they'd covered their mouths with the shock of the decibels, till Murdo appeared outside the study window, looking through the black bars, with his hands over his ears.

Rebecca was expert in taking a pulse from her childhood games. Of course, it was years now since she'd been involved in such practices, but when she tried to find her grandfather's, a slow beat pulsed through her fingertips almost immediately. A very, very slow beat. He could barely open his eyes. He tried to make a word with what breath he had left. Rebecca lowered her ear to his mouth.

'Your mother, darling. Oh you look so like her. Your mother now, darling. Can you hear me.'

Her own words she had to wrestle free from the sorrow which was filling her throat. 'Yes.' She squeezed his hand. 'Yes, I can hear you. Are you going with her?'

'Rebecca. Your mother. You must find her. Listen to your…' a sound she had never heard came from him, as if something else was inside him and trying to get by, to get past, to be dead.

'Gut,' Rebecca said. 'Listen to my gut. I promise. I promise.'

The mice stopped squeaking at the phone and Rebecca could hear a siren wailing up the driveway. She put her grandad's hand back down on the Tiff rug and wondered if this rug was the killer. Had he slipped on the Tiff and split his head? No sign of bruising on his face. Rebecca got up and went into the bathroom. She looked at herself in the mirror and ran the hot tap. She put the facecloth in the hot pool gathering in the sink. She was scared, yet proud of herself.

The flannel didn't lie properly over his face. His lips were not together and it wouldn't be right to prod at them. As the ambulance people let themselves in, Rebecca shouted 'Wait!' and they hesitated at the bottom of the stairs. She lifted the flannel and whispered, 'You are my protector.' But of course he wasn't.

CHAPTER 10

The Aunt

Joya really ought to get herself a new name. That was the only clear thing to Keller in the first weeks at his Aunt's house. His own mother he had no memory of. She had cleared out with some construction worker before Keller was even walking. If he ever tried to get nostalgic over what might have been, his father would throw another crust of reality at him. 'You needed antibiotics just from the diaper rash. Get real, boy. Pity she stayed so long.'

'You mean you wished she'd left before I got born.'

'I didn't say that.'

'Didn't have to.'

*

When Othaniel was incarcerated, his relatives, almost all of which Keller had never set eyes on before, made a big deal of moving the child over to Greensboro, though it was all of thirty miles from Winston Salem. He never quite figured out any kind of family tree or who was what to whom. He didn't care very much anyway and later, not at all. On moving day, the women chattered away, saying the men were to do the heavy lifting but Keller only had one suitcase, a couple of boxes with sports stuff and a rucksack. He could have got the bus over there on his own. But those ladies they liked to direct things and they used the men for verbal target practice, for scorn. Keller thought the men looked like they deserved it, with their flab tipping over the waistband of their pants and their greasy shirt stains.

Aunt Joya had neither a hug nor a smile for him the day she came for his belongings and himself. Joya's relatives commiserated with her on the imposition.

On the journey over to Greensboro, Keller set his hopes for their domestic life together at realistically low. But in fact, he had a room much better than the one at home. It was quite large too, with barn wood walls which he could cover in whatever he liked. Aunt Joya had no children of her own, just a little terrier dog who stayed close to her heel. The dog favoured no-one but Joya, though his Aunt barely spoke to the animal. A week went by before Keller even knew that dog had a name: Peverill. Everyone avoided Peverill. If someone happened to come too close, the terrier flew at their ankles. Keller never had an interest in getting close. He had no intention of working up an affection for the mutt. This was easily achieved with Peverill, a mangy, sly attempt at a pet. Aunt Joya was fond of saying, 'When the dog dies, I die.' But she never smiled at the animal or petted it in Keller's presence.

Neither did Joya Baye lavish any affection on a regular boyfriend. There was the occasional man around, sometimes of a morning too. Or an afternoon. Now and then Keller would come home from school and there would be some workshy fella, slunk low on the sofa and Joya's blouse slipped on her shoulder. But his Aunt had no fixed relationship, nothing extending beyond a night or two.

With this fairly uncomplicated living arrangement, Keller reckoned that with care and attention, he could anticipate difficulty and avoid it. He was a practical sort and he intended to make himself useful at home and in Vandalia Road. Sure, there were plenty of dealers and addicts in the neighborhood, but there were ordinary working folk too and some of them elderly. Keller could mend things and he had a strong back. He was tall for his age and never in any kind of trouble at school.

There was Mrs Bellingham across the street who liked her *Nellie Stevens* hedge trimmed once a week and Mr Soliman who wanted to be escorted to the halal butcher up on Martin Luther King Boulevard, on account of being mugged and beaten senseless outside the meat store a couple months back.

Joya didn't go much to the supermarket. She liked takeout, and fried chicken better than anything. She liked food that could be eaten straight from the carton and when she really had to cook, straight from the pan. She didn't hold with plates and bowls, couldn't be doing with no dish soap. Yes, fried chicken was her all-time favourite and the other thing which wiped that scowl off her brow was playing the lottery. If Keller could have found a way to provide buckets of those things for her from the get go, his life might have been altogether different. But when she wasn't eating fried chicken, she wasn't eating much of anything, and neither was Keller. Before the first month was in, he had learned to steal tins from the Indian grocery. Cheap items which he hoped wouldn't cause too much fuss if he was caught. There was no proper surveillance that he could see, just those big convex mirrors at the end of the aisles. He got into the habit of buying Aunt Joya a Puffball lottery ticket on a Friday and he would leaf through the comic books, smiling if anyone was watching behind the counter and as soon as they were taken with a customer, he'd slip a can of corn into his jacket on one side and some peaches on the other. *Native Forest* was his favourite brand of peaches. He knew that balanced nutrition was important and he tried to vary the products he stole. Soon he learned that tuna was smaller and safer. Tuna was more expensive, therefore a good ratio of dollars to square inch. It was seriously good for him too. But he was never able to steal enough at any one time to satisfy his hunger. He considered going to more than one store and making a stash of cans. But he didn't really want to get that organised, since he didn't like being a thief. And he knew the owner at the Indian. If it came to it, maybe Sanjay would let him off with a smack round the head. Other stores might be harsher.

Now and again, when Joya was happy with the ticket he'd got for her, she'd pluck some dollars from one of her jars and send him back to the store for chicken.

But although she'd had a broad grin for the tickets at first, soon she took the supply for granted and there was nothing he could do to earn decent money for them beyond his odd jobs in the neighborhood. And even there, it was sometimes a question of folks taking pity on him. Not all of them seemed to get that he was working like a full grown man; in fact, harder than many men that Keller could see around. And when some of those neighbors found out that his name wasn't 'Luke', as he had told them (Luke was his favourite name and what he would have chosen for himself) but that he was Keller Baye whose father had murdered that Supreme Court Judge in cold blood, they soon stopped asking him to bag up fallen leaves or sweep out the garage. Mrs Bellingham and Mr Soliman stayed loyal however.

Aunt Joya liked to watch the television. She liked to watch alone. In fact, if she wasn't entertaining a gentleman caller, she liked the house to contain just herself.

In the summer, Keller was happy to oblige, and kicked around with Lemi Kowalski after school. Angelo had dropped out of the gang after the drifter got killed. Lemi couldn't figure it, but Keller just shrugged.

'People come, people go.'

'Are you a mental patient, Kell? We've been buddies for years.'

'That's how it works sometimes. You've seen how the girls—'

'We ain't girls. I can't even get him to talk to me. What the fuck?'

'Drop it, Lem. Will you?'

Eventually, Lemi did drop it. The two boys still wound up at Horsepen Creek most days, weather permitting. Lemi had a curfew and would disappear long before dark. But Keller was free to do as he wished.

*

Occasionally, some of Keller's weird relatives would drop by and they'd go down to the Uwharrie Forest but then Joya set her foot in an old coyote trap there and didn't think to go for a tetanus shot. The rust worked itself into an infection and Keller thought she exaggerated the limp she was left with. Anyway, she was disinclined to go picnicking in the Uwharrie after that.

When fall came, Aunt Joya began locking the door earlier. Keller was not allowed to have his own key. He didn't really mind, he was a skinny boy and could get through almost any window. But when he was around fifteen, his Aunt got a subsidy for insulation and double panes, and after their installation, Keller could no longer get into the house. Everything had a lock on it. He'd ring the doorbell and bang on the door but she didn't answer. Once or twice a neighbor would call her up on the phone and tell her to let the boy in. She'd come thundering down the stairs in a fury and hold the door dramatically aside, sighing and looking heavenwards for recognition at the hardship of it all.

At that time, Keller had no idea that Aunt Joya was getting welfare for housing him; getting real dollar money and doing her level best to keep him out of the house. He found out on a winter's evening. Night had not yet fully descended but it was minus something and he was stuck out on the porch. Keller did not feel well. He was pretty sure he was running a fever. He pleaded with his Aunt to let him in. He promised to fry some chicken, though that was a lie in the making, he had none with him to cook. Not even any tins.

He was a few years older now and was keeping as many jobs after school as he could get. Folks had come around to him some, he didn't have to pretend to be 'Luke' anymore. By and by, they had come to give him a chance and he was a hard worker, they gave him that alright. He still bought the lottery tickets for his Aunt but any spare cash he had left over, went on filling his belly and buying sex. His belly felt like the safest place to stock up. But the sex he paid for with Christie was much more satisfying. Now there was a woman who really would suit the name Joya.

In the beginning, he'd used each of the women out at *Hailey's Whorehouse* but just a few weeks in, he stuck with Christie. On her days off, he didn't even drop by. In terms of tuition, Christie was a professor. She put him on the advanced program. The bird hide had been like kindergarten. Christie filled the gaps in his knowledge and he filled everything he could find in her. It was some months before Keller could see that he could ever be parted from this woman for more than a few days at a time. But he knew the exact moment when his feelings changed. It was the day she told him that Christie was not her real name.

'Don't tell Hailey I said.' But she didn't leave it there. She wanted to talk to him about her boyfriend.

'He the one leaving these marks?' Keller pointed to the bruising across her ribs and Christie nodded, bit her lip.

'I… I guess the truth is, Kell, I think of you as a friend. Oh I know you're under age and all but I'm not so very much older. Guess what age I am. Go on.'

'I don't care.'

'Oh. Really? I thought we'd gotten so close. Leastways that's how I feel.'

But this was the kind of closeness which Keller did not want. It's not that he didn't care about her. He did, in his own way. But he needed her for very specific sex reasons and her deviating into platonic territory was a distinct turnoff.

'See, now I can't even call you Christie without feeling like a prick.'

'Course you can, honey. Aw I'm sorry. I am Christie. I am. For more than ten years. Just, I feel so close to you. I shouldn't have said. I'll keep my trap shut until you tell me to open it.' She began to unbuckle his belt.

'I won't get hard. Not now.'

'Oh that'll be a first. Come on, Kell. Don't be like that. You know I want you.'

'I don't know. It's like you want some kind of brother. I ain't nobody's brother.'

'No, I don't. That's not true. I want you.'

Keller shook his head. 'It's your job.'

'Not always. Not with you.'

'How can I know you want me? How can I tell? You always cover yourself in that lube before I can get near you. You don't want me. You're lying. You don't want me to know that you don't want me, is all.'

'Now you're losing me here, Kell. You don't like me talking? I like it when you talk. I like to hear about your dreams. That pick-up you're gonna buy, the apartment you're—'

'I'm the client. I can say what I like. Me, I can talk. Or not talk. Don't you girls get it?'

'You're right. I get it. Come and put those cupid lips on me.'

Keller stood in front of the full length mirror in her little room at *Hailey's*. With his flies hanging open, he put his hands on his belly. 'You think I'm fat? I'm getting really fat.'

'No, Kell. You're just right. I like a man with a… wait! Where you going?'

Keller buckled up and took off, leaving her door wide open.

Christie hissed after him, 'Don't tell Hailey!'

He never returned.

*

On that winter night when the temperature was a few degrees below zero, Keller was out on the freezing porch, with no gloves. Joya was always rolling her eyes and asking him when would he ever learn. Though from where he was sitting, he learned constantly and she knew nothing. She said she ought to put string over his head and down through his sleeves with the mittens attached, like for little guys. As if she'd ever shift her fat ass to take care of that. He'd like to put string around her neck, and pull real tight.

He'd burned the last pair of gloves he had, after going back to the charred remains of the drifter just before daybreak to check out what was left. He kicked the fire around with his boots and waited for the heat to leave, while he set about making this part of the woods look just as it had before he'd ever set foot in there. He dug up the crossbow. He hadn't had a box to bury it in the day before and he hoped that he hadn't damaged the mechanism with all this earth. It was a small crossbow, compact. He didn't want to part with it and put it carefully into his rucksack with those fine leather shoes which he'd left in that nearby hollow.

The ash and bone in the firepit were still warm but not too hot to go into the thick refuse bags he'd brought. The watch was there too. That wasn't going to ever tell time again. Keller had ten small bags which he loaded into one large sack. He walked back to the town's perimeter and distributed the refuse bags around the public trash cans. He walked a good distance between each and when he was done, he set fire to his dirty gloves.

*

Freezing tonight on the porch, Keller banged his boots on the wooden boards. His feet and fingers were going numb. Maybe he should just get a locksmith to come and change the lock. What the hell, this had got beyond crazy. Aunt Joya had the one master key on a chain around her neck. He'd stared good and hard at that key on many an evening as she dozed off in her armchair, tv fizzing away with her game shows. Yes, a locksmith. He could spin a yarn and get his own master key cut. She was probably out cold, with a couple of rum and Cheerwines swilling around her gut.

It must have been getting down well past zero now. Keller thrust his hands down his pants and between his thighs to get to the last of the warmth. He could go up to the pool hall, but they'd all just stare. He couldn't feel his feet, particularly the left foot where the sensation had gone entirely, right up to the ankle. He could no longer walk upon it. If he tried, he knew he would only fall. He looked at the coal scuttle which always sat out there on the porch, though they had no coal and never used the open fire. That scuttle must have been made out of some kind of metal. Zinc, he reckoned. Too dirty to tell. How much would a thing like that weigh? Enough to shatter through the double pane windows? He had to get inside. The sleepiness was coming. But sleeping outdoors in winter could be fatal. He knew that. They'd scooped up a couple of old homeless crusties with the snowplow last winter. Dead and frozen. They say it is a painless way to die. But Keller wasn't ready to die. He wasn't waiting for that. Not like his dad up at Turville. Year on year, the same prospect. That was a terrible way to go. Crossbow death looked almost painless, as long as you hit the right spot. Perhaps just a few seconds of pain, and then the end.

Keller picked up the broom on the porch and upended it to make a crutch so that he could get along without using his left foot. He went over to the other side of the street, to Peg Bellingham's. Peg was a bit further than one or two of the others but she had a strong dislike of Joya Baye and for all her rantiness, Peg's morals lay on the fair side and her heart hadn't pinched up as the elderly's sometimes do.

Peg was struck with horror when she got Keller's sock off and almost pushed him onto her Davenport sofa. The snow was falling now in beautiful thick flakes and a blue light came through Peg's window, from the police car. There was no siren of course and no tearing rush for the residents from this pocket of the city, but Keller was escorted to the community hospital.

He lost three toes on that left foot, to frostbite. They couldn't get his Aunt to answer her phone, although between curses, Peg was telling them that Joya's lights had been blazing at the house across the street.

Peg stayed for the whole production in the *Emergency Room*, yelping about this and that.

'I don't know what ever got into that Aunt of yours, Kell. We was close once. But over the years, a person gets all bittered up.'

'Lucky you didn't, Peg.'

'She wasn't so bad, Joya. Used to give me them chokeberries. I made jam. Last time I asked, she prackly ran me off the porch with a broom.' Peg stopped and blinked. 'Well I'll be. That same broom you was using, as a crutch.'

Keller was used to the old lady's complaints about Joya Baye. But then she started squawking about the stipend his Aunt was enjoying, for giving him bed and board. At first he didn't recognise the word. She was in her mid-eighties, Peg Bellingham, and given to the use of a bygone language. A stipend, he came to realise, was a sum of money, regular. He thought very hard about that money, but didn't say a word. He wanted to bide his time.

A social worker came to see him and wanted to discuss his living arrangements. Keller did not want to discuss this with a stranger. He did not refuse to answer questions but just kept holding up his hand, like he was getting his breath. It wasn't that long a stretch till he would graduate from Weaver High. After that, he could get properly paid work. He already knew that he would get in at the recycling plant. They always had ads in the paper. And the brighter kids got on the white collar track a year in. He planned to be on that track.

In the end, as the social worker went on and on about benefits at Medicaid for his toe prosthesis and *Temporary Assistance for Needy Families*, Keller became even quieter, and then the anger came. He was not going to be that person. He was going to work for what he needed. And there was nothing this big bosomed lady or his Aunt Joya could do about it. He would be something steady. He wouldn't be *Needy*. He wouldn't be robbing folk anymore. He wouldn't have some crusty old fucker stringing up his pet. He wouldn't be a drunk or a crackhead.

The woman from *Child Protective Services* was banging on about relocating him but it was more trouble than it was worth.

'May I ask you to leave,' he said to the lady who was hell bent on assisting him to live in the manner she recommended. And it seemed that he could ask her to leave, as that is what she promptly did.

He wasn't a child anymore, people had to get that through their thick skulls. And he'd be out of that house soon enough under his own steam. In the meantime, things were going to change. He made his mind up about that in the hospital. Because suddenly, he could see her running scared, Aunt Joya, when she showed up at the hospital the following day, with her hair all done and a soft blue jacket he'd never set eyes on before. Carrying a bag of candy in one hand, she was, and holding it up in front of him with her big grin and an envelope in the other. He wanted to ask her if she'd won the lottery. But all that was going to stop. No more Puffball tickets. He was offering nothing from this day forward. He was going to say only what needed to be said. And when he was good and ready, Keller Baye was going to make his Aunt Joya sit and listen.

The envelope contained a letter, hand delivered, from Makayla. He felt a surge in his chest when Joya told him who it was from. His hopes welled up like a font, he couldn't help it. Keller opened the letter and began reading. Quickly, the implications of her words distracted him, sent him scurrying down complex paths. The police and social services must have been in touch with Weaver High. Those busybody welfare folk must have questioned some pupils because Makayla knew quite a lot. Or was it a felony what Joya did? Were the police up at the school? Keller pictured Angelo's face as the officers approached. He better have held his nerve or he would teach him a lesson he'd never forget. They were no longer friends and if they passed one another in school, Angelo looked the other way. As if the whole thing was Keller Baye's fault. Keller thought about the crossbow buried safely in its crate in the yard now, alongside those handsome shoes. Would the police go to his house? Could dogs sniff for a weapon? Keller smacked himself on the side of his head. No, this was about Aunt Joya. About being locked out. Nothing more.

Keller carried on reading the letter and Makayla came to her point. She wanted to offer her father's assistance:

He's an orthotist at Kindred Hospital. He does a lot of work with veterans. He changes lives.

In this letter, she didn't say any of the sweetheart things he wanted her to say. And why would she, they'd never done anything more intimate than have a sandwich together in the dining hall. But all the same, she still looked at him in that way. Everyone knows when they're being watched and though maybe she didn't want more than that, Keller thought the reasons were mostly circumstantial. She didn't like his circumstances one bit, but what she did like, was the look of him. And here she was offering him help, now that he was an amputee. He'd never heard the word orthotist but he could tell from the note that her dad was some kind of big shot up at Kindred, fixing torn up soldiers with new limbs. Of course her daddy was a hero. You could tell just by looking at his daughter.

That was the problem, you could tell just by looking at Keller, who he was. He knew his head sunk between his shoulders like a dejected turtle. He knew his eyes were shifty, that he scuffed along on the soles of his feet. You could see that he struggled with hope as soon as he got outside of his own bedroom walls. When the wider world and its expectations shone a light on Keller, his heart hammered and his throat dried up. It wouldn't take an expert profiler to figure out Keller Baye's circumstances. They were chiselled into his bones.

He finished reading and muttered, 'I am a moving, living sculpture to those fucking circumstances.' He had half a mind to rip that letter from Makayla into a thousand bits. But then he imagined her taking him to the appointment herself, in that little red Toyota of hers. Always polished up, it was. Maybe she did that polishing with her daddy on a Sunday.

The following week, Makayla did that very thing; she took him to an appointment at Kindred Hospital. He could have taken his clapped out Dodge, since he only needed his right foot to drive it, but she offered, and it was good manners to accept. Keller was so determined not to blow it that he practised everything he might say. He filmed himself and corrected his body language. He could see that he barely moved as he conversed and when he thought his face was expressionless, in fact it scowled. He rehearsed lines, questions that she would like to be asked, just like he used to at the bird hide. Stuff that made girls feel good. Stuff that an older man might think to ask. He even considered going back to Christie for a refresher with some social grace extras thrown in.

'Nah,' he said to the mirror in his bedroom. 'The fuck would Christie know about social graces?'

He watched movie stars on YouTube, not the films, but interviews, when they tried to be at their most charming.

Keller went over to Peg Bellingham's to try out his new persona and she said, 'What in God's name's got into you, Keller Baye?' which he took to mean his strategy was working.

Makayla was on time and he waited by the window so that he could see her Toyota arrive. They hardly talked on the way.

'Nervous, Kell?'

'A little.'

'Don't be.'

That was annoying. Who made her the anxiety judge?

But all went well at the appointment. He was seen by a technician in Outpatients, not by the great man himself. With Medicaid predicting a four month wait for his prosthesis, here they were able to get it to him in just a couple weeks. He could see that this speedy delivery was where Makayla's father came in.

'Get your gait back as quick as we can,' the technician said.

'My what?'

They laughed about that later in Sullivan's Steakhouse. 'You thought, like, he meant a garden gate?' Makayla said.

And Keller took it all, laughed at himself. She hadn't wanted to go to the restaurant but he was determined to persuade her. He'd got her this far, he couldn't let her go now. 'You probably think I'm too fat to be eating in a restaurant. I get it.'

'Oh no, Keller. Not at all.'

'I am planning to go to the gym. I have more money coming in.'

'You're a hard worker. Everyone says so.'

'The gym's on my list, just as soon as I get me a new vehicle. That's my priority.'

'You've got your old Dodge.'

'Uh yeah. Needs a new alternator. With the labour, the estimate's like four times its worth.'

'Can't you fit the alternator? I heard you're great with—'

'I want a decent car, Makayla.'

'I get that. Of course you do. Why do you need a car to get to the gym though? Isn't there one nearby?'

At Keller's local gym, you were more likely to see sloppy batches of crystal meth being brewed than anyone doing physical exercise.

'Oh I have my sights set on one over at Fisher Park.'

'Fisher Park? That's where we live.'

'Really? So anyway, come to Sullivan's. Please. My treat. A way of saying thank you.'

Makayla checked her watch and tilting her head to the side, almost with sympathy, said that she could go to Sullivan's for an hour or so. Like she was doing him a great favor. Like socializing with him was even more generous than offering her father's miraculous services.

When they got settled in the restaurant, he turned his charm offensive right up. He gave the performance his all and before long, he could see her shoulders dropping, so that her collar evened out. She pushed her golden hair back behind one of her ears, a gesture he'd seen so often in class as she got ready to really concentrate. He could see the exquisite line of her collar bone.

They flipped through the catalog of foot prosthetics that he'd been given to take home.

'Hmm.' Keller pointed at one of the glossy shots. 'Silicone flesh with acrylic toe nails. What color should I paint 'em?'

Makayla laughed. 'I have some *Big Apple Red* I could let you borrow. Hell, you could even keep it. My pleasure.'

They both laughed and he inched his hand across the table.

It really could not have gone better. It felt like a date and perhaps he should not have been that surprised then when she asked him to come to the Outer Banks in the Christmas holidays.

'What, you mean like with your family?'

'No, silly. A bunch of us are going to Bodie Island. Rick's parents have a hotel there.'

'Ricky Marjenhoff?'

'Uhuh. It's just lunch though, we're not staying over.'

And here Keller made a misstep. His face clouded over, he could feel it. He had let himself get suddenly carried away with the idea of being with her again, just the two of them. She was probably going out with Ricky Marjenhoff. He hung around her a lot. Why was that dickwang ruining this invitation. He felt a pain in his foot and realised it was where the toes used to be.

'Ok, well, think it over. It's all really mellow out there. Don't sweat it.' She looked at her watch. 'I gotta get going. Let me drop you back at—'

'No, it's fine. It's in the wrong direction for you.' Keller had to bring this meeting to an end. He was making all kinds of mistakes. 'I mean, if you're at Fisher Park.' She must never know that he'd followed her many times to her gorgeous family home. He had run out of charm. Like a potion in a fairytale. His time was up. Keller quickly plastered his grin back on. 'And I'd like to come to the Outers. I'd love to.' He couldn't wait for the check. He slapped down far too many dollar bills and ushered her out of the steakhouse.

*

Keller was running late, on the day of the trip to the Outer Banks. His money was missing from the plastic pouch in the cistern and he'd had to sprint down to the ATM to take some from his savings account. He'd missed his train and consequently the bus in Currituck and so the other guests were already on their main course when he got into the dining room of the Hotel on Bodie Island.

Ricky's guests were eating in a large private room with vast windows overlooking the winter grey waters of the Sound. The light too was grey in the December day but the room was warm and candlelit with a thick red carpet underfoot. The table was laid with crystal and silver cruets. He could see that there was more than one knife and fork to choose from at your place setting.

Keller stood there, still trying to catch his breath. He knew that when he took off his coat, his armpits would be dark with sweat because of running from the bus stop. The stump on his left foot hurt horribly against the prosthesis. He'd only had the fitting a week ago and was only to wear it for an hour each day. He still had the stitches in and was certainly not supposed to be haring along the streets. Also, he had left his gift for the hosts at home on the console by the front door. That'd be gone by the time he got back. He tried to explain to Ricky's mother, as she bustled over with her push up bra cleavage and her big hair but he thought he sounded as if he was lying. He could feel his face flushing. Ricky's mom helped him out of his coat and showed him to his seat, far away from Makayla. Mrs Marjenhoff offered him a leather-bound menu, but he barely recognised the items as food. In a haze of perfume, she leaned over him to help with picking out a dish. He could hardly talk, his mouth was so dry. Eventually, the hostess chose something for Keller and disappeared.

Ricky was sitting next to Makayla, way too close. Keller thought he'd seen her face fall just a little when he appeared. Perhaps she'd been relieved earlier, thinking he hadn't made it. She'd done her good and charitable deed by extending the invitation and now she could get on and enjoy the holidays with Ricky Marjenhoff and his rich parents. But now, damn, Keller Baye was here after all. Was that it?

The group by no means insisted that he join in the conversation. And how could he? They compared the merits of Appaloosas versus Percherons. Keller knew they were talking about horses, but that was it. They discussed their college plans, their upcoming ski trips to Banner Elk and Cataloochee, their hybrid cars. Even when they talked about a TV show which he had seen too, Keller was too slow to come up with an opinion or a witty line.

And why had he thought a football jersey would be the right thing? Mellow, she'd said, but they were in shirts. One of the guys had a bow tie, undone, hanging there, like someone off a fashion poster, the total fucking mouth-breather. Keller could feel his temper simmering away in his chest.

Ricky was drinking red wine and he wanted Makayla to take a sip but she was driving. Great, she'd brought her little red car. Why the fuck hadn't she offered him a ride? Then he wouldn't be in such a state.

God but he was thirsty. Keller grabbed the red wine and poured himself a full glass. There must've been a shaker pint in there. Biggest goddamned wine glass he'd ever seen.

'Wine vandal,' the girl next to him whispered and leaned in. 'Don't you know you only half fill a goblet. If that.'

He pushed her away and there was an awkward silence. Keller picked up his glass and all but drained it. 'Cheers. Sorry, I should've said that first.' He was not used to wine and was quaffing it like water, though it didn't seem to quench his thirst.

'Yes, cheers.' Mrs Marjenhoff came in apace and set some food in front of Keller. It looked like meat, dark and some on the bone, some pulled, with a rice side in the shape of an igloo. Edible enough, he decided and tore in.

Glasses were being refilled and Keller held his up for attention. 'S'good. I don't think I had this one.' He flashed a smile across at Makayla.

Ricky said, 'It's Gevrey Chambertin.'

'I thought so.' Keller kept on grinning. 'I can't quite place the year though.'

They liked that. There was a tinkling of laughter for that and Keller let his grimace slacken off, as he gobbled up another quart of the delicious red Burgundy, imported from France. Then he let a sweet and frank smile settle firmly on his face and looked at Makayla. He couldn't help himself. That was what he was here for, just her. There was suddenly no point in pretending otherwise.

'Hey buddy?' Ricky jerked his chin up at Keller across the table. 'Say buddy?'

Keller came out of his reverie. 'Keller.'

'Yeah Keller. Keller Baye. That football jersey you're wearing. I don't recognise the team. And I know my football. I mean I've been playing since I could walk. You the placekicker, Keller Baye? You kick with the right, or the left?' Ricky looked around his friends and he smiled a crooked smile. 'Try out for the Panthers yet?'

There was complete silence then, not an awkward silence, but an irretrievable soundlessness, sprinkled only with distant conversations from the public restaurant. Keller stood up, unsteady on his new toes, dizzy with the wine.

Makayla's voice was soft but even. 'Ricky, I want you to apologise to Keller. That was totally out of—'

'Ah shut up, Kayla. You made a mistake, asking Keller Baye here. You get to make one mistake. Just one.'

Like a panther, by God, Keller sprang. With the last of his prowess and energy, Keller threw himself right across the fine linen, silver and crystal and got his hands onto Ricky Marjenhoff's beefed up jock chest. It took three of them to get Keller off the host. The damage to Ricky's body was minimal, but the table was wrecked. The Burgundy bled over the white linen and much of the crockery was smashed, as the crippled boy thrashed around with his fists.

THE AUNT

*

Keller had never been what you would call a chatterbox but all the same, Aunt Joya wasn't used to his silence, since the accident with his foot. *Accident* was how she referred to it. She didn't seem to like the silent treatment at all, kept asking him questions. He'd never seen this interest from her. Perhaps she understood there had been a profound change in him and she wanted to see if she could press the reset button.

Joya had noticed it first in the hospital. The boy had looked at her so intensely when she arrived. She couldn't figure it. Bought all those fancy gifts, got herself all dolled up in a nice outfit, for him. When he stared at her, she was reminded of a hound dog they'd had briefly, when she was a child. A dog which had turned and her daddy brought a brick down on its head.

Keller stared at his Aunt until it was clear to her what it was that he had rumbling around inside him. It was hatred. And for the first time in many years, Joya felt truly afraid. She knew one thing for sure: she was never going to lock the door to that boy again.

'Joya?' This was the first time Keller had dropped the *Aunt* from her name. 'I want you go on across to Peg's and invite her to come strip the Chokeberry for her jam.'

'It's winter, Kell. Ain't no berries on that bush. Peg don't want to be—'

'Go. Now. Invite her to come get them berries in the summer.'

Keller watched from the window as Joya went over the street to Peg Bellingham's. She wasn't walking any too quick with that fake limp of hers and he thumped at the glass to shoo her on over. He watched the women's exchange and felt a satisfaction rise up inside him.

Joya's fear of Keller dissipated some over the next weeks but it never left and on the day Keller returned from a trip somewhere, just before Christmas – he wouldn't say where – suddenly here was that same look upon him. Pure hatred. Was it the money she'd taken from the cistern? He didn't seem to mind usually, never made much of a comment. But that sharp, dark look now, she felt the weight of it. He threw it at her, as he mounted the stairs; cast it over her, like a net. She was caught alright and something felt very bad in the pit of her substantial stomach.

*

The next morning when Aunt Joya was coming out of the bathroom, Keller pushed the door back on her. It must have smacked her face, because when he shoved his way in, she was holding one hand over an eye, but there was nothing there, no swelling that he could see. She always did make such a fuss.

'Sit.' He said this softly and in case she was in any doubt where, he pointed at the toilet seat.

Joya hovered over by the toilet and looked over her shoulder through the net of the curtain.

'I'm gonna hold my leg up like this.' Keller lifted his foot so that it rested on the window ledge. 'And you're gonna sit there and take out the stitches. I think it's time you see the consequences of your actions.'

'The nurse is doing that. I know the nurse is doing that. I heard them say.' But she sat down on the toilet.

'Take off the dressing.'

'Kell, you know I'm no good at that kind—'

'You're no good at anything. Take off the dressing.'

'Where's your thing?'

He knew she was talking about the prosthesis.

On the way back from the Outer Banks yesterday, he went straight to the post office on Murrow Boulevard. He bought five dollars of stamps and a padded mail bag. Outside, he sat down on the kerb and removed his temporary prosthesis. It was covered in blood and pus. Passers-by hesitated as they went along the sidewalk. A child of perhaps four managed to say, 'Ewww' before being whisked away by its grown-up. Keller dropped the silicone toes, like horror pan pipes, into the mail bag.

'Like something from a joke shop.' He muttered. 'Fucking joke toes.'

He posted them to Makayla.

*

Now Joya gently unfurled the dressing until the foot was naked. You couldn't even see the original stitching, there was so much gunk covering the wound.

'Any sign of infection? What would you say, Nurse Joya?'

'It looks disgusting. I wouldn't have the first idea how to take out them stitches. Can't even see them. Why don't you just go back up to Kindred and—'

'I'm not seeing any more doctors. You know how much these *things* cost?'

'I'm sorry about the money.'

'What money?' Keller looked at her and pulled his mouth up at one corner, like it was on a thread. 'Forget about it. I don't need my *thing*.' Why was he even talking to her? She deserved zero information, zero insight into his feelings. He had lost some toes. Like her, he walked with a limp. That's who he was. That's who he would be. He was one of the Baye family. Why did he ever think he could cover up his circumstances? Trying just made things worse.

'Kell, I can't do it. I never done anything like it.'

'Sure you have. Bit of needlework. Back when you had some use. Sure you did. Anyhow there ain't nothing to it. I'll talk you through it. I watched a tutorial on YouTube. I know you think the internet is the work of the devil but I find it very helpful. Here.'

He passed Joya a pair of ordinary tweezers. She looked at them with mistrust. 'These mine?'

'Well, they're not mine. And if none of your fellas left 'em behind, I guess they must be yours. Now what you do first, see, is wipe the wound gently with some cotton. Warm water, to loosen any hard bits of blood. Think you can do that?'

'It smells.'

'Well we can stop the smell. By cleaning it. You catching on?'

'I think you better let me up and out of here. Do it yourself. Ain't nothing wrong with your hands.'

'Way I see it, Aunt Joya? You took these toes from me. I've been thinking what to do about that. What the fairest thing would be. Any ideas?'

'I've had enough of your games, Keller Baye. Let me out of here, this minute.' Joya tried to raise herself but there was very little room and his body stood firmly on the spot, his lateral thigh blocking her.

'I don't believe I've ever seen your toes. Come on,' he pushed her back down onto the seat. 'Get 'em out.'

'I will not, what's got into you.'

He could see the change already, in her body language. She had pulled her limbs in just slightly, as an animal would to protect its central organs. He could hear the change too, in her voice, not a tremor quite, not yet, but a higher pitch.

'It will be a thing, won't it, Aunt Joya. You know how people say that. They say, *is that like a thing*? And this'll be ours. A family thing. We never have walked down a street together, have we. Imagine that now. Picture it. You and me. Joya and Keller Baye. Limping.'

There was a scratching at the door.

'Kell, that's Peverill.'

'No shit.'

'Better see what he wants.' The little terrier's paws were frantic to get to Joya.

'Sit, the fuck, back down.'

Keller pulled back the neckline of her blouse and there was the front door key on a string. No need to change the locks. Keller lifted the chain and his Aunt flinched as he took it from her neck and hung it around his own. He would get a spare too, and he knew just where he'd hide it: under that black chokeberry bush that Peg Bellingham was so fond of for her jams.

Peverill barked.

'What is it you always say about the dog? About its passing?'

'I don't remember.'

'Sure you do, Aunt Joya. You always say, *when the dog dies, I die*.'

CHAPTER 11

The Reaper

Once death has a firm hold of you, it is almost impossible to get free. And in any case, Rebecca did not particularly want to be free. She wanted to still be with her grandfather, and that meant sitting alongside death. She spent her time in Ralph's study though she never did any of the things that they had together. Primmy did not instruct Mrs Scattergood to clean the room and over the months the dust became as thick as the gloom. Rebecca listened only to the radio in there until she heard an old story of children in Kosovo being released to run in a field and the soldiers shooting them as their parents watched. She picked up a Sunday supplement and read about a woman who asked a guard if she could finish breast feeding her baby before he raped her. The guard bayoneted the infant and then took its mother. Rebecca made no attempt to shield herself from the world's atrocities. She wanted to hear all of it. She did not know why. She stopped seeing MT in her spare time and stayed in Ralph's study which, with no defined purpose and no-one to care for it, became repellently dishevelled. Things appeared in the study which didn't belong. The others must have been ditching stuff in it whilst she was at school. Rebecca seethed at this unholy invasion. Their wonderful haven, hers and Ralph's, had become a dumping ground. Only a beachcomber would want to enter it now. But it was quiet in there. If you wanted to see how brave you were by burning the fine hairs on your arm, the study was just the place.

She looked at the fireplace which was full of the newspaper knots she and her grandfather used to make for the fire. Ralph taught her to lie the broadsheet out on the diagonal and to roll it reasonably tightly, making a simple knot. From time to time he'd get her to stretch out her arm and he'd thread the knots over her hand till they looked like a row of paper quoits and Rebecca would deliver them to a huge basket in the kitchen, where fire was permitted.

The problem with death for Youngest Brown, was not just the past or even the present. What was preoccupying her currently, was Death's plans for the future. The way she saw it, Death was always hungry. His stomach was always rumbling. Whenever she passed the dining room, she had to wonder if the Reaper was in there, dabbing at the side of his mouth with a crisp linen napkin, ready for its constitutional, ready to walk among them once again.

The only trips Rebecca made now were to the Library at Aird's Crossing. She would have liked to go in disguise, a scarf pulled tight around her head, as Flora MacDonald must have done that night she and Bonnie Prince Charlie set off in their boat over to the Isle of Skye. But Rebecca was too old for dressing up. She could no longer transport herself in that way.

Grandma was with Colette in the kitchen now. They were properly chatting, Rebecca could hear, no doubt seated around the table. Perhaps over a pot of tea. They got along rather well at that time which could never have been predicted a couple of years previously. Rebecca was partially relieved that one pairing in the house did get on, but truthfully, the greater part of her was envious that she no longer had such a pairing.

 Rebecca took the stairs two at a time and went to her room. She had to be called for supper. Grandma hated to call but she certainly wouldn't go chasing up the stairs just to make sure they got fed.

 Rebecca went to bed early and did a very unusual thing: she tidied up. She knew her grandmother would later come in. Primmy was often in a good mood late in the evening, just as she was about to take out her batteries and retire to bed. She sometimes had sleepy, kind words for her grandchildren at that hour. Rebecca wanted her to come in. She wanted her Grandma to sit down beside her and be the lovely one that she could occasionally be. To say words like *insouciant* and *quasi* and *sardonic*. And Primmy did come. She knocked! Rebecca opened the door a little and smiled. Primmy did not notice the tidying, or didn't say so. Compliments did not gush in this part of the British Isles; though they could be forced, but then they weren't worth having. Rebecca swept her hand over the room.

'Look. I've done this.'

'Oh it looks lovely, dear. Well done you.' Primmy hesitated. 'I'm so pleased. I know you miss him. As do I, of course.'

Rebecca could feel a lump swelling in her throat and she bowed her head.

'Well, I'll say goodnight, Becky. There's an envelope with your lunch money on—'

'It's dinner. They all call it dinner.'

'Oh yes, so they do. Well it's on the Mac.' This was the three legged Rene Mackintosh stool by the front door. 'I'm a little late sending the cheque, so do take it straight to the office.'

'Aye aye, cap'n.'

'You've already brushed your teeth?'

'Yup. And gargled.' Rebecca was encouraged to keep infection at bay otherwise she was to get her tonsils and adenoids gouged out. Austen had drawn an illustration for her some years ago. His version did not include anaesthesia. The threat of this operation hung over her constantly like a cartoon rain cloud.

Rebecca would now have liked to ask for a new toothbrush but the conversation had been most agreeable and to prolong it, would have been a danger.

'Goodnight Rebecca dear.'

'Night, skipper.'

*

Rebecca used to pretend that aliens came for her grandparents each night. That they themselves were aliens and went back to the mother ship overnight to eat their real food (they could keep most earthling stuff down but not the chocolates from the box) and recover from planet earth's confusion. They lifted their earthling shirts and the aliens in the lab, popped out a disk from the drive slit in their tummy where a belly button would be for proper earth people, and downloaded the day's experiences. She pretended Austen was complicit in their world and its doings, though not himself an alien.

In the daytime, Rebecca had other fixations. She found ways of not being herself so that if Death were to come for her, it would not find Becky Brown but some other character. Often she became a burglar and would prowl around the house, stealing a holdall full of silver and ornaments. She'd go down to the end of the drive, nipping from tree to tree, and then slither in the back door, returning all the swag to its place.

Her grandmother was to blame, Rebecca was certain of that. She, after all, was supreme teacher of pretence, the one who changed her voice and just wished herself into a new person. If Primmy was on the telephone to a tradesperson, as she called them, she'd hold the apparatus some inches from her ear, as if the low grade of the task was better suited to staff, though she only had Mrs Scattergood and Murdo. She'd say stuff like, 'Well now I don't think that's going to entirely syoot. Relly it won't.' And Rebecca would wonder at this chosen persona and compare it with the real one, who chucked up her pralines of a Sunday evening and slurped loudly at her Hennessy Cognac with Rescue Remedy drops and said when the potion was fully consumed, 'I am such a believer in the Bach Remedies, I do wish the rest of you would try them.' Ralph had disapproved. He'd been a passionate anti-homeopathist but he had simply shaken his head, imperceptibly to all but Rebecca and he'd let his wife witter on to the end of his days.

'Who are you?' Becky would say to herself in the mirror, her head turned slightly to the right. 'But who are you?'

And then she would turn her head to the left. 'I don't know, who do you want me to be?'

And back again. 'It's not who I want you to be. It's who *you* want to be.'

*

Colette and Rebecca encouraged Grandma to find some hobbies for her days. Colette because she was becoming a sensitive and caring teenager, Rebecca because she wanted more freedom and more peace for herself in the house, a trait she was delighted to recognise descended to her from her grandfather.

Primmy Brown did make an effort to find, if not meaning, then interest for her widowhood. She began to make a concerted effort to live the rest of her life. She became a member of the Maillaig Art Society and made shortbread for a charity stall at the Morar Craft Fair. She even tried to join a choir, but quickly gave up.

'My voice is lower than a contralto apparently. That's what they've told me. They don't have a part for me. A singing part. They said I could set up the Baby Burco, for events.'

'What's that?'

'It's a big drum thing for boiling water up. But I do have a voice. I do. There must be something lower than a contralto because I am that. And I know I can sing. There must be something for me.'

'Hormone therapy?' Colette suggested.

'Chh!' Primmy had taken to saying in response to almost anything. Rebecca missed her old rejoinders. She missed her grandmother's outlandish remarks and retorts, her smattering of *plethora* or *mellifluous* or *soi-disant*. Only Austen understood what those words meant but that didn't matter. It was the sound Rebecca liked, the mood Primmy was in when she said those things.

'Chh!' she'd taken to saying instead and then dashed off to try out a new pursuit, grabbing her precise accessories for the sortie. Whereas Rebecca herself was lucky if she remembered her jacket.

*

Colette's new-found grace might have come as a by-product of love. She seemed to be falling for Mister Someone. That's what Primmy called him and for the first time, the old lady tried relentlessly to get an outsider onto the premises, having denied all entrants for a decade. Naturally, Colette was never going to allow this. And hadn't officially declared a relationship with Mister Anyone, let alone Mister Someone. Yet neither had she denied it. It was December and those silly songs on the radio all pointed to available spots beneath mistletoe. Primmy promised to get some, although whenever this had been suggested in previous years, they were subjected to a lecture on the plant's parasitical nature and toxicity if ingested.

'If a pet ate that monstrous stuff, it would die outright. Out *right*!'

'But we haven't got a pet.'

'Less of your lip, Youngest Brown.'

*

Rebecca was a teenager herself now. Fourteen years old. Maria Theresa had not taken kindly to the brush off which had begun since Ralph's death and had asked her friend repeatedly for an explanation. Rebecca did not have one. She had asked herself the same question. There was a need for aloneness, that was all. She couldn't possibly tell her best friend that, not after all these years. To her loyal credit, MT had not given up and had today written her former pal a note:

Beck, I can't believe you would ever be this cruel. It's been so long. I don't understand you but I accept that we're not best friends anymore. I've sent you a crease-me-arse card. In the post. I know you never write them so I won't be expecting one. I love you a lot. That will never ever change. I've left a present for you with Murdo. It's just a pen in Stewart tartan. I'm around all c-m-a holidays, if you want to see me.

MT x

Rebecca got out the letter and re-read it. She'd even drawn a sprig of holly in the top left hand corner. She loved embellishment, did Maria Theresa. It was she who usually decorated the Brown's Christmas tree, so this year, like when Ralph died, the family probably wouldn't bother. They might not even have a tree, because frankly, an undecorated tree is a lot worse than no tree at all.

Rebecca looked over at the chair where her panda sat. It wasn't there. Her panda, Belle, had gone AWOL.

'What the…' Rebecca got up and looked in her cupboard and under her bed. She went along to Colette's room to see if she could possibly have her but of course the door was locked.

Rebecca felt real loss. How long had Belle been gone? Kidnapped? Had Mrs Scattergood stuck her in the washing machine? Taken her off to the jumble? That toy had always been in her life. Perhaps from birth. Perhaps Belle had been bigger than Rebecca for a year or two. Who would have taken her?

There really was only one likely candidate. There was only one person who could find a reason for such a bizarre appropriation. Primmy. Rebecca waited in her room till she heard the front door bang shut in the early afternoon and her grandmother's footsteps in the hall. Rebecca careered down the staircase, almost in flight, to confront Primmy.

'Belle. Where is she?'

'Who?' Primmy strode past and into the kitchen. Now she was at the sink arranging her apron around her and knotting a perfect bow at her back, above her well-maintained bottom.

'You know who. My toy. Who you will never call by her name.'

Primmy released a fierce jet of water from the tap and squirted some washing up liquid into the sink. 'I needed it. You never play with that thing anymore.' She turned off the tap.

'How do you know what I do with her? She's mine. She's the only thing left.'

'I bought it for you. Some trip or other. A gift. From me.' Primmy snapped her green rubber gloves onto her spindly fingers.

'Oh so she was never really mine? She is the one thing I have from—'

'From what? From your mother? Your parents? *I* bought it.'

'Yes, but from that *time*. From *before*.'

Primmy turned around to face Rebecca with a soap-sudded fork in her hand. She turned back around and threw the fork into the washing up. There was a pathetic splash. She had the back of her hand near her eyes.

Rebecca gasped. 'Oh my God! I know what you've done. The eyes! You've given her eyes to the fox.'

Earlier in the week, a lifestyle magazine had requested a visit to *Taransay* because of its unique collection of arts and crafts furniture. The family had all hated the furniture since they'd moved in, but suddenly Primmy was rubbing it down and staring at it from different angles. The vice-chairman of the William Morris Society was coming along with The Glen Tarr Magazine photographer. There was to be a photograph for the front cover: *of the grand fireplace and the exquisite wallpaper above*, they'd said in their letter. The wallpaper pattern was 'Strawberry Thief', a William Morris first edition. And on that Strawberry Thief was a red fox. It was sprawled, spatch-cocked, above the fireplace, but with no eyes. It couldn't easily be taken down, as it had been pinned there for decades, and it had made its mark. If you were to take the fox off the wall, you could still see its outline on the wallpaper. Primmy had lifted its tail to check.

'Where is my panda now?' Rebecca was quivering with injustice.

'I don't think you want to see it.'

'I didn't ask to see it, *her*. I asked where she is.'

'I'm sorry, Becky. I am sorry.' She turned back to face Rebecca. 'They do actually look quite good on the fox, the eyes. It's not something I would have done lightly. I held it up. Her. I held her up there, over the fireplace. And I knew, I just knew it would be perfect. You can go and see, if you—'

'Are you *serious*? I will never enter that room again. In my life.'

Primmy actually laughed a bit. She bit her lip in an attempt to stop. Rebecca could feel the back of her head trembling against the force of her taut neck muscles.

'I will ask you one more time. Where is my panda?'

Rebecca could see now that her grandmother had probably had a little nip. She had that crackly cheek thing going on. And she was inappropriately amused. All the usual signs.

'You see, Becky, I knew you didn't play with it anymore. And, well, my need was great. They are coming the day after tomorrow, you know. The magazine people.'

'How are you going to make it up to me?'

'I see that I would never be able to do that. So I won't.'

'Send me away to school. Where no-one knows me.

'You know I can't. Why?'

'Austen went.'

'Austen was already… Austen's money was put aside. There isn't—'

'Colette goes to a private school.'

'Yes, but she lives at home.'

'I don't want to live here with… with a killer.'

'There just isn't enough money.' She moved towards her granddaughter a little and she raised her hand to form a cupping gesture.

'Don't touch me. So there's money for Austen. And there's money for Colette. But none for me.'

'You are the youngest. You are spoiled in other ways. You've always loved your school, if not the schooling. The girls and boys, I mean to say. Now you have had a slight falling out with Maria, you have become—'

'It's not a falling out. And her name is Maria Theresa.'

'Look dear, I really am sorry. I felt I had no choice. The fox needed eyes. Simple as.'

'I'll never love you now. You've blown it.'

'Well, I'm very sorry to hear that. I left the box of decorations outside your grandfather's study. Did you see them?' Primmy stood up and raised her rubber arms like a surgeon in contemplation. 'No answer. Right. I'll take that as a no. Look, I must get on. You could get me some eggs and we'll have omelettes.'

'I thought we were having pork chops. You said this morning—'

'Rebecca, enough! Do as I ask. Go out now for the eggs. Get plenty. I'm hoping Colette will do us a sponge or something. Austen'll be here tomorrow.' A sudden happiness came to Primmy's face. Genuine glee, as if Christ himself were coming to supper. 'Go on, shoo, shoo, before it's too dark.'

'It's fucking broad daylight! I hate living here with you. Ralph was the only one I had. He loved me all of the time. Not just when he was in a good mood. Anyway, it makes no difference if it's dark for the eggs. Don't you know *anything*? I use a torch in the dark. Ten years we've been in this godforsaken institution. And you don't know jack shit about my life.'

Rebecca had no intention of searching for her panda. Belle suddenly seemed partly responsible. She didn't like that about herself, blaming the innocent. Maria Theresa had fallen prey to that horrid trait. Poor MT, who'd never been anything but a great friend. Rebecca didn't know why she was isolating herself. She could already imagine the panda coming back to her room. She could see herself switching on her torch and shining it into the bear's empty eye sockets. Primmy wasn't the most adroit of women, most of the panda's head would probably be missing.

Rebecca thundered up to her room. She would not be ordered out to the henhouse. She waited till it was velvety dark outside and the air was bristling with frost before lifting the latch quietly on the back door. She went to visit Hennifer first. She was in a separate coop to the others, a converted dog kennel which Murdo gave them when his bearded collie Tam died. Hennifer had to be isolated when the others started attacking her because of the blistery lesions on her eyes. All the chickens saw badly at night, but poor Hennifer could barely see at all. Rebecca knew she wouldn't have an egg but all the same, Rebecca liked to look in and say hello. Perhaps Hennifer would like gouged out Belle for company, as she had nobody now. No, Rebecca would not beg again to know of the panda's whereabouts.

She collected seventeen eggs from the main chicken shed and felt goose bumps creep over her flesh as their glassy eyes stared at her with their harsh indifference.

CHAPTER 12

The Visitors

Keller had liked going to his friend Lemi's house after school. They did their homework there, in companionable silence. Of course, now that Keller had had a good tête-à-tête with Aunt Joya in the bathroom, proper access to his living accommodation was no longer an issue, but for a long time, Lemi Kowalski's place had been a warm haven.

Lemi's mother had always been polite. She liked to get her hands over her son, smooth him down when he got home from school, like a horse after a race. Keller didn't want anyone to do that for him but he thought about what it would feel like from a mother rather than a girl. Mrs Kowalski always had something to eat and drink ready for her boy and she offered Keller whatever Lemi was having. She was close with her sisters, all first generation immigrants. They spoke Polish to one another but Keller didn't feel excluded, since Lemi didn't understand it either. His mom spoke only English to him. She took that very seriously. And the young boys had smiled at one another whilst the grown-up sisters chattered back and forth. It barely seemed possible that those ladies understood what the hell they were saying to one another. It was foreign and then some.

Keller wondered why the Kowalskis had chosen Greensboro, North Carolina, but he never asked. Sometimes the sisters would bake together. Szarlotka cake and packsi which looked like donuts, but without the hole.

In his bed at night, Keller would think about Lemi's mother and guess at what she might be called and what it would feel like to touch her.

The Kowalskis were what they were supposed to be. Yet something about Lemi's excitement with his family on those baking days made Keller very sad. To begin with, the hubbub and cheer would be infectious and he'd feel good to be there but then it would start to fade, as he realised he was just a bystander. Keller didn't understand the feeling, its darkness, its weight, until he was older and his father was finally executed. Then it became clear. Misery's jaws were clamping down and had every intention of devouring him. Only anger could beat it back.

Mrs Kowalski had tried to smile at Keller, but that smile could never quite hitch up to her eyes. She was scared of Keller Baye and though this would generally have enraged him, at Lemi's house it brought the black sorrow, which bedded in for life the day Makayla left.

She had come round to Keller's house in quite a state, after he'd mailed that package. She'd brought those nasty plastic toes with her, hadn't even cleaned them up, by the looks of them. She was mad as hell, standing out there in the street, not even on the porch, shouting up at him. He had never heard her raise her voice before. How did she know his bedroom was at the front? How did she know that was his window? He'd got rid of his dilapidated Dodge, so how did she know that he was even home? He was home though, and he got such a buzz hiding by the bedroom curtain, watching her. Makayla was screaming up at him, brandishing the toes. Well, she lived far from this neighborhood. She didn't know a soul, what did she care, causing a scene. When she started to cry, however, he felt something contract in his chest. And when she turned to leave, he hobbled down the stairs on his crutches and out of the front door.

'Makayla! Maykayla, wait!'

She stopped in her tracks but did not turn to him. He could see the sobs bumping through her shoulders and he called out, 'Please, come inside. Let's not do this out in the street. Let's not make a scene.'

Peg Bellingham opened her front door and shouted, 'Bit late for that!' and slammed it shut again.

Keller negotiated the porch steps, then turned around to face Makayla. The white around her grey eyes was now tinged red from her tears. He felt excited that he had affected her so much. He reached for her hand and stroked it, then held on to her fingertips. 'Let me at least make you a cup of coffee.'

Makayla did not respond to his touch but neither did she withdraw her hand. This was really so easy, Keller thought, without a crowd around. When he was just with a girl alone, that's when he was at his best. 'Come on.'

'Your ghastly Aunt home?'

'Now what do you know about my Aunt?'

'Everyone knows about your Aunt, Keller. They say she let you freeze out there.' Her tears were drying up and being replaced with a calmer curiosity.

'You're not here for some kind of bet?'

'Excuse me?'

'Look. I'm sorry about the package. And I'm sorry about the party. I thought maybe—'

'It wasn't a party. It was just a lunch. You didn't have to be such—'

'You coming in. She's not here. Visiting a relative. I don't know how long she'll be gone. Maybe for good.' It was so easy to lie.

'You don't know? It's Christmas eve.'

Keller shrugged. What would she do if she knew Joya was tied up in her bedroom and gagged? Run a fucking country mile, screaming. 'We're not real close. Monday I think it was she left, just after our… lunch.' Keller looked down Vandalia Road. The weather was unseasonably mild. You could barely tell it was Christmas. He could imagine the fir trees on the avenues of her neighborhood, lights helixed around them and carollers with good coats and lanterns. Only Peg had made an effort here, with an enormous blow up snowman. Peg was nowhere to be seen now. She'd said her bit.

Keller's anxiety was suddenly gone. His tension left his neck and his nerves seemed to drop right out of his sleeves. He felt free. He felt like a force.

'Hey, look at you now.' He smiled at Makayla. Little Miss Fisher Park. What was it about her? He smiled again and this time she took his hand. Then he understood. Underneath all that nurtured upbringing, that *of-course-I-have* confidence, Makayla's appeal for him was her vulnerability. It gave him strength.

Inside the house, Keller locked the door behind them. 'You don't mind, do you? It's a habit I've gotten into.' Nobody but him had the right to enter now. If anyone wanted to see him, well they would have to knock.

Once she'd had a good look around, Makayla seemed pleasantly surprised.

'Not as nasty as you were expecting, huh.'

'I really like those blinds. Where did you get them?' She pointed at the windows.

'Junkyard. Plantation shutters. I painted them white. Well, you can see that.'

'That why you're going up to the Hickory Recycling Center?'

'How do you mean?'

'You like making new things from old.'

'Oh yeah. *Reuse, recycle, reduce.* That's the motto at the Plant.' Keller stood at the foot of the staircase. 'Wanna see my room? I got a fridge and a bar. If it's a little too early in the day, there's coffee. I have an Aeropress.'

'I don't know what that is.'

'I'll show you.' Even on crutches, Keller was able to swing a little nonchalance into those long limbs of his. He was proud of the oak stair treads. He'd sanded and stained them. He could tell she noticed such things. Just because he'd been living with a pig, didn't mean he had to grunt.

She must have come up very slowly behind him because he didn't hear her footsteps. He hoped she was taking her time to get her fill of all his handiwork. He didn't even think of Joya, as Makayla passed by his Aunt's bedroom door. Then the girl of his dreams was standing in the doorway. Keller smiled and flipped through his iPod, looking for the right playlist.

'Hey, know what? You choose.' He gave the device to her and filled the coffee maker with dark roast beans.

He'd set different lights in different nooks. Lots of glass and brushed chrome against shades of grey and beige. A man's room. His bed was large and neatly made. The linen was white. He could tell Makayla was impressed with the space he'd created. The landlord had had to sanction the refurbishment and without offering a dime towards it, stood there in his pissy old clothes saying, 'I guess that'll be alright.' Keller's fists had tightened but he'd nodded and thanked him; showed the property owner to his own door and wanted to kick him down the porch steps.

'You like nice things.' Makayla put down the iPod. 'Books too. I knew you liked to read. Your grades are always so good in literature. Who's your favourite? I mean author.'

'I'd have to say Dostoevsky.'

'Oh.'

'You don't like him?'

'I don't know him. What's he write?'

'Um, I guess his most famous oeuvre would be *Crime and Punishment*.'

'Oeuvre, hmm. You're quite the mystery man, Keller Baye.'

It was a dream. He could have tried for years to lure her into his room, which was as near to a penthouse as he could get it. And now here she was, turned up without so much as an invitation, happy enough by the look of things, and ready for the advance.

'Why did you say at, well, at the lunch that you won't go on with your studies?'

'I want to work. I like working. Nothing else makes much sense. Books are not work. Books are for hot days. Or cold ones in front of a fire. I'll have a big old fire soon. One day soon. And books are for bed. I could read you something if you like.' Keller took her hand and this time he felt the return. Makayla laced her fingers through his.

'Something you wrote?'

He could feel her breath at his neck. 'No. I wouldn't write down my thoughts.' He lifted her chin gently.

'I've never done this, Kell. I never have.'

Oh God that felt so sweet. Marjenhoff hadn't got there first. Jesus, she must be the only virgin in twelfth grade, with the possible exception of Tara Borland who was virtually dead she was off sick so often.

'I know. I know you haven't, sweetheart. And we don't have to. Just coffee, if you like.'

'You have a bit of a reputation, Kell. The girls used to say they'd been hiding.'

'Hiding?'

'The girls you used to take to the bird hide. They called it *hiding*. The stuff that, well, what took place.'

'I didn't take them there. We went together. You make it sound sordid. As if they were unwilling. As if they were—'

'Oh no I didn't mean to make it sound sordid. They… enjoyed it very much.'

Makayla's mouth reached up to his and he slipped his arms around her back. She tasted so fresh. She had brushed her teeth before setting off. He waited for her tongue to search for his and directed her very slightly towards the bed. They sat down and he could feel his erection eager at his flies. He intended to do everything Christie had taught him. Every single thing. He hadn't been to *Hailey's Whorehouse* in a good while or seen any girl. It would be hard to wait.

'You're so beautiful, Makayla.'

'Am I?' She pushed her face back from him. 'You really think so?'

'God, yes. Of course I do. I've never wanted anything, anyone, like I want you right now. But we must take things slow.'

'We must?' She grinned suddenly and threw her head back.

He didn't want her to do that. Virgin, my ass. 'Shall I undress you?'

'Yes. No-one has ever called me *sweetheart*. Well, except my mom.'

The rise and fall of Makayla's chest was a delight, as he unfastened the buttons of her blouse and pushed it back off her shoulders. Her bra fastened at the front. He released the clip and gently pulled the two cups to the sides. The straps fell from her shoulders.

'My God, you're stunning.'

Oh she liked that. She squirmed and took his head in her hands as he reached for her nipple with his tongue. Makayla lay back on the bed and Keller decided that neither of them could wait for the sort of protracted tantric lovemaking that he'd fantasised about with her. They could get to that later. Right now, they had to come. He slipped the palm of his hand up inside her skirt and pulled gently at her pantyhose. She helped him and they came off easily. He didn't throw them aside. He didn't grab or grapple. She had to feel that he was steady and sure. And he most certainly was sure. Now he slid his hand over her thighs. She parted them slightly and he stroked the inner silk of them, till her breathing became ragged. His fingertips rested lightly between her legs. She had shaved, this virgin. He kept his hand still, then pressed very slightly. She moaned softly and he hoped he was finally driving her crazy, just as she had driven him crazy for years.

'Please. Kell, please.'

'Are you ready?'

'Yes. Yes, can't you tell.'

He took as much of her breast into his mouth as he could, letting his teeth graze and bite. He dipped his fingertips into the wet well of her and slid them back and forth. Again, he stopped moving, just pressed very slightly. If she didn't keep her breathing down, she was going to hyperventilate. He'd had that happen once in the bird hide. Damn, he was good. Keller smiled, his top lip trailing across the skin of her belly as he went in for the kill. Makayla gasped as he pushed her legs wide apart and took her into his mouth. In seconds, her orgasm burst at him, and she cried out. The engorged folds of her seemed to reverberate against his face. He could have laughed with joy. He'd never had such an effect on a girl. He wanted more and more. He had only just begun.

He hoped that in her bedroom, his Aunt had heard the girl from Fisher Park coming.

Suddenly, Makayla sat bolt upright. 'What the fuck is that?'

There was a rattling downstairs. Keller knew that rattling sound well since usually he was making it. It was the front door handle.

*

Keller's friendship with Lemi Kowalski spanned several years. Lemi was a remarkably bright student and therefore unpopular. Keller wasn't choosy though. Lemi was applying for Ivy League schools and Keller was hoping to be accepted at the Hickory Recycling Plant. Soon, the boys' paths would veer in different directions. Keller knew that, even if Lemi didn't. They'd been good for each other, good enough. But Keller wasn't going to miss Lemi. Just as he had not missed Angelo, who was already out of Weaver High and working at a car parts store on Landover Road. Doing great, Keller heard.

Towards the end of last summer's term, Lemi and Keller were about to hop on the school bus to go home, when a man reached out a great paw of a hand to separate the boys. He was very tall but what was more impressive, he had a huge torso and a thick neck. The man was bald and suiting it. His muscles strained at his suit jacket and shirt collar.

'You're Keller Baye, aren't you?'

Lemi looked terrified but Keller was only curious. He had gotten very tall himself and he wasn't yet eighteen years old, but he had to look upwards to this man. Keller scrutinised the giant stranger. 'Who wants to know?'

The man laughed and casually saluted the school bus driver.

'My name is Billy Ray Master. You can call me Master. Everyone does.'

Lemi was not impressed. 'C'mon Keller. Get on or get out. You're holding up the line.'

Master smiled at Keller. 'That bother you, Keller Baye? Holding up the line?'

Keller stepped away from Lemi and out of the line. 'What do you want, mister? Mister Master.' Keller grinned and held his hand up on his brow to shield the sun. 'You a boxer?'

'We'll see you later, son.' Master said to Lemi, who was hesitating on the bus steps. The other kids started jostling him and complaining.

Master put his arm lightly across Keller's shoulders and addressed Lemi. 'It's alright, I'm a family friend.' And they turned to walk to Master's car.

Lemi shouted over to them, 'I'll be discussing this with my mother. And my father, when he gets in.' Lemi started questioning the driver, who just threw up harassed hands. Kowalski pushed his way down the aisle and threw his bag on a seat. He fumbled with the window catch and shouted through it. 'I'll see you tomorrow, Kell. Yeah?'

Master opened the door to a black Lincoln and Keller climbed in. He felt no trepidation, only intrigue. He had a sudden feeling that this was supposed to happen, that this was scheduled. He thought maybe his life was about to start, before he even got to Hickory. Master got into the back seat on the far side. Another man was driving. He was older, of regular proportions and he also wore a suit. The Lincoln set off.

'Where you wanna go, Keller?'

Keller was just about say that he didn't know when he changed his mind. 'For a drink?'

'Sure. I was just thinking the same thing.' Master looked to the rear view mirror and the driver nodded.

Keller had hopes that they would be going to some kind of club, owned by the big man. Some place underground, with girls and glitterballs and cocktail shakers but they pulled up at a *Shady Glen* and went upstairs where it was quiet, just a teenage couple in some kind of negotiation: he pleading and she reluctant. The chauffeur did not accompany Master and the boy.

'Order whatever you like, Keller.'

'What're you having?'

'Me? Oh I'm not much one for soda fountains. You choose. No wait, I'll get a shake. I have to watch my monoglycerides but I could use the calcium. How you think I grew these.' Master bared his teeth at the boy and the waitress came flugging up the stairs with her pad. 'You can order from the touchscreen, you know. Never mind, I'm here now.'

Keller wanted to say that he was not much of a one for soda fountains either but that might have been rude, now that they were here. Also, it was a lie.

Keller ordered a maple walnut sundae and Master asked for a strawberry milkshake. He waited for the waitress to go downstairs.

'You're not frightened of me, Keller.'

'No, sir.'

'I meant what I said. I'm a family friend.'

'You know Aunt Joya?'

'I know *of* Aunt Joya. I am a good friend of your father's.'

Keller stiffened. 'My father is in prison. He killed a man.'

'Well now I know that. It was an accident.'

'The jury didn't think so. First they were going to give him life. Ha! That's a funny way of putting it, isn't it. And then they changed their minds. They moved him to the other place. To death row. I don't think he's ever coming out. And he won't let me visit.'

'I am here to tell you that he will allow you to visit.'

'He will?' Keller felt the tears spring to his eyes, like dirty little traitors.

'You know what all happened that day? You know much about it?'

'No, sir. And I don't want to know. I know my father he killed a man. He killed an ex judge. That's all I need to know.'

'Yes, he killed a man. Many men and women were killed on that day. But your father never intended that to happen. No-one did.'

'But he did intend to rob the bank. Well, not him, but he was the getaway guy.'

The waitress clomped up with the shake and sundae. 'If you use the touchscreen, order comes straight up the chute thing automatic, right over there.' She pointed to a little plastic door in the wall. 'Well, next time.'

Keller didn't like impertinent waiting staff. 'You shouldn't be so keen on that chute thing. It's taking your job.'

'It's welcome to it. *Sir.*'

Keller picked up his long spoon and waited for the girl to leave them alone.

Master took a sip of his strawberry milkshake. 'Wow. You forget how good these are, huh. You angry that your daddy was a bank robber?'

'He was the getaway man for a bank robbery. I don't see it as exactly the same thing. He never had a gun before the one they gave him.'

Master doubted that was true but he let it pass. 'You talk to your… your little buddy about this?'

'Who, Lemi? No, sir. I do not. I don't talk to nobody about this. And nobody asks me neither. But they, well, everyone kind of…'

'Everyone knows. They don't say nothing. But they know. You feel he let you down, your old man?'

'He did. He let me down. He put me with her. Aunt Joya. If there's one person who really does need shootin', it's her. But I don't blame him for the robbery. Not really, not in the final analysis.'

Master raised an eyebrow. 'The final analysis. Ok.'

'He owed money. Couldn't find a way out, I guess. Shitty life. He must've had a shitty life 'cause there was never anything to smile about. I can't even imagine my father's face in a smile.' Keller made a false grin. 'He took a chance. He threw the dice, Mister Master. And he lost.'

'You ever steal?'

'Not me, sir, no. I would never do that.'

'Not even from Sanjay's store?'

Keller pressed his lips together and that little pulse thing in his cheek started up.

'I'm going to give you something Keller and I want you to keep it safe.'

'I don't need your money. Your bank money.'

'Nobody got bank money but the bank. It wasn't dollar bills they were after, well was it?'

'I don't know.'

'What do you mean you don't know. Ain't a man or child in the County don't know.'

'Jewels it was. Some fancy diamonds and whatnot. Won't be much use to a dead man. Were you there?'

'At the heist? No. A close relation.'

'Oh, a *close relation*. How illuminating.'

'Hey. You know your words, Keller Baye. You know anyone can go off the rails a little. It's a circumstantial thing.'

'What is?'

'I think you know. Being poor. Being hungry.'

'Yeah, circumstances. I do not accept mine.'

Master laughed and shook his head. 'You a breath of fresh air, Keller.' The big man clinked his glass on Keller's. 'You know, Sanjay is a personal friend of mine.' He nudged Keller's elbow on the table. 'You sure like them peaches, huh?'

Keller pushed the sundae away and sat back on the high leather backed bench. He crossed his arms. 'Well, look at you with your close relations and your personal friends.'

Master smiled. He radiated calm and confidence. Where he got those, Keller couldn't guess.

'Like I said, Keller, I have something for you.'

'I ain't taking your money. I got three paper routes and lawns to cut. Saturdays I wait tables up at Starmount Forest.'

'You're a worker. I heard that. I did not intend offense. This was by means of compensation. For your hardship. I discussed this with your father. He wasn't able to give you what he'd hoped for.' Master was solemn now, which didn't suit him nearly so well.

Keller picked up the spoon and dug deep into his ice cream. 'You said he'd let me go see him?'

'Yes. Your father swore an oath when he was hired. And he kept it. It is my belief that he will continue to do that. Your father made a sacrifice. For you.' Master reached into his pocket and brought out a tiny velvet pochette. He put it in the saucer next to the sundae glass. Master slid out of the seat and straightened his tie. 'I think you will also be a man of honor. Am I right?'

*

Billy Ray Master gave Keller a calling card. Just some digits scribbled on a white background. A cell number. Keller kept it in the lining under his bed. Joya had found this hiding place too. She had emptied that particular nest of dollar bills he'd accumulated from casual work. He didn't stash money there any longer and the little white card was pushed way into the middle of the bed lining, as was the purple velvet pochette. The little bag was secured in a mousetrap, but that was just for Keller's own amusement, a pleasing image. His Aunt would never find anything past arm's length. Joya had a mind for a location, but she was lazy when she got there.

*

It was many years later, when Keller decided to cross the Atlantic, that he looked out that calling card. It wasn't hidden in the bed lining anymore, since by then, Aunt Joya was no longer in the picture. And Keller was living in a brand new apartment up in Fisher Park. Mortgage payments were high but he got plenty of overtime and he didn't go wasting it in bars.

Keller dialled the number and cleared his throat. It was an answering machine. The voice was indistinct. Perhaps a service.

'Uh, Master? That you? This is Keller Baye. I wonder if I might ask a favor of you, sir. I'll be at the *Shady Glen* next Friday 4.30 pm. No, let's say Thursday, the Friday gets busy. Uh, ok then.'

Master was outside in that same Lincoln when Keller arrived. Same driver too. Billy Ray got out of the vehicle, lithe enough still, for a colossus. They shook hands briefly and went upstairs. This time Billy Ray ordered for them on the touchscreen and it came up the chute in moments it seemed. The *Shady Glen* hadn't changed all that much. A brighter color of paint perhaps. Maybe a new floor.

The big man had kept in shape. Still with that smooth head and no appreciable signs of ageing. Some guys were lucky that way and Billy Ray Master was one of them. He carried the tray over to an empty table. As before, there was just one other occupied, this time by a well turned out elderly couple who dressed like New Yorkers.

Master set down the tray. 'Walnut maple sundae. And a strawberry shake. For old time's sake.'

Keller didn't eat that kind of thing any more. He must have been twenty pounds lighter now, but the big man didn't comment.

'Keller, I heard they set a date.'

'June 23rd.'

Master nodded. 'This must be a very difficult time for you.'

'Ain't no picnic for my dad, neither. I'm thinking I should go. I should attend the execution.'

'I think that will be a comfort to him.' Master nodded again, real solemn.

Keller didn't appreciate the tone. Guy behaving like some sort of pastor.

'Did you visit with your father again?'

'No. Just that once. He won't see me. I've tried. Anyways, we didn't get along real well when I did go. I don't think it helped him at all.'

Master put his giant hand around the ice cold shake but he didn't lift it. 'You said on the message I could do you a favor.'

Oh, ok, that's the pleasantries taken care of. 'Yeah. I'm planning a trip. Well, I been planning it for a long time but I wanted to wait, you know, till…'

'Yes, I understand. A trip is a good idea. How can I help?'

Well, he would get to that in all good time. Keller didn't like to be rushed. A lot had happened since they had last met and Keller was no longer weighed down with awe for this suited and booted hulk. Keller Baye would have preferred a little return respect.

'I need a passport, Billy Ray. Is the long and the short of it.'

'You can't get a passport?'

'I need it under a new name.'

'You want to go overseas under an assumed name? Keller no-one does that now. You ever been out of the country? They have all kinds of new technology. They scan your eyes. There, at the airport. Iris recognition. You can't just jump on the dark web, get some dead guy's passport. Some blond dead guy. No.'

The anger was prickling across Keller's shoulders and he rubbed his giveaway cheekbone.

Master leaned forward. 'I mean, I'm not going to ask you what you're up to. I'm not gonna go there, but a false passport these days is a very big deal indeed.'

'Isn't what my father is dying for, a very big deal indeed?'

'I hope this isn't in connection with that.'

Keller did not answer.

'Keller, my mother was Lillius Queen.'

'You think I didn't figure that out. Years ago. I heard she was sick now. Is she dead?'

'No. Not yet.'

'Old Lillius Queen. They have a waxwork of her in the museum in Winston Salem.'

'I know they do.'

'You could get that taken down, I reckon. No way that's legal. She was never convicted.'

Master was staring hard at Keller but he had no wish to continue down this avenue.

'What? Something wrong with my irises?'

'You're different, Keller Baye. I wouldn't know you.'

'You never knew me. You, however, ain't changed a bit. Billy Ray Master.'

'My mother has coronary heart disease. She can't even breathe for herself anymore. In a matter of just weeks, she'll be—'

'So why the fuck is my father about to die for her?' Keller knocked over his sundae and it spattered across Master's black jacket.

Master pulled out an immaculate white handkerchief from his inside pocket and calmly wiped up the worst of it.

The New Yorkers tidied up their tray and hurried on down the stairs.

'Keller, look, I can get you a license. That any good? A fake driver's license?'

Keller just stared at Master's toffee brown eyes. 'Well now, our heist was a fucking sorry tale, wasn't it.'

'Catastrophic.' Master looked sincere. 'Pity of it is,' he threw his soiled handkerchief on the table, 'My mother could've just slept with the fella. Al Mutairi. Or married him, even. She said he was all over her.' Master's chest heaved like a toro in the bullring. 'Or she could have got the codes for the safe deposit boxes. Left the country while that Arab was back in Qatar or Kuwait or wherever. So simple. Isn't that what they say? Keep it simple.'

Was that spittle glistening on Billy Ray's lip there? That really was not nice. Master had lost his cool and Master had lost forever, the admiration of that high school kid he'd plucked out of the bus line all those years ago.

Keller sat back and regarded the hero sized man opposite. He shook his head, real sombre. 'Instead everyone got a death sentence. Now your mom's about to get what's coming to her. And my old man's taking all her blame, in one injection.' Keller mimed a syringe pushing its way into his wrist artery. Then he scooted along the bench and got up. 'You can post me the license. You have my address in Fisher Park?'

'I have it.'

'Shouldn't talk about your mama like she's a whore, my advice. Her on her death bed and all.'

Master got to his feet. He drew himself up to his full height, his chest almost touching Keller's. 'I could kill you with one punch.' He raised his fist and held it inches from Keller's temple. 'Look at you, cheek twitching away. It's all over Keller Baye. Finished. Othaniel. Lillius. She can no longer try to avenge your father's sentence. Do you understand me?'

'I understand that she pretended to try, so's he'd keep his promise.'

'That's a lie. My mother tried so hard. For years she tried. Spent a fortune looking for them Seawhites.'

'You gotta be kidding me. Spent a fortune, my split ass. Well, she had a fortune to spend, didn't she, Miss Lillius Queen. And what did my dad get? Fucking death penalty.'

'She did everything she could to find those people. She's too sick to carry on. We don't know if they're even alive.'

'Why wouldn't they be alive? They're like fifty.'

'I mean that our information could be wrong. Maybe they did die in that crash.'

'Your guy told you categorically it was a set up.'

'Yeah but he was angry. FBI kicked him out, after twenty something years. He'd have done just about anything to make a stink. Jesus, Keller, don't you ever get tired?'

'No.'

'Well, I am. My mother is. That's the last of this chase now. It's over. You hear me? Don't fuck with me, Baye. Only one outcome if you do.'

'I ain't scared of you, Billy Ray. Never have been. Never will be.'

'You got your jewel. You got the biggest prize of all. The rainbow. It'll keep you your whole life. You, your kids, grandkids. And if you're smart—'

'Oh I'm smart, alright. Yeah, I got me a jewel and how many did you get? How you and old Lillius been living all this time while Othaniel's on death row?'

'Fuck, Keller, that's the stupidest part. She couldn't spend it. Felt they were breathing down her neck every minute of the day. Just watching, waiting for her to buy some real estate in Malibu or to take some—'

'Aw you're breaking my heart here, Master. You never got your beach house or your private jet, 'cause the Feds were tailing you. You think I believe that? You're the one with the hard luck story? *Really*? What were y'all eating? Canned tuna? *Native Forest* peaches? I was holed up with the fuckin' chicken lady.'

'Othaniel is dying so that you can keep your rainbow opal.'

'And if he does, then you can keep all the rest of the treasure. That is the plain truth. You miserable son of a bitch.' Keller's cheek was twitching like a bug in a blue grill. 'Should be Lillius Queen they're buckling down for the kill. Fuck me, she's dying anyways. Couldn't she just finally take one for the team?'

Master's whole body was shaking with rage but his eyes were shining with tears.

'Aw hey now, Billy Ray. You're gonna miss your mama. I get that. I do.'

The big man's voice shook. 'I am warning you. No more bloodshed. I will stop you. We've lost everything. It's enough, Baye. Enough. That's the last of it.'

'You're repeating yourself, Billy Ray. Get home to mama now. And don't forget my license.'

A boy who looked about fifteen had climbed the stairs to investigate the shouting, eyes wide with fear. His badge declared him to be:

Daniel

Assistant Manager

How can I help?

'Gentlemen, I'm going to have to ask you to calm down.'

Billy Ray Master cradled his punching fist in his other hand. Suddenly he about-turned and headed for the stairs.

Keller yelled after him. 'Don't you fucking tell me that's the last of it! Who in God's name you think you're talking to?'

Daniel cleared his throat. 'It might be an idea for you to leave too now, sir. Please?'

Keller re-took his seat and looked at Master's untouched strawberry milkshake. He drew back his arm and smashed the shake glass across the wall. As the pink milk dribbled down the tongue in groove washed pine, Keller turned to Daniel.

'You got yourself a decent pair of irises there, Daniel.'

'Sir, I believe one of the customers called the police department.'

Keller started to laugh. 'Police department, is it? I am quaking in my boots.' Keller got up once more and studied the Assistant Manager. 'And now if you'll excuse me, duty calls.'

CHAPTER 13

The Brother

When Rebecca came back in from collecting the eggs, Austen was sitting at the kitchen table. She kicked the door shut behind her. 'Oh! Hello. Weren't you…'

'Due tomorrow. Yes.'

'Ok. Good journey?'

'Hectic. You know the whole way here, everything was shrieking Christmas. Party hats on the train. *Bailey's* in plastic cups. Fucking awful music. Then I get to *Taransay* and…' Austen looks around in mock wonderment. 'Nothing.'

'I know. Nobody could really get behind Christmas this year. I mean not that we ever do, but this year—'

'We've plumbed new depths of humbug.'

'The box of decorations is in the hall. Outside Ralph's study.'

'Yes, I had a strong sense that's what the box was. The word 'Xmas' written on its side was a fair indicator.

'How's uni?'

'*Yooni?* We don't call it yooni at Cambridge.'

'What do you call it?'

'We call it Cambridge.'

'How's Cambridge?'

'Excellent.'

'Right.'

Austen held up a note in their grandmother's writing. 'Primmy's gone to Fort William. Tractor's conked out and she's driving Murdo over to some spare parts place for a magnet and trembler coil, whatever they may be. Where's Colette? I've shouted through the house and no-one stirred.'

'She's, um, she's staying with a friend. Primmy hoped she'd be back. She might come in the morning. She knows Prim wants her to bake something. For you. Did Grandma take the snow chains?'

'How would I know. Yeah I heard about Colette's friend. Do you think they've had the talk. Her and Primmy.'

'The talk?'

'About *it*.'

'You mean babies.'

'Well, not babies. But sex. How to avoid babies.'

'As you say, how would I know.'

'Don't they worry about you here alone? At night?'

'On the whole, no.'

'I wonder if Colette takes a nightie. I can't imagine her with a guy. Can you?'

'I haven't tried.'

'Does she take a bag? With clean underwear? Maybe she's not really thinking clean underwear thoughts.'

'Fucksake, Austen.'

'Grandma's full of it on the phone. She thinks he must be an out of towner. Someone with a holiday home perhaps. A foreigner, d'you reckon? Maybe just a Sassenach, a bone fide English person, with a home counties accent and decent credentials.'

'What's with the penguin suit? Have you been wearing that on the train? Taking your life in your hands.'

'Oh I know how to handle myself. It wasn't all Queensbury rules and fencing at school, you know. I can kick someone in the knackers just as hard as the next posh boy.'

Austen got up and walked into the middle of the kitchen. He turned from Rebecca and kicked his leg out high behind him, at an imaginary opponent.

'Yikes. What's that, Karate?'

'More Taekwondo. My own inimitable version.'

He opened the fridge door. 'Hey, who leaves an empty packet of bacon?' He threw it in Rebecca's direction but she ducked and put her bowl of eggs on the table. 'What are your plans, Youngest Brown? Don't tell me. You have none.'

'Immediate plans? I was wondering how much Campari I could drink without Primmy noticing the level.'

'Ah. Come with me.'

Austen, normally so immaculate, was a mess. Rebecca didn't think she'd ever seen even the hint of a beard on her brother's face before. He was walking funny too, like he was suffering from exhaustion, like he'd walked all the way from Cambridge. He was in a right state. She followed him though.

Austen opened the drawing room door and left it ajar so that some of the heat from the hallway could come in. He went over to the antique radiator. 'This thing doesn't even have a...' He looked for something to make it turn on. 'Several hundred years old. Pretty. But fucked.'

'You think it's pretty. I don't. I don't like any of it.' She looked around the austere drawing room and wondered if there had ever been a jolly gathering within its walls. But it wasn't strictly true, that she didn't like anything in the house. She loved her Victorian bedframe, but didn't want to mention that.

'This is worth a fortune.' Austen opened the art deco drinks cabinet. 'Walnut, with inlaid macassar ebony.' He sniffed at the doors and grinned at Rebecca over his shoulder. 'This is a Cloud design. Primmy's had it all valued. I reckon she's not planning to leave us anything. Each time I come, God I nearly said *home*, she's sold off something else.'

'Perhaps she will sell the whole thing. *Taransay*. And we can all go and live normal lives somewhere else. Separately.' Rebecca watched Austen closely. 'Maybe there was something in a will. From our parents. Stipulating, I don't know, that we be brought up collectively. Here. Except there must have been some sort of codicil for you.'

'Aren't you a little young for codicils?'

'And then... perhaps they put down that when we are twenty-one. Or eighteen. Yes, let's say eighteen, we are all to be set free. From one another.'

'Oh baby, you mean you won't keep in touch?' Austen pinged his fingernail against a crystal glass to make it sing. 'Interesting hypothesis though. But I'm twenty one. Do I look like a free man to you? Hmm? I think what's happening is that the money is running out.'

'At least you got your education.'

'Oh, bitter are we? Is it just all too unfair? You always were a socialist, Becky. You'd never have managed at a fee paying. You're a wee Bolshevik.'

'Something no-one will ever accuse you of being.'

'Oh, let's have these.' Austen took two glasses from the cabinet. They had etched thistles on them and fine green stems. 'Wait a minute, there's a pair of earrings in here.' Austen dipped his nose down to the glass. 'Sitting in, if I'm not mistaken, gin.'

'Those are Prim's diamond studs. She soaks them in gin. It cleans them.'

'Good lord. Grandmother's ear detritus, dropping into this exquisite crystal.' He looked with suspicion at the other glasses. 'I'm inclined to drink straight from the bottle, rather than risk contamination. Here's the Campari. What say we make Americanos.'

'You sound like Bertie Wooster. I can't believe I'm related to you.'

Austen shot her a glance. 'Read a lot of P G Wodehouse do you?'

'You sound like a twat.' Rebecca took the bottle from him and poured a full glass of Campari.

'You're not drinking that without ice.' Austen looked at himself in the fanning deco mirror panes at the back of the cabinet.

'So why the fuck *are* you wearing a tuxedo? I like your silk scarf. And that tartan thing.'

'That tartan thing is a cummerbund. You have a lot to learn.'

'They don't teach us about cummerbunds at my school.'

'No, just codicils.'

'You know what we need to accompany this? *Baxter's* baby beets.'

'We so don't. Olives perhaps.' Austen threw his dinner jacket over the Biedermeyer chaise but he still had the creamy silk scarf with the black tassels around his neck. He was standing at the cabinet, softly singing some half-worded song, pouring himself whisky.

'I've just remembered what your suit smells like.' Rebecca drank off a third of the Campari in her glass. 'Oh that is disgusting.'

'What does my suit smell like?' Austen let the amber whisky tip from side to side, hypnotically.

'Wet pavement. Austen, you're wearing wet pavement.'

'Come on now, let me pour you a proper drink. What'll you have, Youngest? Gin? Vodka? Alright then, what about a little sherry.' He held up a green bottle. '*Tio Pepe* for the lil lady?' He smiled at Rebecca. 'Cheer up! Brother Austen has returned for the Yule feasting.' He cocked his head to one side. 'You look good. Hair's even darker. Have you dyed it?'

'No.'

He poured her sherry and as she reached for it, he jerked his head at the Biedermeyer. 'Go on. Sit. Sit. Fucksake, Becky. Sit. Talk. Haven't seen you for friggin' yonks. What's the matter? Eh? Where's my Wee Lassie MacGraw?'

'Nothing's the matter.' She took the drink and sat down primly on the edge of the chaise.

'Well, there is. You're not still mourning old Ralph, are you?'

'What happened to your face? It's growing.'

He rubbed the stubble on his face. 'How old are you now?'

'Old enough.'

'I suppose you are seven years younger than me. You used to be. That used to be clearer, actually.' He drank off the whisky and his eyelids drooped for a moment. 'You were so young when we came here. You don't know anything do you.' He put down his glass and lifted his hands in front of him, as he often did when he was about to give his family the benefit of his unique intellect. This time though his hands were making some kind of decision, almost as if one of them held a grenade and the other was hovering over the pin. He frowned and his face froze over with some sickening memory. Rebecca was afraid of what he would say next but then he came to once more and grinned his horrible *Here's Johnny* grin.

Rebecca had to get out of there. She rushed to the door.

'What?' Austen opened the whisky once again and started to laugh.

*

Later, when it was fully dark, Austen knocked at his sister's door. 'Becky? Rebecca? Primmy called. Didn't you hear the phone? It's snowing hard.'

'I know.' She needed him to go away. 'I'm going to sleep.'

'Don't you want to know what she said?' He held his ear up to her door, his fringe flopping over a sweaty brow.

'I expect they are staying over. They do that occasionally, if they're out buying at an evening auction.'

'Jesus. What, together? Are they shagging d'you reckon?'

'Goodnight Austen.'

'Aww Becky, don't be like that. I've had such a piss-arse awful time.'

'Sorry to hear that. There's all the decorations to do if you're at a loose end.' She bit her lip over a smile and felt very superior.

Austen opened his sister's door and came into the room. He still wore the silk scarf but not flung all around, just hanging down so that she could see his ruffled shirt and his black bowtie. He looked over all Rebecca's things in her bedroom, scanning her world.

'Remember, Becky, when I used to come home from school in the holidays and Old Ralphie would be so pleased to see me. He would say: *there he is, the boy, home to us Primmy, look at him, de-mob happy.* Do you remember that, Becky?'

'No.' She almost wanted to say yes because he looked so pathetic there, rocking on the door jamb, like he was hanging, not standing. But truthfully, she didn't think her grandfather had ever liked Austen at all.

'My girlfriend Naomi, well she's not exactly my girlfriend, she's, we've been out. Few times.' His lower lip stayed down, wet. He looked tired out. His breathing became heavy and he looked down at her stuff on the floor. Rebecca didn't want him to see her things. She wanted to get up and kick her possessions all under the bed. But that would have been the wrong thing. The wrong thing was to move an inch.

Austen pulled off his scarf and rubbed his face in it. 'It's the big Christmas bash. Tonight. You know, down my way.' He flicked his hand over his ruffles. 'I was trying this lot on.' He cast his hands down over his dress trousers. 'Well, trying a lot on.' He pulled one side of his mouth up into his cheek. 'She wasn't in the mood. I mean, I'm supposed to look handsome! I'm supposed to look my best.' He swayed on his black leather feet and plucked at the cummerbund fastening at the back of his waist. 'Your best is not necessarily comfortable.' He ran his index finger under his wing collar. 'But I don't want to take it off. You know? All this clobber. I don't want that to be the end of… me and her. I don't want it to finish like this.' He shook his finger at me. 'I'm not going into details, Becky.'

'Good. Would you mind getting out.'

'Where's your panda?'

'You're pissed out your head. I want you to leave.'

'Ugly little fucker, that panda. But you loved it madly. Mum got it, didn't she.'

'Grandma said she did.'

'She's lying. Where the hell is it? Honestly, you turn your back for one minute.'

'Austen, please. I want to go to sleep.'

He ducked a little to look under the iron bed frame but kept on fiddling behind his back. The cummerbund wouldn't budge and he looked up at Rebecca. The colour trickled out of his skin and he staggered off, like both ankles were ball and chained.

Rebecca stared at the open door. Then the retching came from the bathroom. Just as it used to with Colette, though that hadn't happened over the last while.

Austen had dropped the lovely scarf on her bedroom floor. She was wearing a nightshirt, a scruffy, striped vintage affair that she'd found at the hospice shop. It had no buttons and was several sizes too large. Rebecca loved the shirt, imagining some army lieutenant had worn it during the Crimean War and she rolled around in that fantasy, trying to conjure a past life, just as she used to with Maria Theresa. Mrs Scattergood had done her usual face when she saw the faded nightshirt, like she'd just withstood a good snort of ammonia.

Rebecca slipped from the bed and went over to the door. It had a loose handle which rattled, and a lock, but no key. She bent down to pick up the scarf and she knew when she straightened up that he was there again. They were inches apart and she feared that she would be able to smell the sick.

'Used your gargle. Hope you don't mind. Like the Jim Hawkins look, by the way. He's the boy in *Treasure Island*.'

'I know who he is.'

'Remember when they told us not to wear underwear in bed? The Grands? Surely choosing when to wear or not wear your own underwear is a human right. What a strange life we've led, eh, Becky?'

She turned quickly around to get away from him and went back to the bed. For a second, she thought he would stop her, grab her hand, but he didn't. She got under the blankets

(Primmy didn't hold with duvets) and Austen took off his bowtie, with fingers more assured now and spinal column more erect.

'Naomi didn't want me. You know what I'm saying.'

'Austen, I really—'

'Oh, she had. She had wanted me from day one. Don't worry about that. Mainly what we did. 90% of what we did was that. But yesterday, no. She wasn't in the mood. Well, not that kind of mood. But she was certainly in a fucking terrible mood.' Austen's head shook quickly from side to side, dismay switching up a gear to fury. 'Becky. She threw me out. In this ridiculous outfit. One minute we're fine. I'm trying on all this gear for the Christmas ball. And the next, kaboom! She's screaming. I'm on the street. No money. Banging on the door like a… I had to borrow cash to even get up here. I made all this effort! To get up here. When this is, God almighty, this is the last place on earth I want to be.'

'What did you do to her?'

'I didn't bloody do anything to her, that's the whole point! She just left me making an arse of myself on the pavement. I had to sell my watch to this migrant bloke in Cambridge to buy a train ticket.'

'Don't you have friends?'

'I couldn't go to them. Mortifying.' Austen stared at the blank space on his wrist where his watch used to be. 'Worth ten times what he gave me. Cunt. I had to fucking hitch from Mallaig Station, in this temperature, in this stupid costume. Couldn't even go into *The Chlachain* for a drink. Look at me. I'm a fish, soooo out of water. I'm wee guppie MacGraw, dying on the side of the road as they blast their horns. Why did we ever live here? Could we say we've been living? *Really*? I think, pretending, would be more honest. You don't understand.'

There was a phone in Grandma's room, Rebecca was thinking.

Austen shrugged and came to sit at the foot of his sister's bed.

'Thank God at least you were here, Becky. You are here.'

He unbuttoned the top two buttons of his shirt. 'Your hair's not just darker. It's grown too. Longer. Much longer.'

'In case I hadn't noticed.' Her voice was shaking.

'You're not frightened are you, darling?'

Rebecca gasped. They both heard it. She couldn't reply. No answer could have been right.

'I've always liked your hair. I like dark girls. Naomi is half Malaysian. Just... gorgeous. Who do you take after, d'you think?'

She knew she looked more like her mother because she'd had dark hair too and her siblings were fair, like the Brown branch.

'I missed you, you know? You know? I mean, I like it. I do. Down there. South.' He smiled at his sister and moved up to the outline of her knees. 'I really like it down there.' He ran his hand up a divide on the blanket, between his sister's thighs.

Rebecca went completely crazy. Everything to hand was used: books, a plastic alarm clock, a tiny framed fishing boat picture on her bedside table, a biro stabbing at his white shirt, a snowglobe which made its mark on his cheekbone, pillows desperately and fists finally. She even stuffed a bookmark into his mouth.

'You bastard! You bastard!'

Eventually, he had her arms tight inside his own, both sitting up, both torsos heaving with the fight, her crying silently and a fine line of saliva spilling down onto his blue inked shirt.

Austen began to stroke the side of her head, to push the hair gently back from her ear. He leaned in to whisper. 'I don't think anyone's ever accused me of that before. We're talking of legitimacy, are we? Well, ok, it's about time.' He took a crushed cigarette packet out of his trouser pocket but he couldn't find a lighter.

'What do you mean, about time?'

'Ach, forget it. Have you got a light?'

'Tell me. There's something. Austen, tell me now. Or I'll…'

'What? What you gonna do, Youngest Brown? Tell Granny?'

'I'll find you a light.' Rebecca pushed him aside and holding her nightshirt together, frantically searched her bedside drawer. She found a book of matches and her fingers trembled as she struck the match. 'Yes, I'll tell Primmy. I will tell Primmy that you… and there's fucking Christmas up shit creek as per fucking usual.'

Austen sucked on his cigarette and hated himself more acutely than ever before. 'Your mother. Now listen carefully and never repeat a word to Primmy, d'you hear?'

'Yes, I swear.'

'Your mother, Rebecca Brown. Your mother, is alive.'

*

At times, there had been hushed conversations; when Rebecca was small, but less so in recent years. And not at all since Ralph died. Times when she was lingering at the door and they regarded Youngest Brown in a very particular, yet mysterious, way. But Rebecca thought this was all part of skirting along the edges of the adult world.

She didn't sleep at all once her brother had left her room that night. She knew he wouldn't be back but she needed all of the darkness to properly explore his words. Something horrid slid around just under her breastbone, each time she replayed the scene. Rebecca wondered if she too needed to be sick.

In the morning, Austen knocked hard on her door and said in a firm and sober tone, 'We need to talk. Kitchen. I've made food.'

Ten minutes later, he was back at his sister's door. 'I'm leaving in half an hour.'

Rebecca fashioned herself a tight ponytail, brushed her teeth till her gums bled and went downstairs.

On the kitchen table, there was a bunch of cutlery, two plates and the butter dish Ralph made the mistake of using once for his pipe ash. Austen was carrying a teapot to the table. Rebecca pulled a wicker mat out of a drawer and slipped it beneath the teapot as he put it down. She could smell toast. She took jars of jam and honey from the fridge. She even got a spoon for them. She searched for the mugs they each liked. Hers covered in Scottie dogs. His with the logo of his old prep school. She searched for order.

He had used the wrong teabags. It was Earl Grey, Rebecca could smell the bergamot as he poured it into the mugs. Primmy thought Earl Grey quite *unsyooted* to breakfast but this was no time to say so.

He laid the teapot down heavily on the table and Rebecca moved it onto the mat again.

'Are you going to tell them, Becky?'

'Tell them what?'

'You know damned well what.'

'That you tried to rape me?'

'You little bitch. I did no such thing.'

'Austen, you stuck your hand right here.' She put her hand on her crotch and stared at him.

'You always were a liar. Everyone knows that. Some kind of fucking sport for you. You wouldn't know the truth if it did stick its hand in your crotch. Fucking little tease. I need some money. I need to get out of here.'

'Well, that's not going to look very good, fleeing the scene of the crime.'

'It was a mistake to come. I need to go before Primmy gets back. Otherwise I'll get stuck here.'

Austen's body snapped around the kitchen cupboards and drawers looking for cash. But all he could find was a jar of five pence pieces which the Grands had used for three card brag. No-one had deposited to or drained from the jar for years. Austen crashed the glass jar down on the worktop. 'Who the fuck would collect these? This is a mad house.'

'I've got money. In my bedside drawer. About sixty pounds.' Austen almost ran out of the kitchen and up the stairs.

Rebecca was suddenly so tired. The sleepless hours piled onto her head and she could hardly hold it up. She opened her mouth but there was nothing to send down from her brain. She didn't even notice him coming back in or sitting down. 'Thank you. Thank you for the money. Hey,' he nudged her, 'you know I'm good for it. That'll get me a bus and a burger. My ATM card's at Naomi's. I'll break her door down if I have to. Sex is one thing. But money, well, money is sacred.'

'Does she know your pin number?'

'Nah. I like women. But I'd never trust one.'

'Trust. Right.'

'Listen Becky, I don't know what's going through your head right now. But let me make this clear. I was never going to have sex with you. You're just a kid.'

'I'm not your sister. It's because I'm not your sister.'

'What?'

'This is not my family.'

'Becky, I'm sorry. It came out all wrong. I shouldn't have said a word. Drink some of that tea.'

'It's too weak.'

He got up and tipped some of her mug into the sink and filled it up again. He sat down closer to his sister.

'Drink it. You've had… you've had a shock. There's toast.'

'I was adopted then. From a baby?' Her head started shaking and Austen tried to hold her face. She made fists of her hands and pushed them into her cheeks. Tears and snot dribbled over her knuckles.

Austen held Rebecca and rocked her a little. 'I've been saying this for years, to the Grands, well, to Primmy now. That you need to know. But they just wouldn't. She won't. Promise me you won't talk to her about last night.' He tried to pull her chin up. 'Please. Promise me.'

'Promise.'

'Drink some tea, Becky. You need to clean yourself up a bit. What if Primmy—'

'Oh fuck off, Austen Brown. Whoever you are. You only care about yourself.'

'Becky, calm down. Let me explain.'

'It wasn't incest then? You and me, we're not related. So that's alright.'

'Becky, I may have been a little pissed but we did not have sex, that much I know.'

'I mean, it wouldn't have been incest then?'

'I was upset. I'd had a rough time, the journey, oh fuck you don't give a shit, women just don't. Not that you are one. You're just a kid.' Austen got up. 'Do what you like. Tell her whatever you want. But if you take that little incest story to her, you'll never see me again. And neither will the others. Your choice, baby. Capeesh?

'Does Colette know about the adoption? Does Murdo? Does everyone?'

Rebecca burst into tears again. 'I just don't understand. When Ralph died he told me, right before he went, he said that I looked so much like my mother. I knew he wanted to tell me something more. But I guess he meant another mother. The mother who gave me away. Oh God! Oh no! It's not Uncle Neil is it? He's not my father?'

'I've said too much already. Stop jumping to conclusions. You and your imagination. It'll be the death of you. Sorry, that's a silly thing to say. God, it's this place. This crazy place.'

'Have you noticed, big brother, that when the going gets tough. I mean, when the chips are down or whatever they say, you stop your Bertie Wooster thing. You just sound the same as everyone else.'

'Becky, listen to me. It's important, it's *vital* that you say nothing of what I told you. About your mother. You understand? Becky? You gave me your word.'

'I did, didn't I. Goodbye Austen.'

CHAPTER 14

Arrivals

Rebecca more or less barricaded herself into her bedroom after Austen's brief visit to *Taransay* that Christmas. She began to skip classes at school over the next years until finally her school career was in ruins.

Primmy was 'concerned'. That's the word she kept using. Rebecca had always been a thoughtful child, introspective. Grandma regarded those adjectives as child markers for difficult teenage times. Primmy went through it all with their GP, Claire Angus, whom she prevailed upon for an urgent home visit. When Dr Angus arrived and Rebecca could not be found, there was a strong case for accusing Primrose Brown of wasting NHS resources, but Claire Angus was a practical woman and kept her feelings to herself. Well, didn't everyone in the Highlands.

They settled in the drawing room and Rebecca listened in on their conversation. She of course had not staged one of her burglaries in many a year, but her stealth in her *stocking soles* – as her grandmother referred to feet clad in socks but no shoes – was still remarkable.

'I'm concerned for her mental health, Doctor Angus.'

'Please, call me Claire.'

'Do you understand? *Concerned*. She's not a bad girl. Never been much of a student. Easily bored, I think. But the main thing is, she spends so much time alone.'

'She's isolated, yes. Geographically of course, too.' (At this point, Dr Angus rifled around in her notes, as if there might be some indicator from a childhood illness like chickenpox. 'Does she have any means of transport?'

'Transport? You mean like a car? Goodness, no.'

'What about a scooter?'

'A scooter? Dear me, no, I can't see Rebecca going for that.'

'A scooter with a motor?'

'You mean like a moped or whatever we call that kind of thing these days?'

'Exactly. Lots of young people have them round here.'

'She doesn't have one. And if she did, she wouldn't use it. She shuns things. She does, Doctor. She shuns. She won't see her friend. And she knew Maria for… well since she started school. Doctor Angus, Rebecca is given to melancholy.'

'The girl lost her parents when she was very young.'

'Yes. But there's something more. Something's wrong. She won't talk to any of us. I'm *concerned*. I… worry that she'll do something silly. You know.'

'You believe that she might take her own life? You think we're at that point?'

'No, well, not really. I just don't *know* Doctor Angus. I don't *know*. God knows I've done my best for those children but I'm not their mother. And I'm not telepathic.'

'No. I'm sure you've done an excellent job. Loss of one parent is so traumatic and Rebecca has lost—'

'And even if that's not the sort of path she's thinking of taking, it's gone on so long, Doctor. There's absolutely no question of her sitting her final exams. Months and months of this. I'm concerned she'll settle into this unhappiness. For good. What can be done?'

'Does she have any hobbies? Any interests? Sport?'

'She likes the Jacobites. That's about it.'

Rebecca enjoyed eavesdropping. She always had. *Taransay* was made for it. And she especially enjoyed it if the conversations were about her. She liked the attention, the *concern*.

Her own personal and chief concern was escape. There had to be a way out. Yes, she'd had a brief look at suicide. She'd felt the call of the kerb on Mallaig's Main Street. But she thought that to take this step, it seemed just too, well, final. She would converse with herself in the bathroom mirror; turn her head directly to the left and say: 'I mean, it's hardly the Gulag after all, is it, the Orphanage.' Then she'd turn to the right. 'Exactly, man the fuck up, wee lassie McGraw.'

However, yes, she was *given to melancholy*. (God, she liked that phrase.) But she had a sense of humour. She still laughed alone in her attic, though quietly. When she wasn't upsetting the Browns, she often amused them. And she was also a pragmatist, deep down. In her life there was still food, water, heating and a prospect of freedom. Death was a constant fear but it did seem to visit only occasionally.

For sure, on the night Austen revealed her adoption, something very cold and heavy had seeped into Rebecca. It slid inside her, slow and steady, like a curling stone across an ice rink. It settled on the bullseye, her heart, for a long time.

And then suddenly, the fog cleared; quite without warning. Rebecca was alone in the house, alone in Ralph's study and leafing through *West Word News* when she saw an ad for *Festival* staff in Edinburgh. She knew immediately that she had to go.

To her astonishment, Primmy was all for it. Colette was also in the capital, studying for a degree in Social Work. Not her grandmother's first choice of career for the girl, but all the same, respectable enough and rapidly becoming admirable, in comparison to her younger sister's general performance.

Colette had moved in with her girlfriend, Alex, in Marchmont. It took Primmy some time to come to terms with the fact that the description 'girlfriend' had a sexual connotation but at least Alex was: *a junior partner in a law firm, several rungs up on the property ladder and privately educated*. Rebecca had shot her grandmother a murderous glance when she made that last observation. She really didn't mind her school at Mallaig. She was indeed a good little Bolshevik, as Austen had said. But she found it difficult to cope with the injustice, the meting out of funds among them and she, Youngest Brown, at the bottom. Of course, she knew now that this was because she was not a Brown at all but she had kept her promise not to reveal this knowledge to Primmy.

She thought, naturally enough, of seeking out her birth mother, whom she just knew would be wonderful. Rebecca thought she could be on that tv programme, *Long Lost Family*, and sob into the arms of the presenters. Her mother of course would love her still, would have thought of her every day of her life, with infinite regret. She would explain to her long lost daughter that she had tried everything to keep her, but had been working in a coal mine back then, for twenty hours a day; stopping only briefly to give birth and then taking up her pickaxe again. Rebecca would nod supportively and hold no grudge. Then when her biological mother heard from Rebecca of the hardship of The Orphanage, the death of her adoptive parents, Julia and Stephen, she would cry too. But not for long. Soon they would be taking holidays together on islands in the Indian Ocean (her mother would by now be extremely wealthy and there would be no other children to share this wealth). That was Rebecca's daydream but she had to first address her own status. She did not want to introduce herself to her mother in her current form. She needed to improve. Rebecca needed to become herself.

*

The *Fringe Festival* in Scotland's capital city was the great illumination. It turned all Rebecca Brown's lights on. She knew what she wanted: to be a comedian. She was just sixteen years old when she left Primmy standing at the front door of *Taransay*, waving Youngest Brown off in her regal manner. Grandma had given her one thousand pounds. Rebecca had hoped for more, since Primmy seemed to indicate that was the lot, some kind of final pay-out. Measly, Rebecca felt, considering what the others had had. How far would that get her in Auld Reekie? A month's rent? Two?

For the first months, she stayed with Colette and Alex in their lovely apartment. Rebecca had a large, double aspect room and to be frank, she could have lodged there indefinitely. Someone was cleaning the place, she didn't know who. Not her, anyway. There was often food in the fridge, and of high quality. Someone was cooking that food, but Rebecca was rarely there in the evening so she didn't know who. Colette didn't cook, that was certain. And her sister hadn't baked a decent cake since that 10th birthday party. Colette was suspicious of food, ill-tempered by its mention. But all the same, the lovely food arrived in its component ingredients and transformed itself into lush dishes. She suspected Alex had a housekeeper who slipped in. She was rather well to do, old Alex. Quite advanced in years, Rebecca surmised, around the thirty mark by now probably.

They all rubbed along rather well in the Marchmont flat, Rebecca had been thinking, so it was something of a surprise when her sister seemed to be sticking to the agreed six month grace period by asking:

'Have you found anything, Becky? A roomshare? Want a hand having a look?'

'I can really only afford a bunk bed in a dorm. And that'll be the bloody top bunk. My career hasn't exactly taken off. I was hoping for something a bit better than *Festival Street Cleanser*.'

'Gotta start somewhere. I know loads of guys who started out on street cleansing. You'll pick up something better at next year's Festival. You work your way up. That's the system. Meantime, diversify. I have complete faith in you.' Colette opened her laptop to start going through roomshares.

Rebecca did indeed diversify. She moved from street cleansing to street food, which had the added bonus of supplying her meals. She ate Creole chicken three times a day. Alex liked the Creole too and Rebecca hoped that she might buy herself a month or two more in Marchmont with its steady provision. She filled the fridge with Gumbo and Jambalaya when she got home in the wee hours, proud to be making a proper hunter gatherer contribution. Then she got a job with an events company with a decent wage, and it really was time to look for her own place.

Rebecca found a two bedroom flat in Muirhouse and a flatmate, Heribert.

Alex bought her a copy of *The Jacobites and The Supernatural*. 'For your bookshelves. Of which I'm sure you'll have many.'

Rebecca kissed Alex on the cheek and as they embraced, Rebecca wondered what it would feel like to be with a woman. Or to be with anyone, for that matter.

Colette cried the day her little sister moved out. 'Come visit whenever you want. I mean it, whenever. And let's do a Sunday lunch thing. Not absolutely every Sunday, but some Sundays. Three Sundays a month. Or at least two.'

*

Rebecca found that once she had shrugged off her old life which was brimming with disappointment, deceit and death, she wanted to fully embrace the future. With the events company, she loved being front of house but took each element of her new job very seriously, tingling with the knowledge that she was getting near to putting herself in the spotlight. She liked the buzz of being in the box office, she liked the feeling of being in control as an usher, she liked selling programmes and merchandise and ice creams, she even became compulsive about picking up litter among the seating and aisles. Her diligence paid off. Her commitment was obvious to her manager, Claude, who was a strong believer in delegation; or bone idle was another way of looking at it. Rebecca was quickly given more responsibility.

This is where she wanted to be, in amongst the stalls, looking down from the balcony and stocking up the dressing rooms, but what she really wanted was the limelight. 'I feel it in my bones,' she'd say to herself in the mirror, then turn her head. 'In your water, lass.' Why hadn't she thought of the stage sooner? The path was so obvious to her now. She could take on all sorts of guises. She could command full attention. It was perfect. The only thing possibly lacking was sheer nerve.

Most of the shows she was involved with at the next *Fringe Festival* were sell-outs. During the performances themselves, Rebecca silently went about her business but her ears were listening keenly to all the artists: their content, their style, their movement as they treaded the boards, their timing. On some nights, Rebecca was totally inspired and knew she herself could do it. On other nights, she was so blown away with the genius she witnessed, she knew she never could.

Colette and Alex encouraged her. They asked to listen to her material. Rebecca refused for a long time, saving her performances for the bedroom mirror and sound recordings on her phone. But after a night of one Tequila too many at a small gathering in the Marchmont flat, Rebecca started to give it a go. There was a veritable small audience before her. The ex landladies had thrown a lavish dinner party for their close friends and the desire to gig forth suddenly came to Rebecca, over the Bendicks Mints.

Rebecca picked up the chocolates. 'Bendicks Mints? Bendickth Minth? What kind of cruel psychopath put the letter 's' in the word 'lisp'?

And then Rebecca began to do her routine so that it merely sounded, in the context of a social gathering, like she was just giving her opinions on this and that. Colette became quickly aware of what was happening, as her little sister got up from her seat at the dining table and started to pace around them, gesticulating in a way that demonstrated performance, in a fashion that evinced command. Rebecca was unrecognisable, and yet completely herself. Everyone fell about and Youngest Brown's heart burst with pride.

She toured with the events company over the next couple of years, learning her trade and becoming an assistant manager. In any spare time, Rebecca got herself a spot on open mic at the clubs.

Although Colette was her biggest supporter, her sister persuaded Rebecca that if comedy did not work out, a solid footing in events was something to fall back on. Life was not cheap in Edinburgh.

'Don't give up the day job. Not till you're sure. Get a bit of cash in the bank, then before you know—'

'You just can't stand the thought of me showing up broke on your doorstep ever again.'

'I just want you to keep safe. I need you safe.'

*

'Beck, Backstage…' was the title of her show for this year's Edinburgh Fringe Festival 2021.

Keller Baye reckoned he was singlehandedly responsible for 95% of video views on her website and on YouTube, but what he liked to watch most, was Rebecca Brown in person; *Beck*, she was now styling herself.

There was a film recording of an interview with *Beck*. The journalist had blue toilet brush hair which Keller took exception to. The title of the clip was *Beck In Her Own Words*. Keller fixed his sleeping bag into a comfortable ball beneath his head and lay back in his bed. He pressed play on the MacBook on his chest.

Blue haired woman: 'Your new show's called *Beck, Backstage*. Is this about your life outside?'

Beck: 'Outside?'

BHW: 'What's it about then?'

Beck: 'Oh everything. I think backstage is just a metaphor, what's going on in my mind. Sorry.'

BHW: 'No worries. You have a reputation for honing your work relentlessly. And touring constantly.'

Beck: 'I do? Why am I broke then? Don't you have to be wealthy to have a reputation? Or corrupt? Sorry, I'm asking too many questions. What did you have for lunch? Just kidding.

BHW: 'Cheerios. Dry, from the box. Do you ever have time for anything else? A private life?'

Beck: 'Ok, so you're hitting on me.'

BHW: 'What?'

Beck: 'I'm still kidding. Occupational hazard. Um, let me see. A private life? Well, I do. But nothing ever happens in it. I'm disappointing you, amn't I.'

Keller clicked pause and touched Rebecca's face on the screen. He had a still of this shot on his phone.

Damn, there was someone outside the wigwam. 'Knock, knock.' A voice said, though there was no knock. Was there no end to British irony? Then came an embarrassed laugh from Denzie, the young girl who collected the fees for the Mortonhall campsite, just south of the city of Edinburgh. Keller got up and flattened out some crushed notes from his pocket. He opened the wigwam door.

'Technically,' Denzie said, 'You're meant to renew payment over at reception.'

'I know. Forgive me. Can I give you this toy money here and now?' He smiled at her and handed over the sterling.

'Another week?'

'Another week. Certainly. Oh Denzie?'

'Yes.'

'Would it be alright if I had a package delivered here. It's just very small.' Keller indicated that the package would fit between his thumb and index finger.'

'Oh, we're not really allowed to take deliveries for guests. I'd have to check.'

'Do you have to check? Don't you ever get stuff delivered? Addressed to Denzie the Devine.'

'Very funny. Like I said, I'd have to check.'

'Ah. Pity.'

'Well I suppose I could, if you address it to me. But I get quite a lot of supplies. I'd have to open it.'

'What's your surname?'

'Lawson.'

'Well how about I make a typo. I put on the delivery name *Lewson* instead of *Lawson* and you'll know that's mine.'

'It's not always me that opens the post though. And what if the sender makes a typo themselves and puts *Lawson* instead of *Lewson*? Eh?' Denzie laughed, thought she'd been very clever.

'Hey, not a problem. In either event. It's not a thermo nuclear device, if that's what you're worrying about. Just a little gadget. Shall we risk it? Delicious Denzie.'

'You're a bam.'

'That a yes?'

'Aye. Go on then.'

*

The wigwam at Mortonhall suited Keller very well. It was considerably more than the kind of tepee he'd envisaged when he'd first heard about this accommodation. In fact, there was a fridge, a tv and a microwave. It was located near to the toilet block, always a plus, and to the Stable Bar where they served amazing ale, for which Keller was acquiring a taste.

He had added considerably to his dossier on Rebecca Brown. He watched the kilobytes build satisfactorily on his Word file each day. Of course, he longed for the day he could introduce himself to her. But he knew the safest thing to do was bide his time, to make it look the casual opposite of what it really was: that he was here to get her.

Keller opened his crossbow file. It was near impossible to buy one in this country. But it was easy enough to make one. He'd got the materials for the stock and prod the day he arrived in Scotland. And already, he had fitted these two components together, to his complete satisfaction. He was good with his hands. All the girls said so. The arrow channel was a fair way along too. Pretty soon he'd be fitting the trigger and rope. The weapon didn't look that special – perhaps he'd paint it – but it would work alright. The anticipation of everything to come, gave him a delicious shiver.

He'd need to set up some target practice. The landscape was a little light on raccoons and feral pigs but he'd find something.

Keller logged on to an amateur porn site. 'Jesus, fella. Your dick's the size of a rolling pin.' Keller scowled at his MacBook. He hated those porn stars, the men and the women, but they were a necessary evil.

The girl in the sex video had very long hair which kept obscuring her face. Someone – the director most likely – was telling her to get the hair sorted so that the audience could see her pleasure. The girl's eyes darted here and there. She was struggling a bit with the pleasure. The moans signified that it was amazing though, unbearably good. Yet she never came, despite the best efforts of her lover, as he plunged into her every orifice. The girl was getting tired. Nothing being done to her seemed to bring any surprise, or discomfort. Was she drugged maybe? The man moved quickly from this thing to that. The moment contact with the girl was broken, the guy grafted away at maintaining his erection. Keller was now struggling to maintain his own. The scene, created for desire, was utterly devoid of it. He needed a real live woman. He needed Rebecca Brown.

Keller traced her comedy tour route: *Udderbelly* on London's South Bank, then over to Bristol, up to Newcastle. When she wanted to test out new material, she seemed to come back home, go along to open mic spots in comedy clubs. She had no manager as far as he could tell and no kind of press agent. At least, nothing was listed on her website. Perhaps she liked to keep a tight rein. He could understand that. Good, he wanted her as isolated as possible. Like a lone deer, distracted with its need to feed, separate from the herd.

Tonight, Beck was playing *The Hob* in Leith, quite aways from the campsite, but she was worth it. *The Hob* hosted the main acts just before they went to the *Fringe* and this evening's show was a sell-out. Keller generally sat well back, in the shadows, but no longer. Tonight, he sat right up front and let Rebecca Brown get a good look at him. It was time to get ahead with his plan. Life, and death, were really all about the timing.

Keller had been observing Rebecca for such a short period in Edinburgh, but it didn't feel like that. How could it, when he'd had her in his sights for so long. And she needed to be attended to with the utmost care. She was capable of rapid movement, jumping on a bus with perhaps just a toothbrush in her bag. She took flight. City to city, gazing up at buildings, her little canvas bag bandoliered across her chest. Sometimes just looking, not even performing, and never visiting people. Then she skipped off somewhere new. Keller could barely keep up.

Her work was imaginative and she often veered from, or embellished, her routine. Rebecca had strong natural responses and an inclination for change, for new. She was a whirlwind of evolution, it seemed. Her act on stage developed greatly in the weeks he'd been watching. Keller Baye had a bulky profile on this young woman but in truth, she was more mysterious than ever.

The first time Keller saw *Beck*, she'd been doing a spot at the *Geffie and Gogie Club*. Gabriella, the girl who was on before, was an opera singer who couldn't get a job. She was wearing dirty overalls and a helmet with miner's lamp (bulb on). Her set was sung in a passionate soprano, mostly bitter jibes about auditions. There was an operatic pop medley to finish: *Rockin' Robin, Oops I did it Again, Tainted Love*. Keller was baffled. He'd never been to a theatre in North Carolina and far as he could tell, he hadn't been missing much. Gabriella announced that this next song would be her last and someone behind Keller shouted 'Thank fuck for that. I've got a razor at my wrist here, doll.'

The girl warbled through *Major Tom* and left the stage to a smattering of applause.

Then Rebecca came on. 'Well, I think we can all agree she sang that in a mostah peculiar way-hay.'

Keller had noticed that Rebecca liked to be spontaneous wherever possible. Though she wasn't terrific with hecklers and she never invited questions or comment from the audience. She turned up her Scottish accent on stage in her home city. She wanted to belong to them. And she put in local landmarks wherever possible. She was a professional. That first gig, *Beck* was talking about sleeplessness, something Keller knew very little about, but then the whole idea of comedy, of standing up and trying to make people laugh, was completely alien to him. The rest of the audience, however, seemed to be made up entirely of insomniacs, as they applauded fiercely and jeered with empathy.

'... that cockerel crowing. You know the one? Or a donkey braying. And this is right here in Leith. This is just outside Tesco's in Park View Road. Who is bringing these farmyard animals into our urban life? Is it you? *(Her eyes scanned a row but did not linger on an individual. She did not want an answer.)* Everything, *everything*, conspires to stop you sleeping. You're so tired, you could be part of some experiment to see at what point tiredness will kill you. You look in the mirror. Your eyes are like a two year old staring out from an airport bus at 1.00 am.' She pulled her eyes down to her cheekbones. 'You know those buses that go to long term parking. Handy, just over in Livingston.'

Presumably this was quite far away from the airport. The British based most of their humour on sarcasm. Keller was coming to understand that.

*

The Hob, like the others, had no curtain on stage. Keller didn't know much about theatre but he knew there ought to be a curtain. The stage was in darkness but as the audience were taking their seats – crazy slow in Keller's opinion, what in God's name could be so complex about finding your seat and sitting in it – you could see folk coming to and from on the stage, blatant, getting the set ready. As far as he was concerned, that was another big mistake.

When they were all settled, there was a voiceover asking them to ensure their mobile phones were on mute and then requesting that audience members with coughs, or *anything viral really*, make their way to the exit. This second request seemed to be a joke, as there was a faint murmur of amusement and nobody got up to leave.

Keller felt distinctly nervous. He couldn't begin to imagine how Rebecca must be feeling, up there, in the dark, everyone's eyes upon her. And tonight she would see him. He would make sure of that. What would it feel like, to finally make eye contact.

The lights went up very gradually, denoting the rising sun, Keller thought. There was a double bed on stage and a body in it, asleep. A phone rang and the person in the bed panicked in their reach to get to it. Then Keller could see for sure that it was her. Rebecca had backcombed her hair and her make-up, which was usually minimal, was now heavy and black and streaking down her face. Her nightgown was stained and its buttons done up irregularly.

'Hello?' Rebecca spoke into a phone.

Voiceover: 'Tracey. It's Neville. I'm in the neighbourhood.'

She looked stricken. 'You are? What time is it?'

'It's 1998. Time to wake up. You know I'm waiting on your exhibit.'

'Ohhh yes, my exhibit.' Rebecca looked around her, she clutched a clump of hair in one hand. Keller noticed that her accent had changed to English, sort of London, and that she spoke with a slight lisp.

'Tracey? Are you there?'

Rebecca let go of her hair and rustled around the bedcovers to retrieve an artist's paintbrush. She looked at it in wonderment, mouth open. 'Yes Neville, I'm here.'

'How's it coming?'

'The exhibit?' She waved the paintbrush inanely.

'Yes, of course, the exhibit for the Tate. Thought I'd drop by and check progress.' There was a toot of a horn. 'I'm outside.'

Rebecca, or rather *Tracey*, threw the phone across the stage and looked around at the disarray of her bedroom. The audience were beginning to laugh but Keller was totally bewildered. Rebecca scrambled out of the bed and messed up the white sheets. She kicked at a pair of dirty slippers. She asked the audience if they had any condoms and cigarettes. Several of these items were handed up to her. She emptied a box of cigarettes on to the bed and the floor. She ripped open a few condoms, dribbled onto them, then pinged them around the set. Breathing heavily, with her tongue hanging out a little, she made a grab for a vodka bottle on the bedside table. She took a long swig and dropped the bottle on the floor. The liquid glugged out onto the boards. She lifted up a full ashtray and scattered the butts over the bed, rubbing in the ash in places and stood back, nodding and smiling.

Then Rebecca looked up coyly and Keller was sure she was looking right at him. She put her hands under her nightgown and removed her underwear. She lifted the panties high into the air, between her thumb and forefinger, and dropped them next to the bed. The doorbell rang. And the lights cut out on stage.

The audience clapped wildly and Keller had no notion as to what was going on. He thought it was going to be a long night. He took off his bomber jacket and placed it gently over his erection.

Between themes, Rebecca would punctuate her act by doing something physical, like having a sniff at something and being unpleasantly surprised, or getting out some cream and applying it to a part of her body, as if there was a mosquito bite. Something to let them know she was moving on.

She always adapted her show to the audience. At the Rotary Club, she asked them if anyone knew about rare great crested newts, since she'd heard if she got one, she could block her neighbour's planning permission. At a student union, she did stuff on Zeno and Descartes. At London Transport, she had a story about a runaway bus with a dog at the wheel.

She tried, Keller had to give her that.

Now the lights rose once more and the set had been cleared. Rebecca was wearing jeans and a t-shirt now. She came up to the stage apron and thumbed over her shoulder. 'Product placement is an interesting thing, isn't it. That phone *Tracey Emin* was using, by the way, was a Samsung Galaxy S10. It's really very nice. But it's just a prop. It's plastic. *Tracey* doesn't really have a Galaxy S10. But *Tracey* would like to.' She nodded.

There was a thunderous clatter offstage. Rebecca excused herself and walked to the back of the stage to bark, 'Can't you learn to knock?' There was another significant clatter. She looked at the audience, rolled her eyes and went offstage. There was a sound effect of a door creaking open and then a soft hum which became a loud buzz. Then a bit of a clatter again and Rebecca offstage said, 'Be careful. You're damaging the box.' Sound effect of a door closing and she came back to the apron with a pizza box. She opened it and started munching away. She tutted and shook her head. 'Fucking drones.'

The audience roared. And Keller was relieved to have understood the joke. Rebecca handed the pizza down to the front row. They each, mostly, took a slice and handed the box along.

At the ten minute interval, a film was run on a drop down screen. It was of Rebecca backstage in her dressing room, making melon balls, ten of them. She placed them on the plate and then in real time, took one ball off each minute and in various poses and states of reflection, ate the lot. The screen rolled back up and Rebecca came back on the stage in person.

'When I stub my toe, I sometimes think, that is SO painful, how will I manage if I get shot?'

'You won't.' Keller hadn't shouted it loudly but everyone heard. Rebecca heard.

*

At the end of the show, Keller was relieved. It was tense, watching live shows. He found that he wasn't becoming used to it, nor enjoying it. Keller knew Rebecca now and that made it more difficult. He wasn't worried for *her* exactly, but he did worry. He didn't care about her feelings, but he did care about the show going well. He didn't know why that would happen but somehow, the tension took hold of him and the need for success. Perhaps it was knowing what was to come, since it was getting near. Maybe the need for control was getting stronger by the day.

As the curtain metaphorically fell, Keller did not get up to leave. He did not even get up to make it easier for the rest of the people in his row. They pushed past his long legs and he waited until the auditorium was quiet.

An usher came up to him and explained that the show was finished.

Keller scowled at the usher. 'I'm waiting for Beck. We're meeting after the show.'

The usher backed off and just moments later, the star herself came up the central aisle at a fair pace and stood with her hands on her hips.

'What's your trouble?'

'Trouble? I ain't looking for no trouble, ma'am.'

'Oh God. Is that your real accent? Don't answer that. You told Harry we're meeting. I don't know who you are but I can tell you that we are not meeting.'

'You don't know who I am? Well let me clear that right up. I'm a fan.'

'I'm going to call security.'

'Now don't be like that… Beck. I'm just a fan in the regular way. Not like that fat dame in *Misery*. Just want to buy you a cup of coffee, is all.'

'Gosh, you're a charmer, aren't you. How could I resist.' She turned on her heel and went over to Harry who stood with his arms crossed and his lips pursed. They were going to call security. Keller got up to leave.

Rebecca generally went to a café after her performances and tonight, despite her 'fan' unnerving her, was no exception. She was an avid note maker and this was part of her routine, as much as the performance. A kind of post-mortem maybe. She had gone immediately to a café after every performance Keller had attended.

Outside tonight's venue, Keller stood in a shop doorway, well away from the streetlight. Just a few doors along was *The Fuse Café* and sure enough in a matter of minutes, this creature of habit, this Beck, walked right past him and into the *Café*. When he reckoned she'd be settled with her stupid cold coffee, which she always ordered, Keller went in to join her.

Rebecca did not see him as he entered. Her nose was already buried in her notebook and her pencil scratched furiously at the page. Keller walked up to the counter. There was a sign by the till: *Bring me my coffee and you may live*. Rebecca was seated on one of the Ercol chairs. She looked upwards for a few seconds. She seemed to be listening intently, her eardrums pulsating for material, for humanity.

Keller came right up to her table and pulled a chair out for himself.

'Why d'you come to dumps like this, Beck? I mean I like a café myself. Get me some reading done.' Keller put a heavy book upon the table, back cover up. 'You're more of a writer than a reader though, aren't ya?'

Rebecca stirred her Frappuccino. 'What is your name?'

'Zachary. Zachary Ness. From Tuscaloosa.'

'Tuscaloosa? Seriously? Sounds like an Italian walrus needing dental treatment.'

'Ah, the quick wit. Yup. Tuscaloosa, Alabama.'

'Ness like the monster?'

Keller could feel that tic start in his cheek. 'I guess.'

'What can I do for you, Mr Ness?'

'Zachary is fine. Just looking for some company is all. Oh and I need you to explain that sketch you did there. Who is Tracey?'

'Tracey Emin? An artist. You didn't get it?'

'Fraid not.'

'Oh that's quite annoying. I worked for ages to make it gettable for foreigners.'

'It's probably just me. I don't get out much.'

'Well Tracey, she did this exhibit thing, an installation we call it. You do too, I imagine. And it was just her bed, her unmade bed, with all the debris of her chaotic life. And people loved it. Or they certainly talked about it.'

'So you… were trying to suppose how she conceived the idea.'

'Yes. It's funny, Zachary. It's comedy. That's what we're her for. That's what we burn for. But maybe not you. That last being a wild shot in the dark.'

Keller shrugged. He tried to look like he was in need of education. Women loved to tell you what's what. He widened his startling green eyes and looked around at the stained walls and ceiling. He could tell that she was watching him. 'I'm sorry. New kid in town. The Eagles sang that. My dad liked them. You know the Eagles?'

'No.' Rebecca's right knee jumped up and down, a trait he had not noticed before. Perhaps they had one thing in common: unwanted spasms.

'Grimy, is a word that might have been invented for a place like this.'

'Hey, if it doesn't suit you, Zachary.' She nodded to the door.

'Oh I'm not saying it doesn't suit me.'

'I find people air their grievances more often, more volubly and more righteously, in these grimy outlets. In short, Mr Ness, Zachary, it's funny in here.' She leaned forward, rubbing at her lumbar region. 'Mind you, these chairs are like fucking egg slicers.'

He hated to hear Rebecca curse. Keller put his hands behind his head and pretended to relax. 'Ain't no-one ever called me that. Mr Ness. I kinda like it.' He turned up his smile to bright.

'I'm not afraid of you. I was. I'll admit I was, back there in *The Hob*. And I've seen you before. Creepy guy, sorry but you are. I don't attract superfans. I'm not famous yet. I'm not pretty. I'm not—'

'Oh you're pretty alright. Who told you that you weren't pretty?'

'Shhh. Listen.'

Two men, far from typical, walked into the café. They looked a bit non-plussed at the décor but decided it was too late to back out. Middle class, in the wrong part of town. Blazers, suede footwear, one had a Worsted cap.

'Why should I listen?' Keller had stopped smiling and she was surprised to see that without showing his teeth, which were a definite asset, he was still handsome.

'Because it'll be funny. Don't listen then. Go away. That'll work for me.'

The two well-heeled gentlemen were having a discussion about one of their wives, Barbara, who had decided to become an AirBnB host. Much to the horror of her husband.

'Honestly, Hugh, I looked into the bay window with its two neatly set breakfast tables and all I could think was, this is the 9th circle of hell.'

Rebecca scribbled it down. She noted his mustard corduroy trousers, the mark of fair success. She noted another man slouched in the corner. He wore shabby leather winkle pickers, the mark of the failed musician.

'What's up with that leaky pen? You're not writing there, you're splodging.'

'I know. It's a bit messy. But it was a gift.'

'From someone special.'

'Yes.'

Keller was immediately jealous. 'Why would you write this stuff out, Beck?'

'Because it's funny. Observational comedy.'

'It's not funny. I'll tell you what's funny. That man over there. He's wearing his pants inside out.'

Rebecca shook her head.

Keller continued, 'He is, look, he's got all the label and seams showing.'

'Yes, he's got his *trousers* on inside out. But that's not funny. Not in the least.'

'You're wrong. You can't see something hilarious staring you in the face.'

'Listen, Ness, it would be fair to say you're not my target audience.'

'Who is your target audience?'

'I don't know.'

'Oh. That's not good. They say you should know your target audience.'

'No they don't, that's for books. For people writing books and shit. A comedian's audience is extremely diverse.'

'No it's not.'

'It fucking is.'

'Depends on the comic.'

'It's different here. People like funny things. In the States, they like jokes, whacky voices, punchlines.'

'Not necessarily.'

'Look, what the fuck are you doing? The Monty Python argument sketch?'

'Who? You shouldn't curse.'

'Fuck you.'

'Yes please.'

'I'm going home.'

'I'm coming with you.'

'Like hell you are.' Rebecca slapped some gold coins on the table and shouted to the guy behind the counter. 'Leaving my money out, Jurgis. Watch out for Hugh and friend. They look light-fingered.'

Hugh and friend looked aghast.

Rebecca jabbed her finger into Keller's chest. 'You're making me behave badly.'

On the way out, Keller tipped the Worsted cap forward. 'Don't mind the lady. She's a comedienne.'

Outside Rebecca told Keller. 'Zachary, I know you follow me. I've seen you before. I thought it was just my paranoia, in shop windows, on street corners. But it's not, is it. You're a...' She didn't want to say the word stalker out loud because that would make this situation properly real and she had to try to stave that off. 'I know you know where I live. But you're not coming with me.'

Rebecca had read this thread about stalkers, on a forum. One girl said, *Meet your stalker, bore them stiff, let them see that whatever they have fantasised you are, you are not. This is the quickest way to get rid of them.*

Keller sighed and held his book close to his chest, the front facing her now, to reveal the title: *Inglorious Rebellion*.

Rebecca stared at the book. 'You're reading about the Jacobites?'

'I think the Rising of 1715 had the best chance. Don't you? I mean they didn't have as big an army as the '45 Rebellion but they did get all the way down to Derby.'

'What the actual fuck? Ok. Meet me here, at *The Fuse*, tomorrow morning. But if you follow me now, I'm calling the police.'

'What time tomorrow?'

'Morning. I can't say a time. I'm an artist.'

'But timing is everything.' He smiled.

'True. Anyone who's ever cooked broccoli knows that. Boom-boom. Go away, creepy Zachary.'

His affable grinning was making his cheeks ache. As soon as Rebecca turned on her heel, Keller swiped that grin from his face. He wanted to kill her. But he wanted to fuck her. Kill her, fuck her, in equal measures.

*

Keller had to get three buses again, to get back there. But he arrived early, as *The Fuse* opened. He ordered so many lemon and ginger teas, Natcha and Jurgis gave him a slice of carrot cake on the house. An old lady came in. She had an electrocution of red veins across her face. She started to cough wildly and grabbed at her crotch with her hand. Natcha led her to the restroom. Jurgis set some free cake down for her return.

The metallic traffic thundered along outside. Rain suddenly fell in thick ropes, not for long, but by the time it was just snivelling from the gutters, Keller was giving up hope. Then when the sun sprang forth once more, that's when Rebecca appeared.

'Apologies, Zachary Ness. I honestly am later than I meant to be. My grandmother has suddenly showed up from the mist. Well not that suddenly, my sister did tell me. But then I forgot. She's in town for a dementia test. Primmy. My grandmother. Not my sister. My sister's fine. What are you drinking? Oh, nice cake.'

Keller forked up a mouthful and held it up. 'So is she?'

'What? Who? I'm not eating off your fork.'

'Your grandmother. Is she demented?'

'Oh God, I haven't even sat down and this is already a mistake.'

'I'm sorry. I'm nervous. I'll leave the jokes to you.'

Rebecca flopped onto the Ercol chair. 'So anyway. That's the kind of thing. Taking my grandmother to the doctor's, dropping her at my sister's. That's my life. My daily life. Stuff like that. Eating. Laundry. Dementia.'

'She showed up from where, your grandmother? Would you like some tea?'

'Certainly not tea. Coffee. An entire jug.' She turned around to smile at Jurgis, who nodded.

'Your grandmother showed up from where?'

'Oh nowhere interesting. North. West. North West. Oh that sounds like a film.'

'Hitchcock. *North by Northwest.*'

'Yeah well it's definitely not like Hitchcock. It's dull. Dull as can be. Duller than ditchwater. Nothing thrillery about Grandma. Or me.'

'What's the matter? Hey.' Keller put his hand lightly on the sleeve of her denim jacket. Jurgis brought her a cafetière of coffee. 'You worried about your grandmother?'

'Broadly, no. Primmy's fine. Apart from the odd bout of pyelonephritis.' Rebecca drank her coffee and licked her lips with satisfaction.

'Pie what? You do drink hot coffee then.'

'Hot coffee in the morning. Cold coffee at night. Pyelonephritis. It's a kidney infection Grandma gets now and then. Anyway, she failed the dementia test, fairly comprehensively. But, fuck me, if she didn't know the prime minister's name! That was a real worry. I'm sure she's never known before. It is good to see her. No, it is. I think she feels… I don't know, it's like she needs to make an excuse to come here.'

'Because she can't just let you know she's visiting because she loves you. Because she misses you.'

Rebecca stared at Keller. 'Where are you staying then?'

'Mortonhall. You?'

'Muirhouse. As if you didn't know. But I'd like to stay in Merchiston. It's nice, Merchiston. I think they'll start walling in the posh parts of the city. Like in London. I think inside the M25, London will start to put up razor wire. There will be passports for—'

'What's the M25?'

'It's a ring road. A road around the city. Everything inside is very expensive. Like a principality. Like Monaco. You know Monaco?'

'I heard of Monaco, yes.'

'Well, only the super rich can afford to live there, so they bus in all the slave people each day, the staff for their casinos and hotels and restaurants. Their chauffeurs. Their mechanics, their personal trainers. Hairdress—'

'I get the picture.'

'Oh, I'm sorry if I'm boring you. I should get going.' Rebecca drained her coffee cup.

'You just got here! Don't you like how they run things at Monte Carlo? My little Bolshevik.'

Rebecca stared at Keller and could feel her face reddening. God, when would she ever grow out of this blushing. 'I'm not your anything. Capeesh?' Oh God, why did she say *capeesh*. It made her sound like her brother, or whoever Austen really was to her.

'I love your accent.' Keller reached out and gently touched the inside of her wrist.

Rebecca caught her breath. 'I love your accent. Oh no, that's not what I want to say. At *all*. What is it with you? Who are you?'

Keller shrugged. 'Just a guy. Came over on the work exchange. You could do that. Maybe they'd like you in New York City. I like you.' Keller let his long legs loose beneath the table. His ankle touched hers.

'The work exchange? Yes, I know a couple of comics who've gone out to try their luck. At *The Gotham* and *The Stand*.'

'I never been to NYC. So tell me about your grandmother. Primmy, you say. That short for something?'

'Primrose. Primrose Anctillious Brown. She's a handful.'

'Well, she would be, she's your grandmother. I'd like to meet her. Listen, don't you think it's about time we exchanged numbers. We've know each other for almost twelve hours.

Here,' Keller gave her the phone he'd bought at Heathrow. 'Put it in. And then I'd like to put mine into yours.' He made a silly face at his hopeless innuendo and she found herself laughing, and handing over her mobile.

CHAPTER 15

The Secret

'Excuse me, Zachary. I need to read this text. My sister.'

'Please.' Keller smiled those wide cupid lips of his.

Rebecca often described her big sister as texting her hair out, ie tearing her hair out by text.

You wouldn't believe the stuff Prim had in her syootcase. A rubber mat to put in the bath. A fucking Lladró horse!! That's a china ornament!!!! She's given me some of our stuff to put away safely to make way for hers. I'm shitting myself she's not going back. Biggest news....

Wait for it....

I said wait for it....

Taransay

Yes Taransay

Is

On

The

Market

As in... for sale

A private sale, she said, through a friend of hers (like she has any). I've had a shufty and I can't find it online.

'Know something?' Keller leaned forward on his Ercol chair. They were back at *The Fuse* again. Rebecca's choice.

Safe ground, she reckoned. He let her call the shots, for now. He gave her the impression that she was in control. That's what they liked. He could tell that she had begun to enjoy his company. He'd studied her for long enough to know that she didn't make friends easily. In his expert opinion, this bothered her, but she pretended it didn't. Perhaps when she did embrace a relationship, though, she took it very seriously. He was happy with that psychology. The back of Rebecca's neck was on his hook and if he let it sink in good and deep, well then the big fish would come.

'What?' Rebecca loved the way he said that: *know sumphmn?*

'On hot days – and admittedly there are few, in Edinburgh.'

'It's Edinburruh, not Edinborrow.'

'If you say so, dear.' He squeezed her hand and she smiled. 'If I may continue. On hot days, out there in Victoria Park, if you lie next to the laburnums, their pods pop in the heat. And old fellas ride by in them carts.'

'Mobility scooters?'

'Yeah. This one guy was holding up a pint of ale and kinda making a figure of eight with his three wheeler. And laughing. Beer all slopping over the side of the glass and splashing onto his pants. Love this town.'

'Me too. I mean, don't get me wrong. Some nights I hear things which make me want to rush to hospital, dash into obstetrics, grab the ventouse and suck out my own inner ear workings. But warts, gashes and all, this is my home.'

'Not North by Northwest?'

Rebecca frowned a little. 'Primmy's got the old place up for sale. That's what my sister was texting about. Between you and me, I think Grandma's visit is taking its toll. I better step up to the plate.'

'She always stay with your sister? Primmy?'

'Yes. It's... well, it's just nicer there. And roomier. This is her September visit. She comes after the *Festival*. The *Wretched Festival*, she calls it. You prolly know my sister, do you? Colette? Follow her?'

'I don't do Twitter.'

'Hilarious. On foot, I mean. Do you follow her?'

'Don't be ridiculous. Why, I believe you're jealous, ma'am.'

'She's prettier than me. Blonde.' Rebecca looked at her mobile.

Keller did not take the bait, for a compliment. He was in charge of the maggots, not her. 'Oh now look. I lost you to your cellphone.'

'I'm sorry. I'm looking for the house. Where Primmy lives. *Taransay*. That's where we grew up. But I can't find it for sale online.'

'What's the matter? You're not upset, are you? Maybe if she's getting to that age, a move near her granddaughters is the right idea.'

'Well, I just wish... I wish she'd told me. I always had this idea that *Taransay* belonged to my parents. But,' Rebecca seemed to be searching her memory, 'No-one ever said that.'

'Why not ask them?'

'Who?'

'Your parents.'

'Oh my parents are dead. They died when I was very young.'

'God, Beck, I'm so very sorry. Damn, I... I want to hold you.'

'Oh it's alright, Zach. Really. It was a hundred years ago. I'm being mercenary anyway. It's probably Primmy's, the house.'

'Who has the deeds?'

'I have no idea. Don't lawyers keep them? I expect Primmy bought the place. Her and old Ralph. That's my grandfather. He's dead too.'

'She lives up there alone, your Granny?'

'Yeah. Now she does. Murdo sort of lived in till last year. Murdo was the… well, anyway, he's gone and all. Cancer. Didn't tell a soul.'

'Is it big? The house?'

'Bloody enormous.' She shook her head. 'Ok, so it's not on Rightmove. That's the online estate agent. Everyone uses that. Except Primmy, it seems.'

'I have an idea. Why don't I go up there?'

'Oh yes? Mosey, as it were?'

'Where is it?' Good, that's good, she would give him all the details now. Reel her in.

'Mallaig. That's the nearest town. I went to school there.'

Excellent. 'Did you wear a uniform?'

'Yes.'

'Mmm. I repeat, I want to hold you.'

In his dossier, Keller had a photo of her in school uniform. 'I could pretend to be a buyer. A rich buyer from Kentucky, or somewheres.'

'No, they wouldn't like that up there. It would come over a bit Donald Trump. They might think you would turn everything into a golf course. Or build a uranium warhead.'

'Well, you take me up there then. Show me around.'

'Really? You… you would like that?'

'Of course I would like that. I'm waiting to ask you out. I'm dying to. A proper date. I want to jump your bones, if I'm honest. But I don't know how it goes, for you. You seem kind of… reticent. Ambivalent?'

'Don't use up all your big words on me.'

'I really have no idea what you think of me, Rebecca Brown.'

'No, me neither. But I do, think of you. Know sumpin? I would be a terrible girlfriend. Lousy, I tell you. That's why I've never been one. A lousy date. A lousy lay. But I'm getting used to you a little. As a friend. I suppose we could go up to *Taransay*. I want to take her back there, Primmy. When she's ready. Escort her, really. She's a little bit upset with all the tests. She says she's not, but she is. She had a CAT scan. And a thorough MOT. You know what that is? It's like a test to see that your car's fit and well. But we say it for humans too.'

'MOT. Oh yeah, we have vehicle inspections in North Carolina.'

'North Carolina? I thought you were from Alabama. Loose Tusk, Alabama.'

'Oh I am. Just, I lived in North Carolina for a while.'

'Say vee hickle again.'

'Vehicle.' He grinned at her but his heart was hammering. This is what happened when he let his guard down. Mistakes. Fatal mistakes. 'Well, if you're escorting Primrose Anctillious back to her Highland home, would she mind if I tag along? Mallaig is so near to Glenfinnan. That's where Bonnie Prince Charlie raised his Standard. On the shores of Loch Shiel. There's a monument there. Sixty feet high and—'

'Zachary, I know. I was raised there. And I happen to know a thing or two about the Jacobites.'

'You do? Well, great! When do we leave? She won't mind, will she. The elderly love Americans. I've noticed that in Edinburgh.'

'I haven't a clue if she'll mind. All my life I've known her. She's been my mother, more or less. Usually less, but someone. She seems to be much more accepting of strangers now than she ever was when we were kids. It's like some danger has passed. We were kept at *Taransay*, like a plague would get us if we ventured out. Well, Austen was at his boarding school but even there, he was kept aside from society too.'

'Now then who would Austen be?'

'Never mind. Listen, if I suggest you come up with us to the old house, she could say *that's a marvellous idea, some male company.* Or she could say that's *the stupidest suggestion I ever heard.* It's not the dementia, she's always been like that.'

'Unpredictable.' Keller didn't like unpredictable people. A man who reminded him of Sanjay came into the Café. Two tiny kids at his hands, like mittens on string. 'You ever gone hungry, Rebecca Brown?'

She wasn't becoming used to his non sequiturs but still, they intrigued her.

*

Keller had visited Sanjay before leaving. He took five hundred dollars as a repayment for the tins he had stolen in those earlier years. But Sanjay wouldn't take it. He said he didn't mind hungry thieves. It was the greedy ones he called the cops on. Besides, Billie Ray had already been by with a recompense. Keller did not ask what form that recompense took. Perhaps gemstones were scattered around the County. One way or other, there was a lot of settling up to do.

*

Keller was not listening to Rebecca's reply about going hungry. He let her prattle on, the way women did. He was looking at her alright, but his ears were closed. He loved to look at her. Such a pleasing face. She liked to think she was smart but there was no real guile there. She was a mouse at his cat's claw.

Rebecca checked her watch. 'Shit, I better run. We're off to lunch. Me and Prim.'

'Oh, hey. They took me on. Start my new job next week. Gotta get some shekels into the coffers.'

'What job? Have I forgotten?'

'Driving a van. It's like an online grocery store. Shoplifter's nightmare.'

'You're a delivery driver?'

'That's me. I am here on a work exchange after all.'

'Well done you. Fantastic.' Rebecca leaned forward and the blushing rushed in.

'Come on, don't be shy. You were going to kiss me. Do it, for luck.'

She kissed his cheek which she could feel raising in a smile. 'Zachary Ness. You can't go swanning about the Highlands looking for Jacobite ghosts when you have proper employment.'

'Well, ma'am, it doesn't start till next week. A lot can happen in a week.'

*

These days, Primmy didn't have anything sweet, dietarily. As they were shown to their table in *Verdi's*, Rebecca was relieved about that. The prospect of her loping with her left shoulder down (as she now did), smartly to the *Ladies* for a purge, made her granddaughter stiff with horror. Rebecca was really hoping that Primmy would insist on paying for the meal, but knew this was unlikely. And then Primmy was *bitterly disappointed* that they weren't staying on for the ballet matinée at *The Festival Theatre*, the lights of which she could see twinkling from the restaurant door. The whole thing started to backfire from the entrance.

A distant memory of a rare meal out once in Arisaig rushed Rebecca's frontal lobe. Primmy had complained that the sherry was corked. Then the lamb was too well done. The mint sauce was below par. The owner appeared and said: *I don't think we are going to be able to please you*, and showed them the door. That same sentence ticker-taped across Rebecca's mind now: *Grandma, I don't think I am going to be able to please you.*

Primmy had a great deal to say about the food on her plate, in the last years. Today she thought she might try something gluten free. When the waiter arrived and Grandma suggested this, Rebecca said, 'Go for your life.' Rebecca herself was having seafood linguine. She ate quite well on the whole. Granola for breakfast with nuts and skimmed milk. Mango, strawberry, grape and banana with Greek yoghurt for lunch. And vodka for tea, if she wasn't performing.

'Where are you living now, dear?'

'Same place.' Primmy had only visited the flat in Muirhouse on one occasion and claimed the air in the vicinity didn't agree with her. She liked it much better in Marchmont with Colette.

'What happened to that nice young man you were sharing with, the one that sounded like a Baltic port?'

'Heribert. Heribert Königshafen.'

'That's him. Wasn't he a sailor or something? I thought he might do rather well for you.'

'Um, no. He's a carpenter. Old school. Mortise and tenon.'

'What was his name? Some kind of Baltic port.'

'Heribert Königshafen.'

'I don't suppose you ever gave him the come hither.' Primmy craned her head back to appraise Youngest Brown. 'You haven't got much in the way of sex appeal. Well, have you.'

'Probably not. But Heri got married to his boyfriend and now they live in Dubrovnik. He's still paying half the rent though, so maybe they'll—'

'Oh. I see.' Primmy's bony hand hovered over a bread roll. 'That's a pity. We could do with a carpenter up at the house. Colette doesn't talk about our projects anymore. Have you noticed? I believe she has quite given up on us.'

'Well no, that's because a decade has passed. And also, what was that other thing? Oh yes, you've put *Taransay* up for sale.'

Primmy put down her knife and fork but kept chewing. Her lips folded inwards now as she worked at food, like she had no teeth. 'How did you know about that?'

'Colette told me. It wasn't a secret, was it?'

'I don't really cook now. Can't seem to fancy anything.'

'I know, Grandma. You must try with the microwave. Just heat up the ones they deliver. They're delicious. Remember we tried them all and you loved—'

'Oh I can't stand those ones. And there's that funny little man who brings them.'

'Ronnie Corbett doesn't bring them. He just advertises them. Or rather he did.'

'I used to work with him, you know. I'm talking about before he died. And I was a dancer. And he was taller then.'

Rebecca didn't correct her grandmother anymore, not unless it was dangerous not to.

'Fantastic. I'll bet you had a lot of—'

'I don't really cook now. Can't seem to fancy anything.'

'I know what you mean.'

Rebecca didn't cook at home. She hadn't turned on an oven since the day she incinerated the King of Diamonds and all in his realm. Anyway, she didn't really get it about cooking. She expanded on this sometimes as a routine in her stand up. She didn't think people were thinking of food when they were watching Nigella. Unless they wanted to quenelle ice cream into her crevices.

'Skipper, I met someone.'

'A girl?'

'No, a man.'

'Oh that's right. Colette has the girl. You're going for a man. So hard to keep up.'

'Well, he's just a friend.' She wanted to say an unusual friend but thought better of it.

Primmy rubbed at her breastbone. She was getting a lot of heartburn. They'd got her Gaviscon but apparently it didn't *syoot*. She was clutching at herself and the whole point of the lunch at Verdi's was to relax her; to treat her, as it turned out.

'Well, Austen doesn't seem to have anyone. Which is good in a way, since he's living so far away. Down under, as they say, which I always worry is a bit rude.'

'I didn't think you worried about being rude. Oh I'm sorry. I'm a little tired.'

'Not pregnant, I hope.'

'No, not pregnant.'

'Menstrual are we?'

'We? Well, I'm guessing you're not. Sorry. I really am just a bit—'

'Ralph always had a steak, didn't he, Youngest.' Primmy prodded at her food. 'He used to say, didn't he, that he wanted to load up on hormones.'

Rebecca nodded, though she did not remember that. It wasn't going to really matter what her grandmother said, either today or in the future, Rebecca was going to try to agree. They would all have to. If there was one pointless thing to do with dementia, it was to try to disagree with it.

'Particularly testosterone,' Primmy said to Rebecca from behind a division she made with her hand, though everyone at the near tables could hear everything she said anyway. Maybe she needed a hearing aid? Her grandmother seemed to regard the hubbub of conversation as some kind of challenge. Primmy pecked hard in some stranger's direction, 'Oh God, he'll have some bad habits, you mark my words.'

In Rebecca's experience, it was an idea not to take the elderly to your favourite haunts because they were fairly critical and their reviews could linger in your psyche. And if that psyche was already troubled, it just wasn't worth it. Go somewhere dispensable with relatives, and make sure the seats are comfy. And avoid technical issues during conversation:

'Who runs the Internet, though?'

'No-one runs it. Different people.'

'Who, Rebecca? You don't even know.'

'Search engines. Companies, selling space.'

'But who owns *them*? Who's in charge overall?'

'There's no one person in charge. Next you'll be saying: but yeah, what is outside of our galaxy?'

'I wouldn't say *yeah*.'

'No. No, you wouldn't. You've hardly touched your steak.'

'It was an error, that choice. I need that thing for these.' She bared her teeth at Rebecca and signalled for her handbag to be passed double quick, though it was just inches from Primmy. 'Come on, Ralph,' she said urgently to her granddaughter, as if awaiting life-saving medication rather than her silver tooth pick. It was a shock to hear that, the first time. Primmy did not correct herself but did not address her late husband again during the meal. She did however want to discuss him.

'I have something very private and personal I want to tell you. Nobody knows. It will be just between us. Youngest and eldest. Would you like that?'

Rebecca was not at all sure if she would like that.

'Once upon a time, your grandfather had an affair. A relationship, I should say, since neither party were married. It was pre-me. Well, just as I was arriving. And Ralph, he was so very much in love. You could tell, just by the look of him.' She fiddled with the toothpick in her hands. The wrinkles in her face stretched and contracted with the ups and downs of a story. She was very expressive, old Primmy, both lingually and facially. 'And when I saw him, well, I set my sights on him. His look of love was very infectious and I fell for him quite without realising.' Primmy's eyes welled suddenly with the memory. 'I didn't understand that if I took away his love, if I took it for myself, then he wouldn't be the same, he wouldn't be the one I wanted anymore. Do you see?'

Of course Rebecca did not see but this was no time to say so.

'Ralph's true love… was not me. I stole his love. I took it from him with threats and lies.'

Rebecca laid her hands over her grandmother's. 'Put down the toothpick, Grandma, please.'

But Primmy pushed off Rebecca's hands and carried on scratching at the translucent skin of her own with the tiny weapon, till blood pricked the white linen tablecloth. The old lady's head started lolling from side to side like a bull speared at the withers. 'He was in love with a man. A man, do you see? Like Colette, but a man. I threatened to expose them. I told them they were obscene. Monsters, I said. Because I had to have him. And then, when I finally did, I wanted him no longer. Because he was gone, changed, empty. I killed him and instead of just hating myself for that, I hated him.'

Rebecca was too stunned to move.

Primmy looked up timidly, 'Have I turned you to stone? I have rather strayed from the point, haven't I?'

Rebecca could not utter a word.

'Why am I talking about Ralph? When what I wanted to talk about was Austen. Can you hear me, Rebecca?'

Rebecca nodded slowly.

Primmy snapped her handbag shut. She was ready to leave. 'Austen is coming home. I said we'd meet him there. At *Taransay*.'

CHAPTER 16

The Coupling

Keller was wearing his smart jeans. They were a little loose. He was eating less and hadn't been to the gym, so his muscle was receding. Last time he dressed up smart was the day he went to get his dad's urn and scattered his ashes in the creek at Horsepen.

Today, he was wearing that same white cotton shirt too, the one with those crazy buttons. Funny kind of thing to pick up for saying goodbye to your old man but the girl in the store had been very enthusiastic. She winked at him and he bought the shirt. Keller liked to think that he had a knack of putting together a room but he had no particular style or interest for adorning his body. On the rare occasion he went shopping, he liked something to simply catch his eye. And if that was just the girl serving behind the counter, fair enough.

Outside Rebecca's apartment block, Keller sat on the stoop, with the grey sandstone edifice climbing up three storeys behind him. It was windy and he hunched his shoulders up, hands tight in his jacket pockets. He hadn't been there long when Rebecca appeared at the end of her street.

She hesitated when she saw him. She had her hair tied up and he could see clearly that she was upset. He had picked a bad moment. She began to walk quickly again, her raincoat gusting up behind her, and as she approached, Rebecca avoided eye contact and busied herself with a search for keys.

'What's the matter, Beck?'

'What are you doing sitting there?'

'Have you been crying?'

'This is not like America. We don't actually sit on these steps. Well, some people do, but they generally have a bottle in a brown paper bag. Can I get past please?'

'Rebecca, wait. I'm sorry about following you. I want to come clean. You know I've been, kind of, obsessing about you. But it comes from a good place. I just… really like you.'

'Zach, I'm tired. I accept that you are one of those people who get hung up on performing folk. But you know me now. A little. I'm nothing special. I just want a bit of peace.'

'Jeez, I'm sorry.' Keller stepped back dramatically. 'I thought things were going well. I mean, slowly, but well. I thought you actually liked me.'

'Oh Zachary, I do. Of course I like you but I just…'

'Didn't go well then? Lunch with Primmy?'

'If you don't mind, I just want to drink some vodka and go to sleep.'

'You *are* special. You *are* something special. Look, vodka is not good for you. Why don't I make you a cup of tea and then, I promise, if you want me to leave, I'll leave.'

'Zachary.' Her mouth started to turn down and something very strange was going on at her chin. 'I… I just got some news.'

'Oh no. What?'

Rebecca shook her head miserably. 'And my grandmother, she wants to go home. Now. Tomorrow. I'm borrowing Colette's car.'

'Tomorrow? But I'm coming too. Aren't I?'

'Zachary, I don't know.'

'What time?'

'About three, I think.'

'Alrighty.'

'*Alrighty*? That's a real word then?'

Keller smiled his charming smile, even put a little tilt on that blond head.

'Nothing seems complicated for you, Zachary. You have an idea, you act. Me, it's all I can do to get by. Whatever it is that you think I am, or want me to be, I'm not. And today… I was coming back from my sister's on the bus. And there was this old woman. She kept saying to her husband, *No seatbelts, not on a train. No seatbelts, not on a train.* And it went on and on, in a loop, in her head. She was still saying it when she got off. Maybe she would all day, or for the rest of their lives. This is what is coming, for Primmy.' She shook her head more vigorously now, trying to expel the image. And for a second Keller was simply entranced with the dark wisps of escaped hair fluttering across her eyes.

'Fuck, it's blowy, huh. Let's get you inside. Wait.' Keller hopped down onto the sidewalk and stood in front of a middle aged man passing by. 'Look at me, sir. Take a good look. I'm going up there with this lovely girl. You are my witness. So if anything happens, be sure and point me out in the lineup.' Both the man and Rebecca looked bewildered. 'Come on, where's your sense of humour? You Brits.'

*

When Keller took off Rebecca's raincoat, she slipped easily into his arms, almost fell. He found himself blinking with astonishment but scooped her up. Their connection was instant, hands on skin like touchpaper and her flimsy claim on tiredness was torn to shreds. This is what they'd both been waiting for.

Neither of them knew just how much till it began. Inside the front door, they pulled each other's clothes off and she cleared the console table with a brush of her arm. Pens, envelopes, desk tidy, all clattered to the floor and he leaned her back over the wooden surface, trying to gauge the table's sturdiness.

She was breathing hard, shoulders lifting off the surface. He stopped for a second to take it in, the vision of her lying there, legs parting, those creamy breasts with hard nipples darkening. She reached for him and he entered her fully with one thrust. Rebecca gasped and tipped up her chin. Her eyes closed briefly and then her hands groped at his chest, like she was searching for her next foothold as she ascended. They were both close and he tried to slow down just a little, his grip more gentle now on her hips. She opened her eyes and stared at him, unsmiling. Lightly, he traced the fingers of one hand down from her hip and between her legs, but he stayed inside her. As he slipped his fingers back and forth, she turned her head to the side, a senseless language streaming from her, as she writhed like an animal caught in a snare. He couldn't tell if she was attempting words. Her voice was transformed. He kept stroking with one hand and with the other, gripped her hip once more. Rebecca arched her back as the orgasm began and Keller thrust harder so that he could come with her. The sound in her throat, became almost a hiss from a tire. He'd never had one like this, and continued to brush along the swollen folds of her so that she climaxed once more, her own hands squeezing the blood out of his biceps.

*

Later, in bed, Rebecca left him sleeping. She gathered up their clothes discarded at the front door and put on his white shirt with the lovely buttons. Something fell out of his jeans pocket.

She picked it up and put it on the console table with all the other bits and pieces she'd swept to the floor.

Her stomach growled and she padded into the kitchen, wondering what on earth she had to eat. When he got his grocery van, would they be able to steal food out of it? She opened the fridge. There was some dubious cheddar that might do for something if she cut the green bits off the sides. And some chorizo. She was sure there was pasta in the cupboard. Heri used to buy tinned tomatoes by the crate. There must be some of them left. Right, that was virtually a meal in the making.

Keller's hands were on her neck.

'Jesus! You scared the living daylights out of me!' Rebecca got such a fright that she felt tears spring to her eyes.

'Oh honey, I'm sorry.' He turned her around and took her in his arms. 'I didn't mean to scare you. Just can't keep my hands off you.'

Her fear was replaced with lust almost instantly. Is this what happens to girls when their virginity goes? They just can't stop? It's a race to catch up? She had thought it would be so awful, or so mediocre or so something that was so far from what it actually was: the best thing she had ever done.

Keller's fingers explored her thighs and then reached inside. By the time she was against the kitchen sink, she could feel the climax rising again. She'd had a thousand orgasms but never at the hand of another. How would she ever leave the flat again? And he, well, he could forget about that job. They'd get their own delivery driver and order in. They could set up a trough at the end of the bed and keep it filled up with lush slops; food requiring no cutlery. They could just guzzle down the calories as fast as possible, so that they could keep on task. The task of gratification. The joy of sex. At last.

'At last?' Keller kissed her throat.

'Nothing. You hungry?' She clung on to him as the last delicious vestiges of climax shivered up her spine.

'Starving. For you. And for food. But mostly for you.'

Her heart skipped a beat, just the way it did in stories. She loved everything about him: the oddness of him, the feel of him, the smell of him, the way he had wandered through naked but for one sock.

'Beck, what say we have a picnic. I love picnics.'

'Sure. Where shall we have it? Paris?' Immediately, she regretted saying that. Keller frowned at her and she could feel the blushing begin. 'Zach, I'm sorry. I was just kidding. You mean now. Well, it's getting dark. And there's the small matter of the food. But yeah, fine, let's have a picnic. The park?'

'The bed. A picnic in bed.'

*

As Keller had planned, he made sure she told him all about herself. Post-coital is the perfect time for revelation and getting her to give him her life story in infinite detail made his position much safer; since he knew so very much of it already. From now on then, if his knowledge should slip from him, he could easily say that she had mentioned whatever fact it was. Naturally, Rebecca Brown wanted to know the same about Zachary Ness. He gave her a mixture of fact and fiction.

Rebecca unscrewed a bottle of red wine. 'This is cheap muck, do you mind?'

'I mind very much, but I'll manage.'

'What was she like, your Aunt? What was her name?'

'Well, her name was Betty. She was alright. She put a roof over my head. Just as your grandmother did for you and Colette. And your brother. Austen, was it?'

'Yes, Austen. Isn't it a ghastly coincidence?'

'What's that, my love?'

Rebecca couldn't help it. She gasped. Yes, so it was a general term of affection but all the same, she was completely taken aback. This morning she had been a red riding hood virgin on her way to Granny and this evening she was a sex fiend with a half dozen orgasms under her belt and declarations of love from a gorgeous but slightly weird American.

'A coincidence that our parents died in car crashes. How old were you, Zach?'

'Oh, bout eight. It's a hazy time. You know. Now will be a hazy time if you ply me with this wine. I ain't used to it.' It was a lot of fun telling her stories though. He would make it all gruesome so's she'd look shocked and then take her in his arms to make her feel good again.

'Silly. Big bloke like you. Did your Auntie love you?'

Keller smiled. 'Auntie?' Fucksake, he'd already forgotten what name he'd given the Aunt. Thought he'd been so prepared for all of this. *Focus!* Keller plucked a hair from his thigh and put down his glass. 'Yeah, Auntie Betty. Well, I think she did, in her own way. She has passed on now too.'

'Is that why you upped sticks?'

'To the British Isles? Sure. Nothin' to keep me. I can always get my old job back though. They liked me there.'

'What happened to Aunt Betty? I mean, if it's alright to ask.'

'Well, it was pretty nasty. I won't get into the detail, but she had this bad leg. Her foot. She tore it on a coyote snare out there in… well, down by the creek. And my Aunt, she wasn't one for no doctors.'

'God, my Grandma neither. We were barely allowed out. School and back. And no loitering. Did your Aunt… what? Get septicaemia?'

'Gangrene. It was a whole lot worse than I realised. She'd just lost her little dog too. I think she just gave up, old Joya.'

'Joya?'

'Yeah. Joya. Uh, Joya was her dog. Died right after.'

'God. Of a broken heart? Like Greyfriar's Bobby. I thought you said she lost the dog before?'

'I get confused. My Aunt was depressed. It was such a depressing time. She locked herself in her room, Betty did. I used to rattle at that handle but she'd just shout for me to go away. Maybe it was her time. Wish I'd broke the door down earlier.'

Rebecca pulled the duvet up over her shoulders. 'She died? Right there in her room? Of gangrene?'

'Wet gangrene. It's a lot worse than dry.'

'My God. That's…' Rebecca swallowed hard. 'That's horrific.'

He liked seeing her unnerved. Gave him a real kick, knowing he could take her to the brink of ecstasy and horror both. 'A sorry sight. Leastways that's what the police said. I was away from Greensboro at the time. With my work. I regret that. I really do.'

'Darling, it must have been *horrible*. To come home to… that.' Rebecca put her arms around Keller and he burrowed his face into her neck, hiding his smile in that delicious nook above her collar bone.

It was true, he had been away at the time. After hooking up with Makayla, he quit school. He wasn't about to limp back into class after the catastrophe lunch out on Bodie Island. Only good thing about school was Makayla and he'd had her now, so he told her goodbye, immediately afterward. Simple as. She cried a lot. He virtually had to push her out the front door. She tripped up on his jacket lying on the porch floor. The rattling at the handle had been that journalist, Quindt. He'd no doubt come around sniffing for a story again, under the premise of returning the jacket Keller had left in his car after the prison visit. Keller wasn't interested in seeing the press guy and suddenly, he wasn't interested in seeing Makayla again. He could still picture her red-rimmed eyes staring at him in disbelief when he said, 'Beat it'. The girl collected her pride finally, he'd give her that. Soon as she understood his certainty, she pulled up her exquisite chin and left. Makayla never made contact again. He hung around her avenue in Fisher Park when he got his apartment up there a few years later. He went only in the holidays because he knew she was studying in Boston. Keller wondered if he could make her fall for him again. But she never appeared.

It was right after Makayla's defloration that Keller applied to the Hickory Recycling Center; that very afternoon in fact, and he was accepted. He knew he would be. He used to take the tourist tours up there and ask intelligent questions. They'd known him for years, used to ruffle his hair and make jokes about him being CEO one day. Soon as the paperwork was done, they wanted to send young Keller Baye on a course with three other new recruits, down in Jacksonville, Florida, the very next week.

Keller had inflicted the wound upon his Aunt in the bathroom, just after supping with those cretins on the Outer Banks. He removed three of her toes, with her own poultry secateurs. She passed out early on and he was able to fashion the wound into a snare injury in relative peace. Peverill barked all the way through.

Then the terrier followed Keller out into the yard, stopping only to cock its head as Keller dug up the crate. It started barking again as Keller held up the crossbow. The dog didn't attempt to move away, wasn't even smart enough to try to escape after the first arrow hissed on by, missing by an inch. The next landed plumb between the eyes.

When the opportunity of the training course arose, it felt providential. A perfect alibi. And the final solution to his domestic woes. Keller hadn't known what he was going to do with Joya after hurting her, but he could never have let her go free, that was sure and certain. With her getting more feeble by the hour, the trip to Jacksonville was timely indeed.

Keller had read up extensively on gangrene and he had a good idea of how long it would take for a woman of her size and age to succumb to the effects of deep tissue infection; and how the process accelerated when a body was deprived of fluid.

Whilst tucked safely away in Florida, it was Angelo who crept into the Baye's back yard in the middle of each night and let himself in to check on Joya. And when she died, two days before the end of Keller's training in extractives and mineral processing, it was Angelo who removed Joya Baye's restraints and unlocked her bedroom door.

It was years since Keller had last spoken to Angelo Peralta and he'd had to spin a yarn to a colleague over at the car accessories place where Angelo worked, just to get his cell number.

'Hey Angelo. You're a hard man to find.' There was silence at the other end of the line. 'Listen, I heard you got a baby. Little girl, that right? Congrats, bro.'

'Who is this?'

'It's me. Keller.'

'Keller. Please don't call this number again.'

'Aw come on. Don't be like that. Listen, I've got a favor to ask.'

It didn't take long to persuade Angelo to help. His old friend had a lot to lose after all, starting with his freedom if Keller were to go to the police with the story he now presented to his friend: of how Angelo alone had killed the tramp.

'It ain't the happiest of childhoods, having your daddy incarcerated for murder. Your little girl wouldn't like it one bit, you can trust old Kell on that one. What's your daughter's name?'

There was a long pause at the other end of the line.

'I said, what's your daughter's name, Peralta?'

'If I do this for you, Keller, I don't want to hear from you ever again. Do we have a deal? If you get in touch, with me or any of my family, I will kill you and then myself, to bring all this to an end. Do you understand me?'

'I understand. It's a deal. If I was standing there, I'd shake your hand. By the way, you'll need a mask.'

Beneath the manacles, Keller had wound thick wads of foam around his Aunt's wrists and ankles. Her jaw was clamped to prevent a powerful scream for help. All she was capable of making was a wild chimp sound which turned quickly to coughing.

Keller had stood outside in the street and you could not hear any noise coming from the upstairs bedroom, but all the same, he gave his prisoner something to think about when she started her muted ape thing. 'You take care with that now, Aunt Joya. Damaging the back of your throat, I reckon. Wouldn't want you to choke when you're all alone.'

Twenty four hours after getting the confirmation text from Angelo, Keller rang Peg Bellingham. She knew he was away. Said she was proud of him. Keller told Peg that his Aunt hadn't been answering his calls. He was worried, naturally. He told his neighbor where she could find his front door key, in a little bamboo box just at the foot of that big chokeberry bush she liked so much. Poor old Peg, having to climb those stairs to find the pitiful body and its hideous decayed stench. Peg Bellingham didn't deserve that.

*

The new couple in Muirhouse did not leave the flat for a picnic or indeed for anything. At one point, they both declared themselves a bit sore to continue but an hour later, they were hard at it again. In between sex bouts, their limbs tied fast like creeper, sucking up the sleep sap.

When hunger for food became overwhelming, Keller boiled up Heribert's pasta and mixed in the other meagre ingredients. Some out of date garlic salt saved the dish. He set the tray down on the ottoman at the end of the bed. Rebecca was standing at the wide open window, wearing his white shirt again. Below in the street, a couple of Russian girls jogged by, their conversation like a runaway typewriter. Rebecca came back to the bed.

'Zach? D'you always keep one sock on during sex?'

'I don't have a rule about it, Rebecca, no.'

She cupped his face with her hand. 'You have a little tic thing. There, in your cheek.'

'It's the burning need.' He threw her onto her back and grinned down at her. But he didn't look happy. He was like a blond wolf. It was the high cheekbones perhaps. Something lupine there. She felt the stirring again but struggled out from under him. 'We must, must, eat!' She crawled like a commando to the food and quickly forked up some pasta.

On his stomach, he did the same, hanging over the end of the bed. Mouth stuffed, he held up his fork. 'Now my girl, tell me all about your grandfather.'

'Oh now my grandfather. He was a character. Well, they both were. I appreciate them so much more now, though he's not here and well, she isn't totally either.'

'Did they get on?' Keller leaned over to lick tomato sauce from the side of her mouth.

'They did, mostly. Of course, she was an outrageous bully, but that kind of worked. They amused each other. Ridiculously eccentric, the pair of them. Goes without saying. They used to replace song lyrics. Silly old songs.'

'For example.'

'For example, you know that song, *There's a hole in my bucket, dear Liza, dear Liza*. Actually, that might be American. A nursery rhyme.'

'I don't know. If it's American. But yes, I know it.'

'Well, they'd just, like, use different words. One time, Ralph sang, *'There's a pube on my dinner plate, dear Liza, dear Liza.'*

'Really?'

'Guess you had to be there. You know my Grandma's greatest regret is that she wasn't one of the Beverley Sisters.'

'Has she got sisters?'

'No. And she used to use beautiful words. And he used to use ones that sounded funny.'

'What do you mean?'

'Like, um, perjink?'

'Perjink? What's that mean?'

'I don't know. It's Scottish, I think. He was a great fan of the Scots.'

'And her? Primmy?'

'Well, no, she wasn't, not at all. She kind of blamed the Scots, and Scotland, for her troubles. I think she likes Scotland now though. Because she could always leave, if she didn't.'

'You said she is leaving. That there was a realtor involved.'

'Oh. Yes. Do you know I hadn't given it any thought. Where she might be thinking of going, I mean. I guess we'll find out soon enough.'

'You could just ask her.'

'I suppose. Everything is so straightforward in your eyes.'

'Oh yeah.'

'Anyway, enough about them. I have a very pressing question, Zachary Ness of Tuscaloosa, Alabama.'

'Mmm.' She noticed that his fork clattered against his teeth with each mouthful he took.

'Have you always been this handsome?'

'I think so. I might have gone off a bit during adolescence. You know how boys do. They have that middle parting thing going on.'

'Oh yes, with the hair sort of slapped firmly down, like an Edwardian.'

'Um, yeah.'

'Another question. Why does your watch have two numbers missing?'

'Why does your body have a shirt around it?'

'Because it's yours. I nearly put on your jeans too. But then I thought… after all this, maybe you wouldn't like that.'

'Wouldn't like you smearing my blue jeans? You kidding?'

'Oh wait, something fell out of your pocket. A label, I think.' Rebecca dashed off to retrieve the label from the console table and then back to bed. 'Must've gone through the wash, I can hardly make out—'

'Give me that.' Keller grabbed the rinsed out label with his father's name and date of death.

'God, I'm sorry. I wasn't looking, I promise you, it was just lying there on the floor, you know when we took off our clothes. And I picked—'

'Shut up! Just shut up will you.' Keller got out of the bed, still clutching the label and went to the bathroom. He sat down on the edge of the bath and studied the label forensically. You could see. You could make it out. Not the date, that wasn't so important, but the name. Although it was faint, you could definitely read the name, *Othaniel Baye,* on the label he'd taken off the urn that day at Horsepen Creek. What a stupid, stupid mistake to keep it.

And he'd made other sloppy mistakes. Keller looked around at all her girly things in the bathroom. He wanted to smash it all up. Why was he fucking her again and again when he was supposed to be doing a professional job.

He'd got Rebecca to open her laptop so that they could look at her website together; like he didn't know it back to front and better than her by now. He made sure to distract her by sending her off to root around for food and whilst she was out of the bedroom, Keller whizzed around her computer files. There was nothing about her parents. Nothing in *documents*, nothing in *pictures*. She didn't seem to know what a USB stick was, so there were unlikely to be any of them kicking about. There wasn't a thing on Julia and Stephen Seawhite and no name pattern recognised in the search box. Why? Why was the next step not apparent? Everything else had fallen into his lap, so where was his objective now?

He looked at himself in the mirror and smacked the tic dancing across his cheekbone. He had been lazy and lustful. He needed to sharpen up.

Keller looked around the bathroom and saw a pink razor on the side of the bath. He grabbed it and slashed at his thigh.

Rebecca could hear the shower turning on, and the water ran for a long time.

CHAPTER 17

The Wigwam

When Keller woke up in his sleeping bag, the memory of Rebecca's shocked face rushed through him. He lifted the makeshift bandage from his leg. It didn't look too bad, considering he'd hacked at it with a razor. What an ass though. How could he lose control so quickly and so entirely? She'd been in tears when he left; fingers all trembling at her mouth, as he dressed to go:

'Zachary! My God, what have you done to your leg?'

'Nothing. I just walked into the thing.'

'What thing?'

'It's nothing. Just leave it.'

'Zach, it looks terrible. Let me get—'

'Will you stop calling me... will you just let me get the hell out of here? Will you, Beck? Can you do that?'

She could do that. Just sat in that bed of hers, covers all pulled up to her neck, like chastity was her overriding concern. And that whispering she did: *I don't understand. I just don't understand.*

But what did she understand by this morning? How in the good fuck was he going to find out what she understood, now that he'd scared the shit out of her and stormed out?

Keller had snatched the urn's label out of her hand, but she'd probably had a good look. She'd have googled his father's name by now. Othaniel Baye was plastered over the internet. And then she might've found a picture of Keller too. There was a photo in an article. Written by that press guy who'd given him a ride from the prison that day. What was his name? Shouldn't have drunk that red wine. Name was on that letter in the dossier. The journalist had written him a letter and left it in Keller's jacket pocket on the porch that day. Makayla had tripped over that jacket when he asked her to leave. He thought she'd tripped over it, but maybe she was kicking it.

Keller threw off the sleeping bag and rifled through the dossier, disgusted to see that his own fingers were trembling. He wasn't scared, it wasn't that. He didn't know fear any longer. But he needed to succeed. He'd worked so hard for all of this. It was his right, his duty. And anything which placed that success in jeopardy, filled him with alarm.

There. He found the letter. More of a note, carefully folded and torn from a lined pad. Neat handwriting.

Dear Keller

Sorry not to catch you at home today. Like I said, I'm working on a book on the Winston Salem Heist. I'd hoped your dad would be able to help me a little more. I have a strong feeling he is covering for the ringleader, the mastermind, if you will. This loyalty I imagine brings a fair recompense, which I believe he will want you to have. But it may cost him his life.

Have a think about that. Get in touch please if you'd like to help. Maybe together we can do something for your father? I believe Othaniel Baye is at heart a good man and he will want only the best for you.

You can reach me at the New York Daily.

Sincerely
Thomas Quindt

Bullshit. Othaniel Baye wanted one thing from his son: revenge.

Keller tried to find the article Quindt had written, where he remembered seeing his own photograph, but it wasn't in the file. Where could that be? He wiped the back of his hand over the sweat beading on his upper lip. He could only hope that if Rebecca found his picture online, she would not see the resemblance between Keller then and Zachary today.

How could his immaculate plan have developed these holes? He grabbed his MacBook to google his dad. He found the article straight away. His own name and his relationship to Othaniel were mentioned, but that was it in terms of *Keller Baye*. However, the picture was there. It was black and white, grainy and Keller scrolled through page after page. But didn't find a color copy. God, he looked like shit back then. His hair was unwashed, long and dishevelled. He was overweight. He had a beard, sort of.

Keller 'after' had very little in physical common with Keller 'before'.

He racked his brain to think of what he could say to Rebecca. He had no idea what she might be piecing together. He looked at the label again. He'd barely worn these jeans. Probably just been through the wash a couple times. But the name really wasn't too legible, particularly if you'd never heard it before. All the same, he had to prepare for the worst case scenario. And he had to win Rebecca back.

He rapped his head hard with the knuckles of both hands. 'Think. Think!'

If she had found Keller from North Carolina on the internet and recognised a resemblance, he could say that he was Keller's cousin. Yes, he could easily say that. He'd revealed by mistake that he had lived in NC. And if she asked about the heist, the execution, all that, he could say that his own family, Ness, was ashamed to be part of the Baye family. That Othaniel had been his uncle and that his mom was devastated by her brother's crime. Of course that wouldn't explain why the label had come to be in his pocket but he would think of something for that. Not too difficult, surely, in the scheme of things. Hell, he could even say he took pity on cousin Kell and helped him scatter the ashes. No, not that. Alright, as a last resort. It sounded convincing enough. Probably since that part was true. If his web of lies got too tangled, he could always become emotional: *Would you mind, baby, if we don't talk about it right now?*

Yes, get up now, clean this wound and re-dress it, and then make amends with Rebecca. What if she had already left with her Grandma for *Taransay*? Did he officially know the name of the house? Had she said it aloud? He just didn't know. But he could wait for her to say it, or manipulate her into saying it. Oh for God's sake, it wouldn't matter. He could just say *north* or *your home*. Jeez, why was he overthinking all of it. It's not like she was recording their every conversation. He slapped his wound and howled. He thought about Rebecca's sweet face as they made love on the table. He remembered the warmth and the scent of her when he awoke later in the bed.

'Knock, knock.'

'Go away, Denzie.'

'What? Was that you squealing?'

'Curtains are shut. That's my *do not disturb* sign. Doing my Jacobite research.'

'Fine. I've got that package. For Lewson? I'll just leave it outside.'

Keller closed the MacBook and got up. She was fifty yards away by the time he got the door open and called, 'Sorry Denzie'.

The package was on the decking. It hadn't been unwrapped. His heart sank as Denzie started to walk back.

Keller leaned around the door, keeping his wounded leg hidden. 'Good of you, Denz. Christ, it took its time, didn't it?'

'Yeah. It arrived last week I think. Someone put it on a shelf. Anyway.' She had her hands in her hoodie pockets and pulled them up towards him like she held little pistols in there. 'Don't suppose you've seen a wee dug.'

'A dug?'

'A dog. A wee dog.'

'Why are you asking me?'

'I'm asking everyone. Sheila's a pure basketcase.'

'Sheila?'

'It's her dog. Wee scruffy thing. Black. Nae pedigree. We're all going for a search of it later if you fancy—'

'No can do, Denzie. Meeting my girlfriend.'

'I see. Right you are, Zach. Good luck with your Jacobites.'

'Yeah, thanks Denzie. Thanks a lot. You're a pal.'

'Sure.'

*

The package was the Kinnect GPS Tracker. People used them for their kids, their pets. Sheila should get Kinnect next time.

Keller put in the tracker's SIM and downloaded the app to his cellphone. It wanted to know the name of the person under surveillance. He typed in *Funny Girl*.

Keller put on his pants and a t shirt. Barefoot, he took the tracker over to the other side of the campsite and hid it under a laurel bush. Then he jogged casually back to his wigwam, gritting his teeth over the pain radiating from his leg wound. Keller opened the app. The screen said:

Funny Girl
147m
26 degrees north east

He imagined making Rebecca swallow the tracker. It was too big really. She would choke. But he liked the idea of keeping things hidden in your insides. Just as he had done with his rainbow opal, before his flight on American Airlines: in his stomach and then his bowel. Keller slapped his leg again. 'Quit your daydreaming and get to work.'

In the shower block, he released his wound to the warm water and after a minute or two, it felt much better. It didn't do to let a wound get infected. He remembered Angelo on the phone, distraught about Joya, sobbing about the smell of rotting meat in her bedroom and begging to be released from the task Keller held him to. But Keller told Angelo to be strong, to just do this one last thing if he wanted freedom for himself and his growing family. Why did the men he admired, like Angelo and Billy Ray, turn to chickenshit.

In the wigwam, it was almost a quarter past ten. Rebecca had said they'd be leaving for *Taransay* in the mid afternoon. She was borrowing her sister's car, so she'd be going over there, most likely. Where was that? Some smart district. Anyway, it was time to make a move. He googled Hertz Rentals and found one downtown at Picardy Place. A *fait accompli* was what he needed to present to Rebecca Brown now.

Keller set his driver's license next to the mirror and tried to arrange his hair in the style of his good pal, Zachary Ness from Tuscaloosa, Alabama. Where was Zachary now? he wondered, as he worked the electric razor around, leaving a darker Ness-like growth above his lip.

'Where'd you go, Zach? Just… took off? Tie a rope around your neck?' Keller drew his fingers down his own neck and lifted his chin to his reflection. He thought he looked pretty much Zachary-ready.

*

Rebecca ignored the horn in the street for the first few blasts. No-one had ever tried to gain her attention in that way, so she assumed it was for someone else. When she eventually went to the window, Zachary was there grinning up from a black Mercedes convertible.

Everything in her head told her to get rid of him but most of her heart and all of her libido told her to unlock her door and lie down on her bed.

She opened the windows and he cupped his hands to shout. 'Not too late, am I? Beautiful day for it. Thought it might suit your big sis to keep her car.' He patted the roof of the Mercedes. Then he reached into the back seat and hoisted aloft a huge bouquet of red roses. 'Can I bring these up?' He got out of the car and locked it without waiting for a reply. Rebecca buzzed him in. She opened the door to the flat and sat down on the sofa. He came in with his big bunch of reconciliation, but she didn't move. He took them to the kitchen and set the roses in the sink.

'I owe you an apology. I'm sorry. I am truly sorry. For snapping at you. For walking out.'

'Zachary, I told you, I'm going to disappoint you. Whatever ideas you have about me, I'd never be able to live up to them. I'm just figuring out who Beck Brown is. I think you're a nice guy but—'

'Ugh. Don't say anymore. Beck please, let me make it up to you. Let me take you up to Mallaig. I'll disappear, do my thing over at Glenfinnan and Culloden Moor, and I'll only come when you call. I promise. I'm falling in love with you, Rebecca Brown. It's such an almighty effort to keep from kissing you right now.'

'What?'

'I mean it, sweet girl. My feelings for you are so strong.'

Oh God, if only he wasn't such a total honey. Rebecca threw herself into his arms, teeth clashing. Their mad Christmas morning hands let loose, tongues lashing, the brightness his eyes seemed to bring to hers and the call of pleasure in their throats.

They had sex like the three minute warning had sounded, ending up on their backs on the sitting room floorboards, semi clothed and sweating buckets. Rebecca smoothed her hand over the slippery ocean of his belly. She paused over each palpable swell of his six pack. How was she supposed to say no?

When they had recovered some breath, Rebecca said, 'Alright, come to *Taransay*. But on your own head be it. Primmy is hard work. Abrasive. Fractious.'

'I think I can handle Primrose Anctillious.'

'Well now, see, I don't like that. I don't like the way you say that. *Handle*.'

'I'm sorry. I'm nervous.'

'That's no excuse. You know, we'll pass Glenfinnan on the way but we need to just get home as directly as possible.

She's quite elderly. I mean, she seems tough, but she's not. Not anymore.'

'Yes, of course. Of course. I can go to Glenfinnan tomorrow. Or the next day. As long as I can be with you. Look at me.' Keller held out his quivering hands for inspection. 'Baby, please. Give me a chance. I want to meet your family. I want to know all of you.'

As he held her firmly in his arms, she hooked her chin over his shoulder, thinking: *In that case, we're going to have a problem, Houston. Because, actually, they're not my family.*

*

Primmy had eyes only for the Mercedes Cabriolet. She barely looked at Keller, just held out her hand meekly and walked around the sleek black sports car. Keller suggested Primmy sit up front. The old lady beamed and commanded her granddaughter to open her syootcase and find an appropriate headscarf.

'Come on, come on, Youngest. While the sun shines. I don't know what the weather is like in your part of the world, Mr… but here, one really must make hay. And it's September! Rebecca dear, do mind the *Lladró*!'

On the pavement, Rebecca rummaged carefully in the case and gave her grandmother a Paisley scarf. Primmy positively hopped into the front passenger seat. Her brain might be shutting down some neural circuits but her joints were still in their forties.

Keller lurched forward as Rebecca went to put the suitcase in the boot. 'No! Allow me. Trunk's a mess already. I'm not the neatest of packers.' The newly completed crossbow was inside a dark nylon carryall but he didn't want her anywhere near his stuff, any of it. He'd made six wooden bolts with steel tips. He'd planned on ten but events had moved quickly all of a sudden.

The journey took around four hours and was punctuated with one brief comfort stop. Whilst Rebecca waited for Primmy to exit the *Ladies*, Keller put his arm around her waist.

'Hey, Beck, we gotta stop meeting like this?'

'Cottaging?'

'What's that?'

'Meeting in toilets for sex.'

'Oh, is there time?'

'Sadly not. Oh Colette has texted.'

He couldn't give a shit who'd texted.

'Sorry. I need to look at this.' Rebecca read the text from Colette.

How's it going?

Austen messaged. He's at Taransay! Taxi dropped him and he says can you get supplies and he'll cook dinner? X

Rebecca's heart thumped in her chest. She replied.

ok

and ok

x

CHAPTER 18

The Browns

When Rebecca saw Austen sitting at the kitchen table, the years fell away. The exact same anxiety, the shape of it and the weight of it, formed in the pit of her stomach. She wondered if she'd ever be free of it.

'Hello Becky.' His hair was shorter but his look was the same. Shirt with button down collar, dark chinos. Austen didn't do sloppy. 'Where's Prim?'

'Austen. When did you get back?'

'Didn't they tell you?'

'Well, yes they did but I'd—'

'Oh God, don't say forgotten.'

'No, no of course not. Just, other events have kind of…'

'Overtaken my significance.'

'Still finishing our sentences.'

'Oh I never had to finish yours, wee lassie MacGraw. Just Colette's. How is she?'

'Very good. She's, well, she's happy.'

'Excellent. Who'd have thought. Now, these other events. You must apprise me of those.'

'You haven't lost your accent then. Or your manner.'

'I think they rather like me the way I am, overseas.'

'And yet you return. Primmy's at the shops. I said I'd change the bedlinen.'

'You've let her loose with the Landrover?'

'No, she hasn't driven that for yonks. It's in the barn. Doesn't even start anymore. We got a lift here.'

'Oh yes?'

'Friend of mine. He's staying. I mean he's going to be staying. They've gone to the Co-op. For shopping.'

Austen smiled. 'Ahh. That's nice. I haven't seen a Co-op in years. Cup a' tea, Youngest?' He filled the kettle. 'Earl Grey, for old time's sake?' He hesitated at the kitchen taps. 'I take that back, Rebecca. Thoroughly inappropriate. Can I say it's the jetlag. Just an hour stopover in Dubai and whoosh.' He made a forty five degree angle with his forearm which his sister took to demonstrate flight.

Rebecca reached into the cupboard for the Earl Grey. 'See now, this is a good time of day for the Earl.' She took the lid off the teapot. 'Been a long time, Austen.'

'Seems like yesterday. I hear you are a great success.'

'I'm not really. But I hear you are.'

'Well, that's grandmothers for you.' Austen put a little boiling water in the pot to heat it up. They prepared tea for two in the way they used to. She finding their favourite mugs, he forgetting the mat for the teapot.

'Your Scottie dogs have taken a few knocks.'

Rebecca looked at the chips on her favourite mug. Austen's was still pristine. Colette and Rebecca would never have dreamed of using it in his absence, particularly as it was emblazoned with the name of his contentious boarding school, *Beaton College*.

'I've missed you, Becky.'

Rebecca looked at Austen. There was something burning behind his eyes. Then to her astonishment those eyes filled with tears and her brother said, 'Why wouldn't you answer my calls?'

'I didn't know what to say. Primmy gave me all your news.' Rebecca waited for him to goad her, to bicker, but he didn't.

'How is Prim? I did ask her about her dementia test, but she was a little vague on it.' He smiled weakly. He looked older. Well, he would, they all would. 'Hey, I made a joke. Must run in the family. I mean, she just said the test went fine.'

'It did, I suppose. Though she does have dementia. She's alright. For her age, she's bloody remarkable.'

'You know, she insists on ringing a landline. I have to get one wherever I am. She is the only person still using a landline.'

'Yes.' Rebecca smiled. 'With me too. When mine rings, I always get a fright. Like it's the police.' This was the first time Rebecca had had Earl Grey since that last breakfast with Austen, all those years ago. 'So how've you been?'

Austen shrugged, nodded. 'Good. Have you ever said that when Grandma asks? *Good, Grandma, I'm good.*'

'Oh yes, I've told her she should get up a petition to reinstate the phrase, *I'm fine.*'

'She hung up on me once, when I said I was *good*. So that's worth bearing in mind, if she's really getting on your tits. Because it's not going to be easy, Becky. You realise that. Alzheimer's. It's not for the faint-hearted.'

'It's not Alzheimer's, Austen. Who told you that? She is forgetful in the way that elderly people are forgetful. This is the beginnings of dementia. Let's not get hysterical.'

He drew breath to object and then capitulated. 'So, a comedienne.'

'A comedian.'

'Whom do you approximate? Whom that I might know?' Austen lifted his chin like he was making way for his high

Victorian collar. He just didn't speak like people of his time. And he tweezed his words from between his sharp teeth.

'I approximate no-one.' She could have told him that critics compare her to Sara Pascoe, (whom she revered) but he wouldn't know who that was.

'You haven't changed, Youngest.'

'Should I have?'

'Can't we just... try and get along. You know, water under the bridge. That kind of thing.'

'Well, the thing about getting along, is, you usually have to get along. What we more realistically could do, is make a good show of it, for Primmy.'

'Agreed. Let's just, uh, turn the clock back. Shall we, Becky?'

'Turn the clock back? To before you set fire to my childhood, you mean?'

'Oh Rebecca, come on now. You know that's not how it was.'

'You never even gave me the fucking sixty quid back.'

He reached into his jacket for his wallet. 'You want it now?'

'Damned right.' She held out her hand.

Rebecca knew that all families had their troubles; that they abused one another as a safety slip road on the carriageway of their life, because no-one else would tolerate that vile behaviour. But was Austen's vile behaviour some kind of front, so that he could hide his loss? Was his expensive education a way of making up for his parents' death? Well, it was a squandered privilege, in her opinion, since Austen was a walking misery. A dark storm was almost visible over her brother's head. If sorrow had made him hastily construct a hard front as a boy, well, that front had well and truly calcified.

'I don't know who you are, Austen. I never did really. What got into you? What got into you your whole life?'

'Ah, well now, that is what I'm here to tell you.'

*

Keller had been a little put out when Rebecca suggested he go to the store with Primmy. He'd just driven a good way north, with the wind battering at his head and shoulders, and now he was being sent on an errand. It didn't seem very hospitable and her explanation of wanting to spend a moment alone with her brother didn't really cut it for Keller.

But then he saw that this invitation to be alone with Primmy was simply his divine right. Like a light being shone on a path, fate was intervening. Keller hardly had to make any decisions for himself now. A higher hand was directing. They were coming to him of their own accord, these *Browns*. Rebecca was asking him to take Primmy. The grandmother was being offered up, like a gift. The pack were gathering on their homeland but Rebecca was allowing one among them to be separated already. She was virtually inviting him to pick Granny off.

'Don't keep her out too long, Zach, will you? She'll be totally knackered. Maybe put the hood up too?'

'The hood? Why what's wrong?' He liked to annoy her, where he could do it undetected.

'No, not the bonnet. The roof of the car. It's cold. It's too cold for Primmy. But she loves it at the shop. Let her get whatever she wants.'

So, she wanted him to carry on shepherding her elderly relative around and hunting down supplies, but now there was a tight time limit and temperature control? The fuck?

Keller pressed the button to retract the roof and glanced sideways at Primrose Anctillious. What age would the old girl be? Eighty? Eighty five? A good age. Look at those old lizard hands, clutched together.

'Cold, Mrs Brown?'

'A little.'

Keller didn't put on the heating.

Once they had shopped for what was, in his opinion, an unlikely combination of ingredients at the local Co-op, Keller expressed a powerful need for a jar of ale.

Primmy was tired and would have liked to get home but she did want to express her gratitude to the kind young man and she too was more than ready for a small restorative.

'There's *The Chlachain* not far from here. Would that syoot? I don't normally set foot in that kind of establishment but I would like to repay you for chauffeuring us all this way.'

Did she really believe the cost of a pint would cover today's expenses? Or did she think he was staff? Stupid old trout. Had she put in one honest day's work in her whole life?

'Mrs Brown, there is no need. It was my pleasure. It's me who must repay you, for your hospitality at *Taransay*.'

'Oh yes.' Primmy had forgotten about that. She didn't have the energy to stifle her sigh.

The inn wasn't quite what Keller was expecting. It was fresh and modern. He'd been hoping for a grand inglenook fireplace with flames crackling over logs and old men in tweed with cowed collie dogs at their heels.

'Now what can I get you?'

'A dram. Thank you, Mr...'

'You look a little pale, Mrs Brown. Can I get you a cup of sweet tea to go with that whisky? By way of a chaser?' Keller smiled warmly at the old lady but it looked more like a sneer to Primmy. She felt uneasy suddenly, but she nodded. Exhaustion from the windy journey pressed down on her slight shoulders and she pulled her wool cardigan over her chest.

When the barman was totting up the bill, Keller slipped the powder from its sachet into the tea.

'There's bowls of sugar at the end of the bar there.' The barman jerked his head over to the spot described.

'Thanks. I guess she's sweet enough.' The ethylene glycol certainly was.

*

Rebecca felt a shiver weave through her vertebrae. Austen was going to make some sort of confession, or revelation. Her brother was suggesting that he'd flown half way across the globe to share a confidence with her. Still reeling from the injustice meted out to her beloved grandfather, Rebecca had to ask herself if she was ready to hear Austen.

'Well, that sounds…'

'Momentous, Rebecca. It is.'

'Right, well perhaps we need to drink something a little stronger?'

'Took the words right out of my mouth. Has the central heating improved?'

'It's worse. Anyway, Primmy won't have it on till October.' Rebecca checked her phone. 'I expect you've noticed there's no signal here. I thought they'd be back by now.'

'What's his name? Your man.'

'He's not… his name's Zachary. Listen, the network kicks in about a half mile up the road. I better tank up there and see if there's a message. They should really have been here by now.'

'I'll come with you. It's pitch black out there. You forget, living in the city, how dark the countryside is. Physically, I mean.'

*

Primmy's speech began to slur before she had even finished her 'tea'. 'You like her, my granddaughter?'

'Oh yes. I like Rebecca very much.'

'We had no idea, about the comedy. You know what she used to have in mind?'

'For what?'

'For a career. Forgive me, I keep forgetting your name. It's nothing personal you understand. My memory's not quite—'

'It's Zachary.'

'Zachary. Oh where was I?'

'You were saying she had an alternate career in mind. Rebecca.'

'Oh yes. Well, she used to think she would visit stately homes which were for sale. All dressed up, she was to be. Passing herself off as Lady So and So. And pretending she was going to buy the property. And in the course of this, well, scam I suppose we'd have to call it, Rebecca would stay for a few days. You know, to get a proper feel of the place, as so much money was involved. And naturally, the incumbent Lord and Lady would wine and dine her. Then she'd planned to tell them she'd go away to think about it. And simply move on to the next one.'

'Not the most secure of career plans. In my humble estimation, ma'am.'

'What age would she have been then? Eleven?'

'Search me.'

'No, but she was funny, Mr…'

'Zachary.'

'Zachary. She'd make us laugh ever such a lot. Anyway, it seems to be an actual profession, the comedy, so good luck to her. What line of work are you in, Mr…?'

'You look tired. I mean, really tired, Mrs Brown. Well, I told Rebecca that I was starting a new job next week. But I just made that up. I'm not great at lying. I could use some practise and so I tried out a bunch of nonsense about being a delivery driver. She believed it.'

Primmy's mouth suddenly sank inwards. 'I say, would you mind, I'm feeling rather dizzy and I really must use the lavatory.'

'Come on, old girl. Let's get you in the car.'

'Old girl? I must go to the lavatory.' Primmy looked for the bartender but he wasn't at the counter.

Keller bundled Primmy out to the Mercedes and by the time he'd belted her into the passenger seat, her eyes were half shut and her protests meek and incoherent.

'C'mon Prim. Let's get you down to Belford Hospital. That's in Fort William. You been? Had one of these replaced?' He prodded Primmy's right hip fairly hard but she didn't respond.

Inside Primmy, her kidneys were battling the first assault of the ethylene glycol. Calcium oxalate crystals were accumulating fast and with a history of pyelonephritis, it wouldn't be long till Primrose Anctillious Brown was in acute renal failure. At her age, there would be no road back.

Keller fetched a Craghopper fleece from the trunk and pulled it on. He could feel the empty sachet in his pocket. He should take care to get rid of it. He didn't want inquisitive Rebecca finding it. He got back in the car and lifted Primmy's wrist. Her pulse was weak.

It hadn't been cheap, buying antifreeze in a powder form. Over three hundred dollars. They would probably have confiscated it at the airport, if some sniffer dog had liked the scent of if in baggage handling. But it wasn't illegal to carry. Just a vehicle product, after all.

'I have a feeling that you are no longer conscious, Mrs Brown. That's just plain rude. And hey, you didn't get to telling me your real surname yet. The one you've been keeping from everyone. Naughty.' Keller slapped Primmy's hand. 'Well, I'm a patient fella. And we ain't in no hurry. Right? Just look at these stars. Do you think it's possible that they're the same as the ones in Greensboro?' Keller thumbed Primmy's eyelids up. 'Yup. Fixed and dilated. I think we need to get you to the Emergency Room.' Keller turned over the engine. 'See who we can get to come follow us.'

*

It was a beautiful night at *Taransay* but once they got past the lamplit driveway, the black came down upon Rebecca and Austen like a velvet cloak.

They shone their phones on the tarmac of the main road and walked briskly towards the hope of a signal.

'It's almost nine o'clock, for crying out loud. Where the hell can they be? He can't have forgotten where *Taransay* is. He dropped me here, like two hours ago.' Rebecca paced and turned on the spot, as if she was dowsing for water. 'We're right on the main road, how hard can it be to find his… oh wait. I've got one bar. There's a message. Zach's written at 8.37.'

Beck, something bads happened to Primmy. Went to the store and on the way home, she kind of collapsed. Im on my way to Fort William. Satnav found Belford. Ring you from there x

'Oh my God.' Rebecca handed her mobile to her brother. 'Read this.'

'Come on, Becky. We'll take the car.'

Rebecca was phoning Zachary but it went to voicemail. 'Bugger. Austen, forget that. The Landrover will never start. We'll need to get a cab. But Gordy's not doing it anymore. I'll ring him and see if someone else—'

'No, we've got a car. Come on. Run!'

'Colette said you came by taxi.'

'I did. Look, we're wasting time. There's a car at the house. Another car. Trust me. Let's go.'

In the light between their phones, Austen held out his hand and she grabbed it. They ran all the way back to *Taransay* and as they got near the red sandstone façade, Rebecca looked up at the arched window which was dimly lit from the floor below. There was someone there. The silhouette of a man. Someone she knew but had not seen for a very long time. Rebecca stopped in her tracks and broke her hand free from her brother's.

'What the fuck is Uncle Neil doing here?'

CHAPTER 19

The Uncle, the day before

On 'Uncle Neil' days, Julia Seawhite was a bag of nerves. The physical persona of the man, his face, and his body of course, had changed a number of times over the years but she only ever knew her contacts as 'Uncle Neil'.

There was news, *important news*. That was the message she got yesterday. The trips were always scheduled within twenty four hours of receiving a message. And whatever Julia had planned - admittedly nothing more interesting than work usually - had to be arranged around Uncle Neil. *Important news*. Of course, there was always news of her family but she tried to remember if the word *news* had ever been preceded by *important*. Could this be it? Could this be what she'd longed for?

Julia felt the itching at her elbows and pulled up her shirt sleeves to apply the E45 cream. As she rubbed it on her skin, she glanced at the clock. He was arriving at 10.00am. They would spend two hours together and then he would leave. That was the drill. The elation she always felt just prior to the meeting with *Uncle Neil* was a stark contrast to the emptiness which engulfed her afterwards. During the two hours, Julia would gobble up and digest all the information and when the wheels of the agent's car started their crunch on the gravel to depart, her chest hollowed out again.

From a limited selection proposed by the Central Bureau of the Witness Protection Programme, Julia Seawhite had chosen this location, Tongue, at the very northern tip of Scotland. This stunning spot mirrored – at a two hundred mile distance – the environment where the children were to grow, for all those years.

And Julia had wanted to grow something by her own hand too. She had to put her very fingers to use in the land, in the icy turquoise sea. Propagation felt crucial, in order to withstand the loss of her family.

Julia Seawhite had secured employment at the oyster farm in Tongue. Last year it had been taken over by a Russian firm but she had kept her position as manager. This morning she'd supervised two newly arrived Ukrainians as they turned all the oysters over in their mesh bags, so that the molluscs could feed more easily on the seaweed free side. The recruits had to turn over a thousand oysters, before the tide came back in.

On her cctv monitor at home, Julia watched a silver saloon car coming down her driveway. Her stomach turned over. How many agents like this one had she met over all these years? How many *Uncle Neils*? Eight? Nine? She couldn't even remember their faces. Though she could recall certain things they'd said about her kids:

Emma got a detention for humming in maths.

Tilly sold her roller blades for diet pills.

Dominic joined the debating society.

Uncle Neil never had all the detail or the exact circumstances. He never knew how Tilly had got the roller blades in the first place. He didn't know what motion Dominic was debating. And Emma was always an enigma. Julia became intensely irritated not to be getting these details about her children's lives and she made notes during every meeting, so that one day, she could ask them in person, and hoped they'd remember.

Of course, the Uncle Neils didn't use the children's real names. The agents referred to the children by their fictional names: Austen, Colette and Rebecca. Their mother remembered the day the new names were picked. Someone suggested they should choose other favourites that had been on the possible lists; the nearly-rans, when the children were born. But that idea hadn't appealed to Julia and at all. They were who they were. It felt like cutting the cord, to give the children new names. It was the hardest thing she had ever done, to give away her own flesh, to Stephen's parents. She had regretted the decision for every minute of her life since, yet Julia knew that it had been the best choice for them, for everyone: to stay alive.

An attempt was made on the Seawhites' lives during the trial, before either Julia or Stephen had even taken the witness stand. It was in the early morning, and there was a brief downpour. You do not expect to be targetted in the rain, as you hurry along in a country where no-one knows you. As they alighted their cab at the North Carolina Supreme Court in Raleigh, the commuters hurried by with their umbrellas aloft and their windshield wipers whipping from side to side. The married couple felt as anonymous as any foreigners, but then a sniper shot at them over the traffic and passers-by. A paid assassin fired bullets at them, from a tree on the north side of East Morgan Street. This beautiful City of Oaks, which they had admired so much and where they had celebrated Julia's victory in the bridge tournament, now held a killer in one of those oaks and his sight was set upon them. They heard the first bullet fizz by on the left and the second one hit Stephen. The bullet passed through his shoulder blade and into his neck, fractionally missing the carotid artery. The police found both the bullets: boat tail with cupronickel jackets, designed for ballistic performance at distance. Of the shooter, however, there was no sign.

The trial was postponed for several days as Stephen received treatment and for the District Attorney to persuade Julia that they needed to go ahead with their essential testimony and get these heist people behind bars. When she refused because her family was in so much danger, the entire West Virginia Judiciary seemed to crowd in on them. The State Governor was deeply concerned. In Winston Salem, the Chief of Police and the Mayor were extremely upset. The families of the victims were distraught. A representative from each official body came to see Mrs Seawhite, as she sat by her bandaged husband in the hospital, with three armed guards outside.

Just days before, they had been so happy: celebrating the win, buying presents for the kids, desperate to get back home. They even talked of having another child. Then with no warning siren, war broke out on the streets of Winston Salem. And Othaniel Baye parked his old cab outside that florist's.

It was the first time Stephen had accompanied Julia to a tournament. She had been selected to play for the United Kingdom in contract bridge's World Olympiad. The dates fell over their 10th anniversary. They'd married a week after Dominic was born, in a registry office with rings from the Kay's catalogue and flowers pinned to their suits, plucked from their witnesses' garden. On each anniversary thereafter, they wore those same flowers, which is why they had gone to the florists in Winston Salem that morning. What were the chances? Julia supposed that is the question every victim and their family asks about every accident. On the day of the heist, Stephen had a black-eyed daisy in his buttonhole and Julia had a peony. As they'd turned to leave the shop, the assistant in the florist's said, 'Hey, don't forget your panda.' And then the gunfire started.

It must have been a good half hour later when William K Yearwood's guts spilled on the pavement. He was the last person to be killed that day.

And the Seawhites lost their lives.

As Julia's protests went on at the hospital in Raleigh, pleading to withdraw her statement and return to her children, the North Carolina Supreme Court were impatient to restart the trial. The sympathetic smiles were put away, one by one. The cajoling stuttered to a stop, and the leather briefcases opened. The Seawhites were given their subpoenas. Stephen's pain medication was taken down a notch so that he was 'fit to receive' the document.

The only people who could help everyone get what they wanted, was a couple from England who'd been there for a game of cards. The jury were given 'unbridled discretion' over the sentencing. The stakes were so very high. North Carolina had never seen such a massacre and they needed justice. The city, the State, the whole country, were gunning for Othaniel Baye and Lillius Queen.

The Seawhites gave their evidence in a private room by audio link to the Supreme Court and after their return to the United Kingdom, they were tragically killed in a motorway accident. That's what the world was asked to believe.

*

The very first *Uncle Neil* wondered, 'Well, what about a name of someone in a book for your kids? Characters from a novel?' Julia could not now remember the first agent's face, nor the voice which had proposed this for the naming. Her initial reaction was that this was quite absurd. What the hell would she pick, Robinson Crusoe? But in fact, she and Stephen did finally settle on favourite authors: Jane Austen, and the French novelist, Colette, who was one of Stephen's heroines. Julia's other choice was Daphne du Maurier but Daphne would have been too much for little Emma, and so her mother picked 'Rebecca', the title character in du Maurier's wonderful book.

Mrs Seawhite herself had another name during her residence in Tongue.

Of course, Julia never referred to the children by their real names. Even when she was speaking with Neil, she would call them Austen, Colette and Rebecca. Not since the trial, had she referred to her children: not once, to another living soul, except those in the Witness Protection Service.

Julia opened the front door to greet the agent this morning. It was the same Neil as last time. In fact, for almost a year this one had been visiting. She was not supposed to ask the Neils anything about themselves. This hadn't been stipulated but had quickly become clear, all the same. Any question or remark that was considered irrelevant to the *case*, was quickly rebuffed or ignored. Julia Seawhite learned to keep herself to herself. That was how it had to be, if they were to be safe in their beds.

Seeing that her kitchen window was open, Uncle Neil called from his car, 'Good morning.' He held up his hands to the sunshine, as if to say *how about that*.

Julia looked at her calendar. Early this morning, she had turned the page to the new month. A picture of sea otters and the logo of her oyster company. Was this the month and the year? Today was the 1st of September 2021. Othaniel Baye had been executed on June 23rd. Lillius Queen was weeks past her expected survival date. Would today, dear God, would today at long last, be the day?

Knock on the door and Julia held her breath for a second before going to answer it.

'Good morning, Neil.' Julia extended her hand towards the agent.

She wanted to pull him by the collar into her sitting room and push him into the armchair. She wanted to jab him with a cattle prod till he spilled all the beans that grew in that other world. But she knew better than to hurry *Uncle Neil*. The Witness

Protection Service knew that haste was how mistakes were made. And mistakes cost lives.

In the kitchen, Julia had the coffee ready and without asking him if he wanted tea – they never did – she lay the jug on the table with mugs and milk. She didn't have any sugar, so she never offered that. She brought the tray into the sitting room where Neil was now seated on the sofa.

'How's the oyster business, Julia? My God, if the weather was like this every day, we'd all live up here.'

'Business? Oh right, well, business is booming. Another farm in Lancashire has been infected with the herpes virus. So we can't meet demand. Could have half a dozen farms here and still not meet demand. How's business down at the International Crime Agency? Steady enough?'

Neil smiled magnanimously and put his pocket file on the coffee table. They never brought laptops and though of course Julia used a computer at work, she was discouraged from having one at home, or any smart device. The temptation at 3.00am would have been too great for her, they all knew that. Sleepless in her bed, she would have succumbed to Google, one of these years, one of these months. Her urges to regain her children had never lessened, in fact the need only strengthened. And it was just too dangerous to search online. Skip tracers could find her all too easily.

The agent snapped the band on his pocket file. 'Oyster prices are rocketing. I read about it. You could open your own farm, you know?'

Now this was new. No *Neil* had ever had any ambition for her in the past.

'That's not really where my hopes lie.'

'No. Well now.' He flipped open the file and brought out the photographs.

Julia Seawhite always cried. Right back at the very beginning, she tried not to, but it was impossible. The Uncle Neils looked on with equanimity. Today's Neil looked sympathetic, caring even. She wasn't used to that, and she didn't like it.

Dominic's picture was first. Julia could barely make him out though. He was wearing a Panama hat and sunglasses. In the next photo, he was in a bar. He was laughing in this shot but she rarely got the impression of happiness from Dominic. She had done a terrible thing to her son. Boys don't let go of their anguish, especially when their mother is the perpetrator.

'He's been in the Bonaparte basin. Western Australia. Doing brilliantly.'

'Oil fields again?'

'No. Condensate and liquefied petroleum gas. He seems to move with great ease between these exports. The brokering is his speciality though. You should be proud.'

How irritating that the agent should tell her what to be feeling. What could he possibly know about getting monthly photographs of your children?

Emma's picture was next. She looked as if she were mid-flow at a gig, the microphone in her hand. Julia knew her younger daughter was funny. She wouldn't have necessarily predicted that Emma would be a stand up comedian but when Julia was informed of this choice, she wasn't surprised in the least.

'Rebecca has a boyfriend.'

'Oh!' Julia's hand flew to her mouth. The tears came again. She needed them to find love, to be in loving arms whenever possible. Now both her daughters had someone. 'Is it serious?'

'Too early to tell. He's from the States.'

Neil could see the fear clouding Julia's eyes.

'No, don't worry. His name is Zachary Ness. From Alabama. Our records show that he is an aid worker in Central America, generally. He's here on that Work Exchange Programme.

'Oh yes, I know it. Something President Descher rigged up, to win over the youth. We get applications at work but Pyotr just deletes them.'

'This is his picture, the boyfriend. Zachary Ness. Handsome. Though I'm no judge.'

'Hmm.' She didn't like the look of him but there was no rational way of explaining that so she withheld judgment and hoped to seem neutral. 'Looks alright. What does Colette think?' Her middle child, Tilly, was her benchmark.

'She hasn't met him. Like I said, it's early days. But Rebecca seems happy.'

'But there's something wrong. What?'

'Well maybe nothing. But an anomaly. You remember when Rebecca started searching for you online last new year. We expected this, of course. We knew she'd want to fill in the detail one day. But she suddenly stopped searching. You remember that? I think it was in the holidays back at—'

'Yes, of course I remember. I live for every morsel you give me. You know that, Neil.'

'Yes, I know that. So, she just started up again. At home, on her laptop. We wonder whether this has some connection to her boyfriend. Perhaps just sharing a confidence. In happiness. This is not necessarily a bad thing. Not at all.'

'But you said back then at New Year, Emma was looking for birth records. You said she was interested in heritage. I distinctly remember that—'

'Yes, I talked to Dominic about it. He said that he had accidentally given Emma a false impression many years ago. And that he had taken care of it.'

'What you do you mean a false impression? You didn't tell me that? What false impression?'

'I didn't know about it till I got in touch with Austen on this new search.'

'Well what did he say?'

'Nothing. Just what I've told you. He said it was something that happened a long time ago. And that he had sorted it. He wouldn't go into detail. Look, Dominic has been with us the whole way. We have to trust him.' Neil didn't trust him though, none of the agents had.

'Of course I trust him. I just… need to know everything.'

'Julia, I don't control them, your children. These blips come up. It's not The Truman Show.'

'No, it's a lot weirder than that. *Blips*?'

'Blips isn't the best word. But anomalies come up. They always have. We deal with it.'

'Neil, I don't mean to be ungracious, but I have been *dealing* with this, for decades. You've been assigned for a year, maybe.'

'Two. Two years I've been working for you. Two and a half, actually. Look, Emma searched briefly about… ancestry. It's normal for orphans. Primrose and Ralph admitted that they were never very good at answering questions. Your daughter has a good life. She is making her way. Like all of us, she looks for… let's say meaning.'

'You're lying. Or omitting. About Emma. I hate it. I hate all of this. It gets worse. Worse and worse, not better. I just keep losing.'

'Julia, try not to let it get to you so much.'

Mrs Seawhite looked at Neil with unabashed loathing. 'I don't think we're going to need two hours today.'

'Don't be foolish.'

'Fuck you.'

'Julia, please. I need you to listen to me. Will you do that? I promise I'll make it worth your while. Rebecca is doing well. She was the one who didn't know. It's natural for her to seek...'

'The truth?'

'Listen, a lot of people search for you. A lot. Random folk, conspiracists, car crash enthusiasts, you'd be surprised. There's even clubs who go in for this kind of thing.'

'Clubs?'

'Yes. Clubs who study, I don't know, freak accidents.'

'Right. That's good to know.'

'And we knew Rebecca would be curious. From the way she conducted the searches, it looked like, well, it seemed that she knew her mother was Julia Seawhite and that she died in the crash. But... I'm not supposed to say this.'

'Tell me. Now.'

'She believed you were, well she thought you were her adoptive mother. And she wanted to find her biological one.'

'That's ridiculous. How could that happen? Why didn't you give me this detail properly?'

'You always get a bit down at New Year. At the time, we thought that—'

'We? Who is *we*? You don't know me, Neil. I don't know you. I need this to stop. My children need this to stop. When in God's name will these people die and leave us in peace? I should never have testified against those monsters. The FBI fucked me over and you lot too, I have no doubt. Collateral damage, that's what I am. And nobody gives a shit. I just want to be a mother. That's all.'

'I know. And talking of motherhood.' He smiled unexpectedly. His teeth were crooked. 'Brace yourself.'

She stared at his wonky teeth. She felt suddenly lightheaded. 'I'm braced.'

'Tilly's partner is expecting a baby.'

'Oh my God.' Julia sandwiched her face with the palms of her hands. 'Oh my dear God.'

Uncle Neil set out a large glossy photo of Tilly. She was looking to her left, at someone.

'They went to a clinic over in Glasgow and Alex has an ovarian condition which means she can't produce eggs, though there is nothing wrong with her womb.' Neil waited for Julia to catch up to the possibilities, but she was so angry with his smug withholding of information that she could have picked up the coffee jug and swung it across his skull. 'Yes, yes. Yes?'

'So, they used Tilly's egg. They fertilised and transplanted it. And now it's growing in Alex's womb.'

Julia was now too stunned to be angry. 'I am going to be a grandmother?'

'Yes, you are, Mrs Seawhite.'

'My God, when you said you had news, I never imagined for a second that it was going to—'

'But wait, that's not the news I was referring to.' He leaned forward. This man was happy in his job. He raised his eyebrows, as if he wanted her to start guessing and her joy about Tilly's news was tinged anew with fury at Neil's abuse of his knowledge and power.

Did he want her to plead? Alright, she would plead. 'Please. Please tell me what news could possibly get near Tilly being a mum.'

'Eight weeks ago, Othaniel Baye was executed.'

The blood drained from Julia's face, as it always did at the mention of the murderer's name. 'Yes, I know that.'

'There have been many executions across the States over the last year. It's a pet project of President Descher's. And Baye's time was up.'

'You are certain? It definitely happened.'

Neil smiled, as if she were a child, and she wanted to clout him again. 'Of course I am certain. You don't come back from a lethal injection. Very few people come back from the dead, as you did. Othaniel Baye is history, cremated, gone.' Neil pushed his hand across the table and Julia thought for a second he was going to touch her. 'You have probably been safe since his death but we had to wait for the demise of Lillius Queen. We had to.' He looked at his watch. 'She died almost thirty hours ago. There is no-one left from the heist. They are all dead and very nearly all buried.'

Julia's hands started shaking and she laced her fingers together, squeezing them tight. 'You mean, no-one is looking for me?'

'No-one is looking for you. And better than that, much better, Queen's son has come forward. Says he has wanted to all along but had to protect his mother. He has given up what jewels remain and his assets are now frozen.'

'Does he know about me?'

'Oh yes. He knows all about you. But he wants no part of the gang's revenge.'

'They're dropping their pledge to kill me?'

'The son, Billy Ray Master's his name, he never was part of this vendetta. And though his mother told him she was trying to find you, there's been no evidence of that for some years. Most likely, she was just trying to protect herself from Othaniel Baye. He had to believe Lillius Queen was keeping her part of the bargain.'

'But who shot Stephen?'

'We still don't know. Frankly, we may never know. Lillius will have organised that, to keep Othaniel on side for his testimony, exonerating her. You have nothing more to fear. There will be a full de-briefing at the Central Bureau. But you can stop worrying.'

'Really. I shall worry every second of every day, for the rest of my life.'

He nodded and tilted his head slightly, as if she was a neurotic spaniel. 'Julia, it's run out of steam. We've been monitoring it with the FBI so carefully. You may be the most expensive woman who ever lived.'

'Oh, should I apologise?'

'Hey. It's going to take time, to get used to the idea—' His hand was too close again.

'I have no more time to give. I want my life back. I want my kids.'

'And you have them. Both sides of the pond feel confident. It's over.'

'Have you told them? Do the children know?'

'Austen does. I mean, Dominic, we can say from now on. He's flying straight home. Primmy knows of course. And Tilly.' Neil looked at his watch again. 'I'm meeting Dominic at *Taransay*.'

'You are? *You*?' Julia didn't recognise the noise coming from her throat. It had no description. It wasn't one thing; not disbelief, nor joy, nor fury, nor relief. It was the sound of her life, her past, present and future.

'Julia, they will all meet at *Taransay*. And you too, you'll be there. But Rebecca, I mean Emma, she doesn't know yet of course. There's a lot to face. She will learn that her father was not killed in the car crash. But then she'll have to hear that he died when she was…'

'She was nine. Long before your time, Neil.'

The agent grasped Julia's hand. 'It's an incredible amount for Emma to take in. Dominic thinks that he should tell her at *Taransay*. Emma is bringing Primmy home tomorrow. But she knows no more than that. And Zachary, Emma's boyfriend, he may be there too. That's what Tilly said.'

'Where is Tilly?'

'She's still in Edinburgh. I need to meet Zachary Ness. So, we'll go down to Mallaig, you and I. I'll drive you. And then—'

'And then I walk in to organ music. That it? Like the Queen of Sheba. What about Tilly?'

'She will be there the following day. She wants Emma to have you to herself first.'

'Dear God. My stomach is in knots. Could you get rid of the boyfriend? What's his name again?'

'It's Zachary. Zachary Ness.'

CHAPTER 20

The End

Uncle Neil stood on the staircase landing at *Taransay*. This is where the old boy had died, Ralph Edward Seawhite. This current Neil, of course, had never met Ralph. He only knew of him from the reports, which is how he read of Stephen Seawhite's death too. Stephen suffered an intracranial aneurism, as his father did just a few years later. The agent at the time reported Stephen's death to Ralph and Primmy. It was noted in the file that the grandmother had pulled off her necklace and shouted at her husband, who bore the brunt of her grief and anger always. Indeed, Primmy had kicked Ralph, as he tried to gather her pearls.

Tonight, Neil looked out of the ornate arched window and down the linden tree driveway. The Seawhites had really gotten under his skin. He had never been so fascinated with an assignment. And his regard for Julia extended well beyond professional care. He was considering his resignation, so that he might make his feelings for her known. Certainly, he could not continue compromising like this.

Neil checked the time on his phone. Why had 'Austen' and 'Rebecca' run suddenly out of the house? That was totally unplanned. And anything unplanned was a threat. The agent looked down the great staircase. This wasn't how it was meant to be. This was the great homecoming, the moment they had all been working and waiting for. He had brought Julia back to *Taransay*. He had given her everything she'd asked for. He'd delivered, and he need her to be grateful. But the woman he had fallen in love with was sitting now in her old study, waiting patiently for the moment she would be reunited with her children.

Austen had asked to have a talk with Rebecca first and Neil had persuaded their mother that they should go along with this. Of course, Julia would never have agreed if she'd known that the children were about to tear off down the driveway and into the night.

*

Julia Seawhite moved heaps of loose books from an armchair to sit down in the study. By the looks of the dust, nobody had been in here for years. There were no curtains and it was getting cold, as the night crowded up to the window bars and around the steading. She tried to imagine Emma in here with her father-in-law, doing all the fun things that had been described to Julia, in the years leading up to Ralph's death; the record playing and their Jacobites. But she couldn't really see it. She pictured instead her old red bridge cloth on the card table. And little bare-chested Emma standing in the kitchen in her pink checked shorts, grilling the tournament pack. As the cards had caught light, she'd shouted at her daughter so hard, and Emma had hidden her face behind those chubby hands.

*

Neil was going to give Rebecca and Austen ten more minutes out there and then the show would be over. He would bring them in and 'Rebecca Brown' would just have to hear it all starkly; and the first thing to be revealed would be her true identity: Emma Seawhite.

There was a creak upstairs but you expected that in a house like *Taransay*. Neil moved his own feet. Yes, creaks everywhere. He looked at his shoes. They needed a polish, and so did he. He'd been doing the job for too long. He was past his sell-by date. His Glock 17 didn't sit right in its holster. He missed his Ruger, now obsolete, like him. How could he allow love to come to work and what could be more deadly? The agent's Bureau phone rang.

'T5, Quindt is on the line. The reporter from the NY Daily. I'm patching him through.'

'Good evening. This is Thomas Quindt.'

'Hello again, Mr Quindt. Where are you?'

'Caught a domestic to Inverness. We're driving now. Just north of Fort William.' Quindt zoomed out on the TomTom screen. 'Spean Bridge on the A82. We can be at *Taransay* in an hour or so.'

'*We*?'

'Jane Rourke is with me. Didn't you get the pdf?'

'Oh yes, of course. Rourke. Well, if your theory holds water, Ms Rourke will be a valuable asset. But Zachary Ness checks out. He's not the one.'

'Have you spoken to him?'

'Not yet. But he arrived here without incident.'

'Keller Baye's not on the roster at the Hickory Plant. And two of his colleagues confirm that he left weeks back, though they don't know where he went. Nobody does. And there's no answer from his apartment. Couldn't get anything out of the mailman but there's no post stacking up, neighbour says.'

'Quindt, Ness checks out. Ok? Unless the guy's got a twin, this is him. You go ahead and make your novel. That's your job. Let me do mine. The Seawhites are coming in tonight.'

'My *novel*? This is not fiction. Can I have your direct number?'

'I'm not permitted to give you that.'

'It's taken me hours to get through. There is no time. You need to understand that. I've just been sent a copy of Angelo Peralta's suicide note. Are you saying you can't receive that on your device? Are you saying you don't want to see it?'

'Of course not. I'll put you back to Central and they'll send it straight on.'

'Where is Julia Seawhite?'

'Quindt, I'm happy for your involvement, but we're right in the middle of the Seawhite closure. Look, we can meet in Mallaig first thing tomorrow morning. Leave your hotel number with—'

'Listen to me, you don't understand. There's no time. You need to hear Peralta's note. I'll have Jane read it out.'

'I don't want you to do that. That's not procedure.'

'Fuck procedure. The Seawhites are in the utmost danger. All of them.'

The sickening truth slithered into the pit of Neil's stomach.

*

Rebecca and Austen ran back into the driveway but she suddenly skidded to a standstill when she saw Uncle Neil's silhouette in the arched window.

'Rebecca, come on! I'll explain who that is up there. But right now, we need to get in the car. It's in the barn.'

Rebecca stared up at Neil, her chest heaving from the sprint. There wasn't enough light around the figure to see. Perhaps it wasn't Uncle Neil, but he had that look, that strange presence in their house. Whoever it was, they were on the phone. She could see the elbow crooked and the hand at his ear. The memory of her grandfather on the landing came flooding back. She remembered Ralph's soft voice, his dying words about her mother. September 17th, the wrong date on the calendar. She'd told Zachary about that day and he'd listened intensely. When she became tearful, he had held her so tenderly and she had waited almost her whole life for someone to do that: to listen to her and to love her, just as she was. Poor Zach, alone at the hospital with a sick old lady. He would be worried to death.

Austen was pulling open the old barn doors where a silver Ford was parked. He switched on the overhead light and pulled open the driver door. 'Fuck! He's got the keys.'

Rebecca glanced up again at the window, but Uncle Neil was gone.

Austen looked wildly around, like there might be a piece of farm equipment to hotwire it.

In the still night, they could hear the creak of *Taransay*'s huge oak door opening. Rebecca could see then that it was not Uncle Neil, and yet he had seemed so similar, so familiar. How long had it been since she'd seen him last; must be years. He held a car key and called out. 'Austen. I just had a call from Central Bureau. A reporter called Quindt has—'

'Neil, give me your car keys. Primmy is…' Austen decided not say that his grandmother was ill. He did not want Neil taking over. He wanted the keys. He wanted his family. Nothing more.

'Listen to me. Austen, we have a problem. A major problem.'

'No shit, Sherlock. We have our own problems. Give me that key, T5. Now!'

'He's here. Keller Baye is here.'

Austen straightened right up, his chin jerking out of his collar, as he approached Neil. 'I don't mean to be rude, but piss off now and let us take care of family business.' Austen turned away but his leg shot out suddenly behind him and into Neil's crotch. The agent doubled up and fell to the ground.

'What in the actual fuck is going on?' Rebecca bent down to the man, her own knees almost buckling.

'Throw me his key. Do it!' Austen held up his hand like a catcher's mitt.

Rebecca snatched the car key from Neil.

*

Keller pulled up in the ambulance bay at Belford Hospital. Inside the Emergency Room entrance, he couldn't see any kind of trolley or wheelchair, so he hauled Primrose Anctillious Seawhite out of the passenger seat and set her against the sliding doors. A fat bloke came out to the doors and as they swung open, Primmy flopped to one side, like an old rag doll.

'Good God,' the guy said and swept the elderly woman out of harm's way before the doors garrotted her. With Primmy in his arms, he looked at Keller. 'Does this lady belong to you?'

'Indeed she does.' Keller clicked the fob to lock the Mercedes. 'Just had to get something out of the trunk of my car. I mean the boot.'

*

Agent T5 opened the door to the study. 'I'm afraid there's been a setback.' He wasn't about to tell her his fears about Zachary Ness.

'Neil, you told me that the next face I'd see would be Emma. You told me that.'

'I know. Julia, a helicopter is on—'

'They're not coming. The children.'

'They've taken my car. Dominic and Emma.'

'Why?'

'They don't know you're here. No-one does.' He couldn't even be sure of that and his uncertainty was written all over his face. 'The Bureau have sent back-up. And…' Neil tried Austen's phone again but it went to voicemail.

'And?'

'They'll find the car immediately. It's fitted with a smart tracker.'

'My kids are on the run? Are you serious? Why are you all huddled over like that?'

'Of course they're not on the run.'

'What will your people do? Put up some big road barrier?'

'No. So much simpler to let them reach their destination. It's not like an action movie. We are discreet. Our intention is always to help. Julia…' He reached for her face and she lurched aside like a boxer dodging a punch.

'I don't want this. I want you lot to get me my children. There's no point without them. Can't you understand? Can't you just tell me what the hell is going on now?'

Neil nodded and his arms hung uselessly at his sides. 'Central Bureau patched through a call from a journalist – his name is Tom Quindt – and he's been researching the Winston Salem heist for a very long time. Would you mind if I sit down?'

'Sit, sit. Researching, yes. Go on.'

'There was a man called Angelo Peralta. He hanged himself last month in Greensboro, North Carolina. Julia, I shouldn't even be telling you this. Not now, not yet. I… I care for you.'

'I care for you too.' She was lying. She would say anything. 'Keep talking.'

'Julia, I just want to protect you.'

'I just want you to protect my children. I kept my part of the bargain. You know, I tried so hard, so so hard, to help them get Othaniel Baye. I worked with the police artist all through that first night. Stephen could barely remember whether the man was black or white. But I gave them every detail. I can see him still. It's etched. *Drilled*. Here.' Julia dug her index finger into the centre of her forehead.

'And they caught him. They caught a murderer. Thanks to you.'

'Christ's sake, Neil, you think I'd do it again, given my time over?'

'You did your duty. You both did.'

'But look at the cost. We were so naïve. Slept in that Courthouse for three days. Guards swarming around, barking orders. Stephen should have stayed in hospital. He never really recovered. But did they give a shit? Oh no, the delay was costing millions of dollars. Dollars, dollars. You could practically see their eyeballs spinning with dollar signs. And after we'd done everything they wanted, they asked us to live apart. Not just from our children but from each other too. Did you know that?'

'Julia, I—'

'There comes a point, when you just think, let me go. If so many people are so determined to kill me, well, just let them. And if I'd known that Stephen would die anyway. If I'd had the first inkling of what it was really like to be apart from my kids, I'd have jumped off a cliff right then.'

'Don't give up now.'

'Have you got a gun? I bet you have a gun. What if I said I have a gun? What if I said, I have a gun and I'm going to blow your Neil brains out unless you give me your gun.'

'You don't have a gun. Even the shittiest agent could tell that. And I'm pretty confident you don't have a stick of dynamite to blast your way out of here.' Neil nodded at the barred windows in the rising moonlight and the noise of helicopter rotor blades whipped up the dark sky. 'I'm sorry, Julia.' Neil went out of the study and as he locked her in, he whispered again, 'I'm sorry.'

Uncle Neil Taransay 5 sat down on the bottom step of the staircase. She must've heard the key turning yet she made no protest. She had nothing left. All year he had seen that coming. Everyone had a limit and Julia Seawhite had reached hers.

It was pointless now for Neil to consider resignation. He would be summarily dismissed. His phone was ringing but he couldn't answer. They'd be asking him about a landing site. They'd be looking up the directory for a spot. The bloody Yellow Pages, for a heliport.

Neil was finished. Julia was never going to be interested in him. They were never going to open their own oyster farm in the Highlands. Might as well tell the helicopter to land on *Taransay*, right on the house. Obliterate the ugly old place. All things come to an end. He hoped those Seawhite kids would get away somehow. Julia was right. The Bureau could not protect them, because ultimately, it didn't care. The only people who can care for your very life, is your family.

Neil thought of Quindt battling on, with Jane Rourke by his side. Americans are so good at this stuff. The agent put his head in his hands. 'You're all washed up, T5.' The latitude he had afforded Austen and Rebecca Brown was wholly unprofessional and there was no doubt that his poor decisions and erratic behaviour originated from his feelings for the children's mother. His career was fucked and he struggled to care. Suicides always got to him. And Angelo Peralta's had truly sickened him.

This death of mine has been many years in the making. As you will discover, I have ingested antifreeze powder. This was an idea that I got from a man who was once my friend. Keller Baye. He came into our shop recently – I am attaching a copy of his till receipt to assist with his arrest – and purchased a quantity of ethylene glycol. Baye showed me a driver's license which I think he had stolen. He asked me if I thought he looked like the man in the photo. I realised then that the killing was not going to stop. That what had begun as an accident, had grown into a monster.

In self defence, Keller and I killed a tramp in the deep woods of Horsepen Creek. The weapon was a small crossbow which the tramp had used on Keller's cat. I do not know the name of the homeless man and I believe that his body was burned. I did not associate with Baye after this incident. And then one day, many years later, he asked me to visit his Aunt who was chained and dying in her bedroom. He said that if I did not tell him when she died, that my family would be harmed. I did not doubt that he meant what he said. I visited Joya Baye each night until she died and then I informed Keller, who was out of town.

I have not been able to live since this moment. Although I have saved my family, I am of no use to them. I must die for what I have done, so that they can be free and innocent.

Angelo Peralta

*

As soon as Austen turned onto the A830 south of Mallaig, Rebecca's patience ran out.

'So, a), you can stop driving like a fucking lunatic. We're no use to Primmy dead. And b), everything else.' Rebecca looked at the satnav destination estimate. You have forty six minutes till we get to Belford. Speak.'

Austen took a deep breath. 'Have you got any water?'

'Why would I have any water? Your phone's ringing.'

'Is it Colette?'

'It says *T5*.'

'That's Neil. Don't answer it.'

'Speak to me!'

'Ok. Ok, ok. Once upon a time—'

'I'm warning you. And slow down. Slow down the speed you're driving. Do not slow down your talking.'

'No really, listen. Let me do it like Primmy does. Do you remember she said, *Once upon a time*… at your tenth birthday party?'

'No. I've wiped that party from my memory bank.'

'She said, *Once upon a time there were three little orphans who lived with their wicked grandparents*. Your eyes were like saucers when she said that.'

'Get on with your story.'

'Ok. Hold tight, Becky. I mean it. Once upon a time, there was a mummy and a daddy. They had three children. Dominic, Tilly and Emma. With me so far?'

'When Prim is better, I'm going to kill you.'

'The mum and dad lived in England, happily, with their children but one day they had to go to America. And whilst they were there, they saw a terrible thing.'

A car coming in the opposite direction blasted its horn.

'Oh God, Austen, you haven't got your lights on. Shall I drive?'

Austen shook his head slowly. 'I don't think you ought to. Not if you want to hear this story.'

'Go on.'

'The couple were called the Seawhites. Julia and Stephen Seawhite.'

Rebecca gasped. 'I know that name. That's the name of... the crash.'

'How do you know that?'

'It was in the paper. I looked it up at the library. I didn't understand. No-one would talk to me. Austen, you have to drop your speed. We'll be killed.'

Austen braked a little. 'So the Seawhites were in North Carolina. Mrs Seawhite was a professional bridge player and she was playing in a very important competition. Not just there, but in a few States.'

'Is this before the crash? How long before the crash? Was I born?'

'Just listen, Youngest. This is hard.'

'Alright.'

'One day they were just minding their own business, in a shop. A florist's, I think. Yes, a florist. And there was this almighty event in the town. Some kind of terrorist plot gone wrong. That's what they thought. Explosions, gunfire, madness. And the Seawhites, like everyone else, sort of took cover. That's when they saw something that would change their lives forever.' Austen started to cough. 'I really do need some water. Running does that to me. I'm so unfit.'

'What! What changed their lives?'

'They saw a man being shot,' Austen croaked. 'Right there, on the street, in front of the shops. And the shooter's name was Othaniel Baye. The man he shot was a judge, well an ex judge. In cold blood.'

A shiver took hold of Rebecca's spine and when she repeated that man's name, it was barely audible: 'Othaniel.'

'Othaniel Baye, yes. B. A. Y. E. Are you alright? Have you heard of him?'

Rebecca's mobile rang and she jumped in her seat like it was an electric chair.

'It's Zach.' A wave of nausea rose up inside her. Rebecca answered. 'Zachary, how is she?'

'Aw honey, she's not great. Can you get here? Can you get here quick?'

'We're on our way. Half hour at most. Can I talk to her?'

'No. I'm afraid not.' She must be bringing the brother. She said *we*. More Seawhites were swimming into his net. 'Sorry, babe. Primmy can't come to the phone.'

'What do you mean? Give the phone to her.'

'I mean she's out, Beck. She's not conscious.'

'Oh lord, no.' Tears pooled up to the surface and Rebecca swallowed hard. 'Can I speak with one of the doctors.'

'Well, they're in there with her now. Doing their thing. I just wanted to touch base. What's that noise?'

'What noise?'

'Like a plane. Oh wait, they're signalling for me to come. I better go. Hang on in there.' Keller hung up and Rebecca stared at her phone.

'Austen. Know how I said slow down? Ignore me. You've always been so good at that.'

'This is not a good time to tell you that my real name is Dominic Seawhite.'

'Now is as good a time as any. I'll wake up in a minute. But while I'm dreaming, you might as well tell me who I am.'

'You are Emma. I'm going to find it hard to get used to that, after all these years.'

'No shit. I hardly dare ask what Primmy is called.'

'She's still Primmy. Listen, we have enough to cope with. Let's get Grandma sorted and worry about who we are later. Ok?'

*

Thomas Quindt first visited Jane Rourke many years ago. He had not been able to get Keller Baye to respond to the note he left in his jacket pocket and he began to dig into the boy's background, particularly school.

Jane was reluctant to entertain Quindt at first, more than reluctant. She felt real pain when Keller's name was mentioned. He could see it in her face. Rourke was now in private practice as a psychotherapist but it was her time as Keller Baye's teacher, that the journalist wanted to discuss. During that first meeting, she was polite and took a cup of coffee with Quindt but she wanted no part in his book. Nor did she want to disclose details of her ex pupil. 'And that's final,' Tom Quindt remembered her saying.

But when Quindt saw Peralta's suicide note, he flew straight back to Jane Rourke.

'Lives depend on you. So many have already been lost, Ms Rourke. You mustn't doubt that. Lives that have been taken, not just in the Winston Salem heist, but also by Keller Baye. Now I am asking you to help *save* some lives, including Keller's.'

That boy had never left Jane Rourke's mind. She'd tried so hard after the death of her own son and all the rumours about Joya Baye's neglect, to persuade the child's Aunt to let her foster Keller or at least share the duties. But Joya would have none of it. She wanted the adoption money for herself and talking of lives depending on you, Joya Baye wouldn't have done a good turn for someone if her own life had depended on it. Later, Jane heard that Joya had met a grim end and she didn't feel as sorry about it as she should have. Mr Thomas Quindt had a theory about Joya's death and he detailed it for the teacher turned therapist. It was a horrific scenario and Jane Rourke could barely listen to another word.

But Quindt made it sound like a crusade, and that only she and him could bring salvation. As the writer made his case to recruit Rourke, she paced around the annexe to her house which served as her therapy room. She took some time to speak, but it seemed to Quindt that she was already preparing to leave: closing files and drawers, pushing in chairs and straightening the drapes.

'Would I need a visa?'

'No. There will be an application form to complete for officials at customs. That's all. Do you have a passport?'

'Yes, I travel quite a bit.'

'It's in date?'

'Yes.'

'Ok. I'm flying out this evening. Will you join me?'

*

Austen grabbed Rebecca by the shirt sleeve as she dashed across Belford Hospital car park.

'Look, Rebecca. It might be an idea to get rid of your boyfriend.'

'What are you talking about? For all we know, Zachary has saved Primmy's life.'

'Listen to me. This is very complicated. You can't tell him about all this stuff.'

'Let go of me. I just need to see my grandmother.'

'Rebecca, you've got to understand. These people… they shot our father.'

'Austen, enough. My head is about to explode. How can I understand? Primmy could be dead in there.' Rebecca pulled away from her brother and ran into the hospital.

*

Quindt's cell pinged again and again. His fingers shook slightly on the steering wheel. He would pay ten thousand dollars right now for a shot of whisky.

'Jane, can you open the emails. Here. Scan my print.' Quindt held out his index fingertip and Jane pressed it to the cellphone scanner. 'Flag up anything relevant.'

Jane Rourke scrolled down his inbox and cleared her throat. 'This address is 6818 dot N dash Y at gmail dot com.'

'That's my ex Fed. Read it, will you.'

Waitress at Clem's Diner, Greensboro remembers Keller Baye well. She knew the date to within a couple days and they have cctv footage of a meeting with Doug Numericki. He's a tracer. Has a website. 'America's Foremost Internet Hunter.' Uses a number of aliases.

Billy Ray Master has confessed in the light of Peralta's suicide note. Central Bureau in the UK know all about it. Master met with Baye at Shady Glen. There is no footage of that but the manager Daniel Kuensberg recalls the pair. There was an altercation and the police were called. Keller Baye received a citation for breach of the peace. He failed to appear in court. No love lost between our man and Master, who is currently spilling his guts to my old employers. Wish I was a fly on the wall.

The mail at Baye's Fisher Park place is being redirected to a Peg Bellingham who knows him from his Vandalia Road days. She's a big fan of 'Kell'. It's fair to say she's the only one.

And now the big one. Peralta was right on the money about a false driver's license. And your hunch on the missing ID photos was right. It is Zachary Ness. He's a Finance Officer for Christian Aid in El Salvador. Employers took care of all the paperwork whilst they're down in El S. Ness didn't even know his license was stolen till he returned to the US on leave. Drum roll. That license was used today at Hertz, Picardy Place, Edinburgh. A black Mercedes Benz E Class, license plate BN20 UYE is out on hire to 'Zachary Ness' right now.

They'll be holding the front page at the Daily. Go get him, Tom.

Be careful.

*

The Kinnect tracker was getting sweaty in Keller's hand. In the waiting area, he kept his eyes fixed on the entrance to *Accident &Emergency*. Primmy never made it to the critical care unit. Perhaps Rebecca would go by the main entrance instead, expecting her grandmother to be in a ward, recovering. But instead, she was dead, and Keller he would be the one to break the news.

He sat well away from the other folk who tended to their cracked limbs and poked at their troubled organs. Then she came, his girl. Keller stood up and shook his head. Rebecca reminded him so much in that moment of Makayla. He had loved Makayla best when she was in a state of devastation and he loved Rebecca now in that exact same way, with the knowledge that he could make them, or break them.

Rebecca did not move towards Keller. She looked all around her, as if she had never seen such a place. A man came in behind her and stood close. This would be the brother then. Austen Brown. Not dissimilar to Keller himself in looks but shorter, neater and possessive, his arm curved around his sister, as he ushered her to a seat. He spoke urgently to Rebecca and then went in search of a doctor.

Keller swiftly approached. 'Darling.' He pulled Rebecca into his arms and though she was tense and taut, she let him gather her up. She had no handbag with her. The Kinnect winked in the darkness of his jeans pocket. 'Primrose Anctillious has died. I am so, so sorry. They say it was fairly quick. I don't think she was aware... of it. Not really. I did what I could.'

When Rebecca looked up again, her face was getting puffy and pink. 'I know you did. My God, like this. Primmy. To go like this? And we were so worried about her bloody dementia.'

Austen returned and looked directly at his sister, as if Keller was not worth seeing. 'Emma, come. We can go and see her. But it's our worst fear. She has passed away.'

Keller held out his hand. 'My name is Zachary. You must be Austen. Can I say how truly sorry I am to meet you in such sad circumstances. Emma?' He looked between the siblings.

Austen ignored the extended hand. 'Rebecca, where is my phone?'

'I think I put it with mine, in my bag. I must have left it in the car.'

Austen held his sister in a kind of soft half nelson and spoke to her gently. 'Go ahead. She is in the end booth. I will be ten seconds.'

Austen took off to retrieve her handbag from the agent's car and when Austen leaned down to the passenger seat footwell, he felt something solid dunt his lower spine.

'Back up very slowly.'

Without turning, Austen said, 'Zachary.'

There was no trajectory, this was point blank; the cocking stirrup was hard against his back. 'Austen. Or should I say Dominic? Dominic Seawhite. As I live and breathe. You told her then? Emma? If I move this crossbow a little to the left, your chances of survival are better. If I go for the stomach, catch the intestines, you will probably die from infection. As opposed to blood loss. Did you know that?'

'Fuck you.'

'Of course, that's in terms of gunshot wounds. There are no statistics for crossbow.'

'Didn't I just say fuck you?'

'Alrighty. Here it is, big brother. Option one: I shoot a steel tipped bolt through your liver. Option two: I shoot you through the liver and then I do the same for your kid sister. Option three: and I'll be honest, I'm right out of options after this one. You tell me where Julia and Stephen are. Right now.'

'They're dead. You better get out of here. You have at best half an hour before all manner of shit descends. Black suits. Weapons. I mean proper weapons, unlike your medieval...'

The tipped arrow did not fizz of course. When Keller pulled the crossbow trigger, there was a muted clunk. Austen's body froze for a second or two, before melting. Keller caught him under one armpit and manoeuvred him to the trunk, bending the body over the edge and then pushing the hips up and into the trunk. Skinny little guy really. But that was an awkward landing. If he was still alive, his neck vertebrae would be screaming. He pulled the car key out of Austen's tight fist and slammed the trunk closed. Keller clicked the Mercedes fob and went to retrieve his carryall.

*

In A&E, Keller waited for Rebecca to come out of the little booth where they had briefly treated Primmy. The old lady had never come round from her loss of consciousness and slipped easily away. He'd done them all a favour, Keller thought. He didn't hold out much hope for leaving this earth in such a peaceful manner as old Granny.

Then Rebecca appeared again. She would never be Emma to him, not after all these years.

'Hey baby, brought your bag.' He held it up. The Kinnect was deep in the bowels of the handbag now, in a little zipped compartment.

'Where's Austen?'

'He got a call. Urgent. I think it might've been your sister.'

'Yes, but where is he?'

'Search me. He got in the car to talk to her. Then he drove off.'

'He drove off? That's...'

'C'mere, honey. Hey, come on. Don't worry about him. You've had a terrible shock. This is just about Primmy now. And my girl. Hmm?' Keller kissed her forehead and swept her hair back. A phone rang in her bag and she unearthed it.

'This is Austen's phone. I thought you said he was speaking to Colette.'

'Maybe he was on your cell. I don't know. Don't answer it. You have to think of yourself for a minute. You've—'

Rebecca held her hand up to Keller's mouth and answered the mobile. 'Austen Brown's phone.' She had turned her back to her boyfriend and failed to see how taken aback he was that she should disobey him. Nor did she see his fury.

'Rebecca, is that you? This is Uncle Neil. Listen to me very carefully. Is Zachary Ness with you? Just say yes or no. Nothing else.'

'Yes. I can hardly hear you.' Rebecca moved away to a quieter spot in the waiting room and signalled to Zach that it was alright. He was holding his fingertips to his ticking cheekbone, looking like he'd been slapped. Rebecca motioned for him to go ahead and sit.

'Rebecca, listen now. I am going to tell you something and you must not react. You must simply say, *It's under the sink*, as if you were talking to Mrs Scattergood. Ok, ready? Zachary Ness is not who he says he is. He is your enemy. Fear him.'

'I... it's under the sink.' Rebecca tried to roll her eyes for Zach. 'My grandmother is dead. Primmy. She's had kidney failure.' Rebecca started to cry. The tears suddenly poured. She remembered a goldfish which she had brought home in a plastic bag and Primmy had stood at the edge of the steading's plateau and threw the fish into the high tide sea. Rebecca remembered pouring the bag of water down the sink. Her tears were like this, like an animation, not real, not here. And not this.

'Rebecca, I'm sorry. Did you understand what I said? About Ness?'

'No.'

'Ok. I want you to make an excuse to go to the toilet. Not right after this call but in a minute or two. Then leave. Leave the building, get into the dark. Keep this phone on—' The line went dead.

Keller took the phone from her.

*

Agent T5 was pacing up and down the hallway with a headset on. Back and forth, past the study door. How in God's name was he going to tell Julia:

That Austen's body was on a gurney, clattering across the tarmac of a hospital car park, with agents and armed police surrounding the building and blocking all exit roads from Fort William.

That a helicopter was hovering over Keller Baye's abandoned Mercedes not a mile from the Accident & Emergency, where her mother-in-law lay dead.

That Primmy's killer now had her daughter captive in a car he had just stolen.

That a middle aged woman had been hauled out of that car at some traffic lights and been knocked senseless.

Neil unlocked the study door and Julia Seawhite sat still in the armchair. She did not look up or react at all.

'Julia. You wouldn't believe the mess I've made of this.'

'I would. Who's dead?'

'Primrose. And…'

'And?'

'Dominic has been hit.'

'Hit? Would you care to elaborate or am I going to have to run you through with this poker?'

'He has been shot at… very close range with a crossbow. In the abdomen. But he's fighting. The doctors have him.'

'Who is in this house? I heard someone arrive. They're not your people. I heard American accents.'

'A man called Quindt. He knows more about this case than you or I put together. He's helping us.'

'I heard a woman's voice.'

'That's Jane Rourke. She's assisting him. She knows Othaniel Baye's son. She knows Keller. She was his teacher, long time ago.'

'And my daughter. Where is she?'

'I'm going to suggest you come out of here now and—'

'Where is Emma?'

'She's with him. They appear to have switched vehicles. Don't worry, all the access points to here are covered.'

'Don't worry. You're saying, don't worry.'

'I mean that you are safe.'

Julia flew at Neil. She beat him across the chest and head, spit flecking his face, as she screamed at him.

Quindt dashed through from the sitting room to help and the two men managed to get control of Julia's arms.

Jane Rourke stood in the study doorway. She waited for the wrestling troupe to still and stood straight-backed. 'I think we should let him come. We should let Keller get to his destination.'

*

'I swear, even in the dark, Beck, this is the most beautiful country I ever seen. Put your seatbelt on, will you, fucking bing bing's driving me nuts.'

Rebecca's wrists were handcuffed. She let them rest in her lap. She wasn't scared anymore. Or she wasn't scared temporarily. There was a kind of hiatus in her mind, in her feelings. She had no way of understanding or controlling this night. The engine of her mind couldn't cope and she'd gone into limp mode.

'You ok, baby?' Keller squeezed her right knee as it spasmed.

'Oh sure.' Rebecca lifted her chains and let her arms drop again. 'I think you killed that woman at the traffic lights. You can't hit someone that hard and expect their brain to survive.'

'I didn't mean to hit her that hard. I never punched anyone before.'

'Yeah, that'll be the whole truth.'

'Anyway, did you see her? Rough as fuck. I hate that kind, with hardware stapled all round the face. No way it was her car. Look at it. She probably stole it.' Keller swiped his hands around the driving wheel. 'Brand new. Cute little stick shift.'

'Where is Austen?'

'You notice that helicopter has gone.'

'I hadn't but now you say, yes. Where's my brother?'

'And all those cops have skedaddled too. Not a blue light to be seen.'

'Not fucking anyone to be seen. Not my fucking brother.'

'That's what Joya used to say. *Skedaddle!* Like she was so clever.'

'It is a clever thing to say. For a dog.'

'Oh yeah, I got my stories and my characters mixed up a little. I'll have to clear that all up for you some time.'

'Can hardly wait.'

'Your knee's pretty much out of control. It did that when we first met. One of the reasons I fell in love with you.'

'Oh you're in love with me, are you.'

'Love and hate mix up in the same bucket.'

'Well, thank you for that, Walt fucking Whitman. You can drop me here if you like. I know my way.'

Keller laughed. 'I'm beginning to get it. Your sense of humour.'

Rebecca lunged for the gear box and pulled the stick into neutral with the join of her handcuffs. When she tried with all her might to strike him with the steel cuffs, Keller leaned forward and took the blow on his shoulder. He stopped the car and cut the engine. He reached over and shook Rebecca hard, so that her head rattled on the stalk of her neck.

Rebecca's mouth widened out into a melting eight, ready to bawl, and Keller stared at that mouth, fascinated. 'I don't want you to die, Beck.'

The girl's head lolled from side to side. 'Where's my brother? Please, *please* tell me.'

'You know what's happening here.' Keller started up the car again. 'Here, I mean.' Keller pointed to the tall pines at the edge of the road. 'And here. And here. They're all in there. Behind them trees. They're all looking for you and me. How far would you say it is now, to *Taransay*?'

'Turn on the satnav.'

'I am asking you, darling.'

'About a mile. And three fifths. Approximately.'

'I love the woods. Spent my whole childhood in woods.'

'Let me guess. Home wasn't quite so good.'

'I killed a man in the woods.'

'Oh for fuck's sake.'

'He had it coming. He killed my cat, Steve Truffaut. For nothing. You don't need to do something wrong for someone to just rub you out.'

'I'm starting to see that.'

'I want to kiss you, Rebecca.'

Now the fear was back, a big dollop of it, swelling up inside. 'We're almost there. The driveway is less than a mile.'

'In the driveway then. I will kiss you.' He smiled and looked at the empty black road ahead.

Rebecca couldn't see the lights from the lamps by the lindens. Nor any coming from the house.

'Now do you believe me, baby? Look. They've turned off all the lights. Lucky we've got these.' Keller flashed the car's full beam. 'It was just a tramp we killed in the woods. Me and my friend Angelo. And the old guy started it. Near ripped my head off. But what I couldn't figure for a long time, was how he got the bolt through the cat and pinned him to the tree like that. No other injury. Took me years to come up with a theory.'

Rebecca wondered what speed they were doing right now. She wondered how the tarmac would feel against her head if she managed to get the door open. First she'd have to negotiate the seatbelt. It would never work.

'See, what I reckon happened is, he killed Steve first, with his hands most likely and then he put a little noose there,' Keller stroked her neck. 'Right around his neck. A rope. By that point, the cat wouldn't have felt nothing, don't worry. He'd have been dead already. And then he must've swung the cat. He had a crossbow. Nice one, too. Not like the one I used on Austen.'

Rebecca felt the vomit working its way up to her throat and she fumbled with the seatbelt catch.

'Stop that, Chrissakes.' Keller pushed her hands back onto her lap. 'Don't shake yourself all up like that. I'm just telling you a story. I think that tramp wanted some target practice. So he put little Steve into the noose and strung him up on a branch. You know that phrase, not big enough to swing a cat? Well, it was plenty big enough in the deep wood at Horsepen. He must've swung the cat back and forth and then, maybe even first time, there weren't no other holes in him, whump, he pinned him to a big old yellow pine.'

Rebecca threw up over the dashboard and the vomit dripped onto the floor.

Keller pulled into the driveway of *Taransay*. 'I ain't kissing you now. Fuck.' Keller cut the engine but left the headlamps on; just two beams of light and not a sound as he opened the driver door. 'Do you ever wonder how long you've got?' Keller looked at his watch. 'Sometimes, now this is a little silly, but sometimes, I like to think that because my watch has missing numbers, whatever happens in those lost hours doesn't really count.'

'Oh yes, absolutely. That'll work. You sick fuck.'

Keller closed his eyes and the tic in his cheek scampered across his fine bones. Then the eyes flashed open again. 'I want you to come out of the vehicle this way, over on my side. Do you want me to say vehicle again?'

'Fucking tadger.'

'I'm sensing a negativity creeping into your noun choices. We need to stick together, Rebecca. Come on now. That's it, just hitch up over that middle bit, I'll help you.'

Keller held Rebecca close as they got out of the car. 'They'll have infrared on us. They will. Maybe sound.' He reverse shuffled them to the rear door and reached in for the crossbow which he then wedged between their bodies, just as he had with Austen. 'Now, Little Miss Seawhite. Let's get you home. It's late.'

*

Jane Rourke made a *calm down* gesture with her hands to Quindt. 'I wonder if you gentlemen would give me a moment alone with Mrs Seawhite. Let's go back into the sitting room. Tom lit a fire. Come. It's icy in here.'

Agent T5 didn't look very keen but Quindt's instincts told him to trust the therapist and he nodded to the British agent.

Julia followed Rourke meekly and grabbed hold of the mantelshelf above the fire. Her fingers shook and then her arms caught the tremor and her legs too. Her whole foundation was crumbling. She could not do this for one moment longer. Despair filled her throat. As the mascara streaked down her cheeks, she made no attempt to clean it up. In the mirror over the fireplace, Julia Seawhite thought she looked just as rotten as she deserved.

'Julia. We must let him come here. That's what he wants. I think he really just needs to… well, to understand. Listen, I have an idea. We're not too dissimilar you and I, are we? In looks. Let me pretend to be you. Keller only knows your picture from such a long time ago. Let me be you. My mother was English. I can do the accent. Let me talk to him.'

Julia was in a rapidly declining state. Her teeth clacked together and she had to hold her jaw still just to get the words out. 'But he'll recognise you.'

'He won't. I wore glasses then, not contacts. And I had red hair.' Jane picked up a lock of her grey hair. 'He was just a boy. Julia, this is our best chance. Let me do it.'

It didn't take Jane Rourke very long to persuade Julia Seawhite to let her swap places.

'I think you have a good heart, Jane Rourke.'

'I want to do this.'

'What if he just kills you straight off.'

'He won't. He'll want to get things off his chest. He's probably been planning this for many years. This is his moment. Do you see?'

'It's a terrible idea. I won't allow it.'

Neil couldn't stay away any longer. He strode into the sitting room and put a blanket around Julia's shoulders. He pulled the thick curtains shut and they all huddled around the fireplace.

Agents were hidden all over the house and grounds, their vehicles half a mile north and the helicopter on neighbouring pasture. Neil was on side too. He told Julia that Quindt and Rourke were in a much better position to judge what to do. They knew Keller Baye well. The agent took Julia's hand which was cold and trembling still.

'Baye's never had sight of you, Julia. You must let Jane handle this. Once she's with him, he'll want to talk. If he wanted to simply shoot us all up, there's many a pub in Edinburgh where he could've procured an automatic weapon. This isn't just about killing for Keller Baye. This is about justice.'

Jane knelt down in front of Julia. 'I've come here for this.'

'To die.'

'No. To try. Look, my husband died when my son Steve was just a baby. Then Steve was taken too. He was Keller's friend. There was four of them in their gang. Great friends. Keller was smart. Super smart. And he had a goodness in him. He did. I know that's hard to believe but when Steve died, I wanted to take Keller in. His Aunt Joya wouldn't allow it. But that's what I wanted. Since losing my family, I haven't been living. Like you. I work. I eat. I exist. But you have a chance now to get your family back. That chance is me. And me, I have nothing to lose.'

Quindt needed a whisky. There was a tray on a dresser behind him. He hadn't had a drink in seven years but he was as close now as he had ever been to falling off the wagon. He could feel his grip loosening. 'Jane. I… I feel responsible for you. I don't know if I can allow you to put yourself in such danger.'

'Duly noted. But this is between me and Julia now.'

Julia took her hand out of Neil's and held it against Jane Rourke's face. 'Be careful, Jane. This cannot now be the boy you knew.'

Neil raised his arm. 'Hear that? Do you hear that? They're in the driveway.' He began hissing instructions on his phone to the waiting agents, then he leaned forward to blow out the candle but Jane Rourke stopped him.

'No. I'll need that.'

*

Keller whispered his own instructions to Rebecca and as he opened the huge oak door, he smiled, as she repeated the words he'd told her to say. 'Hello? Is there anybody home?'

Keller imagined the agents' eyes, beady from behind the furnishings, like vermin; their sniping sights set on him but unable to act whilst the weapon was firmly in Emma Seawhite's back.

'I'm here.' Jane Rourke was standing in the hallway. She held the candle up so that her face was only partially visible.

Keller spoke. 'And who might you be?'

'I am Julia. Julia Seawhite.'

Rebecca's right knee began to flex back and forth, like some drunk puppeteer had lost control of his marionette.

Keller held Rebecca tighter. 'Do you have another candle, Julia Seawhite?'

'Follow me.'

Rourke opened a door which Rebecca knew was the dining room. She didn't want to go in the dining room. She hated it in there.

Jane Rourke took a seat at the grand table. There was a candelabra on the mahogany, with five stubby used red candles, each of which she now lit.

'Keller Baye. Would you like to close the door? So that we can talk in private. Please, take a seat.'

Keller looked around the room, into its dark pouches.

Jane Rourke said, 'I promise you that we are alone in this room. I give you my word.'

'But the butler will be bringing canapes in a minute, right?' Keller relaxed his hold a little on his young prey. 'Rebecca – you will always be Rebecca to me – let me introduce you to your—'

'Keller, I am Jane Rourke.'

Keller pushed Rebecca hard towards the fireplace. She stumbled and as she regained her footing, she could see that his crossbow was fixed upon her, at head height. Rebecca looked up at the red fox's stolen eyes and then at the homemade crossbow. Her world was full of toys, broken toys. And broken people.

Jane Rourke held her palm open. 'I came to help. I just want to talk. Why don't you both take a seat. I'm not asking you to put down your weapon. I just want to talk.'

'Yes, you said that.' Keller squinted at Jane in the candlelight. 'Jane Rourke. I... I know you. Don't I.'

'I was your teacher. I used to lend you books and when you—'

'Oh God. Oh my God. I do remember. I do know you. Miss...'

'Rourke. That's right. This is a lovely dining room, isn't it? A lovely house.'

'I don't think Beck likes it much.' Keller laid the crossbow on the table.

In her mind, Rebecca was simply wandering through the rooms of a haunted mansion in a nightmare. It wouldn't make any difference what she said now because he was right. Those missing hours on his watch had somehow fractured reality. Miss Havisham here, holding court. Any second now, a mad March hare would drop down from the chandelier or they would find they were living at the bottom of the ocean and burst into jolly song.

But this contemporary Miss Havisham had something to say. And the man who had been toying with her heart wanted to hear it.

'Kell, do you know that Steve was my son?'

'Steve?'

'Steve Truffaut. I was his mother. He was real shy about me teaching at the school, so we decided I'd use my maiden name. Rourke. I've used it ever since, for work.'

'Miss Rourke. Yeah. I do remember. Those books. You gave me books. I wish I still had them.'

'I was glad to give them to you.'

'Why don't they shoot me, Miss Rourke? I'm not even holding the weapon.'

'They're not in here. I am here. And this beautiful girl.'

'Do you remember cheerwine? My Aunt used to love that stuff.'

'My mother did too. Cheerwine is ok.'

'Better than Geoffrey Chambertin. You ever hear from the other boys? Lemi? Angelo Peralta?'

'Angelo died. He killed himself Friday before last. He finished work and drove to Grandfather Mountain. Threw himself off the swing bridge.'

'I'm sorry to hear that, Miss.'

'Well. Now there's just you and Lemi.'

'And the Seawhites. And you, Miss Rourke. Angelo, huh. Guess he just didn't have enough in the tank. Like Billy Ray Master. I mean, you'll know this, you're an intelligent sort. You'll know that you have to see things through to the end. Because there is always an end, no point in trying to avoid it. It's just cowardice to duck out before the end.'

'Who decides when the end is though? Or what it should be?'

'Miss Rourke, yeah. You was always asking us questions. I've missed you. Know that? Everything turned to shit right about the last time I saw you.' Keller picked up the crossbow. 'I still have five arrows. And I don't like waste. Aunt Joya would've told you that. You know the story of Nicholas II and Alexandra? They all got shot. Together. The righteous demanded it. And I think if it is your time, and we all have one, don't we. Well, I think it's fitting to die with your family. That's why I watched them kill my father.'

'Keller, why don't we let Rebecca go. I want to tell you about the time I came to see your Aunt.'

'I love Rebecca. There's nothing in a name, is there. I mean, she's Emma Seawhite. But to me it is the sound of her, with the R and the B and the C. She is the sound.'

'I know you love her. I can see that. Why don't we save her now. We can save the girl you love.'

'I should save her. She is innocent. But I was innocent too. And just look at me.'

'Kell, I know that deep inside, you are a good person. A good man. I know it. Let's—'

'What's your plan, Miss Rourke? You're the one who got me started on all those stories. Might as well have been fairy tales, they was so far from my life. What's your plan, teacher?'

'I came to offer you a home. That day on your porch, with your Aunt. I came to offer you, well, to offer you my love. That could have been our story. We can still have a story.'

'We're too near the end now, Miss. We're on the last page. She wanted to keep me, old Joya. She wanted the money. You know she burned them books? *Johnny Tremain* and the others. I gotta figure this out. I bet it's the hardest part, for a writer. The ending.' Keller looked through the dim candlelight at the hounds in the wall paintings. 'I always liked a good hunt. Like these pictures. And look at this fox up here. Skinned. I know what you want, Miss Rourke. You want me to go with you and those nice officers. Back to North Carolina. Get me one of those injections. Painless, they say. But then you have all those folks ogling you, through the one way glass. What in the good fuck is that about? Ain't never gonna evolve, the human. We might as well renovate the Colisseum in Rome. He had the right idea old Emperor Commodus. Get the blood letting done on the weekend, in the arena. That'll keep them satisfied and we can have order in the city Monday through Friday. If your fellas out there could bring me the syringe, I'll do it right here, right now. This is much nicer than the execution chamber, believe you me. Much. And I honestly can't think of two people I'd rather have with me.'

Keller remembered the tempered soda-lime glass in the viewing room. It was entirely sound-proofed. Keller knew that. He'd prepared himself for the execution chamber as best he could. But he hadn't anticipated his father saying, 'I want to know if my son can see me.' Well now, that was a conundrum on June 23rd. Those suits and uniforms weren't more than a minute into their humming and hawing when Keller flew at the toughened glass. He banged on it with his fists and his shoulders and his head, till the guards took him down. They removed Keller Baye from the viewing room.

Later they told him that his father had died in 8 minutes and 47 seconds.

In the *Taransay* dining room, Keller fished the little suede pochette out of his pocket. 'I want to show y'all something.' He extracted the rainbow opal and set it on the table. 'Now doesn't that look fine. This is the perfect setting for such a jewel. It's made quite a journey. You don't really want the detail.'

Rebecca had had enough of Keller's fantasy land. 'You two obviously have a lot to discuss. If you'll forgive me, memory lane is not where I need to be this minute. You won't tell me if my brother is dead, so I'm leaving to find out. I'm leaving the room now. If you want to kill me too, you'll have to shoot me in the back.'

'Wait.' Keller put out his hand to stop her but laid the other on the trigger of the crossbow. 'Give me that terrible pen you like so much. Go on, Beck. Do as I say. While I am making up my mind.'

Jane Rourke said, 'Give him the pen, dear.'

Rebecca opened her bag and as she dug down the Weenect flashed at her. 'What's this? A detonator?'

'It's a tracking device. Funny girl. I always did overthink everything. Just give me the pen now.' Keller pulled hard at the buttons of his shirt and one of them pip-pip-pipped on the mahogany table.

Rebecca thought how aghast her grandmother would be; candle wax and shirt buttons raining down on the pristine mahogany. She handed Keller her old tartan pen.

'What is the tartan?' Keller pulled off the pen's cap.

'It's the Stewart tartan. The Royal House of Stewart. I thought you knew all about the Jacobites.'

'I know nothing about your Jacobites.'

'Every single thing was a lie. Give it back to me.'

'Why do you like this pen so much, darling?'

'It was given to me by someone who loved me. And I let them down.' Rebecca watched him turn the nib towards his own skin. 'I didn't deserve a present. What are you doing?'

'I'm marking the spot.' Keller made a circle of blue on his chest with the leaky pen. 'You see, just an inch left of centre. Damn, I should have made an X. I've made a lot of mistakes. Oh you don't need to look so worried, Miss Rourke. I've rehearsed all this. My arm is plenty long enough to shoot myself. And you are welcome to turn your back.'

'I never turned my back on you. And I won't now.'

'Oh I will.' Rebecca turned to face the fireplace, Belle's eyes glinting in the candlelight still, agog.

'Remember that parents' evening, Miss? My dad came to see you. He was so excited about my IQ test. I could see his chest all pumping up, thinking he had passed on smart genes. He may even have smiled that day. What if he had taken a shine to you. And you to him, Miss Rourke. What if we'd waited in the parking lot and he'd persuaded you to go to a Shady Glen. We all had a shake or a sundae. If we'd known that we could change our circumstances.' Keller pulled the trigger and his breath burst from him. The next words were dying on his lips. 'It's all about the timing. Ten, nine, eight, seven… six, five…'

The End

Acknowledgements

I want to thank you very much for reading my book. My greatest passion in life is people and their stories. It would be lovely to hear from you at www.facebook.com/jennymortonpotts. For more on me and my work, head to my website www.jennymortonpotts.com.

I also want to thank my partner and son for their endless support and love.

Jenny

Printed in Poland
by Amazon Fulfillment
Poland Sp. z o.o., Wrocław